NAN RYAN

The Countess Misbehaves

P9-CPX-491

MIRA®

MIRA

ISBN 1-55166-591-3

THE COUNTESS MISBEHAVES

Copyright © 2000 by Nan Ryan.

MIRA and the Star Colophon are trademarks used under license and registered
in Australia, New Zealand, Philippines, United States Patent and Trademark
Office and in other countries.

Visit us at www.mirabooks.com

Printed in U.S.A.

He had kept her garter all this time.

"I know what that is on your upper arm!" Madeleine hotly accused. Armand de Chevalier smiled, said nothing. "How dare you wear *my* garter for all the world to see!" she raged.

"Now, Maddie, no one but you and I know that it's your garter."

Unconvinced, she charged, "You are bent on ruining my life simply because I...because we..."

"Made memorable love in a summer's storm?" He softly finished her sentence.

"Shhh!" she hissed. "Give that garter back to me!"

"Can't do that," he said, lifting then lowering his wide shoulders. "It's my good luck charm. Besides, it's all I have of you."

"It's all you'll ever have of me, de Chevalier!"

"Ah, you're wrong there, Maddie," he said with irritating cockiness. "You know you are." A sudden warmth radiated from his eyes when he added, "One day we'll be together again."

Countess Madeleine Cavendish swallowed with difficulty. Then she narrowed her eyes and promised him in a soft, acid-laced voice, "You're the one who's wrong, Creole. That day will never come!"

"Yes, it will, *chérie.*" He smiled seductively and predicted, "Perhaps sooner than you think."

Nan Ryan "writes beautifully. Her style, plotting and characterizations are skillfully developed."
—*Wichita Falls Times Record*

For
Katonna Smothermon

A super talented lady, a beautiful woman,
an excellent mother and a treasured friend.

One

Liverpool, England
August 1856

She knew he was trouble the first time she saw him.

And the first time the Countess of Ballarat saw Armand de Chevalier, was as she boarded White Star's luxury liner, the S. S. *Starlight*, for the long voyage to America.

The Countess, known to most as Lady Madeleine Cavendish, lifted her skirts, stepped onto the ship's long gangway, and then paused to look up. She immediately spotted a tall, strikingly handsome, raven-haired man lounging against the ship's railing and boldly giving her the once-over.

He smiled disarmingly at her. But the wise noblewoman did not return his smile. Instead, she quickly looked away. She had no wish to encourage him in any manner. She knew his kind well. Too well. She had married just such a man when she was a young, impulsive girl and it had been a disaster.

Lady Madeleine's delicate jaw hardened at the unpleasant recollection. She had fallen deeply in love with him and the passion between them had raged white hot. In his arms, she had experienced incredible ecstasy, but it had lasted only for a very brief time. They had barely returned from the Italian honeymoon before her bridegroom—a charming commoner her mother had warned her not to wed— began behaving as if he had no wife. He began drinking heavily and gambled away great sums of money. Money that was hers, not his. Worse, he was soon seeking diversion in the arms of other women, humiliating her. It was a nightmare of a kind she was determined never to experience again.

After three miserably unhappy years as the neglected wife, Madeleine Cavendish had been widowed at age twenty-one when her wayward husband was killed in a drunken brawl over another woman.

Now as she ascended the ship's gangway, Lady Madeleine impatiently shook her bonneted head to clear her mind of those events. The action turned her thoughts to the present.

Was the dark, dangerous-looking man still at the ship's railing? When she reached the huge vessel's polished teak deck, she couldn't restrain herself from casting a quick glance in his direction.

He was, to her genuine surprise, still there. Still staring. And still smiling at her in a disturbingly affable way that enforced her earlier impression that he was indeed trouble. Uncharacteristically flustered, Lady Madeleine made a misstep and almost fell. In an instant, the tall, jet-haired admirer was at her side, steadying her.

The startled Countess abruptly experienced an

unwanted rush of excitement when the dark stranger's powerful right arm went around her waist and he pressed her close against his side. Awed by the granite hardness of his lean male frame, she suddenly felt very small and vulnerable.

Lady Madeleine looked up with intent to thank him, but his flashing midnight eyes arrested her so completely she could not speak. She said nothing. Snared by his hot gaze, she felt her heart begin to pound alarmingly and she knew that she *must*, on this long journey to America, stay as far away from this sinfully handsome man as possible.

After a long, awkward moment, she finally recovered. "Let me go!" she ordered in a most imperial tone.

She was totally caught off guard when he immediately released her. Struggling to regain her balance and her dignity, the Countess was shocked and highly incensed that this tall stranger offered no further assistance. Instead he stood there with his arms crossed over his chest, laughing.

He was laughing at her, the rude cad!

Nonplussed, she opened her mouth to hurl stinging oaths at him, but closed it before saying a word. To censure someone with such abominably bad manners and such a twisted sense of humor would be a waste of her precious time. He wasn't worth the effort.

She lifted her noble chin, looked daggers at him, turned about and haughtily flounced away.

Continuing to laugh, an amused Armand de Chevalier watched the angry woman storm off down the crowded promenade deck. Armand liked what he saw. Very much. He decided then and there that he would get to know the lady better during the crossing. He had no idea who she was, but he knew that she possessed a remarkable beauty and fiery spirit.

His kind of woman.

Their face-to-face meeting had been brief, but her image was indelibly etched into his memory. She was, he surmised, about five-six or five-seven. He stood six-two in his stocking feet and the top of her head reached the level of his mouth. Her hair, dressed elaborately atop her head and partially concealed beneath a fussy hat, was an intriguing shade of red-gold. He could all too easily envision it spilling down around her bare shoulders.

A muscle danced in Armand's tanned jaw and his chest grew tight at the pleasant fantasy.

She was such an uncommon beauty. Her pale skin was as flawless as fine alabaster and her large eyes were a deep emerald green. Her mouth, even tightened in anger as it had been when her face was close to his, was full-lipped and decidedly tempting.

Tall, slender, with a natural grace despite her momentary loss of equilibrium, she was a dazzlingly pretty woman and she had effortlessly arrested Armand's attention. He wondered who she was and where she was going. And how long it would be before she was in his arms?

This late-summer crossing was, Armand decided, going to be far more pleasurable than he had hoped.

Once she was safely inside her elegantly appointed stateroom, Lady Madeleine was careful to maintain her calm composure. She didn't want her hired attendant to know that she was upset. She hardly knew Lucinda Montgomery, the young woman who had agreed to be her traveling companion in exchange for passage to America.

"Lucinda, will you please have some ice water sent up at once? I'm very thirsty," the Countess requested in an effort to have a few minutes alone.

"Yes, my Lady," Lucinda replied and she hurried out of the stateroom to do her mistress's bidding.

Alone at last, Lady Madeleine sighed with relief, then immediately shivered and hugged herself. The brief encounter on deck with the impertinent stranger had left her breathless, oddly disturbed and anxious. Which was not at all like her.

She had always led a very social life, one in which she mixed often with the great and near great and took their admiration as her due. She was well aware of her beauty and knew that she possessed a natural talent for charming people. From the time she was a young girl she had been completely comfortable in the company of powerful men. And she had learned early on that she need put forth very little effort to have males, be they young or old, handsome or plain, eating out of hand. She was accustomed to being fawned over, flirted with, panted after and she took it all with good grace and a grain of salt.

So what on earth was bothering her now?

Granted, the stranger was so darkly handsome and potently masculine no female could help but notice and be affected. Tall, slim, impeccably dressed, he appeared to be quite the gentleman. Yet his flashing eyes and audacious manner were contradictory. And, no well-bred gentleman would laugh at a lady the way he had laughed at her.

He was, undoubtedly, a reckless rogue whose outrageous behavior some women would find appealing. Not her. She found him coarse. Common. Vulgar. Not worth wasting another minute's thought on.

Madeleine decisively shook her head, then took off her bonnet and tossed it on a velvet-covered sofa. She crossed to the bed, turned about, and sat down on its edge. She sighed, stretched and slowly sank down onto the brocade-covered bed.

She raised her arms above her head and sighed once more. And she gave silent thanks that the man to whom she was officially engaged, was a kind, cultured nobleman.

Madeleine smiled as she pictured Desmond Chilton, Fourth Earl of Enfield, whom she was to wed next spring. A distant cousin whom she had known since childhood but had rarely seen, Lord Enfield had left their native England more than a decade ago.

The earl had settled in New Orleans where Madeleine's dear uncle, Colfax Sumner—her deceased mother's only sibling—had lived for the past forty-five years. The two men had become good friends and when she had visited her uncle during the past summer, the handsome blond earl had spent a great deal of time at Colfax's French Quarter mansion. A week before she was to return home to England, the earl proposed and she had accepted.

Lord Enfield would, she felt sure, treat her as a wife should be treated. He clearly adored her. And, if she was less than passionately in love, that presented no weighty problem as far as she was concerned. She much preferred being the 'beloved' as opposed to the 'lover.' Desmond was most definitely the lover. She his beloved. Which was as it should be, as it would remain.

Never again would she risk being humiliated by a mere mortal man.

Armand de Chevalier remained on deck for the next hour, strolling unhurriedly from stern to bow as the huge vessel moved slowly out of the Liverpool harbor and made its way to the open sea.

Excited, well-dressed travelers had lined the ship's railing, waving to those left behind. Others, like Armand, promenaded around the ship's polished decks, greeting fellow voyagers, laughing, talking, anticipating an enjoyable adventure.

Many of those happy passengers were, of course, women. Some with husbands or family members. Others traveling together in groups of two or three. Still others were alone, save for a servant or attendant. There were, Armand noted, dozens of unattached, attractive women.

But not one captured his attention as the stunning woman with the red-gold hair. He couldn't get her out of his mind. He wanted to see her again, and he searched the milling crowds, hoping that perhaps she would take a stroll once they were on the open sea.

She did not.

After a couple of frustrating hours, Armand gave up and made his way to the gentleman's tavern. There in the darkly paneled club, he stepped up to the long polished bar, ordered a bourbon straight and downed it in one swallow.

As the barkeep poured another, Armand couldn't help overhearing a conversation taking place between two gentleman standing next to him who were sipping port.

"She's a British noble lady," said a short, balding gentleman with muttonchop sideburns. "The only child of the fifth earl of Ballarat and his American-born wife, both of whom are now deceased."

"Is she now?" replied his drinking companion, a tall, cadaver-thin man in a brown linen suit with a boutonniere in his buttonhole.

Armand knew, instinctively, that they were talking about his red-haired beauty. "Excuse me, gentlemen," he said and the port-drinking pair turned to look at him. "Does the noblewoman of whom you are speaking happen to have red hair?"

The tall, skinny fellow nodded, and said with a slight touch of wistfulness, "An unusual shade of red-gold that is incredibly striking against her pale-white skin."

"Who is she?" Armand asked bluntly.

"Why she's Lady Madeleine Cavendish, the flame-haired Countess," said the short man with the muttonchop sideburns. "One of the most renowned beauties in all Europe."

"Undoubtedly," said Armand before he downed his second whiskey. "Gentlemen," he said as he nodded good-day then turned and walked out of the tavern.

Armand was unfazed by her lofty status. Unbothered by the fact that she was a Countess. An inherently confident man, Armand had learned, long ago, that beneath fine satins and laces, often beat the passionate heart of a hot-blooded woman.

He'd bet everything he owned that the lovely Lady Madeleine Cavendish was such a woman.

Two

After a restful afternoon nap followed by a long leisurely bath, Madeleine Cavendish was again feeling like her old self. Relaxed. Self-assured. Looking forward to her first evening at sea.

When the blinding summer sun had finally slipped below the horizon and full darkness had fallen, Madeleine was humming happily as the surprisingly talented Lucinda meticulously dressed her long hair. It took a good half hour, but when Lucinda had finished, Madeleine's heavy locks were skillfully fashioned into a shiny coronet of thick braids atop her elegant head. The style was quite flattering to Madeleine as it accentuated her graceful, swanlike neck and beautiful throat.

Madeleine had chosen, for the first dinner at sea, a shimmering green silk ball gown with a low-cut bodice, an uncomfortably tight waist, and billowing skirts that spilled attractively over yards and yards of crinoline petticoats.

By ten minutes of nine she was fully dressed and ready for dinner. But she waited another half hour before leaving the stateroom.

Arriving fashionably late, she swept into the immense dining hall with its blazing chandeliers, deep lush carpet and gleaming sandalwood walls. A uniformed steward ushered her directly to the captain's table. A dozen diners were seated at the enormous round, white-clothed table.

All the gentlemen stood as a chair was pulled out for her. Nodding and smiling as she was presented to the well-dressed group, Madeleine noticed that one table companion was even later than she. The gilt chair next to hers was vacant. Perhaps the guest who was to be seated there had come down with a bad case of *mal de mer*. Poor miserable soul. She recalled, all too well, her first crossing years ago, when she had suffered from sea sickness.

As a white-jacketed waiter shook out a large linen dinner napkin and draped it across her silk-covered knees, Madeleine glanced up and saw the stranger from the railing. He was dressed impeccably in evening clothes and was making his way across the crowded room.

Dear lord he was coming straight toward the captain's table!

Lady Madeleine stiffened. She gritted her teeth as he pulled out the empty chair on her right and sat down. The captain made the introductions and she learned her rogue was Armand de Chevalier, a New Orleans native on his way home after a lengthy summer stay in Paris. The elderly, gray-haired gentleman on her left, a New York banker, leaned close and whispered that de Chevalier was an aristocrat. A wealthy Creole who often traveled to Europe. He was, it was rumored, of the *chacalata*—the highest born of the Creole elite. Madeleine nodded. She knew that the haughty Creoles were the descendants of the early French or Spanish settlers who had been born in America. She also knew that they were considered the nobility of New Orleans.

Conversations resumed. Diners began to sample the vichyssoise. Armand de Chevalier turned away to politely reply to a question from a stout, expensively dressed woman seated on his other side.

Lady Madeleine suffered a mild twinge of alarm knowing that she and this raffish Creole were to be dwelling in the very same city. At the unsettling prospect, she involuntarily shivered.

"Are you chilly, my Lady?" Armand de Chevalier, turning his full attention to her, softly inquired. "If so, I could…"

"I am quite comfortable, thank you, Mr. de Chevalier." She icily set him straight and reached for her wineglass.

From the corner of her eye she saw that the Creole's full lips were turned up into a hint of a sardonic grin. Her dislike and distrust of the man increased.

It was, for Madeleine Cavendish, a miserable meal. Her usual healthy appetite missing, she pushed the food around her china plate and forced herself to smile and engage her fellow diners in idle conversation. All but de Chevalier. She said nothing to him. And, further, she silently, subtly let him know that she was not interested in hearing more about him nor did she intend to tell him anything about herself.

He didn't press her.

Still, she was greatly relieved when at last the seven-course meal finally came to an end.

At the captain's insistence, the smiling countess courteously allowed the beaming, white-haired ship's officer to escort her into the ship's mirrored ballroom. Leaving Armand de Chevalier behind, Madeleine immediately began to relax and enjoy herself.

Lavishly dressed dancers were spinning about on the polished parquet floor as a full orchestra in evening wear played a waltz. Warmed by the wine and relieved to be free of the bothersome Creole, Lady Madeleine was gracious when the aging captain lifted his kid-gloved hand and led her onto the floor.

She smiled charmingly as the barrel-chested captain turned her awkwardly about. And she laughed good-naturedly when he stepped on her toes and quickly assured him she was unhurt, no harm done.

Her smile was bright and genuine as the captain, soon wheezing for breath and perspiring heavily, continued to clumsily turn her about on the floor.

But her smile evaporated when Armand de Chevalier appeared and tapped the Captain on the shoulder. He brashly cut in, decisively took her in his arms and deftly spun her away.

She was trapped. Everyone was watching. The other dancers abruptly stopped dancing to watch the Countess and the Creole. Madeleine couldn't make a scene. She couldn't forcefully push de Chevalier away and storm out of the ballroom. She was left with no choice but to smile and endure the dance.

Madeleine's smile was forced.

She was as stiff as a poker.

At least at first. But that quickly changed. The Creole was such a graceful dancer and so incredibly easy to follow, Madeleine—who had always loved dancing—found herself relaxing in his arms. And enjoying herself. Too much.

Soon she was no longer aware of the watching crowd. She was aware of nothing and no one save the man who held her and turned her and spun her about. His lean body barely brushed her own, yet she sensed his every movement as if she were pressed flush against his hard male frame. It was as if they were one body, hers so finely attuned to his, she could easily anticipate even the slightest nuance of movement before it took place.

It was strange.

It was exhilarating.

All her senses seemed suddenly to be heightened. Her vision was so sharp that as she looked at him, the thought struck her that this handsome man's aquiline profile could have been traced from a drawing of a conquistador.

Her hearing, too, was nothing short of incredible. She could hear, above the music and commotion, his deep, steady breathing and even the heavy, rhythmic beating of his heart. His clean, unique masculine scent, so subtle, so intoxicating, caused her to inhale deeply.

Most pronounced of all was her sense of touch. His hand at her back, gently guiding her about, was warm and persuasive, the tapered fingertips only lightly touching her waist, but seeming to burn through the silk of her ball gown. His other hand lightly clutched her own slender fingers and pressed them against the solid wall of his chest. The heat emanating from him was intense; her sensitive fingertips, which touched against his muscled chest, felt as if they were on fire.

A thrill rippled through her.

She was overwhelmed by the sight, sound, smell and touch of this sinfully handsome man. Guiltily she wondered about that other sense. The sense of taste. What would it taste like to be kissed by him? Covertly, she glanced at his sensual lips and felt butterflies take wing inside.

Quickly she looked away.

And saw—reflected in the ballroom's mirrored walls—duplicate pairs of the dancing duo. He so tall and dark and broad-shouldered. She so pale and slender and bare-shouldered. The two of them moving perfectly together. Swaying seductively to the music.

It was a powerful image and Madeleine felt quite faint. Her partner immediately sensed her condition and artfully danced her out of the warm ballroom and onto the ship's deserted deck.

Armand solicitously steered Madeleine to the railing where the salt-laden sea breeze cooled them. He gave her a chance to catch her breath, watched as some of the color returned to her cheeks.

"Better?" he asked.

She nodded and took a couple of long, deep breaths. Then she gripped the railing tightly, lifted her face into the wind and closed her eyes. In silence Armand stared at her in frank admiration. What a lovely vision she was with her noble head thrown back, her delicate chin lifted, her long dark

lashes fluttering restlessly over her closed, beautiful
eyes. He noted, and not for the first time that evening, that she possessed the most exquisite shoulders and bosom he had ever seen.

The bodice of her emerald-green gown was cut
low enough to reveal the tempting swell of her
milky-white bosom. At the same time the gown's
fabric rose high enough to modestly conceal her
soft, rounded breasts.

Madeleine opened her eyes. She turned to look
at Armand and some of the disturbing warmth
quickly returned. Struck by his imposing height, the
width of his shoulders and the way the moonlight
silvered his raven-black hair, she said anxiously,
"Good night to you, Mr. de Chevalier. I...I must
retire to my...my...stateroom." She stammered as
she stared at his mouth and tingles of excitement
swept though her. "I hardly know you and it's im-
proper for the two of us to be here alone."

Armand smiled at her and asked, "Would it have
been better to have stayed inside where you would
have fainted before all those staring people?"

"I never faint!" she promptly defended herself.

"Ah, I see. My mistake," he replied in a low,
teasing voice. "I thought that you were feeling a
little dizzy and..."

"I was, but I am perfectly fine, Mr. de Chevalier.
Now if you'll kindly excuse me."

She turned away.

He followed.

"I will see you to your stateroom, Lady Madeleine," he said.

She was quick to protest. "That isn't necessary, I can find my way...."

"You heard me, Countess," he interrupted as he commandingly took her arm and escorted her to her cabin.

Outside the closed door of her stateroom, Armand stood facing her. He raised a long arm above her head and rested his hand on the door frame. Leaning close, he said, "Have lunch with me tomorrow."

Her back pressed against the carved door, Madeleine said, "That, sir, is out of the question. You see, I am...that is, I..." She started to inform him that she was an engaged lady, but decided against it. She owed him no explanations. She owed him nothing. She said pointedly, "I am not interested in sharing lunch, or anything else, with you, sir."

Unperturbed, Armand lowered his raised arm, brushed the tips of his fingers along her bare white shoulder, smiled easily and said, "Well, I can take a hint. Good night, Madeleine."

She scornfully corrected him, "That's Lady Madeleine to you, Mr. de Chevalier!"

Armand shrugged, grinned and said, "Now, Maddie, you are not *my* lady." She whirled about, opened the door, and rushed inside as he silently added, *Yet.*

Three

Lady Madeleine Cavendish had a difficult time falling asleep that night. Armand de Chevalier was responsible. As she restlessly tossed and turned, Madeleine reluctantly conceded it was impossible to deny that the insolent Creole had aroused an unsettling emotion in her she'd long thought dead.

She promptly told herself that it was completely normal, nothing to be concerned about. It was quite simple, really. De Chevalier was formidably masculine. She, totally feminine. The polarity generated its own dynamic tension, engendered a natural curiosity and fascination. That was it. Nothing more.

Thank heaven she was wise enough to recognize the attraction for what was. That elementary knowledge was a valuable aid in building total immunity to the Creole's questionable charms.

There was no need to worry about the handsome de Chevalier. Even if he refused to leave her alone—and she strongly suspected that would be the case—it was no great cause for concern. She was not some flighty, starry-eyed eighteen-year-old. She was an intelligent, levelheaded woman of twenty-seven whose knees did not go weak every time a strikingly handsome man smiled at her.

Decisively dismissing the vexing Creole from her mind, Madeleine let her thoughts drift across the ocean to the two fine men who were waiting for her in New Orleans. She was anxious to reach her destination and genuinely delighted that the charming river city was now to be her home.

With both parents dead and no close family left in England, she would live with her dear Uncle Colfax until next spring when she wed Lord Enfield. Her uncle had assured her that the earl was a gentleman of sterling character, well thought of and quite wealthy after more than a decade in America.

Madeleine smiled in the darkness, pleased that her uncle and her fiancé were such good friends. It was important to her that her Uncle Colfax fully approve of the man she was to marry.

She knew how much her bachelor uncle doted on her, loved her as if she were his own daughter. He had told her, on more than one occasion, that she was the sole heir to his sizable fortune. But she loved her uncle as he loved her and hoped that it would be many long years before she claimed her inheritance.

Besides, she would have no need of her uncle's fortune. Lord Enfield was a wealthy man in his own right.

Madeleine sighed heavily, then yawned. Sleepy at last, she turned over onto her stomach, hugged her pillow, and closed her eyes.

And was soon sound asleep.

On that first full day at sea, Madeleine awakened to the bright August sun spilling through the portholes of her luxurious stateroom. A woman who loved excitement and adventure, she dressed hurriedly and rushed out on deck.

A yellow parasol raised above her head to protect her fair skin, Lady Madeleine smiled and nodded to fellow passengers as she strolled along the promenade deck.

Inhaling deeply of the fresh sea air and looking out with pleasure at the calm blue ocean, Madeleine was enjoying herself immensely.

The gentlemen she passed tipped their hats or bowed slightly from the waist, acknowledging her. The ladies smiled and greeted her and several asked her to join them for high tea that afternoon in the ladies' salon.

On she strolled.

Taking her time. No destination in mind. Smiling easily. Savoring the beauty of the warm August day at sea. Then all at once Madeleine abruptly blinked. She stopped walking. Stood stock-still. She squinted against the brightness of the sun, staring.

Several yards ahead a couple stood at the ship's railing. They were laughing merrily and in their hands, each held a long-stemmed glass of what appeared to be champagne, although it was only ten o'clock in the morning. The woman, looking up at the man as if he were a god, was a voluptuous brunette dressed in an expensive-looking traveling suit of pale-blue cotton. The man, who was smiling down at the alluring brunette as if they shared some exciting secret, wore a finely tailored summer suit of crisp beige linen.

Armand de Chevalier!

Lady Madeleine felt her jaw tighten and her brows knit. She straightened her spine, threw her head back and started walking. Directly toward the laughing, champagne-sipping couple. As she approached, she waited expectantly for de Chevalier to look up, see her and perhaps motion her over.

It never happened.

Madeleine drew up even with the laughing pair and purposely paused not twelve feet away. She stood there for several long seconds, giving both the opportunity to acknowledge her. Neither seemed aware of her presence. Neither so much as glanced in her direction. They had eyes only for each other.

Madeleine hurried away, admittedly stung by the Creole's pointed neglect and shocked by such callous behavior. Here was the man who, only last night, had held her in his arms. He had danced with her and escorted her to her stateroom, where he had asked her to have lunch with him today.

Had he already forgotten her? Had she made absolutely no impression on him? Had it not bothered him in the slightest that she had turned down his luncheon invitation? It would seem not. It was as if she didn't exist. Well, what did she care? It was, after all, she who had advised him to leave her alone. She should be grateful that he was honoring that request. And she was. She was glad he had found someone else with whom to amuse himself. Someone with whom he could share lunch.

By evening, Lady Madeleine had begun to wonder if de Chevalier and the buxom brunette weren't sharing a great deal more than lunch. At dinner the pair were together at a table close by and they seemed to be having quite a gay time.

After the evening meal, Madeleine joined some of her table companions in the ship's ballroom. There she spotted, swaying on the floor, the Creole and his enchanted companion. Madeleine swallowed with difficulty. Watching the two of them glide about the floor brought back the vivid recollection of being in de Chevalier's arms.

Suffering the onset of a sudden headache, Lady Madeleine made her apologies and said good-night. She hurried to the haven of her stateroom. There she stormed around, pacing back and forth, curiously angry and upset.

And much, much later after she had retired and lay sleepless in a shaft of summer moonlight, she heard a deep, masculine voice that she instantly recognized. Curious, she tossed back the silky sheets, got out of bed, hurried across the carpeted stateroom to an open porthole and peered out.

Directly below, at the railing, a lone couple stood bathed in moonlight. While Madeleine watched, wide-eyed, the provocative brunette who had spent the day with the Creole, slipped her bare arms up around his neck and lifted her face for his kiss.

Madeleine quickly turned away in disgust.

She had been so right about de Chevalier! He was nothing but a rogue and a scoundrel. She felt sorry for his enthralled victim.

In the days and nights that followed, Madeleine found that the pretty brunette was not the only woman who was entranced with de Chevalier. The handsome Creole never lacked for feminine companionship. Each time she saw him he was with a beautiful woman. A different woman each evening. And each of those beautiful women clung possessively to his arm, gazed adoringly at him and laughed at his every word.

Lady Madeleine pitied them, making such fools of themselves over a charming scamp who changed women as often as he changed shirts. Seeing him for the cad he was helped to extinguish the troublesome heat she had felt for him that first night at sea.

The Creole was somebody else's problem, not hers.

But the Countess was bored.

As several long days and longer nights at sea passed by uneventfully, Madeleine grew weary of the journey, the idleness. She was tired of being trapped on a ship in the middle of the ocean. She was anxious to step onto terra firma. Anxious to reach New Orleans. Anxious to see Lord Enfield and Uncle Colfax. Anxious to go out to dinner and the theater and the opera.

So she was relieved when finally the long journey neared its end. She experienced an escalating degree of excitement when Lucinda awakened her with the news the ship was rounding the southernmost tip of the Florida Keys before it headed up into the Gulf of Mexico. Sometime within the next forty-eight hours, she would be disembarking at New Orleans' busy port.

Humming happily, Madeleine quickly dressed

and eagerly made her way out onto the deck, blithely ignoring the strong winds that had risen with the red dawn. She shaded her eyes and gazed, smiling, at the old lighthouse rising majestically from the very last island of the Keys. And she laughed when a great gust of wind caught her yellow silk parasol, tore it out of her hands, and sent it skittering away.

Several gentlemen, immediately aware of her plight, went after the dainty umbrella, but each time one of them bent to pluck it up from the deck, another puff of wind sent it toppling out of reach.

Instantly, it became a highly competitive game to see who could successfully seize Lady Madeleine's tumbling, wind-tossed parasol. Determined gentlemen scrambled to recover the colorful article, each eager to be the lucky one who could present it to its lovely owner.

As fate would have it, the parasol was effortlessly retrieved by a disinterested gentleman who was not in on the game. The flapping, fluttering object slammed up against the trousered leg of none other than Armand de Chevalier. He placed his well-shod foot gingerly on the parasol's handle to secure it. Then bent from the waist, picked it up and slyly raised it over his head. Turning slowly, he stood there twirling the parasol playfully, waiting for its owner to reclaim it.

Good sports all, the gentlemen who had been chasing the wayward umbrella laughed and applauded de Chevalier's good fortune. Armand nodded and accepted their congratulations. When the small crowd dispersed and the laughing gentlemen went on their way, Armand stayed where he was.

The Countess, several yards down the deck, also stayed put. She naturally assumed de Chevalier would bring the parasol to her.

So she waited.

And waited.

Frowning she motioned for him to come. He shrugged wide shoulders and a look of puzzlement crossed his face as if he had no idea what she wanted.

Madeleine's hands went to her hips. She glanced cautiously around, not wishing to attract attention. She looked directly at Armand and, without sound, mouthed the words, "Bring me that parasol!"

"Not a chance," Armand replied in a firm, loud voice. He grinned devilishly and added, "Come and get it, Countess."

Taken aback and instantly irritated, Madeleine said, loudly enough to be heard by him as well as by passersby, "Sir, I *command* you to return my personal property."

Ignoring her queenly command, Armand's devilish smile remained solidly in place. "You may have your little umbrella anytime you want it. All you have to do is take the few short steps to me." His smile grew even broader. "Or, you could stop by my stateroom late this evening and we'll..."

"Shhh!" Madeleine hissed and hurried toward him, looking furiously around, afraid someone had heard. Reaching him, she stepped up close and said angrily, "How dare you make such a suggestion for all to hear! Your behavior is inexcusable! You would lead our fellow passengers to believe that I might actually come to your stateroom when you know very well I would *never* do such a disgraceful thing!''

Continuing to twirl the yellow silk parasol above his dark head, Armand said, "Calm down, Countess. I'm quite sure everyone knows you would never consort with the likes of me."

"I should certainly hope so," she replied haughtily.

Armand smiled easily, handed her the parasol and then reached out to push a windblown lock of red-gold hair off her forehead. "It's getting awfully blustery, Lady Madeleine. You might consider retiring to your stateroom."

"You might consider not telling me what to do, Mr. de Chevalier."

"You might consider listening when someone gives you a bit of sound advice."

"You might consider that I neither need nor want any advice from you."

"You might consider occasionally behaving like the lady you're supposed to be, my lady."

Madeleine's red face grew redder. A strong gust of wind assaulted her just as she started to speak. It caught the umbrella and again tore it from her hands. She anxiously looked at Armand and pointed to the fluttering parasol. Armand didn't move a muscle.

He smiled and said, "You might consider fetching it yourself, Countess."

Anger and frustration flashing out of her emerald

eyes, she said, "You might consider leaping overboard and ridding this vessel of its vermin!"

She stepped around Armand and took a few tentative steps toward the parasol. Then stopped
abruptly. She wasn't about to chase after anything.
Let it go. And let him go.

She spun on her heel and majestically marched
over to the railing. Muttering under her breath,
wondering if he was still there, she soon hazarded
a glance over her shoulder.

Strong west winds pressed the fabric of his slate-
gray trousers against his long legs and lifted locks
of his jet-black hair. As Armand started toward her
she hastily turned back around. He walked up beside her and, without saying a word, put a leather-
shod foot on the lower rung of the railing. He
swung up onto the wooden railing, straddling it.

Staring, she said, "You fool, what are you doing?"

"I've decided you are right, Lady Madeleine. I
should just go ahead and leap overboard."

He threw his other leg over and came to his feet,
balanced precariously on the decorative molding
outside of the railing.

Her heart in her throat and her eyes wide with
fear, Madeleine impulsively threw her protective
arms around his lean thighs and shouted, "No!
Don't do it. I was only teasing."

"You don't want me to jump? You want me to
live?"

"No! Yes! Please, Mr. de Chevalier, come back
inside before you fall to your death."

"Would you care?"

"Of course, I would care. Stop scaring me."

"Okay," he said as he agilely turned and jumped down onto the deck. He stood facing her. "Were you really afraid? Did you think you might lose me?"

His safety now ensured, Madeleine felt her anger quickly returning. She was furious that he had frightened her. And annoyed that he knew that she was frightened.

"Mr. de Chevalier, you might consider joining the children down in their play lounge. Your childish stunts clearly reveal that you have the intellect of a backward ten-year-old."

Four

Later that morning, Lady Madeleine was alone at the ship's railing, gazing expectantly out over the churning blue waters. A couple of hours had passed since she had spotted the ancient lighthouse rising majestically from the very last island of the Florida Keys. She had experienced a great rush of excitement when the huge ship had rounded that final spit of land and headed northward into the Gulf of Mexico. Now the Keys had been left far behind and no land was visible.

The winds, she suddenly realized, had risen dramatically since she'd first come out on deck that morning. She now had to cling tenaciously to the railing to keep her balance. And she noted that the waves had grown much higher, so high they were actually lifting and tossing the heavy vessel. Her breath caught when, all at once, deep swells rose beneath the huge craft and it swung and rolled violently.

Madeleine became curious, and increasingly anxious, when the ship's crewmen began rushing about, hurrying to obey shouted commands from the stern-faced first officer. There was a sudden burst of activity as passengers hurried onto the decks. She heard a gentleman shouting to his companion as they passed that a West Indian cyclone was upon them.

Alarmed, Madeleine started toward her stateroom when the ship took a frenzied swing. As she struggled against the rising winds, she overheard two crewman speaking softly. One claimed the ship was taking on water.

Seconds later, the captain appeared on the promenade deck. Calm, collected, he walked briskly among the passengers speaking quietly, yet with clarity. "Passengers should return to their staterooms," he instructed. "No need to rush, no reason to panic," he said, although he was more worried than anyone would ever know. Not only were there not enough lifeboats, they were painfully short of life preservers. And the waterproof integrity of those pitiful few vests on board was in doubt. "Return to your staterooms and secure the portholes," he repeated again and again. On encountering her, the captain said reassuringly, "Merely a safety precaution, Lady Madeleine."

She smiled and nodded, but she knew better. A full-fledged hurricane was racing toward them.

Struggling against the worsening winds and dodging scrambling passengers as they fled to their cabins, Madeleine finally reached the door of her stateroom. She banged on the solid wood and Lucinda yanked the door open and anxiously drew her mistress inside.

There the two women huddled together in growing fear as the S. S. *Starlight* pitched and rolled in the punishing winds as if it were a child's toy. The

roar was deafening as mountainous seas and fear-
some gales assaulted the mighty vessel.

While the fierce storm raged, sending the huge
ship into fits of savage rocking and lurching, the
Starlight's crew and many of the male passengers—
including Armand de Chevalier with his suit jacket
cast aside and his shirtsleeves rolled up—toiled tirelessly at three bucket brigades to reduce the flooding in the engine room.

Soaked to the skin, striving to stay on their feet,
the contingent labored manfully to keep five hundred tons of boilers and engines afloat in the angry,
storm-tossed Gulf of Mexico. But it was a losing
battle. Soon it became evident. The S. S. *Starlight*
was irreparably breached. The huge ocean liner was
going down.

The ship now badly listing, a terrified Lady Madeleine and Lucinda rushed back outside. Terror-
stricken passengers ran about on the slippery, slant-
ing decks shouting, ''Where are we to go? What
are we to do?''

Families hugged their loved ones to them and
herded them toward the ship's railing where lifeboats were being deployed. Frightened people were
pushing and shoving, fighting to gain a coveted spot
in one of the lifeboats.

''Hurry!'' shouted Lucinda to Madeleine, ''we
must hurry!''

The servant clung to her mistress's hand and
pulled her along through the pressing crush of humanity. But when Lucinda realized that most of the
lifeboats, filled to capacity, had already dropped
into the sea, she panicked. Survival her only in-

stinct, she dropped Madeleine's hand and elbowed her way through the mob, desperate to flee the sinking ship and a drowning death in the ocean's depths.

Lucinda made it to the railing, climbed over, and jumped down into an overflowing lifeboat as it was being lowered down the ship's tilting side.

The countess, struggling against the ferocious winds and screaming passengers, anxiously followed. Fighting her way toward the lowering lifeboat, badly hampered by her heavy hoop skirts, she was struck by a giant wave and flung violently against the railing and momentarily stunned.

If not for the strong hands that reached out and caught her, she would have been washed overboard.

"My God!" shouted Armand de Chevalier, "why have you waited this long? We must get you into a lifeboat at once!"

Madeleine's head snapped around and she stared up at him in shocked surprise. She would have supposed that this self-absorbed Creole would have shoved women and children out his way to get to a lifeboat and save his own hide.

"Why have *you* waited?" she shouted against the wind.

Ignoring the question, Armand firmly propelled her through the hysterical crowd to the railing. Armand looked over the ship's side and saw the last of the lifeboats splash down into the boiling sea.

Against Madeleine's left ear he shouted, "We have to make it to the other side of the ship. There may still be lifeboats off the port that have not yet been deployed!"

The pair fought their way up across the badly listing deck, falling once, slipping back downward toward starboard. But Armand managed to rise again and pull Madeleine up. Holding on to anything they could find to steady themselves, the pair fought on.

It was far from easy.

The howling winds kept ballooning Madeleine's skirts, threatening to lift her off her feet. Quickly assessing the situation, Armand propelled her to a deck chair that was bolted to the deck. While she held tightly to the chair's back, Armand took a small, sharp-bladed knife from a leather holster at his ankle. He lifted Madeleine's damp dress and slashed the threads that held her fashionable crinoline petticoats. In seconds the heavy crinoline frame fell away and Armand lifted her out of it. Free of the impeding contraption, it was easier for Madeleine to keep up with him.

After what seemed an eternity, the embattled pair finally reached the ship's rising port side. Gripping the wet wooden railing, Armand drew Madeleine in front of him, enclosing her in his arms as he clutched the rail. His eyes watering from the wind and salt spray of the sea, he anxiously peered over the ship's side in search of a lifeboat.

There were none.

All the lifeboats had cast off and were rapidly rowing away from the doomed ship.

"God in heaven!" Armand swore in frustration. "There are no more lifeboats!"

"I know," Madeleine said, exhaling resignedly

as she pushed a soaked lock of hair off her cheek and gazed wistfully after the departing boats.

For a long uncertain moment the couple stood there together on the badly listing deck of the sinking vessel. The winds roared relentlessly and the huge waves rose to awesome heights, badly buffeting the crippled ship. Dozens of people, washed overboard, clung to wreckage. Others bobbed about like corks in the roiling sea, supported by life belts. And above the din, the terrible screams of people filled the air as they flailed about and drowned.

Madeleine trembled and a sob of fear escaped her lips.

"Come," Armand shouted, "let's get in out of the wind."

His arm firmly around her, Armand guided the frightened Madeleine back across the slick deck and up the tilting bridge to the captain's cabin, just off the wheelhouse. Sheltering her against his tall body, Armand tried the door. It was jammed. He pressed a muscular shoulder against it, pushed with all his strength and it flew open.

Quickly he handed Madeleine inside and followed, closing the door behind him. The cabin was deserted. The captain was gone. The crew was gone. They had either been swept overboard or had fled cowardly in one of the lifeboats.

Madeleine stood in the center of the small, tidy cabin, hugging herself. Chilled with fear, she thanked Armand with her eyes when he took a large white towel from a sea chest and handed it to her.

She blotted her wet shiny face, then began rubbing her thick, soaked hair. She watched as Armand took another towel, peeled off his drenched white shirt and dried his dark chest and wide shoulders.

"I'm sorry there are no dry clothes here for you to…" he began.

Swearing, he tore a clean gray blanket from a narrow bunk that hung from the far bulkhead by strong link chains. He wrapped the blanket around her trembling shoulders and suggested she sit down. She looked around, realizing the bed was the only place to sit. Madeleine shook her head and said she'd rather stand. The words had hardly passed her lips before a giant wave crashed against the cabin, sending her sprawling on the sharply canted deck.

Armand reached her in an instant, drawing her to her feet. "Are you all right?" he shouted, clasping her upper arms.

"Yes," she shouted back, "but maybe I had better sit down."

He guided her to the bunk and she sank down onto the mattress's edge. Armand drew down the bunk's canvas restraining straps and cinched them around her waist. "That should hold you," he said. Then he exhaled heavily and sat down on the bed beside her, realizing there was nothing more to be done.

The ship continued to pitch and roll and plunge and rise as the hurricane-force winds slammed mercilessly into the crippled vessel. Strapped down in the captain's bunk beside a virtual stranger, Lady Madeleine Cavendish tried very hard to be brave. She had been reared to keep a stiff upper lip in moments of crisis and to never let others know she was upset.

But she had never faced anything like this. It was impossible to hide the fact that she was terrified.

"We are going to die, aren't we, Mr. de Chevalier?" the shivering Madeleine asked, her eyes round with fear.

Armand was quick to offer hope to the frightened woman. "No. Certainly not. This vessel has a wooden hull, which means it can stay afloat for hours," he said and slid a comforting arm around her shaking shoulders. "There's every chance that we will be picked up." He gave her shoulder a reassuring squeeze, then dropped his hand away, bracing a stiffened arm behind her on the mattress.

"You don't believe that," she accused, studying his dark face for signs of sincerity. His unchanged countenance revealed nothing. "Do you?" She pulled the blanket closer around her shoulders.

"Yes, I do." Armand insisted, keeping up the pretense for her sake. "With any luck another ship will pass by here within the hour and take us onboard."

She nodded, but she was not fooled.

Her shoulders slumped with despair and try as she might, she could no longer hold back the tears that were stinging her eyes. Madeleine began to quietly cry. Armand didn't hesitate. He took her in his arms and pressed her wet cheek to his bare chest. He stroked the crown of her damp hair, gently patted her slender back and comforted her with soft spoken words of solace.

In her rising fear, Madeleine put her arms around his trim waist, clasping her hands together behind his back. The blanket fell away from her shoulders.

She clung to Armand as if he were her lifeline to survival. Tears spilling down her cheeks, she buried her face in the warm solidness of his naked chest and closed her eyes. Above her bent head, his deep, calm voice soothed and reassured.

Madeleine's tears soon ceased, but Armand continued to hold her in his arms. On a soft inhalation of breath, she raised her head and looked up at him apologetically.

"I'm sorry," she said.

"For what?" He replied, then smiled at her in that devil-may-care way of his as if nothing were amiss. She knew that he was being brave and strong for her sake. And it touched her. She smiled back at him and realized, as she did so, that it was the first time she had ever really smiled at him. His dark, beautiful eyes lighted in response.

And as she smiled at him the thought struck her that his handsomely chiseled features would be the last face she saw this side of heaven. The two of them were going to die together in this tiny cabin. It might be an hour. It might be less. But soon the sinking ship would plunge with decisive finality into the dark, fathomless depths of ocean and she and de Chevalier would drown.

They were going to die together, two strangers who knew nothing about each other. Neither of them would ever see their homes or loved ones again. They would never again eat a sumptuous meal. Or drink chilled champagne. Or warm themselves before a roaring fire. Or laugh in the rain. Or dance beneath the stars.

Or make love.

Madeleine stirred against the handsome man who held her. The sea pounded against the ship. Waves slapped against the cabin. She clung to Armand, her arms wrapped around him, her head on his shoulder.

It was crazy, she knew, totally insane, but she wondered—as she had that first night when they had danced—what it would be like to kiss him. To be kissed by him. Through the cover of her half-lowered lashes, she gazed with interest at his sensual mouth.

And was amazed when Armand said, as if he could read her thoughts, "Kiss me, Countess." He gently drew her closer, pushing the blanket completely away. Her head fell back against his supporting arm. He slowly bent his dark head to her upturned face. "Kiss me, once."

Not waiting for permission, Armand kissed Madeleine. It was not a soft, feathery kiss of two people slowly becoming better acquainted. It was not a tender, closed-mouth caress of a lover who had forever and a day to win and woo his reluctant lady fair. It was not a brief, introductory meeting of two tentative pairs of lips.

It was a kiss of such flaring fire and primordial passion that Madeleine was instantly overwhelmed. Dazed and clutching at his smooth, deeply clefted back, she felt herself go limp in his strong arms as he swiftly deepened the blazing kiss. He thrust his tongue inside her mouth, boldly exploring all the highly sensitive regions, stroking her tongue with his own, sending her wits scattering and her pulses pounding.

Madeleine realized, as her lips were combined with his, that she wanted this handsome, hard-faced rogue. Before she died she wanted to know—one last time—the kind of passion she barely remembered from her first nights as a newlywed.

If any man could give her even the slightest taste of that kind of rapture, it was surely this dark, seductive Creole who was kissing her with such unrestrained passion. She sighed into Armand's mouth and her nails raked down his warm smooth back. The more she considered the two of them making love, the more she wanted it.

The more she wanted him.

When at long last his conquering lips released hers, her head fell back against his rock-hard biceps. She looked into his eyes and trembled with rising desire.

"Mr. de Chevalier," she said finally, almost shouting to be heard above the wind's constant roar, "will you...that is, I...could we...?"

"What? I can't hear you." He leaned down, placed his ear close to her lips.

"Make love to me, Mr. de Chevalier," she blurted out. Armand raised his head, looked at her, one dark eyebrow lifting slightly. She rushed her words, "We are going to go down with this ship. You know we are, I know we are. So what difference would it make if we...we..." Her words trailed away and she lowered her eyes, sorry that she had made such a preposterous proposal.

Until he put his thumb and forefinger to her chin, raised her face to his, and looking straight into her eyes, said, "I'll make love to you on one condition.'' He brushed a kiss to her temple. Madeleine's brows knitted in puzzlement. He smiled and said, "If you'll stop calling me Mr. de Chevalier. Say 'Armand, make love to me.'''

Aroused by his stirring kiss and the granite hardness and awesome heat of his lean body, Lady Madeleine eagerly said, "Armand, make love to me.''

"With pleasure, Countess.''

Five

For a long, tense moment, Armand de Chevalier did nothing, didn't move a muscle. He simply held Madeleine in his arms and looked into her eyes. Unable to look away or even to breathe properly, Madeleine felt as if she were being pulled into the fathomless depths of his unforgettable black eyes.

The winds howled and the cabin plunged sharply into the sea, then rose again. Madeleine hardly noticed. She was totally mesmerized by this dark stranger with whom she wanted desperately to be intimate.

She drew a sharp intake of air as Armand slowly lowered his face to hers. Expecting another of those instantly ardent, breath-stealing kisses, she was surprised when he brushed his smooth, warm lips ever so lightly against hers. For several sweet, unhurried moments, he kissed her softly, undemandingly, as if she were actually his treasured love.

Madeleine found it incredibly moving. Stirring. Exciting. Each gentle, unhurried kiss became more thrilling than the last. His mouth seemed to fit so perfectly with hers. As if their lips were made solely for each other's kisses.

Pressing one last feathery kiss to her slightly

parted lips, Armand flipped open the buckle to the restraints holding her in place. He lifted her and sat her on his right knee and both were almost dumped to the floor when a great gust of wind hit the ship. Armand gripped the bunk's frame with one hand and held Madeleine with the other. Then quickly drew the restraints around both of them, buckling them loosely behind her back.

Clutching his neck, Madeleine was both astonished and thrilled when he took her hand, placed it directly over his heart and said in a low, husky voice, "Touch me. Feel me, sweetheart."

She immediately complied. Her fingers spread, palm flush against him, she eagerly explored the perfect symmetry of his naked bronzed torso. She stroked and rubbed and examined him thoroughly, letting her fingertips circle the flat brown nipples almost hidden in the dense black chest hair. She felt a small tremor surge through him at her touch and was excited by the knowledge that she had so titillated him. Her eyes focused on the broad expanse of bare flesh before her, she popped her finger into her mouth and sucked it briefly. She then circled his left nipple with her wet fingertip before looking up to get his reaction.

Incredible heat radiated from his dark eyes and he wrapped a hand around the back of her neck, drew her to him and kissed her hungrily. As he kissed her, Madeleine continued to toy with him, raking her nails down his chest, fanning her hand over his hot skin, tangling her fingertips in the crisp, springy hair.

When their heated lips finally separated, Made-

leine was surprised to find that Armand had managed—during the prolonged kiss—to completely
unbutton the jacket of her peach traveling suit.
When he pushed it apart, she suffered a mild twinge
of doubt. But when he bent his head and placed the
gentlest of kisses in the valley between her breasts,
all misgivings fled. She felt her nipples tighten and
her stomach contract. And she made no move to
stop him when he pushed the open jacket down her
arms and tossed it aside.

"God, you are so sweet, so beautiful," he said,
placing the tip of his little finger under the lacy
strap of her camisole.

Madeleine felt the strap being slipped off her
shoulder and sliding down her upper arm. She took
a quick excited breath through her mouth and heard
him say, "Look at me, *chérie.*"

Her eyes met his and again she experienced the
feeling of being pulled into him.

"Trust me. I won't hurt you," he promised and
as her gaze stayed locked with his, he raised her
damp skirts and ran a hand up her stockinged left
leg. When his fingers encountered the ruffled border
of her knee-length pantalets, he gave the lacy trim
a playful tug, then urged her knees apart.

Madeleine inhaled anxiously as his warm fingers
moved steadily upward along the inside of her
thigh.

"Kiss me," he coaxed and she eagerly obeyed.

Wildly she kissed him, cupping his lean cheeks
in her hands, anxiously moving her questing lips
against his and thrusting her tongue deep into his
mouth. During the fervent kiss she felt his lean fin-

gers move all the way up between her legs to touch her in that most intimate spot.

Through the soft cotton of her pantalets he slowly, expertly caressed her until the fabric, which was the only barrier between his moving fingers and her tingling flesh, was damp from her body's response.

Sucking anxiously at his lips, she sighed and squirmed and became more aroused with each passing second.

"Feel good, sweetheart?" Armand murmured against her lips.

"Mmm," was all she could manage in reply.

"I want you to feel even better," Armand told her, and with the speed and wizardry of a trained magician, he deftly relieved her of her pantelets.

Naked now beneath the skirts of her damp dress, Madeleine held her breath, waiting expectantly for him to touch her again. Armand made her wait. But only long enough to unhook her lace-trimmed camisole and remove it.

"I knew it," he said, when she was bare to the waist.

"W-what?" she asked, trembling.

"That you don't wear those horrible corsets. You have no need for them. Your waist is naturally small and your breasts—" his eyes lowered to the twin mounds of pale flesh topped with satiny pink nipples "—are full and need no stays to enhance or lift them." As if to punctuate the sentence, he bent his head and kissed the rising swell of Madeleine's left breast.

After that, everything became an electrifying blur

of sheer ecstasy to the highly aroused Madeleine. While the storm raged on with winds so forceful that the couple was at constant risk of being dumped onto the rolling, pitching floor, Armand de Chevalier made passionate, prolonged love to Lady Madeleine Cavendish as if they had forever.

Madeleine wiggled and sighed with pleasure as Armand's warm hand again stole up under her skirts to touch and tease and toy. His fingers slid easily in the silky wetness flowing freely from her, as he leaned to her and brushed a kiss to her right nipple. Instinctively Madeleine arched her back, thrusting her breasts more fully against his hot, handsome face. Armand kissed her, then opened his mouth and gently nibbled on her rapidly stiffening nipples.

Dizzy with desire, Madeleine hugged Armand's dark head to her while he sucked on her responsive nipples and his fingers gently circled that ultrasensitive button of pure sensation between her parted legs.

Armand felt her climax beginning even before Madeleine realized it was happening. He gave her nipple one last plucking kiss, raised his head, and watched the changing expressions march across her beautiful face as she ascended steadily toward total release.

And all the while she was pleading, "Don't stop, don't stop, please, please."

"Never, my love," he assured her, not rushing her, patiently taking her all the way, carefully guiding her to an all-encompassing climax.

"Armand! Armand! Armand!" she cried out at

last and dug her nails into his muscular biceps as she reached the shattering zenith.

"Yes, baby, yes," he soothed, continuing to caress her until he was certain her powerful orgasm was totally completed.

Frantically she grabbed his arm to stay his hand, then went limp against him, shaking and trembling with emotion. He pressed her head onto his shoulder and kissed her parted lips, her closed eyes, her flushed cheeks.

Gale-force winds continued to buffet the sinking ship and the bunk upon which the two were strapped rose and fell with the high, tossing waves. It had little effect on the pair. Hot for each other, determined to fill their last minutes on earth with abandoned carnal joy, they ignored the roar of the wind, the rolling of the ship.

When Madeleine had calmed a little and had caught her breath, Armand finished undressing her. He managed the pleasant task as she continued to sit on his right knee. And as he disrobed her, he lovingly caressed each portion of bare skin he exposed. She was like malleable clay in his artistic hands, stirring to the slightest touch of his fiery fingertips.

When she was as naked as the day she was born, save for her silk stockings and leather slippers, Armand placed a hand behind her right knee and raised it, lifting her foot up onto his own left knee. He took the slipper from her foot and dropped it to the floor. Then he smiled at her, slipped a hand under her lace-trimmed, blue satin garter and peeled it down her leg.

Madeleine watched, puzzled and amused, as he slid the garter up his bare right arm, and released it when it tightly encircled his biceps.

"A keepsake from you," he explained and she nodded.

He stripped the silken stocking down her bent leg and tossed it aside. She suddenly felt very foolish and awkward. Here she was, naked, sitting on his knee with one of her legs bent and raised, her bare foot propped on his knee. She shuddered when he cupped her foot in his palm, raised it slightly and bent to kiss her instep. Then she giggled uncontrollably when she felt his tongue go between her ticklish toes.

He laughed, raised his head and lowered her bare foot to the floor. She waited for him to remove the other stocking. But he didn't do it and she didn't complain although she was sure she looked quite silly wearing nothing but one stocking and one garter.

He didn't think so. "God, you're desirable," he murmured, his hand sweeping down her silk-encased leg. "I want you to leave this one stocking on for me."

"Whatever you want," she said, unhampered by conscience or inhibitions or thoughts of tomorrow, "I want."

"I want *you*," he said. "I want you to give me every kind of love you can possibly express. I want you to tell me everything you've ever wanted to do and never did. I want you to reveal to me every secret yearning you've ever had and never told. I want you share with me every craving you've ever

experienced. I want you to give yourself to me
completely and let me love you as no one ever has.
I want you. I want you, over and over again.''

Already aroused, his bold words further awakened Madeleine's innate sensuality. The things he
said excited her, made her want to give him all she
had to give, to lose herself in him and his lovemaking, to actually do all the forbidden things she
had never done with anyone.

Armand kissed her, took her hand, and placed it
on the waistband of his dark trousers. Her lips fused
with his, her fingers found the buttons of his trousers and she hastily undid them. Then, without his
urging, she laid her hand against the ridge of hard
flesh restrained by his white linen underwear. As
the probing kiss continued, Armand made a half-
strangled sound that Madeleine easily interpreted.

She pulled the white underwear out and away
from his flat belly, freeing his straining masculinity.
Her hand was back on him then, stroking, caressing,
arousing.

Until Armand could stand it no more.

He clasped her fragile wrist, stayed her hand and
said, ''I can't wait any longer, sweetheart.''

In seconds he was naked and Madeleine was
stretched out on her back on the bunk with Armand
lying atop her. The restraining straps were buckled
loosely behind his back. His weight supported on
stiffened arms, Armand lay between Madeleine's
parted legs, kissing her, murmuring shockingly forbidden words of passion, arousing her to a fever
pitch by carefully positioning himself so that his

heavy, pulsing erection was warmly cradled by her open female flesh.

Madeleine lay squirming beneath him, gazing into his eyes and clutching his upper arms. His handsome face, broad chest and muscular shoulders filled the entire scope of her vision. She could see nothing else. Nothing but him. He was her whole world, this giver of such exquisite erotic pleasure.

When Armand bent his head to press a kiss to her breasts, she sighed with prickling pleasure as his silky hair ruffled against her chin and his lips tugged at her nipple. She turned her head on the pillow and smiled dreamily at the sight of her blue satin garter encircling his muscular upper arm.

But when he raised his head and put his hand between their pressing bodies, Madeleine automatically tensed for what was to come.

"Don't, *chérie*," he said. "Relax. I'll be gentle. Let me love you."

She did.

And he did.

She released a shallow breath as she felt his throbbing tumescence slide slowly, cautiously into her. She knew that he was watching her face for signs of pain so she was very careful not to exhibit any traces of the discomfort she briefly experienced. It did hurt. It had been a long, long time. And he was so...so big. She felt as if her body were being filled and stretched far beyond its capacity.

But not for long. Amazingly enough, she found that her yielding flesh was indeed able to accommodate his impressive erection. And when he began to move inside her, Madeleine gave silent thanks that this stranger to whom she was willingly surrendering her body was so very well endowed.

In this dark lover's arms, Madeleine became oblivious to the raging storm. Swept away in a tempest of white-hot passion, deeply impaled upon his thrusting flesh, she rocked and bucked against him, finding the rhythm of the rocking, bucking bunk beneath them.

It was a wild, erotic ride as neither Madeleine nor Armand held anything back. Mating in an almost animalistic manner, they moaned and gasped as they made hot, totally uninhibited love as the ship rose and fell violently, the fierce movements only adding to the savage joy of their vigorous coupling.

Glorying in the intimacy and the ecstasy, Madeleine was certain that this handsome Creole was indisputably the world's most thrilling lover. She was totally enchanted, loving the look in his flashing black eyes, the taste of his burning lips and the splendid feel of his lean body on hers—and in hers.

She was amazed that he had the power and the stamina and the skill to make her climax again and again until she was practically weeping his name in near sexual hysteria. And she was shocked that he could attain his own hot, spurting orgasm and then be able and ready to pleasure her again within just a few short minutes.

And so it went.

While the hurricane howled and punished and threatened to capsize the already sinking ship, the lovers continued to thrill and please and pleasure each other as if there were no tomorrow.

And there wasn't. But it didn't matter.

As Madeleine again felt her lover's hard flesh seek the soft warmth of hers, she sighed and gazed at him, enthralled.

He was everything. He was the only thing. There was no future and no past. Only now with him moving inside her as he looked into her eyes and murmured her name in low, soft tones that she magically managed to hear above the deafening din.

Only him.

Only now.

And now was forever.

Six

Forever came to the end seconds later.

The world intruded.

Loud shouts from out on deck brought the lovers abruptly back to reality. Heads snapped around, listening intently, Armand and Madeleine learned that the sudden flurry of excitement was over a coastal steamer that had been spotted making its way toward the crippled ship.

The sea, they now realized with some surprise, had calmed dramatically in the last few minutes of their lovemaking. They were not going to die after all.

Armand gave Madeleine a quick kiss, levered himself up and drew her to her feet. In haste they dressed and hurried out on deck, hearts pumping with adrenaline.

The steamer had reached the sinking ship, but it was a small vessel. Passengers were already clamoring over the *Starlight's* railing and crowding onto the steamer's deck, endangering the vessel that offered safety.

"No more!" shouted the worried steamer captain, "we can't take any more passengers. We'll swamp if we do! Water's already to the gunnels! Get back, get back!"

A cry of protest rose from the pushing, shoving mob of men. Determined to get Madeleine on the steamer and save her life, Armand swept her up into his arms and forced his way through the crowd.

"Wait!" he shouted to the captain of the *City of Mobile*, handing Madeleine down onto its decks, "You must take her! She's the last woman on board. Show a little mercy, Captain!"

"Very well," the frowning captain reluctantly agreed, "but she's the last one I'll take." He drew a pistol from his waistband and shouted, "I'll shoot the next man who tries to board this vessel!"

Amidst curses and threats from those left behind, the dangerously overloaded steamboat backed away from the sinking ocean liner. Jostled and pushed about, Lady Madeleine stood on the crowded deck and looked back at the sinking ship.

Her tear-filled eyes clung to Armand de Chevalier as he gallantly smiled, waved and threw her a kiss. The lump in her throat grew bigger as she kissed her fingertips and threw the kiss back. And when he hastily unbuttoned his soiled white shirt and whipped it off his left shoulder to reveal her blue satin garter encircling his hard brown biceps, she laughed and sobbed at the same time.

"Armand," she said without sound, realizing that her lover was going to die. She would never see him again.

After many long, nightmarish hours spent on the badly over-crowded *City of Mobile* as it steamed through the Gulf and made its slow way upriver, Lady Madeleine at long last arrived in New Orleans.

It was sunset.

Wan and exhausted from the ordeal, Madeleine stood at the riverboat's lacy railing wondering if her Uncle Colfax and Lord Enfield would be at the landing to meet her. She wondered if they had heard of the hurricane in the Gulf and the sinking of the S. S. *Starlight.* Would they think she had perished? Gone down with the ship? They would have no way of knowing that she had been spared.

Madeleine sighed as she shaded her eyes from the dying summer sun. She couldn't expect them to meet every river steamer making port in hopes she would be on it. It didn't matter. As soon as she reached the levee, she'd hire a carriage to drive her straight to her Uncle Colfax's French Quarter mansion.

Her eyes lighted in anticipation of seeing her adored uncle. It would be so pleasant to have a little time alone with him before she had to face her fiancé, Lord Enfield. The prospect of looking the lord in the eye and pretending that she was still the high-moraled lady he thought her to be, filled Madeleine with dread and apprehension. She was eager to see him, of course, but now that reality had sunk in, she was so riddled with guilt she wasn't sure she could conceal her anxiety.

Dear, kind, unsuspecting Desmond. If he knew what she had done, his heart would break and he would surely hate her for all eternity.

The Louisiana sun finally sank beneath the horizon as the slow-moving riverboat approached the levee. In the lingering orange afterglow Madeleine spotted, standing side-by-side on the bustling levee, her Uncle Colfax Sumner and Desmond Chilton.

Torn by conflicting emotions, she raised a hand and waved madly.

"My sweet little Madeleine!" exclaimed her beaming uncle after the riverboat captain had personally escorted her down the gangway and into the outstretched arms of the spry, sixty-seven-year-old Colfax Sumner. "We heard about the terrible storm," he said, embracing Madeleine, but addressing the captain. "The S. S. *Starlight*, did she make it?"

Madeleine's heart hurt when the captain replied, "Afraid not, sir. The last we saw of her, she was swiftly going down. Those left on board most surely perished."

"Such a tragedy," said Colfax, then hugged his precious niece so tightly he almost crushed her ribs, unaware of his own strength. Against her ear, he said, "I never gave up hope. Thank the Almighty you're safe!"

He released her and Madeleine stiffened slightly when the tall, blondly handsome Lord Enfield immediately took her in his arms. He hugged her, but made no attempt to kiss her and for that she was grateful. He was a well-mannered, blue-blooded nobleman who thought it common and vulgar to demonstrate affection in public. Thank heaven. She was not yet ready to kiss him. She needed a few days, or at least a few hours, before she kissed anyone again.

Holding her in a much gentler embrace than her spirited uncle, Lord Enfield said softly, "My dear, we were so worried." He pulled back to look down at her. "Are you unharmed?"

"I'm fine," she assured him, not feeling fine at

all. Forcing a smile, she glanced at her uncle and added, "Now that I'm here with the two of you."

The trio climbed into the waiting carriage and Colfax himself drove them directly to his Royal Street town house. The troubled Madeleine experienced a measure of well-being when the carriage passed through the mansion's heavy iron gates and rolled through the porte cochere.

She loved this comfortable French Quarter home with its captivating gardens and private courtyard. A charming Creole town house, the structure consisted of a ground floor containing the kitchen and service rooms that opened onto the courtyard. Stairs to the living quarters were mounted outside the galleries in the courtyard. At the far back edge of the property, beyond the courtyard, were a couple of two-story *garçonnières,* carriage houses that had originally been built for male relatives or guests. Their only occupant was the indomitable black woman, Avalina, who single-handedly tended the Sumner house.

On the second floor of the main house were the entertaining rooms: drawing room, dining room, small ballroom, and Colfax's book-lined study and spacious bedroom suite. On the third floor were a number of bedrooms, one of which belonged to Madeleine, even though she had stayed in it only two or three times in her life.

As she alighted from the carriage, Madeleine automatically inhaled deeply and sighed with satisfaction. The sweet scent of magnolias and azaleas and honeysuckle and japonica and Cherokee roses made her realize fully that she was back in the seductive semitropics of New Orleans.

That, and the damp, muggy heat that caused her hair to curl around her face and beads of perspiration to stand out on her forehead.

Eagerly climbing the stairs to the second floor gallery that was embellished with fancy iron lace, Madeleine hurried through the tall, fan-lighted double doors and stepped into the spacious entryway. She had taken but a few short steps before Avalina, her signature white *tignon* on her head, her broad black face radiating pleasure, was there to meet her.

"My stars above, Lady Madeleine, you had us all worried sick," exclaimed the smiling woman who for the past thirty-one years had demonstrated unquestioned efficiency, style and undying loyalty to the man whose home she so capably ran.

"I know and I'm so sorry," Madeleine replied, wrapping her arms around the stout woman.

Half embarrassed, as she always was, when the spirited young noblewoman embraced her—a mere servant—Avalina quickly pulled away, nodded to Lord Enfield and said to Colfax Sumner, "Welcoming celebrations and countless questions about her ordeal will have to wait until Lady Madeleine has fully recovered. She looks weak and pallid and she needs rest."

Nodding, Colfax Sumner quickly agreed with the intuitive Avalina. Lord Enfield similarly demonstrated his caring and kindness, insisting, along with her concerned uncle, that she go directly up to bed and remain there for a least a week. She surely needed that long to recover from all she'd been through.

Madeleine put up no arguments. There was nothing she desired more than to escape the unsettling presence of her devoted fiancé, whom she could hardly face, so plagued was she with guilt.

"You go on now, dearest," said Lord Enfield. "I'll come up to say good-night once you're settled in bed." He glanced at Colfax Sumner. "That is, with your permission, sir."

"Permission granted," said Colfax, smiling.

The lord turned his attention back to Madeleine. "Dear?"

Madeleine inwardly cringed, but managed a smile as she said, "Yes, that would be nice." She turned and hugged her uncle, then followed Avalina.

Upstairs, Madeleine released a soft sigh of relief and nodded gratefully when Avalina asked if she would like to take a nice, long bath.

Moments later Madeleine sank down into the depths of a tub filled to the brim with hot sudsy water. While Avalina gathered up her soiled clothing and laid out a clean white nightgown, Madeleine laid her head back against the tub's rim, closed her eyes and began to unwind as she tried to fully relax.

But with her eyes closed she saw again the handsome face that had been just above her own when the Creole had made love to her during the storm. She was heartsick to think that Armand de Chevalier had drowned, but she knew that it was true. She was genuinely saddened by his death and at the same time filled with remorse for what she had done.

Madeleine opened her eyes and reached for a loofah and bar of sweet-scented soap. She began to anxiously lather her body and to scrub vigorously, determined to wash away any lingering traces of Armand de Chevalier.

As she avidly lathered every inch of her flesh with the soap and hot water, Madeleine told herself that this cleansing bath was exactly what she needed to put everything right. She would, she was determined, successfully wash away even the nagging memories of what she and Armand de Chevalier had impetuously done.

But when, fresh and clean from the bath, she lay in the big four-poster awaiting Lord Enfield, Armand de Chevalier was still very much in her thoughts. It was, she realized, going to take more than a hot bath to free her from the clutches of the Creole.

At the gentle knock on the door, Madeleine glanced at Avalina, half tempted to ask her to stay. "Please invite Desmond in," she said to the housekeeper.

Avalina nodded, opened the door and left as Lord Enfield entered. When he quietly closed the door, Madeleine automatically stiffened. Smiling, he crossed to her, sat down on the edge of the bed facing her and held out his arms.

"Alone at last," he said and reached for her.

He drew her up into his arms and Madeleine fought a perplexing desire to push him away, to order him out of her room, to tell him to leave her alone, that she wasn't feeling well. She sat there in bed with her arms around his neck, her cheek pressed to his chest, feeling trapped and uneasy.

She felt his lips in her hair as he murmured, "How I yearn for the day when we're married and I no longer have to leave you at bedtime." He pulled back to look at her and said, "If only we were already man and wife. I could undress, get into bed with you and hold you all through the night."

Madeleine swallowed convulsively. "Yes, that would be…wonderful."

He read the anxiety in her expressive emerald eyes and felt her slender body tremble. He gave her a puzzled look. "What is it, my dear? You're not yourself. Why, you're trembling."

"It's just…well, I am very tired and I…"

"Oh, of course you are." He was immediately contrite and sympathetic. "How thoughtless and selfish of me. I'll run along now and let you get some rest."

"Thank you, Desmond."

"Good night, my dearest love," he said softly, and his face slowly descended to hers. Terrified he was going to kiss her, Madeleine sighed with relief when he merely brushed his lips to her forehead.

"I love you very much, Madeleine," he whispered, "and I'm so relieved that you came through that terrible disaster unharmed."

Lord Enfield rose to his feet, smiled down at her, and said, "Dream of me tonight, darling."

"I will," she said.

But after he had gone and she'd put out the lamp and lowered the gauzy mosquito *baire* around the bed, it was not Desmond Chilton who filled her thoughts. Armand de Chevalier again intruded.

Madeleine impatiently kicked off the covering sheet, yanked her long nightgown up around her thighs in an effort to battle the sultry New Orleans heat, and closed her eyes.

Exhausted, she fell instantly asleep. But the man who tortured her waking hours followed her into her dreams to hold her and kiss her and make her misbehave.

"She's sound asleep." Avalina, having looked in on Madeleine after Lord Enfield left, announced to Colfax Sumner. "I expect she'll sleep round the clock."

"Yes, bless her heart. She needs the rest," he said. Then he stated, pleased, "It sure is good to have her here."

"It is," Avalina agreed. "And the best part is, she'll be right here at home with us for eight full months."

"That's right," said Colfax. "The wedding is planned for April. We'll have time to enjoy her before she marries and leaves us."

"Indeed," Avalina replied.

"Well, I think I'll retire myself," said Colfax. "It's been an exciting day." He turned, started down the hall toward his bedroom suite, but stopped after taking only a few steps. "Avalina, be sure all the doors have been locked before you go to bed."

"I always do, sir."

"I know you do." He nodded, smiled and went on to his room.

There he disrobed, slipped into the nightshirt Avalina had laid out for him, and got into bed to read. But soon he was yawning sleepily, the words blurring on the pages. He laid the book aside, blew out the lamp, and stretched out on his back, folding his hands beneath his head. He sighed in the quiet darkness, content as he hadn't been in a long time. His only niece was now in his house, safe and sound upstairs, sleeping the sleep of the innocent.

In minutes he, too, was sleeping soundly.

But in the middle of that hot dark night, Colfax Sumner was abruptly awakened by the sound of something hitting the streetside balcony just outside the open French doors. Heart hammering, he lunged up, grabbed his dressing gown and hurried out to investigate.

There on the balcony lay a small leather pouch. Colfax gingerly picked it up, took it inside, lit a lamp and examined the contents of the bag.

Several locks of human hair. Some nail parings. The skin of a reptile. A couple of chicken bones tied together to form a crude cross.

Colfax Sumner had learned enough about the practice of voodoo from Avalina to know that a bundle like this left in the dark of the moon was supposed to work incalculable harm on the occupant of the house.

An intelligent, logical man, Sumner did not believe in black magic. But he did believe that someone wanted to frighten or even harm him. Or someone in his house.

He decisively shook his head and told himself he was being foolish. He had no enemies that he knew of. No one who would wish harm on him or his. Most likely the sneaky person who had tossed the bundle of *gris-gris* onto his balcony had, in the darkness, gotten the wrong house.

Still, as Colfax threw the offensive pouch into

the trash before he took off his dressing gown, he trembled.

And it was a long time before he fell back to sleep.

Seven

It was nearing ten the next morning when Lady Madeleine awakened to the sound of a feminine voice with a pronounced southern drawl excitedly calling her name. Madeleine struggled to open her eyes as a young, pretty woman with coal-black hair and pale-white skin stepped close to the bed and yanked up the mosquito *baire*.

"Lady Madeleine Cavendish!" the young woman happily exclaimed as she sank down onto the bed facing Madeleine.

"Melissa Ann Ledette!" replied Madeleine, lunging up, smiling broadly.

The two young women threw their arms around each other and hugged like long-lost sisters. Madeleine was genuinely delighted to see this raven-haired Creole belle with whom she had become close friends on her last visit to New Orleans. Full of vim, always animated and ready to gossip and laugh, Melissa was the pampered only daughter of prominent New Orleans physician, Dr. Jean Paul Ledette.

"Oh, Maddie, I couldn't wait one second longer to see you," exclaimed Melissa, finally releasing her friend.

"Well, I expected you last night," Madeleine responded.

Melissa's pale, pretty face immediately screwed up into a frown. "But I didn't know you were here last night!"

"I know you didn't," Madeleine said. "I was teasing you."

"Oh, of course." The bright smile was back on Melissa's face. Then, the questions began. Taking Madeleine's hand in both of her own, Melissa said, "Now you must tell me all about the terrible sea disaster. Weren't you absolutely terrified? Did you think you were going to die? Did you actually see people drown? Were there women and children who...who..." Melissa abruptly interrupted herself to say, with a sudden look of sorrow, "Oh, Maddie, the saddest thing...a New Orleans native was on that ill-fated vessel and he didn't make it. He went down with the ship. He drowned."

"I—I'm sorry to hear that," said Madeleine, feeling suddenly as if a band had tightened around her chest.

"I just can't believe he's really gone. He was so handsome and charming and half the women in this city were hopelessly in love with him, including me." Melissa bowed her head and tears welled up in her large, dark eyes. "New Orleans will never be the same without Armand de Chevalier." She immediately raised her head and asked, "Maybe you met Armand on the ship and..."

"I don't think so," said Madeleine, "the name doesn't ring a bell."

Melissa nodded. "If you'd met Armand, you would remember him."

Madeleine gave no reply.

"Forgive me for being so maudlin," said Melissa. "From now on I'll speak of only pleasant things. Want to hear all that's happened in the year since you were here?"

Madeleine finally relaxed a little. "You know I do."

"All right. Let's see, oh yes, you remember Prudence Picard? That prissy girl with the frizzy blond hair and the high-pitched voice? Well, she up and married old Louis Jaubert. It's scandalous, if you ask me. Prudence is barely eighteen and Jaubert is well into his seventies." Melissa immediately burst into laughter and added, "He can't hear and he can't see too well, but apparently one part him still functions. Prudence is pregnant!"

"Oh, no!"

"Oh, yes!" Melissa bobbed her head for emphasis. "Let me see, what else? The youngest Le Blanc boy got killed in a duel last Thanksgiving. No one was surprised. He swaggered around asking for trouble all the time. Pierre Lemonnier's widow ran off with a cabinetmaker from Mobile before her dear-departed was cold in the ground. Abigail Stuart called off her wedding at the last minute and..."

Melissa continued to talk, to inform her friend of all that had happened in the river city since they had last seen each other. Finally she paused, took a breath, and said, "I declare, what gets into me? Momma says I just never shut my mouth. Forgive me, Maddie. I really do want to hear about the shipwreck and all."

Madeleine relayed, in the briefest terms, the events of the disaster, concluding with, "And then a small steamer appeared, took me onboard and saved my life. I'm sure the ocean liner went down less than an hour later.''

"What a terrible nightmare," Melissa commented. Then patted Madeleine's hand and said, "But it's over and now you must put it behind you."

"Yes, I know."

"It's so great to have you here and…and…oh, did I tell you? This year we're planning a big holiday bazaar in December to aid Florence Nightingale and her brave nurses in the Crimea. You'll help out, won't you?"

"Certainly," Madeleine said.

"It'll be great fun. Then, after the holidays we'll have to start planning your wedding! I will be maid of honor, won't I?" Not giving Madeleine a chance to respond, she gushed, "You are so lucky. Lord Enfield will make the perfect husband. He is handsome and distinguished and respected and…and he's rich. Isn't he? I mean, I assume he is, everyone says he is."

Madeleine smiled. "Desmond has, for years now, worked very hard and has made a great deal of money in the cotton and sugar markets. The profits were wisely invested in various other enterprises, such as real estate. Yes, he is a wealthy man."

Melissa sighed. "Well, I'm green with envy. He's so madly in love with you. You'll be pleased to know that I have attended numerous social functions where beautiful women openly flirted with your blond nobleman, but to absolutely no avail. Lord Enfield's heart belongs solely to you." She gazed dreamily at Madeleine.

Feeling as if she had to comment, Madeleine said, "And mine belongs to him."

"Oh, it's all so romantic," said Melissa, clasping her hands together beneath her chin.

The two young woman continued to talk and laugh until Avalina, knocking softly on the door, entered and said, "Miss Melissa, you have been here for over two hours. Time for you go so Lady Madeleine can rest."

"Avalina's right," Melissa said to Madeleine and rose from the bed. She leaned down, pressed her cheek to Madeleine's, and promised, "I'll be back to see you real soon."

Lord Enfield's many business interests required all of his time and attention during the daylight hours. But he visited the Royal Street town house and his cherished fiancée each evening. Taking care not to overstay his welcome and tire his bride-to-be, he would ascend the stairs to her bedroom every evening, bringing with him a bouquet of fresh-cut flowers, or a book, or a box of bonbons. He would pull up a chair and visit with Madeleine, gently holding her hand and smiling at her as they talked quietly together.

Concern for her welfare always uppermost in his mind, the lord never stayed longer than an hour or two. And when it was time for him to depart, he would lean down and brush a brief kiss to her forehead or her cheek.

"I love you so much it hurts to leave you," he'd whisper. "But I want you to get plenty of rest, so I'll go now."

Madeleine was touched by his thoughtfulness.

Most men would have already been pressing her for intimate kisses and caresses, but the blond nobleman was chivalrous. He realized fully that she was not yet well enough to be receptive to displays of passion.

His unfailing kindness and astute understanding caused Madeleine to suffer even greater bouts of guilt. It would have been easier if he had behaved the impatient male and attempted to make love to her. Then she could have blamed him for being so unfeeling and intolerant.

As it was, she could blame him for nothing. He was consistently the empathetic, compassionate fiancé who cared only for her well-being. She was, she knew, a most fortunate woman to have such discerning gentleman eager to make her his wife.

Nonetheless, when Lord Enfield was not there with her, when Madeleine was alone, her thoughts unfailingly returned to the darkly handsome Creole who had gone down with the sinking ship. Armand de Chevalier was, she knew, dead. She knew, as well, that she would never completely forget him.

Fortunately, Madeleine was seldom left alone to brood. Overjoyed to have her in his home, her uncle Colfax spent long hours with her, talking, reminiscing, enthusiastically discussing her upcoming marriage to Lord Enfield.

On a hot, sunny day in early September after spending a full week in bed, Madeleine awakened feeling rested and eager to get up. She reached out and pulled the bell cord that would summon Avalina.

When the woman appeared, Madeleine said, "I can stand this bed no longer. I want to get up. I am

feeling well enough to join Uncle Colfax downstairs for breakfast.''

Indulgent, Avalina smiled. ''The master will be
delighted and I will fix something special for the
momentous occasion.''

Shortly before 9:00 a.m., Madeleine, aided by the
stalwart Avalina, descended the stairs. Colfax
waited at the base. When the two women reached
him, Avalina turned and hurried downstairs to her
kitchen, while Colfax ushered his niece into his
paneled, book-lined study.

''Are you sure you feel like being up?'' he asked,
noting that she was still quite pale.

''I'm fine, Uncle Colfax, really I am.''

''Well, then we've a few minutes before Avalina
calls us to breakfast and there's something I want
to show you.''

He led her across the carpeted study to where a
portrait of LaFayette hung directly behind his mahogany desk. While she watched, curious, he slid
the heavy portrait aside to reveal a hidden wall safe.
A small round safe with a heavy bronze door.

''I keep my most valuable documents here,'' he
explained, then beckoned her forward. ''I will tell
you the combination and I want you to open the
safe.''

When she had opened the safe, Madeleine
stepped back. Colfax reached inside and withdrew
a legal-looking vellum document. He handed it to
her.

''My last will and testament,'' he explained. As
Madeleine unfolded and skimmed the document, he
said, ''Upon my death everything I own will belong
to you, and as you surely know, I have accumulated

a vast fortune over the years.'' He smiled then and added, ''Fortunately, we live in Louisiana, the only state in America where a woman can own property. Much of my fortune in is real estate holdings.''

Madeleine looked up and handed the will back without reading further. With a smile she said, ''Uncle, let's not talk about wills and dying. You are going to be around for at least another twenty or thirty years!''

''Perhaps,'' he said, but with little conviction.

Madeleine noticed and asked, ''Uncle Colfax, you're not...you're not ill, are you?'' Worriedly, she studied his face.

''No, no, child,'' he quickly assured her. ''I'm in excellent health.''

He returned the will to the wall safe, but withdrew a second document. He began to smile as he told her that it was a provisional will that he had had drawn up some eight or nine years ago.

''You were,'' he explained, ''a rather flighty young woman then, as I fondly recall, and I wanted to make certain that you would be protected.'' Madeleine stared at him, her eyes questioning. He continued, ''As you well know, Lord Enfield has been a loyal, trusted friend almost from the minute our cousin arrived in New Orleans. I realized back then—well before the two of you discovered each other and became engaged—that he was an honorable, trustworthy man who would, I felt confident, look after your best interests.''

She nodded her agreement.

''So I wrote up a provisional will making Chilton coexecutor along with a couple of other old friends, giving the three of them total control over my estate, on your behalf." Colfax frowned then and added, "Unfortunately, the other two gentlemen have since passed away." He shook his graying head, then continued, "But I digress. The provisional will remained in effect for seven years. Then, a few months before you and Lord Enfield fell in love and decided to marry, I drafted my last will and testament making you the sole heir."

She smiled at him and said, "As usual, you left no stone unturned. My inheritance had been protected all these years."

"Indeed it has," he replied. "Now I want you to memorize the safe's combination."

"I already have," she said and then proved it by flawlessly reciting it.

He beamed with pride and said, "You always were a very clever girl."

She slid her hand around his arm and said, "Well, of course, I am. I take after my brilliant uncle."

Eight

Soon Lady Madeleine had regained her strength, had pushed Armand de Chevalier and her guilt to the back of her mind and was eager to get out and enjoy the many pleasures of New Orleans.

Lord Enfield, delighted that the roses were back in her cheeks, said at dinner, "My love, I will take you anywhere you wish to go this evening."

"You won't laugh if I tell you where I really want to go?"

"I would never laugh at you, Madeleine," was his gallant reply.

Her emerald eyes lighted and she said, "To Le Circus de Paris! I saw handbills posted that the circus is in town and Avalina said the show is drawing huge crowds every night. I want to go. Say we can, Desmond, please."

Lord Enfield was indulgent. "The circus it is," he said and smiled warmly at her.

Moments later the handsome pair stepped down from Lord Enfield's chauffeured carriage and onto the banquette at St. Ann's. They crossed the street to Jackson Square where a large gathering had assembled to watch the circus.

Sword swallowers. Fire eaters. Jugglers. Trained animals. Colorful clowns. All delighted the spectators. Madeleine applauded like everyone else, fully enjoying herself.

Midway through the performance, the red-coated ringmaster stepped into the center ring and raised his hands for silence.

"*Mesdames et Messieurs,* ladies and gentlemen," he shouted loudly enough for all to hear, "our next performer is a man of great strength."

A ripple of excitement swept through the crowd and they began to chant, "Big Montro! Big Montro! Big Montro!"

The ringmaster again signaled for silence and announced, "The moment you've been waiting for has arrived, my friends. It is with great pleasure that I present to you the amazing Big Montro!"

A gigantic man stepped into the center ring amidst loud applause and whistles and admirers shouting his name. He wore nothing but a low-riding pair of loose white linen trousers. His massive chest was bare, as were his feet.

Like everyone else, Madeleine stared in awe at the imposing giant. Knotted muscles rippled in his gargantuan arms and across his mammoth chest. He slowly turned round and round to afford everyone a good long look at him.

Ironically, his face was round and smooth—a baby face at complete odds with his powerful body. And his dark-brown hair had a little boy's cowlick at the crown. He was smiling shyly, as if embarrassed by all the attention.

He went immediately into his act when a quartet of laughing, tumbling clowns joined him in the ring. The clowns circled the strong man, taunting and teasing him until he reached out and plucked one off the ground. Gripping both the clown's feet in one hand, Montro lifted the laughing man high over his head, extending his long, muscled arm full-length.

The crowd roared.

In minutes Big Montro had scooped up all four clowns and held them easily on his outstretched arms, turning slowly about as the crowd screamed its approval.

For the next half hour the strong man demonstrated his astounding strength and Madeleine applauded as enthusiastically as all the others. She was so caught up in the amazing spectacle, she never noticed that Lord Enfield was not particularly enchanted by Montro's crowd-pleasing act.

At breakfast the next morning, Madeleine excitedly told her Uncle Colfax and the attentive Avalina about the circus and how thrilling it had been.

She took a sip of freshly squeezed orange juice and said, "The very best part was the strong man. Big Montro. You wouldn't believe the things he did!" And she proceeded to tell them of the many incredible feats he had performed.

Colfax smiled and nodded as she spoke. She was, in many ways, still quite childlike, a trait he found most engaging. But she possessed another trait, one that concerned him.

She was a strong-willed woman and so she ignored the frown of worry that immediately crossed her uncle's face when she announced, "I'm going down to the French Market this morning to…"

"Oh, child, I'm afraid a visit to the market will have to wait," Colfax interrupted. "Unfortunately,

I have an important business engagement that I simply cannot break.''

''And why should you?'' she replied. ''I never expected you to go with me.'' She glanced at the black woman pouring another cup of coffee for Colfax. ''Avalina will accompany me to the market,'' she stated in tones that brooked no argument.

Colfax's frown deepened, but he acquiesced.

Lady Madeleine and Avalina walked the three short blocks down to the French Market on the riverfront. The place was humming—women with baskets over their arms were carefully choosing fruits, loaves of bread and freshly caught fish.

Pausing before the many stalls, interested in all that was for sale, Madeleine savored every sight and smell and sound. She loved this busy market where all the varied factions of New Orleans shopped. The haughty French Creoles, the Spanish, the Germans, the Irish, the Americans. People who would normally not even speak to each other rubbed elbows here and haggled over prices.

Drawn to the booth where fresh, hot *beignets* were being served, Madeleine bought one for herself and one for Avalina. Rolling her eyes with pleasure, she quickly devoured the delicious diamond-shaped doughnut that was generously dusted with sweet powdered sugar.

Madeleine was having such a good time she hated to leave. But they had been out in the sultry summer heat now for well over an hour and she was beginning to feel flushed and faint. So, with their many treasures in a big basket over Avalina's arm, the two started home.

They had gone but one short block when a trio of unkempt ruffians suddenly stepped into their path and began making crude, suggestive remarks to Lady Madeleine. One, a big, ugly brute moved in so close Madeleine could smell the strong offensive odor of stale sweat and unwashed flesh.

Horrified, her heart beating in her throat, she said with as much authority as she could muster, "You get away from me! Step out of my way or I'll..."

"Or you'll what, my pretty," mocked the monster, "have a case of the vapors and fall into my arms?"

While Avalina cursed the men in gumbo French, Madeleine looked anxiously about for help.

Help appeared in the form of the six-foot-six giant who Madeleine recognized as the strong man from Le Circus de Paris. Big Montro stepped out of an alley and onto the banquette. Without lifting so much as a finger, the giant, his arms crossed over his massive chest, planted himself squarely in front of the frightened women, sending their tormentors scurrying for cover.

Once the ruffians had gone, he turned, smiled at the grateful ladies and said in a deep, surprisingly soft voice, "I am Montro. I will escort you to your home."

They both nodded, still badly shaken and more appreciative than he would ever know.

The very next morning when Lady Madeleine and Avalina again ventured out, Big Montro was there below on the cobblestone banquette, waiting for them.

"Montro," Madeleine exclaimed when she

reached him, "I thought the circus was leaving New Orleans today."

"It is," he said without emotion, "I am staying here."

"I see," she replied. "Well, Avalina and I are going to meet with a dressmaker over on Toulesse and…"

"I will see you safely there," he said and did.

From that morning on the gentle giant accompanied the two women wherever they went. Very soon, without any formal arrangements, Big Montro became Lady Madeleine's faithful bodyguard.

Madeleine was somewhat surprised that her uncle offered no protests to including Big Montro in his household. It was Colfax who suggested that Montro move into the vacant *garçonnière* across the courtyard at the back edge of the property. And, he agreed to pay him a generous monthly salary, much more than he'd made with the circus.

The truth was that Colfax Sumner was quietly relieved that the strong man would be watching over them. Colfax would never have mentioned it to Madeleine or Avalina or anyone else, but he had felt increasingly threatened of late. Plagued with a nagging sense of foreboding that he couldn't seem to shake.

It was as if some unseen danger lurked in the shadowy streets directly below the mansion's iron lace galleries.

Nine

On a blistering-hot day in September, a tall, dark man stood on the wooden wharf in Havana, Cuba.

Armand de Chevalier patiently waited his turn to board the cargo ship that would take him to New Orleans. Armand was smiling, as usual. He knew how lucky he was to be alive. Plucked from the sea by a small trader bound for Cuba late that fateful August afternoon, he hadn't complained when he learned it was headed for Havana.

"Sounds good to me," he had said with a laugh, after having spent hours bobbing in the water under a burning summer sun.

Now, after three long weeks of rest and boredom in Havana, Armand was as robust as ever and more than ready to go home.

"*Señor,*" said one of the crewman, motioning him forward.

Armand nodded and climbed the gangway, whistling merrily.

The days were the drowsy ones of late summer. The weather in New Orleans stayed hot and muggy throughout the month of September. The hot mist off the bayous seemed to scald the skin.

Along with the humid heat was the constant irritant of the buzzing, biting mosquitoes. The residents of the low-lying river city didn't dare try sleeping without a mosquito *baire* protecting them.

The mosquitoes had been worse than usual this summer, but Colfax Sumner told his niece it was a good thing, really. There had been very few cases of yellow fever this year, thanks to the mosquitoes. He was convinced that the swarms of mosquitoes purified the miasmic swamp airs that caused the deadly disease.

"You actually believe that?" Madeleine asked, skeptical, as the two of them sat together in the shaded courtyard on a sweltering September afternoon.

"Indeed. If the fever had been rampant this year as it was in '53, I would never have allowed you to come near New Orleans. Or, if you had come, you'd have had to stay upriver at the plantation or else have shut yourself up inside this house and never have gone outdoors. You wouldn't have liked that."

"Heavens, no. I do so enjoy going out."

As if she hadn't spoken, Colfax mused, "I recall that the mosquito population was so sparse in '53 one could sleep without the *baire* enclosing the bed. But *bronze john* swept through this city all summer and took countless lives. Barrels of burning tar constantly blackened the skies and burned our eyes and choked us. The cathedral bell tolled each time another poor soul died and it seemed that the terrible tolling never stopped. Night and day it pealed."

"You were in no danger since you had the fever all those years ago?"

"That's true. I've been immune ever since...

since the summer of..." He shook his head sadly, fell silent, and his eyes clouded.

Madeleine knew he was looking back into the past, to that dreadful summer of 1816 and the sad events that had changed his life forever. He had been a young man who was to be married to a beautiful Creole belle. The two had been madly in love, but a yellow fever epidemic had ended their dreams. Both contracted the fever, but Colfax survived. His beloved had not. Twenty-four hours before they were to be married, she died in his arms and was buried in her white wedding gown.

As if there had been no lapse in the conversation, Colfax said, "Yes, thankfully, I am immune. That's why I didn't flee upriver to the safety of the plantation with Avalina in '53. Many of the sick were good friends and they needed me. I did what I could for them, but in many cases it wasn't enough."

"I know you did," Madeleine said and affectionately patted his arm. Quickly changing the subject, she said, "Desmond is coming for dinner and afterward we are going to the theater. Why don't you come with us?"

"Some other time," he begged off. "I've some reading and paperwork to catch up on."

"Well, don't say I didn't ask," she said, giving him a quick kiss on the cheek before she hurried upstairs to dress.

On those evenings when Lord Enfield wasn't taking Lady Madeleine out to dinner or to the theater, he dined with her and her uncle at the Royal Street town house. Or else he invited them to join him for the evening meal at his own Dumaine Street home.

Whether at the Sumner town house or his own home, the earl, ever the caring consort, was careful not to keep either of them up too late. He insisted that the countess should continue to get plenty of rest. Colfax readily concurred, pleased that Lord Enfield was such a thoughtful man.

Madeleine, too, was grateful that Desmond was concerned for her welfare. A true blue-blooded gentleman, he expected nothing more from her than brief good-night kisses in the flower-filled courtyard. Which made her feel terribly guilty. What would he think if he knew how wantonly she had behaved with a total stranger?

One such evening, Madeleine returned to the parlor after kissing Desmond good-night beneath the porte cochere. When she came into the room, Avalina looked at her, then looked at the French clock on the white marble mantel. Nine-thirty. Avalina pursed her lips.

"What? What is it?" Madeleine asked, puzzled.

The black woman shrugged. "Nothing."

"I know better," said Madeleine. "Something's on your mind. What is it?"

Avalina made a face. "Seems to me it's mighty early for a lovestruck gentleman to be leaving his fiancée."

"For heaven's sake, Desmond's only being considerate," Madeleine promptly defended him. "And I appreciate it."

Avalina rolled her eyes heavenward and said, "Will you need me anymore this evening?"

"No. No, I can undress without you."

"Then, good night, my lady." Avalina turned and left the room.

Madeleine stared after her. She had the distinct impression that Avalina did not like Lord Enfield. But why? Desmond was unfailingly cordial to Avalina and even brought her little presents on occasion. Which she accepted almost grudgingly.

Madeleine sighed and climbed the stairs to her room. It was too early for bed. She wasn't sleepy. She was hot and she was restless. The latitude and climate of New Orleans had a disturbingly potent effect on her. The tropical heat of the sultry summer days made her feel lazy and content.

But the long languorous nights had the opposite effect. The New Orleans nights were powerfully provocative. The humid, heavy air. The moonlight on the Mississippi. The sweet scent of jasmine and gardenias. The faint sound of music from a street musician's banjo.

Madeleine wandered out onto the streetside iron lace balcony and inhaled deeply of the warm moist air. Almost wistfully, she looked out over the sprawling city.

Under a beguiling tropic sky, carriages noisily rolled down the streets and laughing people crowded the banquettes. At 10:00 p.m., the Crescent City was alive with merrymakers hurrying to the restaurants and theaters and gaming palaces.

Many were just now leaving their homes to go out for the evening. Avalina was right. It *was* early for Desmond to have gone. He could have stayed a while longer.

She frowned and went back inside.

Madeleine began to undress in the darkness, knowing that she would not sleep. It would be another of those nights when, tormented by the heat and the buzzing of mosquitoes and a shameful yearning for a dead, dark lover, she would toss and turn and sigh.

Feeling edgy and irritated, Madeleine finished undressing. She picked up the fresh nightgown Avalina had laid out for her, then shook her head and tossed the gown across the back of a chair. Naked, her russet hair pinned atop her head for coolness, she climbed into the big four-poster bed. She lowered the mosquito *baire,* punched the feather pillows and lay down on her back.

Her eyes on the cream satin bed hangings above, she exhaled heavily and stretched her long, slender legs, wiggling her toes, ordering herself to think only of Desmond and their wonderful future together.

She assumed that her fiancé was home by now. He lived only a few short blocks away. He was probably having a nightcap before bed.

The weather finally turned.

The damp, sticky heat of summer gave way to clear, brisk autumn air. The mosquitoes subsided and a cool breeze blew in off the river.

On a chilly evening in early October, Lady Madeleine was extraordinarily excited. She was to attend, with her tall blond earl, the first masked ball of the season. She was in high spirits. Memories and regrets had begun to fade. The dark, handsome face that had haunted her dreams was less clear. It blurred. She couldn't recall exactly what Armand de Chevalier looked like.

And she vowed to herself that she would be a

faithful, loving wife to Lord Enfield and never look at another man for as long as she lived.

Now as she finished dressing for the momentous occasion, Madeleine smiled as she gazed at herself in the mirror. She had kept her choice of costumes a secret, except from Avalina, who was helping her dress. She was going to the ball as Shakespeare's tragic heroine, Juliet. Biting her lips to give them color, Madeleine idly wondered, would the earl guess and show up dressed as her Romeo?

At shortly after 8:00 p.m., a cortege of carriages rolled up before the French Quarter's grand St. Louis Hotel. The hotel's façade boasted no out-thrust portico, but instead a line of six graceful columns. In the New Orleans tradition, intricate iron-work galleries opened before the outer rooms. The structure was impressive in every way, but a large domed rotunda was the hotel's real marvel.

The imposing Creole hotel was the center of the city's French business, entertainment and cultural district. It was here that throngs attended the *bals de société,* subscription affairs given by the aristo-cratic Creoles.

On this evening, gorgeously costumed ladies and gentlemen alighted from gleaming coaches and hur-ried inside and through the rotunda. Beautiful milky-skinned, dark-eyed Creole belles clung to the arms of the city's gay handsome blades.

This glittering gala in the hotel's opulent ball-room was one of the season's major affairs, at-tended by the city's elite. Bowers of fresh-cut flow-ers sweetened the air. French champagne flowed freely. An orchestra, in full evening dress, played waltzes.

And Lady Madeleine, in a flowing gown of virginal white chiffon, her russet hair hidden beneath the long conical hennan headdress with shimmering white silk streamers trailing from its tip, wore an elaborate mask adorned with semiprecious jewels. She fairly glowed as she turned about on the dance floor in Lord Enfield's arms. Her fiancé was dressed as Robin Hood.

She waved to Melissa Ann Ledette, an exotic Cleopatra, as Melissa danced by in the arms of her latest beau, a striking young man wearing the robes of a desert sheik. Madeleine nodded to others on the floor. She was having a wonderful time.

In fact, Madeleine felt more carefree and gay than she had since arriving in New Orleans.

But that warm sense of well-being faltered when she spotted, across the crowded dance floor, a tall, raven-haired, masked Romeo in a brilliant Harlequin vest. She couldn't see his face—most of it was covered with a jet-back mask—but there was something disturbingly familiar about the set of his wide shoulders, the tilt of his dark head and the easy, fluid way he danced. He moved with a provocative, feline grace that instantly set off alarm bells in Madeleine's head.

She told herself that she was being silly.

Returning her full attention to her fiancé, Madeleine was more than gracious when—at the request of the orchestra leader—everyone changed partners. She laughed merrily at the stricken look on the lord's face when a short, rotund Maid Marion with bouncing sausage curls eagerly grabbed him and lifted her short, plump arms up around his neck. Still laughing, Madeleine turned to receive her new partner.

The tall, dark, masked Romeo.

His black eyes glittering dangerously through the twin holes in his mask, he smiled engagingly, drew her close, and waited for her acknowledgement.

Her breath now short, her heart pounding furiously, she said as he began to slowly move to the music, "And who are you?"

"Why, Juliet," he said, "I'm your brave and handsome Romeo."

The deep, pleasing baritone was vaguely familiar, but still she was uncertain. It couldn't be. He had drowned. He was dead. He couldn't possibly be here in New Orleans at the St. Louis Hotel.

But then he bent his head, put his lips near her ear, and repeated the words she had once so foolishly said to him.

"Make love to me."

Lady Madeleine was struck speechless. Aghast. Unable to respond. He quickly took advantage of the situation. As he had on the ship, Armand de Chevalier smoothly danced her out of the stuffy, crowded ballroom and onto the deserted stone balcony.

There he repeated what he had said on the doomed ocean liner, "Kiss me, Countess. Kiss me once."

Before she could protest, Armand kissed Madeleine, sending her wits scattering. He raised his head, looked about and swiftly guided her to a secluded alcove hidden between two tall stone pillars.

He drew her closer and kissed her again.

It was a kiss of such potent heat, she melted in his arms. Nobody had ever kissed her the way this masked man kissed her and she couldn't bring herself to resist. Their masks still firmly in place, the tall, dark Romeo and the beautiful russet-haired Juliet stood on the chill, windswept balcony embracing ardently like two long-lost lovers.

They kissed greedily. They gasped for breath. They changed positions and kissed again. They clung to each other in a daze of building passion.

But finally, when Armand's warm, lean hand slipped down inside her low-cut bodice to cup and caress her soft, warm breast, Lady Madeleine came to her senses. She pushed his hand away and began to struggle.

"You!" she cried. "What are you doing here? I thought that you…you…"

"Drowned?" He supplied the word she was searching for and again reached for her.

"Yes." She was almost shouting now, anxiously tearing his lean fingers away from her waist.

"Now, Countess, you of all people should have known that I'm not that easy to kill," he said with a self-deprecating smile as he stripped off his black mask.

She stared at him, her lips parted, her breath caught in her throat. She had forgotten how devastatingly handsome he was. The imposing height. The smooth olive skin. The dark flashing eyes. The arrogant nose. The explicitly sensual mouth.

Seeing him again—kissing him again—brought back vivid memories of their unforgettable lovemaking.

And with them returned the shame and remorse.

Confused and upset, she said quickly, "Mr. de Chevalier, I must tell you that I am engaged to be married, and so…"

"You forgot me that quickly?" he quipped, shaking his head as if in disbelief. "I am deeply wounded," he said, placing a spread hand over his heart.

As if he hadn't spoken, she said, "If there is an ounce of decency in you, you will *not*…you must promise me that…surely no gentleman would…"

Smoothly interrupting, Armand said, "But as you learned firsthand, I'm no gentleman."

Taken aback, for a moment she said nothing. Just gritted her teeth and looked daggers at him.

"Oh you—you blackhearted knave!" she finally sniffed indignantly and turned to flee. "Say anything you please!"

Armand called after her, "Relax, Countess, your guilty secret is safe with me."

She was not convinced.

Ten

At the Royal Street town house that same October evening, Avalina stood in the foyer holding Colfax Sumner's cloak as the tall cased clock struck the hour of nine. She had been standing there for a full fifteen minutes, wondering what could be keeping him. She was beginning to grow annoyed.

Late getting home from his office. Now late getting ready for the gala. It wasn't like him.

Colfax had intended to go to the masked ball with Lady Madeleine and Lord Enfield. But since he been late coming home, he had urged them to go on without him; he would meet them there. They had agreed and, accompanied by the ever watchful Big Montro, had gone on ahead.

Now, more than an hour later, Colfax was still in his room. With each tick of the clock, Avalina felt her irritation rising. Big Montro had returned a good forty-five minutes ago and was patiently waiting down in the porte cochere to see Colfax safely to the hotel.

Avalina finally huffed and hung the dark evening cloak on the coat tree. Hands going to her hips, she marched down the hall to Colfax's quarters.

Pausing before the closed door, she rapped loudly on it and shouted, "A vain woman could have been dressed by now! You're late and it's high time…''

The door opened and Colfax Sumner stood there, dressed in evening attire. He looked pale and drawn and Avalina's aggravation instantly evaporated.

"Colfax," she said, using his given name, which she only did when the two of them were alone. "What is it? What's wrong?"

"Nothing's wrong," he said to the loyal black woman who was his trusted friend as well as his valued housekeeper. He tried a faint smile. "Guess I'm just getting slow in my old age."

"You don't look well, Colfax. Maybe you should stay home this evening. Get to bed early."

He shook his gray head. "I promised Madeleine I would be there." He coughed needlessly then and, attempting to sound casual, asked, "Did Montro come back?"

She nodded. "He's down in the courtyard waiting for you."

"Ah, good," he said, and the astute Avalina noted the look of relief that came into his pale eyes.

He was afraid of something. She could sense it. And that made her afraid.

Together they walked down the hall to the front door. When they paused in the foyer and she took his evening cloak from the tree and draped it around his shoulders, a slight shudder swept through his body.

She felt it, stepped around in front of him, and said, "There *is* something wrong, Colfax. You are trembling." Her voice was low, soft and her big, dark eyes were wide with worry.

"Just one of those times when a cat walked

across my grave,'' he said with a smile, making
light of it. "Now, good night, Avalina, I must be
on my way."

"Very well, but you be very careful, you hear?"

"I hear."

As soon as he was gone, a troubled Avalina hurried out to her *garçonnière*. She went into her bedroom, fell to her knees before a heavy oak chest
and pulled out the bottom drawer. After rummaging
around beneath some folded winter clothes, she
withdrew a small velvet pouch with a drawstring.

She rose and hurried back across the courtyard
to the main house. Inside she went directly to Colfax's bedroom. From a small compartment within
the velvet pouch, she withdrew an amulet she had
gotten years ago from an old voodoo queen. Softly
uttering incantations that she hoped would cast a
magical spell of safekeeping over the house and its
occupants, she placed the sacred charm beneath
Colfax Sumner's four-poster bed.

Then she rose and hurrying to the streetside balcony, pushed the double doors open. There she
carefully sprinkled some magical powders from the
velvet pouch. She repeated the exercise on the balcony opening onto the courtyard. She even sprinkled some of the precious powder on each win-
dowsill.

Rising to her feet, she left his room, went down
the corridor to the front door. There she sprinkled
more powder. Softly chanting as she worked, Avalina didn't stop until all the doors on all three levels
of the town house had been lightly dusted with the
magical powder.

Colfax would surely laugh and tease her if he

knew what she was doing. But she didn't care. She fully believed in the evil power of voodoo and knew that it was up to her to try to ward away the danger threatening the master of the house.

Finally Avalina pulled the velvet bag's drawstring tight, and looked about, nodding her *tignon*ed head approvingly. She felt better.

Colfax should be safe now.

At least in his own home.

Back inside the ballroom, Lady Madeleine stopped and leaned against the wall for a minute to catch her breath and calm herself. Pale and shaken, she searched anxiously for Lord Enfield. Nervously scanning the crowd, she saw her Uncle Colfax, arriving late for the ball, warmly greeting none other than Armand de Chevalier as if the Creole were a long-lost son.

Her lips fell open and her eyes widened.

Madeleine cringed inwardly when her uncle caught sight of her and immediately motioned for her to join them. She had no choice. If she refused, it would look suspicious. Dear lord, how did she get herself into these terrible predicaments?

Swallowing hard, drawing a spine-stiffening breath, Madeleine started toward the two men.

"My dear," said her uncle, smiling broadly, when she reached them, "I want to introduce you to a good friend."

She glanced warily at Armand and caught the gleam of mischief in his eyes. She wanted to choke him.

"Armand," Colfax stated proudly, "this is my beautiful red-haired niece, Lady Madeleine Cavendish." Armand reached for her hand as her uncle continued, "Madeleine, may I present Mr. Armand de Chevalier, a true Creole whose ancestors came to New Orleans from France more than a hundred years ago."

"A genuine honor, Lady Madeleine," Armand said before he bent and brushed his lips lightly across the back of her hand.

"Can you believe it, my dear?" Colfax Sumner added, "Armand was on the same ill-fated vessel as you!"

Attempting to unobtrusively free her hand of Armand's, Madeleine feigned surprise. "Indeed? That certainly is a coincidence."

"Isn't it a miracle that you both survived?" said Colfax. Before either could reply, he asked, "Did the two of you happen to meet on board?"

Madeleine felt her heart stop beating. Terrified the devilish Armand would give her away, she anxiously clasped his hand in a pleading request that he remain quiet.

He gently squeezed her slender fingers and replied graciously, "Unfortunately, I didn't have the pleasure."

"Too bad, too bad," said Colfax, then, "Armand, my boy, next time you have a free evening, please come round for dinner."

Twin points of impish light flashing in his night-black eyes, Armand stated, "Why, luckily I'm free tomorrow evening."

"Then we insist you join us for dinner at eight," Colfax said, and looked at his niece as she withdrew her hand from Armand's, "don't we, my dear?"

"By all means," she replied calmly, favoring Armand with a self-assured smile. But the pulse in her bare throat was beating double time and he was not fooled.

In the next breath, her uncle informed Armand that, unfortunately, he wouldn't be having his only niece with him for very long.

"Oh?" Armand looked from uncle to niece. "A short visit? You'll soon be returning to England, Lady Madeleine?"

"No, no," Colfax answered for her. "New Orleans is to be her home. She'll continue to live right in the city, but not with me. You see, she is engaged to be married next spring."

"May I wish you every happiness," Armand addressed Madeleine. Smiling easily, he asked, "And who is the lucky fellow?"

"Desmond Chilton, the Earl of Enfield," she haughtily informed him.

And was taken aback by the fleeting look of shock or dismay that came into his expressive black eyes at her smug announcement. It vanished so quickly she wondered if she had imagined it. Surely she had. After all, she had told him out on the balcony that she was engaged and he hadn't seemed to care one whit.

She stiffened when she heard Armand say, "Sir, may I have your permission to dance with Lady Madeleine?"

Colfax knew his niece well. He chuckled and said, "You have my permission, but you'd better ask Madeleine if she..."

Armand didn't. He knew she'd refuse. So he simply wrapped his long fingers firmly around her upper arm, assertively guided her out onto the floor and took her in his arms.

Flashing him a dazzling smile to ensure that no one would know how she really felt, Madeleine informed him, "If you possessed even the tiniest bit of sensitivity, you would know that you are the last man on earth with whom I wish to dance."

"Why is that, Countess?" He grinned wickedly at her. "Think you'll enjoy it more than you should?"

She laughed in his face. "I think, Creole, that you greatly over estimate your appeal."

"Do I?" he responded, drawing her closer. He put his lips near her ear and whispered, "Tell me your heart is not fluttering just as mine is. Declare here and now that you dislike having my arms around you. Swear to me that you're not experiencing even a hint of that uncontrollable passion we knew on the ship."

Her angry reply was, "You are mad, de Chevalier. Totally insane. And you're unprincipled, as well! Indecent. Vulgar. Disgusting. Repulsive. Loathsome and...and..."

"Revolting?" he prompted with a grin, unfazed by her insults.

"That, too!" she said. "Now won't you please take me to my fiancé, Lord Enfield, at once."

"Are you afraid of me, Countess?" He lifted a dark eyebrow and added, "Or are you afraid of yourself?"

"Afraid? I?" She gave him a wilting look. "I'm afraid of nothing, de Chevalier."

"Then finish the dance and I won't say another word."

She sighed and reluctantly agreed. And then wished that she had not. As he slowly, seductively turned her about the polished floor beneath the blazing chandeliers, Madeleine experienced all the things of which he just accused her.

Her heart, pressed against his solid chest, was pounding with excitement. His arms, those long, powerful arms, felt splendid around her. Her temperature swiftly rising, she found herself suffering from more than just a hint of the uncontrollable passion they had known on the ship.

When at last the dance ended, she felt quite faint and unnerved. Armand cupped her elbow and ushered her back to her uncle. Madeleine was so shaken from the close contact with the Creole she was glad that Lord Enfield was engaged in conversation across the ballroom, lest he notice.

"Child, you look flushed," said her Uncle Colfax, his brows knitting. "Are you feeling okay?"

"Just a little overheated," she said with a weak smile.

"Ah, what you need is some refreshment," said her uncle. "I'll go get you a nice cup of iced fruit punch."

"I'll go with you," she said, and grabbed Colfax's arm. Glancing at Armand, she said, "You'll excuse us, sir?"

"Why, certainly, Lady Madeleine."

Colfax Sumner smiled at the younger, taller man. "Now don't forget dinner tomorrow night."

"I'll be there," Armand promised.

Eleven

Armand arrived at the Royal Street town house next evening at eight sharp. In one hand was a bouquet of long-stemmed white roses; in the other a box of Swiss chocolates.

Avalina let him in and Madeleine, seated on one of the twin damask sofas in the spacious drawing room, watched in annoyance as Armand effortlessly charmed the usually sedate housekeeper. Avalina squealed like a schoolgirl when he kissed her hand and teased her.

"The roses are for Lady Madeleine," he told the laughing black woman. "The chocolates are for no one but you."

Madeleine, overhearing, rolled her eyes heavenward. Then braced herself as the Creole stepped into the arched doorway of the parlor. Looking suave and handsome, he was smiling easily, his neatly brushed raven hair gleaming in the lamplight, his clothes perfectly tailored, the crease in his buff trousers breaking at just the right spot atop his leather shoes.

Madeleine felt her pulse quicken at the sight of him. Such potent masculinity. Such dynamic magnetism.

Much as she hated to admit it, the handsome Creole need do nothing more than enter a drawing room to disturb the entire atmosphere. An electricity immediately filled the air and Madeleine knew instinctively that hers was not the only feminine bosom in which he stirred shameful thoughts.

"My boy, we're so glad you could come," Colfax rose to greet Armand. "Come in, come in, and we'll have a glass of tafia before dinner." He shared Armand's fondness for the potent sugarcane rum. "Lord Enfield's running a little late. Should be along any minute."

"Good evening, Lady Madeleine," Armand acknowledged.

She nodded almost imperceptibly. And to her chagrin, he, grinning and looking for all the world like a charming, spoiled little boy, crossed the elegantly appointed room and sat down right beside her on the sofa. He was seated there, with a long arm resting behind her on the sofa's tall back, when Lord Enfield arrived. Desmond walked into the room and Armand unhurriedly came to his feet, as did Colfax Sumner.

"I believe the two you know each other," said Colfax to Desmond.

"Yes, we do. De Chevalier," Desmond said, smiling, and thrust out his hand.

"Lord Enfield, good to see you," Armand responded and the two men shook hands.

"My love," Lord Enfield quickly turned his attention to Madeleine. "Forgive me for my tardiness."

"Of course, I forgive you," she said, then blinked in genuine surprise when he came to her, reached for her hands, drew her to her feet, and warmly embraced her before her uncle and Armand de Chevalier.

Beaming, Colfax said to the couple, "Now, now, none of that romantic foolishness before dinner, you two." And to Armand, "Guess we'll have to forgive them for being so much in love they hardly know we're here."

Colfax laughed jovially.

So did Armand.

Soon the foursome went in to dinner in the candlelit dining room. Madeleine was seated across from Armand, Desmond at her side. Within minutes she wished it had been the other way around. If the Creole was sitting beside her, she wouldn't have to look at him. As it was, each time she lifted her eyes she caught sight of the dark, handsome face, half shadowed in the candlelight, the gleaming raven hair, the beautifully tapered brown fingers holding the heavy cutlery or lifting the wineglass.

And, it did not escape her attention that Armand's bold dark gaze, too often, touched her cleavage. She wished now that she had worn a different gown. The one she had carelessly chosen for the evening was an unquestionably lovely creation of rich turquoise merino wool, but the bodice, fashioned into a deep V between her breasts, was quite low, revealing, perhaps, a bit too much flesh.

Aware that de Chevalier had noticed her decolletage, Madeleine self-consciously drew quick, nervous breaths. Which only served to accentuate her dilemma. Mortified, Madeleine was tempted to snatch up her dinner napkin and pointedly cover herself.

But then her Cavendish pride asserted itself and

she decided she was not about to let the brash Creole think he was embarrassing her. She knew that she had a magnificent bosom and she was vain enough to be proud of it.

Madeleine quickly glanced at her uncle to be sure he was not looking at her. He wasn't. He was focused fully on Desmond, shaking his heavy silver fork to make a point. Desmond was thoughtfully nodding his head, agreeing.

So Madeleine, her lowered lashes fluttering over mischievous emerald eyes, pointedly glanced at Armand to make sure she had his attention. She did. She sat up very straight, moved her arms back until her elbows touched the plush fabric of the chair, allowed her hands fall to her lap, and then took a long, deep, slow breath, the deliberate gesture swelling her full bosom against the gown's tight bodice until her pale white breasts were nearly spilling out of the dress.

She felt a pleasing degree of victory when she caught the flash of fire in Armand's black eyes and saw him swallow hard and reach for his wineglass.

Trifle with her? She'd show him! Madeleine gave Armand a smug look and turned her attention to Lord Enfield.

Her victory was short-lived. At her uncle's urging, Armand began to talk about the shipwreck and the events leading up to it. As Madeleine listened to him speak in a low, clear baritone, she was on pins and needles. Would he, as he had at the masked ball, keep quiet about her? Or would he tell what really happened that day? Would he carelessly reveal that the two of them had not only met, but had been together in that last hour she spent on the sinking ship?

Avalina interrupted when she came into the dining room bearing a heavy silver tray. Madeleine gave silent thanks and exhaled heavily.

Avalina had outdone herself on the dinner.

She had prepared not one, but two, tempting entrees. And so many mouthwatering side dishes Madeleine lost count. Smiling broadly, Avalina served Armand a huge helping of her own special brand of succulent gumbo; a rich combination of shrimp, crab, bits of ham and spicy herbs served over a heaping bed of rice.

Then she brought in a plump roast duckling, covered in a thick rich brown sauce. While Madeleine was well aware that roasted duckling was one of Desmond's favorites, it was obvious that de Chevalier couldn't get enough of the spicy gumbo. How, Madeleine idly wondered, did Avalina know that gumbo was one of the Creole's preferred dishes?

Madeleine had never liked roast duckling. She loved Avalina's rich gumbo. But tonight she chose the duck, shaking her head no to the tempting gumbo. She didn't want de Chevalier to think they shared anything, even the appreciation of a good, spicy dish.

The three men ate with genuine relish. Madeleine had no appetite. She just wanted the meal to end so that the vexing Creole would leave and she could relax. She noticed, as the table conversation went spiritedly on about her, that Armand seemed perfectly comfortable and at ease.

Damn him. Shouldn't he feel awkward and

ashamed to be sitting at the table with Desmond? Didn't it bother de Chevalier that he had been intimate with her when she was Lord Enfield's fiancée? Did the man have no conscience?

Apparently not.

Desmond, too, appeared to be perfectly placid. Uncle Colfax, who loved entertaining, was clearly having a delightful time. While she was in agony, the men were thoroughly enjoying themselves. Apparently none of them cared how she felt. She wondered if a single one of them knew that she was sitting here wanting to scream.

Finally, after more than an hour, the miserable meal ended. The quartet rose from the table and strolled leisurely back toward the drawing room. Desmond and Madeleine were in the lead, Colfax and Armand following. Madeleine was smiling now, relieved the nightmarish evening was coming to an end.

Or so she thought.

"It's early," she heard her uncle say. "Let's have a spot of brandy with our coffee and visit some more."

Madeleine held her breath, praying that de Chevalier would graciously decline.

"I'd love a brandy," Armand said and without being able to see his face, she knew that his black eyes were twinkling evilly.

The three gentlemen drank cognac while Madeleine sipped an apricot brandy. She heard the tall cased clock in the hall strike the hour of ten. Surely the Creole would leave now.

He did not.

He stayed on, talking, laughing, swapping amusing tales with her uncle and Desmond.

It well past eleven when, at long last, Armand rose and said, "I had no idea it was getting so late. Forgive me, I've overstayed my welcome."

"No, no, not at all," assured Colfax.

"It was a most enjoyable evening," Armand said, shaking the shorter, older man's hand. "Thank you so much for having me."

"Any time, any time," said Colfax, smiling, patting Armand on the back. "Promise you'll come back soon."

Both Madeleine and Desmond had risen to their feet. Armand turned to them, bade them good evening and was gone.

Stifling a yawn, Colfax immediately said, "It's past my bedtime. Good night, children."

"Good night," they said in unison.

"Walk me down to the carriage?" Desmond said to Madeleine and she nodded.

In the courtyard, she was surprised when instead of going directly to his waiting carriage he guided her to one of the many iron lace benches that graced the garden. They sat down and he immediately took her in his arms and kissed her. A warmer, longer kiss than his norm.

But nothing to compare with the blazing hot kisses of Armand de Chevalier.

"It was an enjoyable evening, wasn't it?" he said.

"Yes, it was. Mr. de Chevalier can be quite amusing," she offered. "How well do you know him, Desmond?"

He answered with a smile and question. "How well do you know him?"

Madeleine panicked. "Me? Why, I don't know him at all. I met him for the first time last night at the masked ball." She hoped the Almighty wouldn't strike her dead for lying.

"Well, watch him, my dear. He's a bit of a devil."

"A devil? What do you mean?"

Still smiling, Desmond shook his blond head and told her, "I like de Chevalier, he can be most entertaining, a pleasure to be around. But, he's a typical Creole, lazy and unprincipled, caring only for his own pleasure. His habits are quite scandalous. His only ambition, it seems to me, is to live a life of indolent ease, without aim or purpose."

Her heart hammering, Madeleine said softly, "If this it true, why does my uncle—"

Desmond laughed and said, "De Chevalier is one of those people who can get away with murder. Colfax, like everyone else, is willing to turn a blind eye to the Creole's shortcomings. Which is fine, so long as he never has any business dealings with de Chevalier. I wouldn't trust the carefree Creole as far as I could throw him."

Madeleine listened intently, learning that Armand de Chevalier was exactly the kind of man she had thought him to be the first moment she laid eyes on him. A rogue. An adventurer. A disbarred attorney who owned and operated The Beaufort, one of New Orleans' many gambling establishments.

De Chevalier, Desmond told Madeleine, had made so much money from his popular gambling den, that he had invested in other, more respectable businesses and had made huge profits.

Madeleine made no comment. She didn't want Desmond to think she was interested in anything the Creole did.

But without her prompting, the lord continued to talk about Armand de Chevalier. "The Creole has been so prosperous he has several abodes. I'm told he maintains luxurious quarters upstairs above his gaming palace. And, he has an elegant apartment in the new Pontalba Building on Jackson Square. A lake house out on Pontchartrain." Lord Enfield shook his head. "He even has a big plantation mansion upriver, not far from your uncle's place."

"He must be very wealthy," said Madeleine.

"No doubt, but then it's relatively easy to amass great sums of money if one has no qualms about how it is made," said Desmond.

"That's true," Madeleine replied, hearing the censure in his tone.

"De Chevalier not only likes to make money, he likes to spend it as well. Which is probably why he manages to attract an ever changing parade of exquisitely lovely women."

"Are there many?"

Desmond nodded. "He's rarely seen without a pale-skinned Creole beauty on his arm, but none mean anything to him. He treats them all like physical playthings, caring nothing for their tender feelings, callously exchanging them for a new one after he tires of them."

"Sounds like he's a heartless scoundrel," Madeleine said, silently praying that Desmond would never, ever find out she had once—for one brief unforgettable hour—been the reckless Creole's physical plaything.

"Yes, but then he's not our problem, is he, my love?"

"No. Of course not."

"Kiss me good-night. It's late and I must go."

Madeleine stood in the moonlight and watched as the lord's carriage rolled through the porte cochere and turned into the street. Once again she reminded herself how fortunate she was that Lord Enfield was such a good, admirable, honest man who loved and respected her.

Nothing at all like the wicked Armand de Chevalier.

Twelve

November settled over New Orleans with a cold, raw dampness. The long, somnolent afternoons of summer were now gone and the sunny Louisiana skies changed from a dazzling azure blue to a depressing gunmetal gray. A chill, foggy mist often blanketed the River City.

Winds swept fallen leaves across dim winter courtyards and cobblestone banquettes. The bright yellow, green and peach-hued stucco houses of the French Quarter seemed to lose their cheerful colors in the cloudy autumn gloom.

The dramatic change in the weather did little to dampen the spirits of New Orleans native, Armand de Chevalier. The climate of the old River City suited him fine. The warm sunny days in the spring of the year were as near to perfect as could be found this side of paradise. And the long, lazy days of the hot summertime had a calming effect; a sweet lassitude went hand in hand with the muggy heat. And then, when finally the scorching, humid days grudgingly gave way to the coming chill of autumn, he felt pleasantly invigorated and optimistic.

On a nippy November evening, Armand de Chevalier stood naked, save for a white towel knotted at his waist, in the bathroom of his elegant second-floor apartment in the Pontalba Building on St. Peter Street. Armand, just out of his bath, was humming as he shaved, feeling good, looking forward to the evening.

When he had completed the task of shaving his dark, heavy beard, he picked up twin, soft-bristled, wooden-backed brushes, and ran them through his black hair several times at the temples. He tossed the brushes on the marble vanity and started to turn away from the mirror.

But he stopped.

And he grinned.

And he reached for the sun-faded, water-damaged blue satin garter that hung on one of the ornamental gold leaf flowers framing the heavy mirror. Armand lifted the garter away from the mirror frame as if it were fragile and might break into a million pieces. His black eyes flashed as he slipped the garter over his right hand and slid it up his arm and over his hard biceps.

Armand had, since the stormy August afternoon when he had taken the garter from the shapely leg of the beautiful Lady Madeleine, never been without it. He had continued to wear it throughout that long summer day and he'd been saved when it looked like all hope was lost. It had been nothing short of a maritime miracle. So from that fateful day he had thought of the garter as his good luck charm.

He never left his house without it.

At times he wore the garter around his upper arm, as tonight. Other times it encircled his lower calf, just above the ankle. When he didn't wear it, he stuffed it in the inside breast pocket of his frock coat. Or he put it in his trouser pocket. Or a vest pocket. Each time he ventured from his home, Madeleine's garter was somewhere on his person.

Looking in the mirror at a bare-chested man wearing a women's garter on his arm, Armand laughed at himself for his foolishness. Then he turned away from the mirror and went into the bedroom to dress.

He drew on freshly laundered white underwear, then shoved his long arms into the sleeves of a crisp white shirt with a fancy pleated yoke. His cravat was of shimmering black silk and his stick pin and cuff links were black onyx trimmed in gold. Next came stockings and a pair of gleaming patent-leather shoes. Then he stepped into snug-fitting black trousers, sharply creased, and drew on the matching coat that flared at just the proper angle.

Armand de Chevalier was ready for an evening at The Beaufort.

Extending his arms so that an inch of white cuff would show beneath the coat sleeve's edge, he went into the drawing room. The double doors to the gallery were open despite the pervasive chill of the gathering dusk. Armand poured himself a shot of Kentucky bourbon and went out onto the iron lace gallery.

He squinted in the foggy twilight. Cold mist kissed his freshly shaven face, but it felt good. In the dense fog he could barely make out the huge statue of Andrew Jackson astride a rearing steed, which his landlady, the Baroness Micaela de Pontalba, had recently had erected at the center of the Vieux Carré parade ground. The plaza had been renamed Jackson Square to honor the hero of the

1815 Battle of New Orleans. But to Armand, it would always be the Place D'Armes.

A bell tolled and Armand shifted his gaze to the twin-towered St. Louis Cathedral that dominated the plaza's north side. It was there that his parents had been married. Now both lay buried in the old St. Louis cemetery, having died within hours of each other in the yellow fever epidemic of '43. Armand shook his dark head. He couldn't recall the last time he had been inside the old church or to the cemetery.

His squint-eyed gaze moved on to the left of the Cathedral to the old Cabildo government building. Next to the Cabildo was the Presbytère, which served as a courthouse. Armand had spent a great deal of time in both buildings when he was a practicing attorney. Now he rarely entered either.

He shifted his attention, directly across the square. But could only make out the hazy outline of the Pontalba apartments on St. Ann, which matched those where he stood. Lastly, he turned and looked toward the riverfront bordering the south side of the square.

A few people walked beneath the street lamps along the banquette near the river. But the mist was so thick, he couldn't see the many vessels lining the wharf. He could, however, hear the frogs croaking at water's edge and an occasional shout from a flatboatman.

Armand drew a deep breath of the chill, wet air and smiled. How he loved this old city. He had traveled extensively, both in America and on the Continent, but there was no place on earth he would rather be than right here in New Orleans.

He stood on the gallery for another minute or two before spotting his chauffeur-driven carriage pull in at the banquette directly below. He waved to the driver, turned, grabbed his dark evening cloak from the coat tree, and hurried downstairs.

It was a short ride from his Pontalba apartment to his Carondelet Street gambling palace. In minutes he was stepping down from the carriage and climbing the stone steps to the heavy front doors of The Beaufort, an opulent, three-story gambling club.

In the huge marble foyer, Armand handed his cloak to a smiling employee whose sole job it was to check the wraps of the club's patrons.

Nodding and smiling, the man took Armand's cloak and said, "Good evening, boss."

"Evening, Sam. We doing any business tonight?"

"A little early yet," said Sam.

"That's true. It'll pick up around nine or so."

"You bet," Sam said as Armand turned away.

Straightening his cravat and smoothing his hair, Armand paused on the jutting lip of the raised foyer. He stood at the edge of the curved, elevated entrance, below which was the main gaming salon. Wide marble steps led down into the vast, plushly carpeted room. Crystal chandeliers, suspended from the twenty-foot ceiling, cast prisms of light on elaborate marble statuary, white marble fireplaces, heavy damask curtains, burgundy velvet carpets, and green baize tables where nimble-fingered dealers stood ready for the night's action.

The Beaufort was the only gambling establishment in the city, and perhaps America, where the croupiers and dealers were required to wear evening dress. Armand thought it gave the place a touch of class. So did the patrons. The richness of appointments, the elegance of the club drew the city's elite to try their luck at games of chance.

New Orleans' young, rich, good-looking blades and their beautiful Creole sweethearts, garbed in gorgeous evening gowns, frequented The Beaufort. Not all the lovely ladies who visited the club came in the company of a gentleman. Some of the bolder, more adventurous belles showed up without escorts. It was common knowledge that the brazen beauties were hoping to catch the eye of the club's darkly handsome owner.

Many had.

In the five years that Armand had owned The Beaufort, he had enjoyed numerous dalliances with young ladies—and some who were not so young— that he had met at his club. He told himself that the reason he hadn't invited any of the ladies from the gaming tables to join him for dinner of late was because none had struck his fancy. And it was true. He kept involuntarily comparing every woman he saw with a fiery, russet-haired Countess and none measured up. The mere thought of Lady Madeleine sent a little tingle of pleasure down his spine.

Armand's swank club was not only famous for the attire and demeanor of its croupiers, but for the sumptuous buffet suppers served free of charge each evening. He had employed a trio of talented chefs to cook up delicacies to tempt the most discriminating of palates. There were, Armand knew, people who came to The Beaufort and never went near a gaming table. After a few minutes of me-

andering around, acting as if they were trying to
decide what game to play, which wheel to spin,
they would gravitate to the heavily laden buffet table. Once there they would glance anxiously
around, pick up one of the heavy china plates, and
fill it to overflowing.

Armand didn't care. Let them eat. There was always plenty. So much, he had the excess bounty
taken, early each morning before dawn, to the Ur-
suline nuns. The sisters were happy to get it and
each time any of them passed him on the street,
they smiled, thanked him and told him they prayed
for him.

By nine the club was beginning to hum. By ten
the place was alive with handsomely dressed,
champagne-sipping gamblers. The green baize tables were filled with players and a blue haze of
smoke from dozens of lighted cigars hung heavily
in the air.

Armand had been greeting patrons for two solid
hours without a pause. Shaking hands and kissing
cheeks and wishing everyone good luck and making sure the gamblers were enjoying themselves.
When finally there was a lull he made his way
through the noisy cavernous room, climbed the
marble steps, crossed the wide foyer, and slipped
out the heavy double doors.

There, under the scarlet canopy, he leaned a muscular shoulder against a lamppost and drew a long
refreshing breath of the misty night air. He took a
thin, black cigar from the inside pocket of his black
frock coat, stuck it between his lips, and lit it with
a Lucifer he struck with his thumbnail. He shook
the match out, dropped it and drew on the cigar.

Standing there, enjoying the relative solitude and the cigar, he saw a distinctive carriage coming up Carondelet. There was an impressive gold crest on the black coach's door. Lord Enfield's carriage.

Armand shook his dark head.

It was just past ten o'clock and the nobleman had already bade good-night to his beloved. But, if Chilton was heading to his own home after an evening with his fiancée, he was going in the wrong direction.

Armand's black eyes narrowed.

Desmond Chilton had no intention of going home. He was heading toward North Rampart street. Armand knew his destination.

Thirteen

Inside the roomy crested coach, a smug, smiling Lord Enfield was so lost in pleasant anticipation of what the next hour would bring, he never so much as glanced out the window. Pleasingly full after a lavish meal shared with Colfax and Madeleine, he was now eager to satisfy another, more insatiable appetite.

The lord was still smiling when his carriage rolled up before a small white house on North Rampart street. The house was identical to all the others lining both sides of the street. But inside the unimposing structure was a unique and priceless treasure.

Lord Enfield looked warily about. He saw no one on the street. Warning his driver, as he always did, of the constant need to be discreet, he quickly alighted and the carriage immediately drove away.

Using his key, Desmond let himself in the front door of the white cottage, shrugged out of his great coat and tossed it aside. He hurried through the parlor and went directly to the bedroom at the back of the small house.

His heartbeat beginning to quicken with growing excitement, he stepped into the doorway of the shadowy room.

And his smile broadened.

A beautiful quadroon awaited him. Quadroons, the preferred mistresses of many New Orleans gentlemen, were the offspring of a white and a mulatto, a mulatto being the issue of a white and a black. His lovely nineteen-year-old quadroon was dressed as if she were going out for the evening in an elegant ball gown of shimmering rose satin. Her long, dark hair had been swept atop her head and the lustrous curls were embellished with a scattering of tiny rose satin bows that matched her gown. She wore long white satin gloves and at her throat was a cameo brooch on a velvet ribbon.

She looked very young and quite prim and proper. And innocent. So sweet and innocent. It was a look that greatly excited her blond male visitor. Laughing girlishly and daintily lifting the hem of her satin skirts and crinoline petticoats, she crossed to him.

"*Bonsoir*, my lord," she said, went up on tiptoe and brushed a quick kiss to his lips.

"My darling Dominique," he murmured.

She smiled saucily and helped him get undressed.

When he was naked, the satin-gowned Dominique indicated a lyre-backed chair that had been placed at the room's center.

"Sit down, my lord," she softly commanded.

Desmond Chilton sat down. Once he was seated, the beautiful quadroon, standing a few short feet from him, began to seductively undress. She was deliberately slow in disrobing. She took an inordinate amount of time simply peeling the long satin gloves down her arms. Then, starting on the tiny satin-covered buttons going down the center of the gown's bodice, she paused between each button. A good ten minutes had passed by the time she stepped out of the shimmering rose satin gown and carelessly tossed it to the floor.

Next came the crinoline petticoats and when she was free of them, the naked man watching her murmured approvingly, "Yes, oh yes."

Now wearing only a camisole and pantalets, Dominique, smiling and pushing one of the camisole's lace-trimmed straps off her shoulder, turned slowly about to give her admirer a good look at her shapely backside.

When she was again facing him, she flicked open the hooks of the camisole, laughed and flipped one side open, revealing her heavy left breast. Then she quickly covered it and exposed her right breast. Again she turned her back to him, took off the camisole and dropped it to her feet.

"Please, my sweet angel," he begged, beseeching her to turn around.

Slowly she pivoted and his chest tightened and his mouth watered. The quadroon had huge, heavy breasts with large dark nipples. He could hardly wait to get his mouth on them. Knowing exactly what was going through his mind, the playful Dominique put her hands under the heavy breasts, lifted them and pushed them together. While she wet her lips with the tip of her pink tongue, she ran her thumbs over her jutting nipples, causing them to stiffen and stick straight out.

Excited, Lord Chilton started to come up off his chair.

"No, my lord!" she ordered and he reluctantly sat back down, knowing that if he didn't behave, she might tie him up and torture him for hours before allowing him to touch her.

Dominique yanked on the tape of her pantalets, then slowly, provocatively let the gauzy underwear slip down her belly. The pantalets caught low on her flaring hips and for a long moment she allowed them to stay like that, coyly concealing the part of her anatomy her lover most wanted to see.

Finally she eased the filmy undergarment on down and let it fall to the floor. She stepped out of the pantalets and kicked them aside. She wore no shoes, no stockings, so she was now as naked as he.

"Oh, God! Please, come here, Dom," Desmond rasped, the blood pounding in his ears and in his erection.

But the woman who best knew how to excite the blond nobleman shook her head and did not go to him. Instead she took a crystal vial of sweetly scented oil from the table by the bed and began to languidly spread it over her bare golden-brown body while her tortured lover squirmed and breathed heavily.

Desmond watched, intrigued and aroused, as she expertly rubbed the oil on her throat and arms. Next came her full breasts and flat belly. He moaned in sweet agony as she smoothed the oil down a leg, bending from the waist, stroking her shapely left thigh until it glistened in the lamplight. She straightened, gave him a naughty look and turned her back to him.

She again bent from the waist to spread oil down her right leg, and in so doing, purposely turned up her bare, slippery bottom to him. He groaned aloud, swallowed hard, and then leaned forward to grip his spread knees.

Dominique laughed evilly, straightened and turned back to face him.

The muscles across Desmond's naked belly contracted sharply when she poured a few drops of the oil into the palm of her hand, set the vial aside, put her hand between her legs and enticingly spread the oil all through the dark springy curls of her groin and over the wet pink flesh beneath.

The lord was now panting like a puppy.

The sight of that thick triangle of dense black coils gleaming with oil almost pushed him over the edge.

With a wicked smile on her lovely face, Dominique reached up and withdrew the combs holding her hair in place. It spilled down over her shoulders and reached to her waist. Some of the tiny satin bows fell to the floor, others stayed snagged in the long black locks.

At last, she went to him.

"Turn and sit sideways on the chair," she instructed and he quickly complied.

Then she very slowly, very sensuously rubbed her oiled body on his. She stood before him, leaned down close and let her pendulous, well-greased breasts brush back and forth against his naked chest. She moved around in back of him, agilely lifted a long leg, draped it over his shoulder and slid it up against his neck and face and then out over his shoulder and down his arm. She put her foot back on the floor, turned about so that her back was to his back, and slithered up and down against him several times.

She came around in front of him, climbed astride his left knee, and ordered him to move to the edge of the chair and straighten his long legs out before him. He eagerly did as he was told. She let herself slowly slip and slide all the way down his straightened leg to his bare foot, leaving a residue of oil in her wake. She repeated the exercise on his right leg. Then she came to her feet and searched for spots of flesh on his body that had not been oiled.

As she had done with herself, she saved his groin until last. A wildness shining out of her big, dark eyes, she indicated that he was to return to his former position, with his back flush against the chair's back. He did so hurriedly. And then sighed with pleasure when she slid down astride his lap with her legs open wide. While she clung to his neck, Dominique thrust her pelvis forward, pressed her slippery groin to his, and squirmed and rubbed and slipped against him until his thrusting masculinity and the blond coils surrounding it were shiny with oil from her hot body.

Sliding his oil-covered hands beneath her slick buttocks, Desmond said, "You're a witch, a cruel enchantress."

"A complaint, my lord?"

"Never," he assured her with a kiss.

The eager lord rose with her in his arms and sank down to the carpet. He anxiously laid her on her back beneath him. He rose to his knees to look down at her. She *was* a witch, a beautiful, dangerous witch with tan satin skin and big tempting breasts and wide shapely hips and strong young thighs meant to hold a man and drive him half-crazy.

And he couldn't live without her.

The well-oiled lord excitedly flipped Dominique onto her stomach, then drew her up onto her hands and knees. He roughly thrust his throbbing flesh deeply into her from behind. He was so aroused, he came almost instantly. He knew she wouldn't complain and she didn't. They had all night and both knew that before he was finished with her, she would be begging him to stop.

Her task, right now, was to arouse him again. Dominique wasted no time. She went to work on him and within minutes he was hard and ready again. There on the carpet, they made wild, lusty love.

Deep in the stillness of that same chill November night, while Lord Enfield and his quadroon mistress romped naked on the floor of her Rampart Street cottage and the rest of the city slept, a darkly cloaked figure stole silently through the thick mist along the riverfront toward an elegant French Quarter mansion.

A pale white moon had risen above the bayous beyond the city. It slowly sailed over the rooftops and cast patches of silver and black into the empty, silent streets. A coal-black cat slithered from one side of the cobblestone street to the other.

The ghostlike invader quietly approached the Royal Street town house of Colfax Sumner, looked up at the iron lace gallery above, and started toward a sturdy pilaster that supported the veranda.

He never reached it.

Big Montro silently stepped out of the deep shadows.

The intruder turned and fled.

Fourteen

The last day of November was extraordinarily mild and sunny. It might have been spring, so warm and pleasant was the air. A gentle breeze off the Gulf leisurely nudged billowy white clouds across an azure sky and from the waterfront came the sounds of laborers singing as they loaded cargo.

Madeleine hummed happily as she descended the stairs shortly after 10:00 a.m. She had been invited to the home of Melissa Ann Ledette to help plan the upcoming holiday bazaar. Since it was such a beautiful day, she insisted on walking to the Ledette's, which was only a few blocks away.

Big Montro, materializing the moment she skipped down the outside stairs into the courtyard, greeted her with a boyish grin, followed her through the heavy wrought-iron gates, and fell into step beside her.

Madeleine didn't mind his shadowing her. She liked this gentle giant who was unfailingly there when she needed him. Avalina had confided that it wasn't only in the daylight hours that this conscientious strong man guarded the Sumner household. She had seen him from the bedroom window of her *garçonnière* in the middle of the night, quietly patrolling the shadowy courtyard and slipping out the heavy iron gates to check the darkened street.

Madeleine had, from the beginning, been curious about this big man who seemed so dedicated and content to be a bodyguard. She wondered where he came from, if he had a family, why he had chosen to attach himself to her.

He was a private man, so it had taken a while, but she had, in the past days and weeks, managed to draw him out, to question him, to learn something of his background. To gently probe into his past.

She was fascinated when finally he had opened up and told her that he had been raised in an orphan's asylum in Birmingham, Alabama. He had never known his mother and father, nor if he had brothers and sisters.

At thirteen, he ran away from the asylum. He had walked all the way to Mobile where he found work loading and unloading cargo down on the docks. He had saved almost every cent he made, because his dream was to own a little piece of land, to have a home just like other people.

At twenty, he saw a pretty young woman with flaxen hair step off a paddle wheeler in the bright Alabama sunshine and he'd fallen in love at first sight. Against her parents' wishes, they soon married, and when they'd saved enough, he bought a small piece of property across the bay. Heavily timbered and miles from the nearest neighbor, it was a private paradise to the newlyweds. There on his land, Montro had built a log cabin and it was the first home he had ever had.

Soon the couple had a child, a baby girl, and life was sweet indeed.

But when the baby was two years old, she came down with a touch of fever. Montro was instantly worried. His wife told him it was nothing, babies occasionally ran a fever. But when she, too, developed a temperature, Montro was beside himself.

He had no choice. He had to leave his feverish wife and daughter alone while he went for help. He ran every step of the way into the village of Spanish Fort. When he returned to the cabin with the doctor in tow, both his wife and baby girl were dead. Scarlet fever, the doctor said, shaking his head.

Montro blamed himself. He should never have left them alone.

With them gone, their cabin was no longer home to him. He buried his loved ones, burned the cabin down, and walked to Louisiana. There he drifted from one odd job to another until he saw a handbill advertising Le Circus de Paris which was coming to New Orleans.

He hired on to help the troop unload and set up for the show. The promoter saw him and offered him a position as the show's strong man. He took it and spent the next ten years traveling abroad and throughout America with the circus.

"Montro, why did you decide to leave the circus?" Madeleine asked him now as they strolled leisurely along the banquette toward the Ledette's house.

"I had a dream," he said, totally serious. "In the dream I was shown that my place was here guarding you and Master Colfax."

"But, Montro," she countered, smiling, "you

didn't even know we existed when you left the circus.''

Montro grinned, lifted a huge hand, smoothed down the unruly cowlick at the back of his head and said with calm authority, ''I knew. I saw you in the audience at the circus. You were with Lord Enfield. Later that night, I had the dream.''

''And the very next morning you saved me from those horrible ruffians.''

''That I did,'' he said with pride. Then frowning, he added, ''New Orleans is a very dangerous place, my lady. You must never forget that. It is city unlike any other. As you know, rowdy grog shops and cheap bordellos and gambling hells are not a stone's throw from some of the most aristocratic streets in New Orleans, including the one on which we live.''

''I know,'' Madeleine said, ''but then that's what gives New Orleans its unique charm and flavor.'' She smiled and said, ''Ah, look, Montro. We're here.'' They stood before the magnificent mansion of Dr. Jean Paul Ledette. Madeleine touched Montro's forearm and said, ''I'm late so I'll hurry on in. See you this afternoon.''

''At what hour shall I come for you?''

''Mmm. Make it three. I'm sure I'll be ready to go home by then.''

''As you wish,'' he said and then stood there unmoving on the banquette until his mistress was safely inside.

''You're late, Madeleine!'' the pretty, dark-haired Melissa Ann Ledette good-naturedly accused.

"I know and I apologize," said Madeleine as Melissa linked their arms and ushered her into the spacious drawing room.

There, a dozen well-dressed ladies—half young women in their twenties and early thirties, the other half matrons with graying hair and spreading waistlines—awaited. Some Madeleine knew. Others she met for the first time. All were cordial and friendly. All knew her Uncle Colfax and all had heard that she was the fiancée of Lord Enfield. They remarked that she was a fortunate young woman, that her intended was one of the finest gentleman in New Orleans.

Madeleine graciously agreed, took a chair, and the group spent the morning planning the upcoming holiday bazaar.

"I think we should have the bazaar outdoors," said the young woman seated beside Madeleine. "We could use the booths in the French Market and rope off the street for the dance that evening."

"No, no," one of the older ladies quickly vetoed the idea. "You don't know what kind of weather we'll be having in mid-December. It could be pouring rain or freezing cold. I say we engage the Orleans Ballroom for the event."

"My stars, that's where they have those scandalous quadroon balls, Harriet!" said an incensed Letisha Bradford.

"So what if they do? I'm told it is a large, beautiful ballroom with the finest dance floor to be found in America. It will be perfect for our needs."

"I wholeheartedly agree, Harriet," offered the aging Grandmère Douglas, bobbing her white head in approval. "That way, if the weather is nice, we can serve wines and cordials down in the back courtyard.''

The talk turned to decorations and games and contests and who would work what booth at the bazaar before it drifted into spirited feminine gossip. Madeleine pretended nonchalance and disinterest when one of the ladies gleefully confided that she had it on good authority that the rich, recently widowed Raphelle Delion had set her cap for New Orleans' most charming scamp, the handsome Creole, Armand de Chevalier.

A lively conversation followed in which he was the topic. It seemed to Madeleine that the genteel ladies had an unhealthy interest in de Chevalier's escapades. They all laughed when old Grandmère Douglas stated, "No doubt about it, any woman who dallies with de Chevalier is asking for heartbreak. Still, if I were fifty years younger..."

She was interrupted when a uniformed butler appeared to announce that lunch was ready. The ladies were ushered into the huge dining room where a light meal was served. The talk, much to Madeleine's relief, turned to food.

By one o'clock the ladies began leaving. By two all had gone home.

"Is Montro waiting for you?" Melissa asked Madeleine.

"No. I told him to come for me at three."

"Good!" said the smiling Melissa. "We've a whole hour. Let's go to that fancy new coffee shop that just opened around the corner."

"By ourselves? Just the two of us?"

Hands going to her hips, Melissa said, "Yes, by ourselves. Good heavens, it is broad daylight and

I'm told it's a very ritzy café where unescorted ladies are more than welcome. Let's go.''

The Sans Souci was all Melissa had promised and more. It was an intimate room, richly appointed, immaculate and cozy. The clientele was clearly New Orleans' uppercrust and at more than one round marble-topped table were ladies without male escorts.

Madeleine and Melissa chose a table on the wall and had just ordered their favorite, *café brulet,* when the shop's front door opened and through it stepped Armand de Chevalier. He looked devastatingly handsome in a pair of fawn-colored trousers that clung to his lean hips and long legs and a white linen shirt with no jacket.

Every head turned. Every eye fastened on the tall, dark Creole. Electricity seemed to crackle in the air as he effortlessly took command of the room and everyone in it. It was evident that more than half the patrons in the café hoped that he would join them.

Melissa excitedly raised a hand and waved to Armand. Madeleine, horrified, reached across the table and pinched Melissa's arm.

"Ouch." Melissa frowned, puzzled. "What did you do that for?"

Madeleine never got the opportunity to answer. Armand, having smoothly weaved his way through the scattered tables, smiling and nodding to friends and acquaintances, stood looming above her. At once she felt the male power emanating from him, stirring her blood, making her nervous, frightening her.

"Ladies," he greeted them, his voice low, calm. "May I join you?"

"Why, certainly!" Melissa said and patted the empty chair beside her.

But Armand slid down onto the chair beside Madeleine. He smiled at her and, beneath the table, reached for her hand. No one but the two of them knew when he took her hand in his. His touch instantly filled her with indescribable excitement. It was wrong and incredibly foolish, but she sat there allowing him to secretly hold her hand beneath the table as he talked.

Fear and guilt and pleasure swept through her as his little finger teasingly stroked the length of hers. He could, she realized with alarm, make simply holding hands thrilling, almost erotic. As if he read her thoughts, Armand's hand closed possessively over hers and she felt her fingers crushed in the warmth of his palm.

Madeleine suddenly flushed at the recollection of how the hand that now imprisoned hers had once intimately touched every part of her bare trembling body. His beautiful hand with its long, tapered fingers and square, short-clipped nails had given her such exquisite pleasure she grew breathless at the memory.

Cursing herself for being a fool, Madeleine quietly attempted to free her hand from Armand's. But he refused to let it go and she was forced to sit there pretending nothing was going on while he sensuously rubbed her fingers, one at a time, and tickled her palm with the tip of his middle finger, and brushed the pad of his thumb back and forth over the inside of her wrist where the pulse was now hammering.

She shot him a mean look, but his black eyes were flashing with pure devilment and she knew he was enjoying her discomfort.

"...and it's going to be the best bazaar ever," Melissa was saying. "You'll be there won't you, Armand?"

He squeezed Madeleine's hand. "Why, I wouldn't miss it for the world."

"Good!" Melissa said. "There's going to be all kinds of food and games and dancing and..."

Madeleine, only half listening to Melissa chatter on, cast a sidelong glance at Armand and noticed a narrow band of fabric encircling his upper arm, barely visible through the fine linen of his white shirt. She frowned, puzzled. What, she wondered, was around his arm? A bandage of some sort?

Curious, she raised her eyes to his face and caught him grinning wickedly. Almost imperceptibly, he nodded his dark head and abruptly it registered. Her heart stopped. Then raced out of control. She knew instinctively what was around his bulging biceps. Her garter! The lacy blue satin garter he had taken off her leg during their lovemaking. She was at once angry and flattered. Annoyed and surprised. Irritated and thrilled.

He had kept her garter all this time.

Madeleine felt light-headed. The conversations going on around her became an indecipherable buzz until she heard Armand saying, "Melissa, that lady in the lavender dress is motioning to you."

Melissa turned her head, smiled, and said, "Yes, that's Mrs. Foster, a good friend of my mother's. I must go over and say hello." She rose and Armand promptly released Madeleine's hand and got to his feet. "If you two will excuse me..." And with that Melissa was gone.

Armand sat back down to face an upset Madeleine. Her emerald eyes snapping green fire, she said under her breath, "Are you totally insane?"

"What would give you that impression?" he replied with a crazy grin.

"I know what that is on your upper arm!" she hotly accused. He smiled, said nothing. She raged on, "How dare you wear *my* garter for all the world to see!"

"Now, Maddie, no one but you and I know that it's your garter."

Unconvinced, she charged, "You are bent on ruining my life simply because I...because we..."

"Made memorable love in a summer storm?" he softly finished her sentence.

"Shh!" she hissed. "You give that garter back to me!"

"Can't do that," he said, lifting then lowering his wide shoulders. "It's my good luck charm. Besides, it's all I have of you."

"Yes, well, it's all you'll ever have of me, de Chevalier!"

"Ah, you're wrong there, Maddie," he said with irritating cockiness. "You know you are." A sudden warmth radiated from eyes when he added, "One day we'll be together again."

Madeleine swallowed with difficulty. Then she narrowed her eyes and promised him in a soft, acid-laced voice, "You're the one who's wrong, Creole. The day will never come!"

"Yes, it will, *chérie*." He smiled seductively and predicted, "Perhaps sooner than you think."

Fifteen

"*T*hey'll see us," she warned, anxiously.

"Let them," he said, unconcerned.

She gazed at him, openmouthed, as he moved steadily closer, unmindful of the crowds of people gathering around, peering at him, watching.

He was naked and obviously unashamed. She gazed in awe upon the beauty of his lean, brown body, a body more perfect than any she had ever seen. The curious crowd, some wearing colorful Mardi Gras masks, some not, oohed and ahhed as they stared at him.

There was an evil splendor about him that was irresistible. Women swooned and a few fainted at the sight of him in his stark naked beauty.

Madeleine's eyes clung to him as he approached. He was surely the most wicked man she'd even known, but he was also the most exciting. She wished the voyeurs would magically disappear so that she could go to him, run her hands over the flesh of his beautiful body. Let her eager fingers explore the hard-muscled arms and long, lean legs. She could almost feel the smoothness of his deeply clefted back and tight buttocks. How she longed to entwine her fingers in the dense, dark hair covering his broad chest.

But no one left.

Others came.

More and more people eagerly crowded around to gaze upon the naked Adonis who was in her bedroom. She didn't know how they had gotten there. She didn't know how he had gotten there. He had simply appeared and with him came the crowd and she wondered if he was Armand de Chevalier or if he were actually Lucifer. No doubt Lucifer himself was handsome, attractive and daring.

That was it. He was Lucifer and he knew that she hadn't the will to resist his vitality, his beauty, his fierce animal appeal.

He reached the bed and she saw that her faded blue garter encircled his dark upper arm, so perhaps he wasn't Lucifer after all, but Armand. She knew in the next moment that he was Lucifer when he coolly commanded her to take off her nightgown.

"No!" she argued, wanting to disrobe and be in his arms, but mindful of the prying eyes. "All these people."

"Forget them," he said in a low, commanding voice. "If they want to watch, let them."

He was evil.

He was the devil.

And yet, the prospect of making love with him while others watched was incredibly tempting. She glanced past him across the room and spotted a stern, disapproving Lord Enfield in the sea of curious faces. She was horrified and immediately remorseful.

But then her naked master stepped between her and the crowd and Lord Enfield was instantly for-

gotten. There was no one but him, no one but this dark, sensuous devil-man.

He was magnificent. Tall and lean and tanned. His broad, symmetrical chest was covered with an appealing pattern of coal-black hair that narrowed to a thick line going down his flat belly and blossoming again at his groin where his awesome, fully formed erection, thick and long and hard, sprang proudly from the crisp black curls.

The sight of him standing there in all his naked glory made her shiver with a mixture of fear and desire. He snapped his fingers and she rose to her knees on the bed. Anxiously, lest he tear it from her, she lifted the nightgown over her head and tossed it to him.

He held it to his chest for a long moment while he looked at her. Under his intense gaze her nipples hardened and her belly jerked spasmodically. She knelt there on the mattress waiting for his next command.

She shivered when he raised the nightgown to his handsome face, closed his darkly lashed eyes, and inhaled deeply, his broad chest expanding as he drank in the subtle feminine fragrance that clung to the gossamer garment.

His eyes opened and they gleamed with fierce animal passion. Her heart began to pound and she was both afraid and impatient. He tossed the gown aside, stepped closer to the bed, took hold of her bare shoulders, bent his head and kissed her forcefully, thrusting his tongue deep into her mouth.

She was vaguely aware of the burst of applause from the crowd.

He tore his burning lips from hers, put his hands

behind her knees, and toppled her over onto her back. His lean fingers still gripping the backs of her knees, he drew her to the edge of the mattress, urged her legs widely apart and stepped between.

Cheers of approval rose from the excited crowd when he leaned over, put one hand on the mattress beside her head, rested his weight on his stiffened arm, took his hard, heavy flesh in his hand and placed the tip inside her.

"No, no!" She heard a lone voice desperately shouting for them to stop. The voice of a distraught Lord Enfield. "She's mine, not yours! Let her go! Let her go!"

Poised above her, Armand or Lucifer or whoever it was so deliciously seducing her, smiled down at her and said, "Tell him. Tell him you belong to me, not him."

She hesitated, so he swiftly thrust his hot throbbing flesh deeply into her. Lips parted, eyes wide, she stared up at her dark, demon lover and felt her body begin to eagerly grip and hold and squeeze him.

"I belong to you," she said to her dark lover. Then speaking more loudly, she shouted, "I belong to the Creole. I'm his to do with as he pleases."

"No, Lady Madeleine, no!" wailed Lord Enfield. "Where's your sense of decency?" Soundly hissed and restrained by the crowd, his protests fell on deaf ears.

Madeleine clasped Armand's upper arms so tightly her nails drew blood. She murmured his name again and again and bucked wildly against him and behaved the total wanton, much to the delight of the crowd. She realized that she was not *the least bit ashamed and it made her wonder if it was she, not he, who was the devil incarnate. Perhaps she was a succubus—the demon of the old witch stories who assumed female form to lie with men as they slept—and him not know it.*

"Armand," she said, "you know who I am, don't you?"

"Yes," he assured her. "You're mine, Madeleine. You belong to me, now and forever."

She sighed. She wasn't sure which one of them was the imp from Hades and she really didn't care. The only thing she was sure of was that the two of them were making hot demon love before an audience of masked men and women and it was exciting beyond belief.

They purposely kept each other on the very verge of fulfillment, not allowing full release. They played to their appreciative fans. They changed positions often and languidly performed the most intimate of acts in full view of the gasping onlookers, smiling with shared satisfaction when some the more timid spectators registered shock and disbelief at their sexual calisthenics.

As imaginative and uninhibited as he, she abruptly raised herself off him, where she'd been seated astride, got out of bed, and scampered around to one of the tall, carved posts at the foot of the four-poster. She wrapped her arms around the heavy carved post and gave a triumphant laugh when he followed, just as she'd known he would.

She felt his hands skim over her back, down her sides, to her hips. He leaned his face up beside hers and said, "Stand on tiptoe and spread your legs a little."

She quickly obeyed. He moved closer, bent his knees and thrust into her from behind. They made lusty love standing there with her clinging tightly to the bedpost and he pounding into her, his hands on her hips, guiding her, controlling her, conquering her.

Whistles erupted from the onlookers and the applause became deafening. She looked over her shoulder at the stirred-up crowd and suspected that some of the eager voyeurs were experiencing their own orgasms from merely watching the two of them make love.

She wanted to climax, too.

She couldn't wait much longer. She was so hot and excited she felt as if she were dangerously close to hysteria. She made a moaning sound in the back of her throat and he stopped pumping into her. She pulled away, ducked under his arm, and got back into bed. She stretched out on her back with her head on the pillow and sighed with happiness when he joined her there.

She looked up into his eyes and said, "Give it to me now."

"Soon," he said. "Very soon."

"Now, right now. Take me all the way. I'm hot and hurting. Make me climax. Please, Armand, please."

"Yes," he said, but even as he spoke he mysteriously began to float away from her. While she stared in horror and anxiously reached for him, he dissipated into the thin air before her very eyes, as if he were just an illusion.

"Please, Armand, please," Madeleine was murmuring as she abruptly awakened from the erotic

dream, her head tossing about on the pillow, her heart racing. "Please, Armand, please."

"Please...please..." Her eyes opened and she looked anxiously around, half expecting to see him there.

Her nightgown was damp with perspiration and her breath was short and raspy. She was almost painfully aroused from the disturbingly indecent dream. She lunged up into a sitting position and hugged herself, trembling with fear and desire.

Hot shame burned her cheeks because even now, wide-awake, she yearned for the touch of the dark, dangerous man who had been in her dream.

"No!" she said aloud. "I don't want you, Armand, I don't, I don't!"

Restless, worried, she got out of bed, crossed to the streetside double doors. She pushed them open, stepped out onto the gallery and drew a deep refreshing breath of the heavy night air.

She stood there trembling with emotion until finally her blood began to cool. Her pulse began to slow. There was nothing to worry about. She'd had a dream. No, a nightmare. She'd had a terrible nightmare and in the morning she wouldn't even remember it. That's the way bad dreams were. Vivid upon awakening, then quickly fading.

Soon forgotten.

Unfortunately, Madeleine's disturbing dream did not dim and pale with the morning light. Upon awakening, she could recall every intimate detail of the carnal dream with vivid, face-reddening clarity.

And the unsettling recollection continued to

plague her throughout the day. She felt guilty and upset and yes, aroused.

When Lord Enfield arrived at eight that evening, Madeleine anxiously called out to Avalina, "I'll get it!"

She dashed to the front door and when her fiancé stepped into the foyer, she impulsively threw her arms around his neck and said, "Kiss me, Desmond!"

Taken aback, he said, "Dear, is something wrong?"

"No, no, nothing's wrong. Kiss me, please." When he still hesitated, she said impatiently, "Uncle Colfax isn't home. Avalina's in the kitchen. Montro's down in the courtyard. No one will see us. Kiss me."

He smiled, framed her upturned face in his hands, leaned down and kissed her.

"There," he said, when he took his lips from hers after a brief, less than passionate kiss, "satisfied?"

"Yes," she lied, feeling far from satisfied, but blaming herself, not him.

As usual he was the consummate gentleman while she was less of a lady than he deserved.

Sixteen

December came to the Crescent City and with it contagious holiday merriment. The lampposts bordering the narrow streets in the Quarter were gaily festooned with holly and red ribbons. Wreaths of fragrant green cedar graced the front doors of homes. Tall pine trees, embellished with a myriad of fancy decorations, stood majestically in the drawing rooms of the city's mansions.

Cheerful warming fires blazed in the grates of marble fireplaces all over town and heavenly scents wafted into the streets from kitchens where cooks were busy baking holiday treats.

Smiling shoppers in woolens and furs swept in and out of the many shops in the Quarter, searching for just the right gifts for those on their Christmas lists. And when they bumped into a friend or neighbor, the first question either asked was, "You'll be at the bazaar, won't you?"

Creoles loved social affairs of any and all kinds. Picnics. Soirees. Balls. Dinner parties. Horse races. Wine suppers. Any excuse to get together and drink and eat and enjoy themselves.

So the holiday season in New Orleans was one long gala celebration, topped only by the unrestrained merriment of the Mardi Gras festival.

The lighthearted mood of the city had rubbed off on Madeleine and, on a cold, but crisp December day with a bright Louisiana sun shining down, she decided to go Christmas shopping. She asked Avalina to join her, but Avalina politely declined. She didn't like cold weather. She would stay home and make pralines for Saturday's bazaar.

With the ever watchful Montro at her side, Madeleine set out to accomplish some serious Christmas shopping. Against his will, she bullied him into going inside the shops with her, urged him to help her pick out gifts. She was amazed by his impeccable taste and insight. She would hold up a sweater or a muffler with her Uncle Colfax in mind and Montro would shake his big head. He had, obviously, closely observed the kind of clothing Colfax Sumner preferred. He also knew the type of delicate little trinkets Avalina favored.

Glad she had brought him along, Madeleine laughed and joked with him as they went from one shop to another. After a couple of hours of intense shopping, Madeleine had bought so many gifts Montro was loaded down with her packages.

She looked up at him and asked, "Are those things too heavy? I promised Avalina we'd go by the French Market and pick her up some cinnamon and cloves."

Montro smiled. "You're forgetting, Countess, I was the circus strong man. I could carry you and Avalina and all these packages from here to Lake Ponchartrain without tiring."

"I forgot," she said with a laugh.

The two strolled unhurriedly toward the riverfront in the strong winter sunlight. The levee was lined with vessels of all sizes, shapes and colors. Steam packets, oceangoing ships, flatboats, keelboats, and small river craft were crowded together at the wooden wharf. Strong-backed laborers shouted to each other as they unloaded exotic fabrics, tobacco, hemp, salted meats, kegs of pork, barrels full of pickled foods, rum and coffee.

A normal day in one of the world's busiest ports.

Madeleine and Montro soon reached the bustling French Market and Madeleine pointed to a small outdoor table and suggested he sit and enjoy a hot cup of *café au lait* while she shopped.

"You won't get out my sight?" he asked, unsure.

She exhaled in mild irritation. "I'll be right here in the market at one of the booths. If I step out of your sight, it won't be for a minute or two, okay?"

"I guess," he said, skeptical, and sat down on a delicate iron lace chair before a small café table, dwarfing both. He realized he looked foolish sitting there, so he favored Madeleine with a knowing wink. She laughed, patted him on the shoulder, and turned away.

Madeleine walked among the busy booths. Wrinkling her regal nose, she passed hurriedly by the stalls filled with wiggling crawfish and crabs and a variety of silver-skinned fish shining in the sun. She knew the spices were located at the far south end of the market so she headed in that direction.

But as she passed stands filled with fruits and vegetables, a pyramid of pomegranates caught her eye. She paused, smiled, and ventured closer. She stood there examining the fruit for a long moment before finally reaching out and taking one.

"That one's not ripe," came a low, familiar

voice from very near and Madeleine dropped the pomegranate as if it were hot.

She whirled around to find Armand de Chevalier standing dangerously close, smiling down at her. It was the first time she'd seen him since she'd had the disturbing dream and she felt her face grow instantly hot.

She quickly turned back to the stack of pomegranates and said, "If I want your opinion, Mr. de Chevalier, I will ask for it."

"Just trying to be helpful."

He pointed out a pomegranate that was fully ripened. But she was no longer interested in the fruit. She just wanted to get away from him. It wasn't that easy.

She gave him a weak, obligatory smile and said dismissively, "Nice to see you, Mr. de Chevalier, but I was on my way to the spices so..."

"I'll go with you," he said with a grin. Then casually asked, "You ready for Saturday's big holiday bazaar?"

"Not particularly, but I'm sure you are," she said, giving him a wilting look. "You Creoles seem to care for nothing but your own pleasure."

"Guilty as charged," he said, unperturbed. "It's been said that a Creole gentleman likes his liquor, his food, his races and his women." He cocked his dark head to one side and added, "Not necessarily in that order, at least not for me."

"I really don't care in what order you list your hedonistic diversions, de Chevalier," she haughtily informed him.

"Maddie, don't you think you should call me Armand, our relationship being what it is?"

She exploded in anger. "We have no relationship, Creole!"

People turned to stare. "Better lower your voice or everyone will know about us," Armand warned, took her arm and propelled her down the alley of booths.

"There is no *us*," Madeleine said through gritted teeth.

Ignoring her outburst, Armand let his fingers slide down her arm to enclose her small hand and said, "It's such a beautiful day. Let's slip over to the St. Louis Hotel and have an absinthe."

She snatched her hand from his. "I'm going nowhere with you, now or ever."

"Why?" he looked puzzled. "You afraid to join me for a harmless little cordial? Afraid I'll try to make..."

"I have told you before, I am afraid of nothing. Now if you'll kindly excuse me..." She quickened her steps. Armand followed, easily catching up with her.

She shook her head and said sarcastically, "Tell me, de Chevalier, is pursuing me your main goal in life?"

"Oui, c'est ça," he said, the deep, low timbre of his voice strangely compelling. "Yes it is, Maddie. My *only* goal. I want you." His eyes darkened and a muscle danced in his lean jaw when he added, unsmiling, "And I am going to have you."

"Will you be quiet!" she snapped, looking anxiously around to see if anyone had heard. But her heart fluttered erratically at the straightforward confession which both frightened and flattered her.

"I'll be anything you want, sweetheart," he said with a note of sincerity.

"What I want is you out of my sight, Creole. I am going to leave the market. I want you to stay right here, do not follow me. Do not take another step!"

"Sorry, I can't do that."

Frustrated, she said, "You can't...why?"

Armand shrugged. "I promised Montro I'd join him for a *café au lait.*"

"You saw Montro outside?" she asked. Armand nodded. "He told you I was in the market?" Again Armand nodded. Madeleine's chin lifted. "I didn't realize that the two of you knew each other."

"Well, we do," was his curt reply.

"Yes, well, I shall reprimand him for telling you that I..."

"Don't. I wheedled it out of him and no harm's been done. I haven't accosted you or frightened you or put your life in danger, have I?"

Grudgingly, she admitted, "No, of course not."

"Well, there you have it," he said. "If you ask me..."

"I didn't ask you. Let me make something clear to you, de Chevalier," she lectured brittlely. "I do *not* want to have anything further to do with you. Not now, not ever. Can you understand that? Can you remember?"

His answer was, "Can you forget making love on the ship?"

"What happened between us on that ship was a terrible mistake that was made because...because...I was terrified and under great duress. It was a monumental blunder that I shall regret until my last breath. But I do not intend to pay for it forever. I've told you before, I will tell you again, you do not belong in my life. I am engaged to a fine man who loves me and..."

"You love him?" Armand interrupted.

"What?" His question caught her off guard, momentarily flustered her. "Why, yes, yes I'm very much in love with him and I—I—" She stopped speaking, glared at him. "Why are you smiling?"

"Because you are so cute and earnest when you attempt to make an argument."

"I'm not making an argument, I am stating a fact!"

"Ah, I stand corrected," he said as he reached up and crooked his little finger through a wayward russet curl at her cheek.

She slapped his hand away and told him, "I will waste no more of my time parrying with fools, Creole!"

With that she whirled about and marched off, her long skirts swishing with her steps. Watching the seductive sway of her hips, Armand smiled with pleasure.

He allowed her to go only a few short feet before he called out to her. "Lady Madeleine!" Madeleine didn't stop walking, wasn't about to turn around. Armand quickly glanced about to make sure no one either of them knew was within earshot. Then he said in a clear, baritone voice, "Maddie, do you ever dream of me at night?"

Seventeen

From the outside, the Orleans Ballroom was not impressive. Just an ordinary building whose low, wide façade was totally devoid of any architectural style or grace.

But inside was a different story.

While the ground floor, which had been divided into card rooms and private reception rooms, was nothing special, the second-floor ballroom was spectacular.

The large, long ballroom with its lofty ceiling was elaborately embellished with crystal chandeliers, costly paintings and statuary, and inlays and paneling of fine wood. The dance floor was constructed of three thicknesses of cypress topped by a layer of quarter-sawed oak. It was said to be the finest dance floor in the entire United States.

Balconies overlooked the gardens at the back of the St. Louis Cathedral and at the rear of the beautiful ballroom a wide stairway led down to a courtyard where, on festive occasions when the weather permitted, wines and cordials were served.

On this gray and chilly December Saturday, the elegant Orleans ballroom was brightly decorated for the Yuletide Bazaar. Red and green bunting graced makeshift booths that had been constructed along both sides of the room. Sprigs of mistletoe hung from the crystal chandeliers and wide satin ribbons adorned the marble statuary.

By midafternoon the room was filled and the ladies working in the booths were kept constantly busy selling their wares or daring passersby to try their luck at various games of skill. Manning a booth at the far end of the ballroom, Madeleine had found no time to take a breather since arriving before noon.

The attraction of winning one of the prizes lining the shelves at the back of her booth kept a steady stream of hopefuls pressing up to take a chance. For a mere picayune a player got three chances at striking the bull's-eye of a corkboard mounted at the booth's back wall with a well-aimed dart.

It was, of course, a game that almost exclusively attracted males and when she had been assigned to this particular booth, Madeleine had quickly protested, appealing to the bazaar committee to allow her to work in one of the booths selling homemade candies or embroidered linens or whatnots.

Anything but this.

But when the committee had asked why she was so opposed to working the darts booth, she had no feasible answer. She couldn't very well admit the real reason. She couldn't tell these genteel ladies that if she worked in a booth that catered to gentleman, Armand de Chevalier would have the perfect excuse to come around and torment her.

All afternoon Madeleine had been nervously scanning the crowd. She had expected at any minute to see the arrogant Armand coming toward her. The prospect ruined any pleasure she might have taken from this social charity function. The Creole had warned her that he would come and she didn't doubt his word. He would be there if for no other reason than to upset her.

"Good for you," she said now to a young, gangly boy who had successfully placed his three darts squarely in the corkboard's bull's-eye. She extended her hand to the shelves of prizes, "Choose anything you like from one of the lower shelves," she invited.

"Ah, I—I guess I'll take that china pitcher there on the second shelf." He flushed and hastily added, "It's for my mother."

Madeleine took down the pitcher, handed it to the boy, congratulated him and told him he was welcome to try again. He grinned and said he might be back later. He and his young friends moved on to other stalls.

Madeleine drew a deep breath. For the first time all afternoon, no one waited in line to throw darts. She was grateful for the opportunity to rest a minute. She glanced across the crowded room to the big-faced clock mounted above a set of doors leading onto the balcony.

She couldn't believe how fast the afternoon had passed. It was now after six.

Full darkness had fallen an hour ago and Armand hadn't shown up. Maybe he wasn't coming. Maybe he'd just told her he would come to aggravate her. Maybe she could relax and enjoy herself like everyone else. Perhaps she and Desmond could... could...

Suddenly it dawned on her. De Chevalier was not the only one missing.

So was Desmond.

The earl had told her he had an important business affair to attend to that afternoon, but promised he would be there no later than five. She looked about, searching, but didn't see him. Besides, if he had arrived, he would have come directly to her booth. Madeleine frowned slightly. He was more than an hour late. What could possibly be keeping him?

"I'm keeping you here."

"You can't. I have to go."

"No!" An angry Dominique pushed the fully-dressed Desmond down onto his back on her bed and threw herself atop him. "It is early. Stay with me. Love me."

Desmond sighed. "Behave yourself, love. It's past six and I promised I'd be there by five."

Her dark eyes smoldering dangerously, Dominique slowly raised herself to a sitting position astride her prostrate lover, untied the sash of the black silk wrapper she wore, took the robe off and dropped it to the carpeted floor. Naked, she sat there on the fully clothed lord and began the grinding, thrusting movements of her hips. She smiled wickedly down at him. Her long dark hair spilled around her shoulders and her heavy breasts swayed seductively as she moved.

"Stay here with me, my lord," she entreated, leaned down and kissed him. Her mouth moving against his, she whispered, "Show me it's me you really love." She licked his lips, bit his chin, rubbed herself against him, determined to arouse him.

"Darling, you know I love only you," he tried

to placate her, tried to lift her off him, but she wouldn't be deterred.

Desmond knew her all too well. If he didn't make love to her again, she would never let him leave. She was jealous and possessive and insatiable. They had been in bed all afternoon, but that wasn't enough for her. She wanted him again and more than that, she wanted to make him late for the bazaar.

Lord Enfield resignedly began unbuttoning his shirt. Dominique, smiling catlike, quickly got up off him and left the bedroom. He rose to his feet and finished undressing. In seconds he was as naked as she. He called out to her. She didn't come. He walked into the parlor, but no Dominique. He ventured into the dining room, which was lighted only by candles in silver holders placed at each end of the table.

The naked, naughty Dominique was seated atop the gleaming cherrywood table, leaning back on stiffened arms, her parted legs dangling over the table's edge.

With no buildup or preliminaries, Lord Enfield stepped up between her spread legs and said, "It belongs to you, so if you want it, go ahead and take it."

With dexterous hands, the beautiful quadroon eagerly guided him into her and the naked pair made earthy love there on the dining table in the mellow candlelight. As her hot, wet flesh closed around him, Dominique looked into his eyes and said, "It does belong to me and you must never put it in her."

His hands filled with the twin cheeks of her generous bottom, his pelvis thrusting against hers, Lord Chilton said, "Be reasonable, love, she's to be my wife. I'll have to put it in her once we're married."

With a skill known by very few, save the world's highest-paid courtesans, the quadroon used her accomplished muscles to rhythmically squeeze and release, squeeze and release, so that Chilton groaned with indescribable pleasure and lost himself in her.

"Don't marry her," said the beautiful satin-skinned woman who could turn him to quivering jelly. "I don't want you marrying her!"

"All right, all right, I won't," he rasped, willing to agree to anything as his shattering climax began.

But when it was finished, Lord Enfield reminded the petulant Dominique that they had been over their well-laid plans at least a thousand times and had agreed to go through with them if necessary.

"Darling, say you understand," he urged, attempting to humor her. "You know I don't want to marry Lady Madeleine, but I must. As I've told you, over a year ago Colfax Sumner drew up a new will leaving everything to Madeleine. That cuts me out. The provisional will, in which I would gain control over his estate, has been superseded by the final will. So I'm left with no choice. I have to marry Madeleine if I'm to get my hands on Sumner's money."

Frowning, Dominique whined, "Didn't you tell me that Sumner never bothered to destroy the provisional will?"

"That's correct. As far as I know, it's still in his safe, but it is nothing more than a worthless piece of paper."

"It wouldn't be worthless if the final will should disappear, would it?"

"No, but that's not going happen. Now, please, darling, stop this foolishness and allow me to go to the bazaar."

Already so late he would have some serious explaining to do, Lord Enfield had time only for a hasty washup. Dominique watched as he soaped his belly and groin. Without benefit of a full, cleansing bath, her scent and the scent of her perfume would surely continue to cling to him.

Let him explain that.

It was nearing seven when Lord Enfield hurried into the Orleans Ballroom. Madeleine saw him anxiously making his way through the crowd. When he reached her booth, he had to wait to speak with her. A quartet of young gentlemen, laughing and scuffling, were loudly bragging to one another about their skill with the darts.

It was at least fifteen minutes before the last of the group had had a go at the game.

Desmond eagerly stepped up to the booth and smiled apologetically at Madeleine. "My dear, I'm so sorry I'm late and..."

"What kept you, Desmond?" She was irritated and wanted him to know it.

He knew it.

He reached for her hand, held it in both of his own. "I tried to get away, honest I did," he said, and it was true. He had tried to get away from Dominique, but she wouldn't let him go. "That boring business appointment dragged on and on, but it was a very important meeting, for both of us. For you and me, I mean." He favored her with a smile and said, "My darling, you must know that everything I do is for you. I have worked extra hard this past year so that when we are married, you'll want for nothing."

She nodded, half convinced, half suspicious. She asked, "Who was the long business meeting with, Desmond?"

"A London cotton buyer who quibbles over every last detail of a contract." He shook his blond head, as if in disgust. "I kept telling him I had a prior engagement and he kept arguing over everything. Finally, I told him I was going and he could take the deal or leave it."

"Did he take it?"

"He did," Lord Enfield said, "but he made me earn my money."

Madeleine finally smiled and sympathized. "You must be exhausted," she said and squeezed his hand. "They've set up a gentlemen's bar down in the courtyard. Uncle Colfax is out there. If it's not too chilly, why don't you go on down, have a drink, relax?"

"What have I done to deserve you?" he asked earnestly, gazing adoringly at her. "My sweet, you have no idea how much I love you."

Flattered, Madeleine urged, "Go on down and have a drink, dear." She smiled at him and added, "Be sure to save a dance for me this evening."

"Every dance," he said, backing away.

Madeleine sighed. She felt better. Her fiancé was late because he had been conducting important business that would benefit them both. Better yet, the Creole still had not shown up and she was beginning to feel confident that he wouldn't come.

A group of gentlemen crowded up to the booth to throw the darts. Once they had gone, there was another lull in business, and Madeleine took the opportunity to carefully survey the crowd. She searched for the dark-haired de Chevalier, hoping, praying she wouldn't find him.

She didn't.

It was after eight. He wasn't coming. If he was, he would have arrived by now. And if he had arrived, she would surely have seen him. She released a long sigh of relief. She turned away to rearrange the prizes still resting on the shelves. Only one remained on the very top shelf. A beautiful, expensive, miniature mother-of-pearl music box trimmed in filigreed gold.

To win it, the player had to sink not three, but six darts squarely in the center of the bull's-eye. Several had tried. All had failed. She doubted that anyone would win the delicate music box, which was a shame because it was a gift any woman would love to get.

"May I give it try?" came a low, drawling voice, and Madeleine whirled about to see de Chevalier standing before her, smiling easily.

She did not smile back at him. She said coolly, "For a picayune, anyone may try."

He reached into his trouser pockets, searched for a coin. "What would it take to win that little white music box up there on the top shelf?"

"Nothing to it, really," she said with a derisive smirk. "Just pay two picayunes and then sink six darts into the center of the bull's-eye.'' She crossed her arms over her chest and continued to sneer.

"Is that all?" said Armand as he handed her two picayunes and reached for six feather-tipped darts.

Madeleine quickly moved to safety at the side of the booth, having little confidence in his dart-throwing ability. She watched, irritably, as he leisurely shrugged out of his dark frock coat and carefully draped it across the booth's counter. He then meticulously lined up the six darts, placing them in a neat row on the wooden makeshift counter, fussing with them, annoying her.

"For heaven sake," she finally snapped, "you're not allowed to take all day!"

Still Armand did not hurry. He grinned at her, reached up and loosened his silk cravat, then carefully undid the top two buttons of his fine white shirt. She exhaled loudly when he lifted his right wrist and took the gold link from his shirt cuff. He repeated the exercise with his left wrist. He dropped the gold cufflinks down inside his trouser pocket, then made a big show of rolling up his shirtsleeves, making sure the folds were neat and that they matched perfectly on each arm.

Afraid his antics would soon draw a crowd, Madeleine stepped up directly before him and said under her breath, "That's it, Creole. Throw the darts or move away and give someone else a chance."

"I'm ready," he announced, his sleeves tidily rolled up over his tanned forearms, a devilish smile on his handsome face.

Madeleine again retreated to safety. Armand picked up the first dart, closed one eye and threw the dart. Dead center of the bull's-eye. In quick succession the other five darts followed. Each struck the bull's-eye to Armand's delight and Madeleine's dismay.

"Are you properly impressed?" he teased her. "Choose a prize."

He pointed. "That little gold-trimmed mother-of-pearl music box up there on the top shelf."

She ground her teeth. She didn't want him to have the beautiful miniature music box. She had hoped it would go to some sentimental gentleman who wanted it for his treasured sweetheart.

Rules were rules. De Chevalier had won it fair and square and she had no choice but to give it to him. She stood on tiptoe and took down the exquisite mother-of-pearl music box, turned and crossed to him. She reluctantly placed the beautiful box on the rough wooden counter.

"There," she said, "it's yours."

She watched, thoroughly miffed, as he reached out and touched the dainty box. His long, lean fingers lightly stroking the smooth surface of the lid, he flipped it open with the tip of his thumb. Music tinkled softly from it. A sweet romantic love song.

Both were staring at the music box. Both glanced up at the same time. Their eyes met and held.

"I want you to have the music box," he said.

"I don't want it," she replied.

"Yes, you do."

"No, I don't."

"Take it home with you, Maddie," he said with that male cockiness she despised. He gently pushed it toward her. "Tonight when you get into bed, open the box, listen to the music—" he paused, leaned a trifle closer, and predicted "—and dream of me, *chérie*."

Eighteen

Downstairs, in one of the private reception halls, a long buffet table laden with hot and cold edibles graced one end of the room. White-jacketed waiters stood behind the table, serving up broiled pompano, steaming crawfish, baked ham and roast of beef to hungry revelers attending the holiday bazaar. A myriad of vegetables, salads and desserts complimented the entrees. And at the very center of the long, white-clothed table stood a huge crystal bowl filled with thick, rich eggnog liberally laced with Jamaican rum and heavily garnished with cinnamon.

Madeleine, having finally been relieved of her post, joined her Uncle Colfax and Desmond at the buffet table. They moved along, hurrying to fill their plates to enjoy the meal before the dancing began upstairs at nine.

Most of the crowd had already dined, so the three of them sat at a table by a window in the almost deserted room and sampled the many tempting foods, commenting on how delicious everything was.

When Madeleine took the last bite of a *cala,* she rolled her eyes with pleasure. She had come to like the rich rice cakes so favored by the Orleanians.

"Aren't you having dessert, Madeleine?" asked her Uncle Colfax.

She smiled and patted the tight midriff of her wine velvet dress. "No room."

"Well, you don't know what you're missing," he said. "This peach melba is absolutely superb."

She laughed and said, "If I take one more bite, I won't be able to dance." She glanced at Lord Enfield. "Feel like dancing, Desmond?"

The lord nodded, set his coffee cup in the china saucer, and said, "If we're to dance the first dance, we'd better go. I hear the orchestra tuning up."

"You two run on along," said Colfax Sumner, indicating his half-full dish of peach melba. "When you reach my age, good food interests you a great deal more than dancing."

Madeleine and Desmond laughed, then rose to their feet. Madeleine leaned down and kissed her uncle's cheek. "See you upstairs in a few minutes."

Hand in hand the couple rushed up the stairs and entered the ballroom just as the orchestra began to play. Within seconds the floor was crowded with dancers.

Madeleine looked up at her fiancé and said, "Well? Shall we dance the first dance?"

"The first and the last," he said, agreeable, and led her onto the floor.

As they spun about the polished floor, Madeleine, recalling what the ladies of the bazaar committee had told her about the beautiful ballroom, looked up at Lord Enfield and said, "Darling, did you know that quadroon balls are regularly held in this very room?" She was looking directly at him and it seemed to her that he suddenly grew pale. He blinked nervously. Puzzled, she cocked her head to one side, and accused, "Then you did know."

"For God's sake, Madeleine, everyone in New Orleans knows about the quadroon balls."

"Oh, I see." She stared at him, wondering why merely mentioning the balls seemed to aggravate him. She took a deep breath, and asked, "Have you ever...?"

"Certainly not!" he said sharply, obviously offended. "And I don't think a lady of your station should be gossiping about such things."

"Oh, come now, Desmond," she said, "don't you think you're being a bit stuffy?" He did not reply. Madeleine pressed on. "Melissa Ann Ledette swears that some of the city's most respected and aristocratic gentleman—both single and married— attend the quadroon balls."

"That could be, I wouldn't know."

"They go to the balls to choose a lovely quadroon mistress and then they keep the women in neat little white houses up on..."

"Madeleine," he interrupted, "could we please listen to the music and enjoy the dance?"

"Yes, I'm sorry."

The lord held his lady at arm's length as they danced, gently swaying to the music, not talking. Halfway through the number, he turned her about and Madeleine caught sight of Armand de Chevalier, his raven hair gleaming in the light of a chandelier.

In his arms was a glowing Melissa Ann Ledette. Melissa was gazing up at Armand as if he were a god. Her slender arms were wrapped around Armand's neck and she was apparently attempting to draw him nearer, to close the space between them. Shameless little fool.

Watching the pair, Madeleine felt a jolt of jealousy slam through her. She remembered all too well what it was like to dance with the handsome Creole. She wondered if, when she and Armand had danced on the ship, she had worn the same idiotic, worshipful expression that was on Melissa's pretty face now.

Armand turned his head and caught Madeleine looking at him. He impudently winked at her. She was appalled. Here he was, openly flirting with her right under her fiancé's nose. She glared at him, tightened her arm around Desmond's neck, and moved more fully into his embrace.

She closed her eyes and tried to recapture the dreamy delight she had found in de Chevalier's arms when they'd danced that evening on board. She sighed and snuggled close and attempted to lose herself in the dance with her handsome, blond earl.

It didn't work.

While Lord Enfield was an accomplished dancer and she had no trouble following his lead, the magic was missing. She didn't experience that forbidden thrill, didn't feel as if she were dying to get closer to him. Her heart did not pound. Her breath was not short. Her limbs didn't tingle and her stomach didn't do flip-flops.

She was comfortable in the lord's arms, that was all. Her eyes still closed, Madeleine gritted her even white teeth and reprimanded herself strongly. She was being even sillier than Melissa Ann Ledette and she was past the age for foolishness.

She reminded herself of the misery she had suffered at the hands of the good-looking scoundrel to whom she was married for three horrible years. Men like Armand de Chevalier were reckless heartbreakers. Perhaps that's what made them so exciting. But she had no intention of letting any man break her heart, no matter how charming or exciting.

She was, she knew, in the arms of the man who was right for her. The upstanding, trustworthy man with whom her wise uncle had trusted her large inheritance. The man who would make a faithful and loving husband. They belonged together, she and Desmond. They came from similar backgrounds. They were both titled Britishers. They enjoyed the same pleasures and pastimes. They liked the same books, the same art, the same operas. They agreed on what was important in life. And it wasn't storybook romance that everyone knew faded too quickly. It was mutual respect and fondness and the desire to build a strong, sold future together.

Let others court danger.

She wanted safety and security.

Madeleine opened her eyes and looked up at Lord Enfield. He smiled at her. She returned his smile, then pressed her face against his throat and again closed her eyes. She inhaled deeply and was assailed by a foreign scent. She opened her eyes and quietly sniffed at his collar, the side of his neck, his jaw.

She smelled…she smelled…perfume? The scent of perfume. Subtle, but unmistakable. She sniffed again. A sickly sweet aroma. She raised her head, looked up at him. She was frowning.

"What? What is it?" Desmond asked.

"Desmond, are you…are you wearing some kind of strong cologne?"

For the second time that evening he paled. But he quickly regained control and said, "I was at the barbershop for a quick hair clipping this morning." He laughed then, shook his head, and said, "Before I could stop him, Barber William drenched me in some awful-smelling concoction. Dreadful, isn't it?"

"Yes," she said, "dreadful."

"Sorry, darling," he said.

Anxiously he pressed his cheek to hers so he wouldn't have to look her in the eye. His heart was hammering in his chest and a vein throbbed on his forehead. A close call. He should have known better than to carelessly come here smelling of Dominique. He was a fool to endanger his relationship with Madeleine. If she should ever so much as suspect anything… He shuddered at the thought and drew her closer.

Madeleine quietly made it a point to closely examine his neatly brushed blond hair.

It looked to be the same length it had been yesterday.

The celebration continued.

The children who had been there throughout the afternoon had now been taken home to bed. Only the adults remained.

The freshly replenished bowl of eggnog was brought upstairs and a bar was set up at one end of the ballroom. Jeraboams of champagne, chilling down in the icy depths of huge silver buckets, filled glass after glass of thirsty dancers. There was also plenty of wine and sangaree and absinthe and tafia and bourbon and brandy.

The gentlemen were not the only ones who imbibed. The ladies, too, drank of the heavily spiked eggnog and sipped chilled champagne from stemmed glasses.

Conversations became louder. Laughter more frequent. The music more spirited. Everyone was having a grand time.

Determined that she, too, would enjoy herself, Madeleine reached out and took another glass of champagne from the silver tray of a passing waiter.

"My dear," cautioned Lord Enfield, "I do believe that's your third glass of bubbly. Do you think it wise to continue drinking?"

Already feeling the effects of the smooth wine, Madeleine took a drink from the glass, licked her lips, and said with a coquettish smile, "Don't you ever tire of being wise, Desmond?"

"Well, no, I..."

"Madeleine, excuse me," Melissa Ann Ledette stepped up and interrupted them, "Will you do me a big, big favor?"

"I'll try."

"Oh, good," Melissa said, and touched Madeleine's arm. "We need someone to fill in down at booth number eleven." She pointed across the room. "Just for a half hour or so. Are you up to it?"

"Of course." Madeleine was gracious. She

turned to Lord Enfield and raised her glass in salute. "You'll wait for me?"

"I shall count the minutes until you return," he said and affectionately touched her cheek.

He stood and watched her walk away, wondering what would happen if she ever found out about Dominique. Would she accept it as the way of life here and allow him to keep his treasured quadroon? No. She certainly would not. She would call off the wedding and then everything he had worked so hard for all these years would be forever lost.

He could not let that happen. He wouldn't let it happen. He had, up until this evening, been very careful not to arouse anyone's suspicions. He hadn't, like some of New Orleans' bolder gentlemen, come here to this notorious ballroom to pick a beautiful quadroon mistress.

He wasn't that foolish. He had happened to spot the youthful Dominique outside a milliner's shop one morning and had immediately sent an aid to fetch her.

She had been brought directly to his carriage, which was prudently parked in an alley two blocks away. Dominique had eagerly gotten into the carriage, smiled seductively at him, and climbed onto his lap. Within minutes she'd had his cock hard and his head spinning and he had promised her that if she told no one about him, he would install her in a nice little house on the Ramparts and bring her presents and fine clothes and spend his every free moment with her.

That had been two and a half years ago.

So far as he knew, there had never been a whisper of scandal about the two of them. He had purposely kept Dominique half afraid of him, had warned of what he would do to her if she ever exposed him. And he had always taken the proper precautions. He never traveled the same route to her house and he never alighted from the carriage if anyone was on the street.

No, no one knew.

And this was the perfect arrangement. Dominique more than satisfied his raging sexual hunger, and that kept him from misbehaving with the prim Lady Madeleine and frightening her half to death. Actually, Madeleine should be grateful to Dominique for satisfying his sexual hunger and catering to his baser needs. He couldn't imagine the patrician Lady Madeleine engaging in the forbidden acts of lust which he and Dominique so enjoyed. Madeleine would be shocked and horrified if she knew the truth about him. She would break their engagement. Refuse to marry him. The prospect terrified him. He *had* to have her fortune.

He trembled inwardly as the grim face and grimmer words of Burton Abbot, his broker, came back to him. The long cash position he had taken in sugar futures had been completely wiped out. Bumper crops in Jamaica and Cuba had flooded the market. Desmond knew he was perilously close to ruin. His need for cash was acute. He only hoped he could hold out until the April wedding.

No, Madeleine never would know. She would never know about Dominique and she would never know his real reason for proposing marriage. He would continue to be the caring consort to her until they were safely married and he was in firm and total control of her vast estate. He would marry

Lady Madeleine no matter how loudly Dominique protested.

And how bad could that be, he asked himself as he watched the skirts of Madeleine's wine velvet dress sway seductively as she walked away.

Not bad at all.

Madeleine took another drink of champagne as she cut through the dancers on the floor and headed for the other side of the ballroom. When she approached the booths lining the far wall, she glanced up to check the numbers. Each had a number and the number was painted on decorative bunting that was wrapped around the top of the booth.

"Number six," she said aloud and moved on down the row, dodging dancers and drinkers. Soon she stood before number eleven.

"Oh, thank you for coming to my rescue," said Betsy Barringer, the young pretty wife of a prominent New Orleans banker, as she eagerly ducked out from beneath the counter. "My feet are killing me and I just have to sit down for a while."

Madeleine glanced at the empty booth, then gave Betsy a puzzled look. "Where is your merchandise? I don't see…"

"You're the merchandise, Lady Madeleine," Betsy said with a chuckle.

"I'm afraid I don't understand."

"Melissa didn't tell you? She should have. We're selling dances here." Betsy pointed to a small, hand-painted sign at the back of the booth which said A Dollar a Dance.

"Selling dances?"

"Yes. For a silver dollar, a gentleman gets one

dance with you." Betsy laughed again, and added, "For a five-dollar gold piece, he gets five."

"But I…"

"See you in a while. Thanks for being a good sport."

"No, wait, please…"

Lady Madeleine sighed, set her champagne glass on the wooden counter and ducked under. The prospect of dancing with a bunch of drunken, awkward old gentlemen was less than pleasing. Maybe she would be lucky. Maybe everyone was already dancing with the partner of his choice and for free. Maybe if she halfway hid, everyone would think the booth was deserted.

She grabbed up her glass of champagne and retreated to the back of the booth. She moved the booth's folding chair until it was directly in front of the sign that said A Dollar a Dance. She quickly sat down and smoothed her long velvet skirts around her. No one could see her without really taking the trouble to search. She would just sit and relax and drink her champagne in peace.

She exhaled, set her champagne glass aside, slipped the drawstrings of her velvet reticule off her wrist and set the reticule on her lap. Taking one cautious look around, seeing no one coming toward her, she carefully pulled the reticule's drawstrings until the velvet bag was open.

Inside was the miniature mother-of-pearl music box. She had told herself not to take it, to leave it on the shelf at the dart booth and let someone else win it.

But she hadn't done it. She had wanted the beautiful music box like a child might want a special trinket. Armand de Chevalier had won it and he had insisted that she take it. She had quickly told him she didn't want it, wasn't about to take it.

"You will take it," he had arrogantly predicted.

And when he had walked away and she was left alone in the booth, she had battled with herself, only to end up slipping the tiny music box into her reticule. She smiled now as she covertly examined the exquisite little box. She ran her thumb over its smooth lid and was tempted to flip it open to let the music play, but knew better than to do such a foolish thing.

Finally she sighed, drew the reticule's strings tight again, and placed the velvet reticule on the floor beside her chair.

She picked up her glass of champagne, took a refreshing drink, and savored this moment of peace.

In a heartbeat, her peace was shattered.

A tall, imposing man stepped up to the booth. His perfectly tailored frock coat was as black as the darkest midnight and his shirt was as white as an angel's wings. He was handsome in such a born-to-break-hearts way that Madeleine couldn't take her eyes off him.

He was smiling.

And there was something about that smile—the exotic way his lips curled in sensual triumph—and something about the way his eyes conveyed both mischief and danger at the same time.

Madeleine felt a great rush of heat engulf her, yet she was icy cold.

He placed a shiny twenty-dollar gold piece on the wooden counter.

"The way I figure it," said Armand de Chevalier, "this coin buys me twenty dances with you, Countess."

Nineteen

Madeleine remained seated long enough to fully compose herself, fighting the uneasy feelings this man so effortlessly aroused in her. She hated him for being able to do this to her, hated him more because she was never able to unnerve him.

He stood before her, totally confident, smiling easily, his white teeth flashing in the darkness of his face, an exasperating gleam flashing from his eyes.

Madeleine would have been very surprised had she known what was going through Armand's mind as he smiled at her.

Projecting a nonchalance he didn't feel, Armand gazed steadily at the russet-haired beauty in the low-cut velvet dress and his heart thumped violently against his ribs. She was looking straight into his eyes, assuring him she was not afraid, daring him to try to misbehave, warning him that she could and would easily hold her own against him.

Armand vowed he would never give her the satisfaction of knowing that she possessed the power to make him weak in the knees, to cause his heart to race out of control. But she did have that power. And it was not solely because she was a dazzling fair-skinned beauty with hair that flamed in the sunlight and a perfect willowy body that made him want her with a hot, eternal passion.

It was more, much more than just her beauty. He'd had many beautiful women, some even more beautiful that she. But none had had the ability to twist his insides into knots the way she could. Everything about her charmed him. Her irrepressible spirit and the regal way she held her head and the brilliant green fire that flashed from her eyes and the pugnacious lift of her chin when she was angry.

And she was angry now.

Madeleine reached down and picked up her velvet reticule, slipped the drawstrings around her wrist and regally rose.

She crossed to the smiling Armand, lifted her noble chin a trifle higher and said scathingly, "I would rather be burned at the stake than dance twenty times with you, de Chevalier."

"In that case I'll pay twenty dollars for *one* dance," he said as he reached out, took her hand, and placed the twenty-dollar gold piece in her palm. He grinned then and, unceremoniously sliding her reticule's drawstrings down over her hand, told her, "You can leave this here. No one's going to steal your little music box."

Madeleine's emerald eyes widened, then narrowed and blazed with anger. "There's no music box in my..."

"Maddie, Maddie, I hate to point this out," he gently scolded, shaking his dark head, "but you're becoming quite the little liar."

"I am not a liar!"

"No? Then open that velvet bag and show me what's inside."

"I will do nothing of the kind!" she informed him icily. "But here's a bit of truth for you, Creole, I do *not* want to dance even one dance with you!"

Armand shrugged wide shoulders. "Perhaps I can make you change your mind." He grinned impishly and added, "Or at least your heart."

"Never in a million years," she sarcastically informed him, crossing her arms over her chest.

He continued to grin. "I paid twenty dollars to try, so quit hiding behind that counter and give me a chance."

She flashed him a bored, impatient look. Then sighed irritably and ducked under the counter and rose to face him.

"I think you'll find, de Chevalier," she said, "that you have wasted your twenty dollars."

"Perhaps," he said, still smiling, cocksure as always. "It's too soon to tell." He took her arm, guided her toward the floor.

"You never tire of tormenting me, do you?"

Armand stopped, lifted his hands and, clasping her upper arms, gently turned her to face him. "You let me know if this dance is torment, Countess."

With that he commandingly took her in his arms and began to slowly dance her across the floor. He held her no closer than he'd held Melissa Ann Ledette, no closer than Desmond had held her when they had danced. Yet she felt as if she were being forcefully pulled against the heat and hardness of his tall, lean frame. It was as if there were some strange electrical field between them, drawing them together like powerful magnets, making it nearly impossible to stay decently apart. It was all she could do to keep herself from pressing closer to the potent lure of his athletic body.

Did he feel it too?

All at once she found herself much closer to him, so close she could feel the heavy beating of his heart against her breasts, the hardness of his long legs brushing against hers through the velvet skirts of her dress. She swallowed hard and nervously glanced up at him.

Her head was tipped back, face lifted to his. His head was bent, face lowered to hers. Their gazes locked. Her breath caught in her throat.

His eyes gleamed with heat and his lips—those beautifully sculptured, sinfully sensual lips—were mere scant inches from her own. She felt her own parted lips quiver and for a moment she was afraid he was actually going to kiss her.

She was equally afraid that he was not.

She saw the muscles in his tanned throat work convulsively as he swallowed with difficulty and she knew that he wanted to kiss her as much as she wanted to kiss him. For one wild, insane second, she was tempted to throw away her nice, safe future, pull Armand's handsome head down to her and kiss him as he'd never been kissed before.

And let the devil take the hindermost.

It was Armand who saved her from herself when he said, with a cynical curve to his tempting mouth and a subtle rotation of his slim hips, "Tell me the truth, *chérie*, is this torment?"

"Yes, it most certainly is!" she was able to say with total honesty.

And it was.

It was torture of a kind against which she was

totally powerless. This dark, dangerous Creole had awakened in her a long-sleeping passion. When he had made love to her on that sinking ship, he had shown her a kind of ecstasy she had never known existed. Ever since that stormy afternoon she had yearned to experience it again. Yes, yes it was torment to be held by him, and not to be loved by him. Not to be kissed and touched and caressed by him. Not to know again the wonder of his passionate lovemaking.

Armand smiled and let her know that he was on to her. "But a highly enjoyable kind of torment, *oui, chérie?*"

Trying desperately to sound incensed, she said, "Don't be ridiculous, Creole!"

"Am I?" he said. "Ah, Countess, don't. Don't pretend that nothing has happened between us during this dance."

"I'm not pretending! Nothing *has* happened. What could have possibly happened on a dance floor with dozens of people around?"

"The sweet stirring of shared desire?"

"Hardly!" She made a face at him.

He smiled at her. "Don't say that you don't want me to hold you closer in my arms."

"I do not want any such thing!"

"Don't tell me that you don't want to kiss me."

His last statement silenced her. She stared at him, mute, and made a misstep. He smoothly caught her, kept her from tripping. He hadn't said "Don't tell me you don't want to kiss you." He had said "Don't tell me you don't want to kiss me." Which was exactly the way it was. She had, only seconds ago, wanted to kiss him so badly she had almost stupidly jeopardized her future and ruined her life.

Mercifully the music stopped. Madeleine anxiously pulled out of Armand's embrace.

He said, "The best twenty dollars I ever spent."

She replied hatefully, "For your sake I certainly hope so, because that dance is all you'll ever get from me, Creole."

"You're wrong, Countess," he said and his dark, hooded eyes held both warning and promise. "You know you are."

Alarmed, she exploded in anger. "Dear lord, how I hate you!" Her emerald eyes flashed and spots of high color stained her pale cheeks.

She had never looked prettier and Armand was totally enchanted.

"You know what they say, Countess," he leaned close and whispered, "There's a fine line between hate and love. Perhaps the reason you hate me so much is because actually you love me."

Her hands immediately went to her velvet-covered hips. She said, "If you were the only man left on this earth, I would leap to my death in the Mississippi before I'd allow you to touch me! Does that sound like love, Creole?"

"What's going on, Madeleine?"

"Going on?"

"Yes," said Lord Enfield. "I saw you dancing with de Chevalier and…"

"Oh, that."

"Yes, that."

"I had absolutely no choice, Desmond," Madeleine quickly assured him. "You recall Melissa asking if I'd help out in one the booths for a while?"

"Yes, I remember."

"Well, it turns out that they were selling dances there," Madeleine said, shaking her head as if disgusted. "De Chevalier bought a dance and I..."

"I see," Desmond interrupted, nodding. "It looked as if the two of you were...ah...well... should I be worried?"

"Good heavens, no!" Madeleine said emphatically as if that were the most ridiculous thing she'd ever heard in her life.

Realizing with a stab of guilt that she was once again being "quite the little liar" Armand had accused her of becoming, she was tempted to shout at her fiancé, "Yes, you should be worried! You should be very worried because I have been in Armand's arms, have made passionate love with him when I've never made love to you. Worse, the Creole's trying to get me into his bed again and I'm not certain how long I can hold out against such overwhelming magnetism. Yes, yes, yes! You should be worried and insanely jealous!"

Instead she smiled sweetly at the earl and said again, "No, darling. I was only doing my duty, raising funds for our brave British Florence Nightingale."

"I'm relieved to hear you say that," he told her as he took her hand and led her onto the dance floor. As they began to dance, he whispered in her ear, "De Chevalier wants you. Desires you. I can tell by the way he looks at you."

"Oh, Desmond, that's not..."

"Shh," he gently chided. "It's okay. Doesn't

matter. In fact, I find it rather satisfying knowing that while he wants you, I have you. And although I don't trust the Creole as far as I can throw him, I have the utmost faith in you, my love."

For the remainder of the evening, Madeleine stayed safely close to her fiancé, silently vowing to behave herself and earn the deep trust Desmond had in her. The couple danced and talked with friends and accepted congratulations on their engagement.

Madeleine was disappointed when Desmond told her that her Uncle Colfax had grown weary and had left the dance early.

"That's not like him," Madeleine said with a worried frown.

"Now, darling, don't make more of it than is there," cautioned Lord Enfield. "He told me to assure you that nothing's wrong, he's just a bit tired from all the excitement and activity."

"Mmm," Madeleine murmured. "Montro drove him home?"

"Yes, of course," said Desmond. "Now stop your fretting and let's dance again."

Madeleine finally smiled and stepped into his arms. But as they danced she caught herself involuntarily searching the crowd for the Creole. She finally found him. He was standing alone on the perimeter of the dance floor, a drink in his hand. When she caught sight of him, his eyes were fastened on her and in them was a puzzling sadness.

It was gone the instant she caught him looking at her. Replaced by that cool, cynical appraisal she'd come to expect from him. Then he looked away as an elegantly gowned woman approached him and touched his forearm. Madeleine recognized the dark-haired, milky-skinned widow, Raphelle Delion.

Madeleine's eyes clouded slightly. She remembered the gossips saying that the rich, beautiful widow Delion had set her cap for Armand de Chevalier. Perhaps there was some truth to the rumor.

Madeleine watched as the tall, shapely brunette smiled seductively, laid a hand on Armand's arm, and said something to him. Armand immediately set his liquor glass aside, led Raphelle Delion onto the dance floor, and took her in his arms.

Raphelle smiled up at Armand, wet her lips with the tip of her tongue, and said, "It's getting late, Armand, and I'm getting tired."

"Are you?" he replied, noncommittally.

"I am," she said and pressed aggressively closer, subtly, but provocatively thrusting her pelvis against his groin. "I keep thinking of my big, comfortable four-poster and the blaze in the fireplace across from it. My maid's laid out a naughty black lace nightgown for me to slip into when I get home."

Armand studied the forward young widow whose pale breasts were resting against his chest. She was a voluptuous southern beauty with soft, generous curves, milky-white skin, dark, lustrous hair and big bedroom eyes. And this was not the first time she had made an overture to him. He had no doubt he could be in her bed within the hour and stay there for as long as he wished.

Raphelle was waiting for him to say something. When he did not, she said, "Take me home, Armand. Enjoy my big four-poster and the blazing fire

and my naughty nightie. And most of all, enjoy me.
We can sip chilled champagne and make hot love
all night.''

Armand was tempted.

His blood was up. He was edgy, restless, yearning. Coiled as tightly as a watch spring. He badly
needed release. If he could enjoy Raphelle's ample
charms for the night with no strings attached, he
would take her up on the offer. But he knew her
game. She wanted a great deal more than one night
of passion.

Taking her to bed would be a big mistake. She
would, he felt sure, be the clinging, weeping type
who would make his life hell and getting out of her
clutches would be a full-time occupation. She had
told friends that she wanted him, hoped to marry
him.

He had enough trouble.

He didn't want any more.

''Armand?'' Raphelle was gazing hungrily at
him, hoping he'd say yes.

''I'm very flattered, but...'' He shrugged. Her
face fell and she looked as if she might be going
to cry. Quickly, he said, ''Good night, Raphelle,''
and made a hasty exit.

Twenty

The pale winter moon had risen and the night air was damp and bitterly cold when Madeleine and Desmond left the dance shortly after midnight. Madeleine began shivering as the pair climbed into Lord Enfield's waiting carriage.

"My dear, you're freezing," he said, wrapping an arm around her and drawing her close.

Madeleine's right hand, with her reticule dangling from her wrist, got wedged between them. She felt the sharp corner of the miniature music box jab her in the ribs. She held her breath, hoping that it wasn't touching Desmond.

It was.

Frowning, he reached between them and lifted the reticule. "Darling, what's in your evening bag?" He felt it, confounded by the shape. "Something in here stuck me in the side."

Anxiously snatching the reticule away from him, Madeleine laughed nervously and said, "I'm sorry, Desmond." She cleared her throat needlessly and explained, "The head of the bazaar committee gave me a little gift for helping out."

"I see. What is it?"

"Ah—a—it's a tin box of chocolates." Another lie. "Would you like one?"

"No, thanks," he said, and she released a soft sigh of relief.

She quickly switched the telltale reticule to her other hand and out of the way. Desmond again drew her close as the carriage wheels rumbled over the cobblestone street in the cold winter darkness.

Her head tucked beneath his chin, cheek resting on his chest, Madeleine closed her eyes and berated herself for lying to him. Again. She who hated lies and deceptions. She who had always prided herself on being totally honest with everyone and fully expecting the same from them.

It was astounding how one lie led to another.

And another.

"We're here, darling." Desmond abruptly shook her from her painful reveries.

She raised her head as the carriage rolled through the iron gates of home. Big Montro immediately stepped out of the shadows and opened the carriage door.

"Give us a minute, will you, Montro!" Lord Enfield said sharply.

"Yes, sir," said Montro, contrite as he quickly closed the door.

"Desmond," Madeleine scolded, brows knitted, "why did you speak to him like that? I'm afraid you've hurt his feelings."

"Madeleine, good God, the man's a common servant," Desmond replied. "Why should I be worried about his feelings?"

"Because he is a human being and a very kind one at that."

"Yes, well he's often an irritant if you ask me.

Always underfoot. Every time I look up, there he is, in my way. It's a bit tiresome."

"I had no idea you felt that way, Desmond," she said, staring at him.

He quickly softened his expression, touched her cheek, and answered, "I'm sorry, darling. It's just that...well, I wanted to give you a nice, long goodnight kiss here in the warmth of the carriage and..."

"You aren't coming up?"

"Not tonight, sweet. It's been a long, trying day and I'm exhausted."

Secretly glad that he wasn't coming inside, she said, "Then I shall see you tomorrow."

"Indeed you will," he agreed, taking her chin in his hand, leaning close to kiss her.

"Good night, dear."

"Good night, Desmond."

He rapped on the carriage door. Big Montro came forward and opened it. As the mannerly giant gently lifted his mistress to the ground, Lord Enfield stuck his head out and said, "I say, Montro, do forgive me for being testy. I'm overly tired, but that's no excuse. I do apologize."

"Apology accepted," replied Big Montro before he closed the carriage door.

Ushering Madeleine up the outside staircase in the cold, Montro asked, "Did you enjoy the bazaar, my lady?"

"Very much," she responded. "We raised a tidy sum for the Crimea and I had a wonderful time." She mentally kicked herself. Here she was lying again. She had *not* had a wonderful time. Armand de Chevalier had seen to that.

At the door, Montro handed her inside the foyer, smiled, and said, "Sleep well, sleep warm."

"You too," she returned, "and thanks, Montro, for consistently being here when I need you."

The big man beamed. "Always a pleasure, my lady."

Madeleine closed and locked the door, glanced down the wide center hall and saw that no lights were visible under her uncle's closed door. She climbed the stairs to her room and found the ever efficient Avalina awake and waiting for her.

"Oh, Avalina," Madeleine said, "you didn't need to wait up for me. Bless your heart, I know you must be sleepy."

Avalina shook her head, setting the points of her ever present white *tignon* to trembling. "A little, but I knew you'd be very tired when you got in and might need my help."

Madeleine nodded, shrugged out of her long, ermine-lined cape and asked, "Did you see Uncle Colfax when he came in?"

"Yes, I did."

"Was he all right? He left the dance early and…"

"He's fine. Or at least he told me he was," Avalina stated. She tilted her head to one side thoughtfully and added, "I'm afraid the master's age is beginning to catch up with him. Seems to me these past few months he's often tired."

Madeleine offered, "Well, he was at the bazaar all afternoon. I'm not old and I'm tired to the bone."

"I'm sure you are," said Avalina. "Here, let me help you with that dress."

Madeleine nodded, sighed. "What would we do without you and Big Montro?"

"You'll never have to find out," said the indomitable black woman who took great pride in tending them all.

Madeleine was delighted to find that the thoughtful Avalina had readied a hot tub for her. Within minutes she was sinking down into its sudsy depths and telling Avalina about the bazaar. Who was there. Who danced with whom. Who drank too much. Whose gown was the loveliest, whose the tackiest. The two women gossiped and giggled like young schoolgirls.

But Madeleine's laughter died when, out of the blue, Avalina asked, "Was that handsome-as-sin Armand de Chevalier there?"

Once Avalina had gone and the yawning, peignoir-clad Madeleine was finally in bed, she lay on her side in the pale winter moonlight. On the mattress before her rested the miniature music box. She toyed with the lid, but did not open it.

As she gazed at her gift Madeleine bit her bottom lip. The last glimpse she'd had of Armand, he was dancing with Raphelle Delion. The wealthy widow whom everyone said was openly after him.

Madeleine knew she shouldn't care one way or the other, but she couldn't help but wonder. Was Raphelle still in Armand's arms?

In his bed?

Sudden, unreasonable fury flooded through her and, like an angry child, she impulsively swept the music box off the bed. It bounced on the deep carpet. The lid fell open. Sweet music tinkled forth.

"Damn you, Creole!" Madeleine swore, as tears

of frustration sprang to her eyes. "I don't want the silly music box and I don't want you!"

Armand, in a dark caped cloak and soft kid gloves, hurriedly exited the Orleans Ballroom. His carriage and driver were waiting.

"Home, sir?" the driver asked, as he opened the carriage door for Armand.

"Yes, Philip, home." Armand said, as he started to climb up into the carriage. He stopped, turned and said, "I've changed my mind. Drive me up to Lulu St. Clair's."

"Yes, sir," Philip said, his expression unchanged.

Armand sat in the back of the shadowy carriage with his arms crossed over his chest and his hooded eyes narrowed. He was nervous, edgy, frustrated. And it was his own fault. Nobody else's. So he was disgusted with himself. He had allowed a beautiful russet-haired noblewoman—who belonged to another man—to get under his skin and into his blood. All because on a stormy summer afternoon she'd lain naked in arms and loved him in a sweet, fiery way he couldn't seem to forget.

A muscle spasmed in Armand's dark jaw. He gritted his teeth and his black eyes flashed with resolution. He *would* forget. He was going to forget. And he knew how to do it. What he needed on this cold December night was a few hours in the warm arms of one of Madame Lulu's exotic girls.

He had been told by a discerning gentleman who frequented Lulu's, that she employed the most beautiful, and therefore expensive, women in the entire South. The girls, it was said, were incredibly lovely, highly cultured, boldly adventuresome and eternally discreet. Elegance and excessive formality were said to be the keynote of the swanky establishment and only high-class trade was welcome there.

The carriage rolled to a stop before the imposing three-story mansion on Bourbon Street. Armand's driver jumped down off the box and hurried to assist his master. When Armand stepped out into the cold, he said, "Philip, I plan on staying all night, so you may go."

"Yes, sir. Whatever you say," Philip replied. "Shall I come for you tomorrow morning?"

"No earlier than noon," Armand instructed, planning a long night of lovemaking and a longer sleep afterward.

Twenty-One

Armand hurried up the front walk, climbed the steps to the gallery and lifted the heavy door knocker. A liveried butler opened the door, smiled politely and invited Armand inside.

Armand was shedding his gloves and cloak and handing them to the butler when the handsomely gowned Lulu St. Clair swept regally into the foyer and greeted him warmly.

"Ah, Mr. de Chevalier," she said, beaming. "Welcome, welcome. We were beginning to wonder if you'd ever find your way to our modest abode."

"Here I am," he replied with a grin.

She laughed and tapped him on the chest with her collapsible fan. "So you are. We'll see to it that you have such an enjoyable visit you'll want to return again and again." She wrapped a plump, bejeweled hand around his arm and led him into a spacious, elegantly appointed parlor. Fireplaces and mantels were of gleaming white marble and the furniture, upholstered in fine burgundy damask, was of highly polished mahogany. The mahogany floors were covered by plush velvet carpets.

The large, candlelit room was almost deserted. A well-dressed couple sat on a damask sofa, sipping champagne and whispering. And in the corner a man in evening clothes played a square, heavily carved pianoforte.

Madame Lulu was quick to explain, "It is quite late."

"If it's too late, I'll…"

"No, no, Mr. de Chevalier. Never too late and I've got just the right girl for you." She beamed as if she knew a delicious secret. She yanked on a nearby bell cord and within seconds a strikingly pretty young woman entered the parlor. As the tall, gorgeously gowned, red-haired beauty slowly approached, Madam Lulu told Armand about her. "Her name is Gytha. That's old English. It means 'a gift.' She'll be your gift, if you like."

"No!" Armand said with such firmness, Madam Lulu was taken aback.

"You do not find Gytha to your liking?" Lulu raised her plump hand, motioned the red-haired woman to stay where she was. "Is she not beautiful?"

"She's exquisite," Armand agreed, "but I want a brunette. Or a blonde. Or a…"

"Ah, I see, I see. You do not like the red hair, Mr. de Chevalier?"

"No, no I don't."

Madame Lulu was smiling again as she snapped her fingers and sent Gytha away. Seconds later another beautiful woman descended the wide staircase and came into the parlor. She was also tall and quite voluptuous. Her hair was as black as Armand's and her skin held the hint of an olive hue, though lighter than his own. She wore a becoming evening gown of black velvet that was cut so daringly low he expected to see the flash of a nipple any minute. Her hips were concealed by the hooped bell of her full skirts, but he would bet good money that they were generously rounded. Her full-lipped mouth was turned up into a seductive smile and in her dark, flashing eyes was the promise of prolonged pleasure.

"You like, *monsieur?*" asked Madame Lulu.

"Very much," said Armand.

"Ah, bon, bon," gushed the madam. "Her name is Jade. She's of Spanish descent and she knows how to please the most discriminate of lovers."

"I'm sure she does," said Armand. "I'll want her for the entire night."

"A wise decision," said Madame Lulu as Armand moved toward the dark-haired beauty.

He reached her, smiled, and said, "Jade, I'm Armand de Chevalier. You're stunningly beautiful and I want to spend the night with you."

She flashed him a dazzling smile and said, "I'll make it a night you will never forget, Armand."

She took his hand and led him up the wide, carpeted stairway. At the top of the stairs, Jade guided Armand to the third door down, and into her private quarters. Once they were inside, she locked the door, turned, leaned back against it and gazed at the man who was to spend the night in her bed. Jade couldn't believe her good fortune. For the first time in her professional life she looked forward to her work. The majority of the gentlemen who visited Lulu's were well into their fifties, some sixty, some even seventy and beyond. All were wealthy and cultured and often she thoroughly enjoyed talking with them. But it was always a dreaded chore to climb into bed with a pasty, droopy-skinned man with skinny arms and legs who had to be painstakingly stimulated—sometimes for hours—before he was able to perform.

One look at this tall, young, virile Creole and Jade knew it was going to be a highly enjoyable experience. She was glad he was spending the entire night. While she spent her life servicing gentlemen, she seldom achieved any satisfaction. She was only human. She needed a good strong dose of abandoned lovemaking with a skilled partner that would leave her limp and satiated.

This sinfully handsome Creole could easily give that to her.

While Jade looked only at him, Armand casually glanced around her luxurious lair. Priceless statuettes, the work of renowned artists, were displayed on floor-to-ceiling shelves. Nearby stood a tall, glass-doored armoire filled with fancy linen-wear and bedsheets.

Over the mantel of the fireplace was a costly French mirror in a gilt frame. A pair of armchairs and a sofa, all of which were covered with damask, were arranged before the fire.

Directly across from the fireplace and visible in the huge mirror, was the bed. Specially built to accommodate the tallest of men, the bed had hangings of fine lace, sheets of clean snowy white, and a fragrant basket of fresh-cut flowers hung suspended from the bed's tester.

The richly appointed room and its incredible occupant were conducive to the pursuit of sexual pleasure. And Armand was ready to pursue plenty of sexual pleasure.

Excited by the prospect of being in this man's arms, Jade crossed to Armand, laid her soft hands on his chest and said, "I want to please you. Anything you want, you may have."

"A nice, hot bath for starters," he said, shrugging out of his dark evening jacket.

"You shall have it," she said, crossing to the bed and pulling the bell cord.

Moments later Armand was seated in a claw-footed tub filled with thick suds and steaming hot water. And the beautiful Jade—now wearing only a skimpy black lace chemise and silk stockings—was scrubbing his back with a long-handled brush.

When he was clean and glistening, Armand rose and allowed Jade to towel his body dry. She made a sensuous exercise of it, teasing him with the towel, rubbing it lightly over his skin and sinking to her knees to blot the water from his long muscular legs.

Finally she dropped the towel, rose to her feet, smiled at Armand and said, "I will be waiting for you."

She turned and left the bath dressing room. Armand stayed. He lifted a dainty, feminine-looking hairbrush from the vanity and brushed his damp hair back. He dropped the brush and ran both hands through the thick hair at his temples. He took another fresh towel from the shelf, finished drying the spots Jade had missed, then swirled the towel around his body and knotted it atop his right hip.

He went back into the bedroom.

Jade's black lace chemise and silk stockings had been discarded carelessly to the carpet. Totally naked, she lay stretched out in the bed, her voluptuous body covered with the soft white bedsheet. Her dark hair was swirled seductively on the lace-trimmed pillow. Her bare shoulders and the tops of her full breasts were visible above the sheet's top edge.

Her dark eyes blazed with hunger and fire.

His gaze holding hers, Armand dropped his covering towel and went naked to the bed. He bent and slowly peeled the sheet away from her body. Then he gave the sheet a quick, firm jerk, completely pulling it free of the bed. He dropped it to the carpet and got into bed with Jade.

He ran a caressing hand down her beautiful body and, his fingers caressing her thigh, said, "You'll make love to me all through the night and into the morning?"

"Yes, oh yes," she said, her tingling body responding to his touch.

"All night long," he repeated and pulled her into his arms.

But not a half hour later, Armand was drawing on his dark trousers while Jade sat cross-legged in the middle of the rumpled bed, pouting.

"You paid for the entire night," she reminded him.

"I know," he said, stuffing his shirttails down into his trousers. Trying to spare her feelings, he said, "And it was worth it, Jade. Really it was."

"Then why are you leaving?" she asked. "I will give you incredible pleasure if only you'll stay."

"You already have," he told her, but she was not placated.

"What's wrong with you?" she demanded, insulted and miffed. "You can't get it up but once a night? Is that it?"

"That's it," Armand said with a self-deprecating smile. "Guess I'm not much of a man."

"No, you're not!" she said and angrily sailed a pillow at him as he exited the room.

Downstairs Armand hurriedly collected his cloak and gloves and stepped out into the darkness. He glanced up and down the silent street. Then he remembered. He had told Philip he would be staying at Lulu's until noon tomorrow.

No matter. A moonlight walk in the cold night air might do him some good. Something had to do him some good. There had to be balm for this misery.

He had assumed that a night with a beautiful woman would do the trick. And when he had taken the voluptuous Jade in his arms he'd had no trouble performing sexually. He had been hot and so had she, and together they had attained a shuddering climax.

It had been a draining release, so why did he still feel so edgy, so restless, so unfulfilled?

Armand didn't actually plan it, but he found himself taking the long way home. He could have walked straight down St. Peter to his Pontalba apartment. But he hadn't. He headed west on Bourbon. When he reached Conti, he turned south and walked the block to Royal.

Soon he was pausing before the town house of Colfax Sumner and gazing wistfully up at the second-floor windows. He shivered in the cold, thrust his hands deep down into his cloak's pockets, and stood on the banquette picturing the lovely redhaired Madeleine in her soft, warm bed.

"Everything all right, Mr. de Chevalier?" a low,

deep voice startled him and Armand looked up to find the giant, Montro, approaching.

"I—I'm fine," Armand stammered. "I was just…I…I…was walking home and I…"

"From your club?"

"Yes, from the Beaufort."

Montro smiled knowingly. "A little out of the way, isn't it?"

"You've got me cold," Armand said and he, too, smiled. "Jesus, don't tell anyone. Especially not her."

"Never," promised Montro, knowing that Armand was referring to Madeleine. Armand sighed wearily. "I mean her no harm, it's just…"

"I know you don't," said the wise giant. "You worry about her, as I do."

Armand's dark brows knitted. "You worry about her, too?"

Big Montro nodded. "There's something about Lord Enfield," he muttered, shaking his head. "I can't put my finger on it, but…"

Armand simply said, "Yes. I know what you mean." He turned up the collar of his cloak, and added, "Guess I best be on my way and let you get in out of the cold. Good night, Montro."

"Good night, sir."

His wide shoulders hunched, Armand walked away. In minutes he was home and inside the warmth of his apartment. He tossed his cloak over the back of a chair and headed for the bedroom. Yawning, he stripped to the skin, letting his clothes lie where they fell.

But before he got into bed, he picked up his discarded trousers, reached inside a pocket, and carefully withdrew the faded, slightly tattered blue garter. His good-luck charm. Madeleine's garter. All he had of her. All he would ever have?

Armand blew out the lamp, got into bed, turned onto his side and placed the garter on the mattress before him.

As he stared at it he saw again the beautiful Madeleine asleep in her bed, her pale body warm with sleep beneath the covers. He quickly imagined himself in that warm bed with her. The vision was so real, so stirring he found himself aching to hold her in his arms. He longed to kiss her and make sweet love to her.

Armand's belly tightened and he bit the inside of his jaw as rash desire seized him. He cursed the throbbing, jerking erection that pressed against his belly, mocking him, ridiculing him. Angered by his weakness, light-headed from his need, he impulsively swept the garter off the bed and turned onto his back.

He forced himself to picture the russet-haired witch responsible for this agony in the arms of her fiancé.

Gritting his teeth so viciously his jaws ached, he envisioned an eager Madeleine writhing naked beneath the blond nobleman. Sickened by the vivid vision, Armand's blood soon began to cool, his pulsing erection to deflate.

Burning desire fled.

The terrible yearning did not.

Twenty-Two

'Twas the season to be jolly.

But the Countess wasn't.

Because of the Creole.

Madeleine couldn't enjoy the continuous round of Christmas luncheons, receptions and soirees for fear of finding Armand de Chevalier at every gala gathering.

That fear was well-founded. The fact that his reputation was less than sterling apparently had little or no negative effect on the number of invitations he received. The celebrated hostesses of New Orleans unfailingly put Armand de Chevalier's name at the top of their guest lists.

He was warmly welcomed into the opulent drawing rooms of the city's monied elite. Indeed, the privileged doyennes fought over him, knowing that his presence at a party ensured its success. Armand was, to Madeleine's despair, well-liked by the city's Old Guard. The gentlemen enjoyed his company, the ladies were drawn to him like moths to a flame.

Madeleine had learned, early on, that if she was going to live in New Orleans, avoiding Armand de Chevalier would be next to impossible. After all, they were part of the very same social circle. So while she should have been enjoying the Christmas season, she was, instead, counting the days until it was over.

By New Year's Eve she was a bundle of nerves. She and Desmond had attended at least two dozen holiday events in the past three weeks and Armand had been at the majority of them. At each and every party or ball, she had tenaciously stayed close to Desmond, hardly letting him out of her sight.

But the tension had taken its toll. While she had said little more than hello to Armand since the holiday bazaar, she had been achingly aware of his presence at all the glittering events. She'd had difficulty keeping her eyes off him. It seemed he grew a little handsomer each night and a great deal harder to ignore.

Lord, she hated the Christmas holidays!

But now, as she dressed for the final celebration of the season, she was at last beginning to breathe a little easier. With the holidays behind her, she would not be attending nightly parties. Which meant she wouldn't be seeing the devilish Creole. It was entirely possible that she might be able to go for weeks without running into him.

Which was exactly what she needed. Out of sight, out of mind. If she no longer saw him, she would no longer think about him. She would turn her attention to the things that were important. Like her upcoming marriage to Desmond. She could focus fully on planning their spring wedding.

Convinced everything would soon return to normal, Madeleine was, in fact, rather looking forward to this New Year's evening. While she and Desmond had received numerous invitations to private parties, the earl had graciously deferred to her, suggesting she choose where they would spend their last evening of the old year.

She had quickly decided upon the New Year's Eve ball at the St. Charles Hotel. The St. Charles was in the American section of the city. What could be safer? As a general rule, the snobbish Creoles hated and snubbed the Americans. And vice versa. The St. Charles would surely be the last place on earth where a haughty Creole would be caught dead.

Nonetheless, when Lord Enfield's carriage rolled to a stop on St. Charles Avenue and the couple joined other revelers who were hurrying into the hotel, she automatically searched the crowd for Armand.

As she danced the evening away in the impressive ballroom, which rivaled the palace of the czar in St. Petersburg, Madeleine continued to nervously look for Armand. But when the hours passed with no sight of him, the last traces of her tenseness finally fled and she congratulated herself. She had been right in choosing the St. Charles.

Armand would not appear.

The hour of midnight struck.

The brand-new year had arrived.

Bells chimed in the tower of the St. Louis Cathedral and the crowded dance floor of the St. Charles hotel immediately erupted into pandemonium. Couples were hugging and kissing and there were deafening chants of "Happy New Year!" echoing throughout the massive ballroom. Smiling, Desmond bent and gave Madeleine a brief buss, then turned abruptly when a drunken gentleman clasped his shoulder and wished him a Happy New Year. A good sport, Desmond politely brushed a kiss to the plump cheek of the man's tipsy wife.

The orchestra struck up "Auld Lang Syne." People sang and swayed and applauded and whistled and stomped their feet. Pushed and jostled by the swarm of happy revelers, in seconds Madeleine was separated from Desmond. Shuffled about by the crush of exuberant humanity, she grew mildly alarmed. Standing on tiptoe, she anxiously looked around, straining to see over heads and between bodies, searching for Desmond.

She couldn't find him.

Then she felt a firm hand on her arm and was relieved that Desmond had rescued her. Smiling, she quickly turned to him. Only it wasn't her fiancé.

Armand de Chevalier loomed before her, tall and handsome and intimidating.

"Happy New Year, Maddie," he mouthed the words above the deafening den, bent his dark head and kissed Madeleine with such swift, fiery passion she felt her knees buckle.

Then he was gone.

Disappearing back into the crowd, leaving Madeleine to wonder if he had only been an illusion. She touched her tingling lips.

That was no illusion.

That was the Creole.

"My dear," she heard Lord Enfield say, "we got separated somehow. I'm so sorry. I looked around and couldn't find you anywhere. I was quite worried."

"I know, I looked for you, too," she said, wondering exactly when he had managed to spot her.

Wondering if he had seen Armand kissing her. Wondering what he would say if he had. She braced herself for the worst.

"Dear, this crowd has become unruly," he said, shaking his head. "I think we should go." He possessively took her arm.

"Yes, I agree," she said, certain by his calm demeanor that he hadn't seen her with the Creole. She breathed a sigh of relief once they were safely in their carriage and then began to look forward to their next stop at the Hamiltons'. When she realized they were heading home to the Royal Street town house, she said, "Desmond, aren't we going to the breakfast party at the Hamiltons'?"

"I think not, dear," he said matter-of-factly. "I'll make our apologies when next I see them."

"But, I thought that we…"

"Haven't you had enough celebrating? I, myself, can hardly wait to get into bed. I'm so sleepy I can't keep my eyes open." He yawned dramatically.

At the front door of the town house, Madeleine said good night, turned her cheek up for Desmond's kiss and then went inside. Silently she climbed the stairs and was relieved to see that Avalina was not there waiting for her.

She had told Avalina that she and Desmond would not be home until the wee small hours. After the ball at the St. Charles, they were to go to an early-morning breakfast celebration at the Lawford Hamilton's. Afterward, the two had planned to retire to Desmond's house where they would see in the dawn of the new year sipping brandy before a blazing fire.

Madeleine sighed heavily.

She should, she knew, be very disappointed that Desmond had wanted to cut their evening short. But she wasn't. She had wanted to come home from the minute Armand had kissed her and left her flustered and frightened.

She was, however, beginning to seriously wonder about Lord Enfield. Either he was, as she constantly assured herself, the most self-disciplined man in all the world or else she aroused no more passion in him than he did in her.

Perhaps there was no passion in him.

"Oh, darling, yes," Lord Enfield was groaning with desire not fifteen minutes after leaving Madeleine. "Please, now, please."

Too aroused to take the time to fully undress, Desmond Chilton, his long dark cloak pushed back over his shoulders, sat on an easy chair in the parlor of Dominique's Rampart Street cottage. He still wore his fine black evening jacket, shirt and black satin cravat with its pearl stickpin.

But from the waist down, he was naked.

Dominique, dressed in an azure taffeta evening gown that was adorned with a sapphire-and-diamond necklace he had given her, knelt between the lord's spread knees and cunningly tortured him. She knew exactly what he wanted. So she withheld it.

Because there was something she wanted.

When she got what she wanted, he would get what he wanted.

"God have mercy!" Desmond groaned, his pulsing erection dictating to him. "I'm begging you, Dom. Do it."

"Oh—I will, my love," she said, sinking back onto her heels and folding her hands demurely in her lap. "Just as soon as you agree."

"Agree? Agree to what?" His face was blood-red, eyes wild. He was in agony. "I don't know what you're talking about."

"I want you to promise you'll go with me to visit Mama Cecile."

"Oh, God, don't start that now…"

Dominique smiled wickedly and then abruptly rose to her feet.

"No! Come back here. Don't leave me, darling, I…"

Looking down at him, Dominique asked, "You will agree to go to Mama Cecile's?"

"Yes, yes, I will. I'll go anywhere you say. I'll do anything you want, but, please…"

"We will go to see the voodoo priestess one night next week," she announced decisively.

At that moment, he would have agreed to anything. "Yes, yes, next week. We'll go, I promise." He gave her a pleading look. "Dom, please."

Dominique smiled triumphantly and slowly sank back to her knees between his spread legs. Lord Enfield was trembling now, his throbbing erection jerking rhythmically against the long tails of his white shirt, his breath coming in loud, shallow spurts.

Ah yes, thought Dominique, her lord was quite the eager lover. She had never known such a passionate man. She had only to touch him and he was instantly rock-hard with need. She was glad he was this way. And not just because she, too, was highly passionate.

Dominique knew, and had known, from the day she first climbed into his carriage and kissed him senseless, that she could make him hers and that she could get anything out of him she wanted by sexually exciting him. So she made it a point to keep him excited and aroused.

And hers.

When he was a good boy, when he did exactly what she wanted him to do, she was more than happy to reward him.

Like now.

Dominique felt certain that the answer to their problem could be found at Mama Cecile's. And now Lord Enfield had agreed to go there with her. He wouldn't regret that decision.

"My lusty lord," she murmured lovingly as she leaned closer and, bowing her dark head, opened her mouth.

"Happy New Year," she whispered and put him out of his misery.

Twenty-Three

The first few days of the new year were cold, damp and dismal. The skies were heavy with the constant threat of rain and the weak winter sun was unable to penetrate the low, dense cloud cover.

The weather matched Madeleine's melancholy mood. She was troubled about her own personal problems, but more importantly she was worried about her beloved uncle.

Colfax Sumner had always been such a vigorous, outgoing man. Old friends had often commented on his zest for life, his wide-ranging interests, his childlike curiosity and his incredible physical stamina.

A gregarious man who loved parties and galas almost as much as the pleasure-seeking Creoles, he never missed a social event. Or, at least, there had been a time that he hadn't.

That had changed.

In the past few weeks, Uncle Colfax had turned down more invitations than he had accepted. When darkness fell each evening, he seemed more than a little reluctant to leave the comfortable confines of his home.

Madeleine had discussed her concerns with both Big Montro and Avalina. She knew that they, too, were worried about Uncle Colfax and it showed. Avalina went out of her way to coddle and care for Colfax, while Big Montro doggedly watched over him, alert for the least little sign of trouble.

Deciding she would simply confront her uncle, Madeleine caught him in his study late one dreary afternoon and announced that the two of them needed to talk.

At her words, a worried expression crossed his face, and he said, "Child, is something wrong? Tell me and I'll fix it."

Madeleine smiled at hearing the familiar statement. That was so like him. He had said those words to her dozens of times in her life. She knew that he loved her dearly and that her happiness was his main concern. He did everything in his power to make her life a lovely fairy tale. Dear lord, what would she ever do without him?

"Nothing for you to fix, Uncle," she said cheerfully, "but there's something for me to fix." She sat down on the camel-backed sofa beside him.

"Something for you to fix?" He looked puzzled. "I'm afraid I don't follow."

Madeleine drew a deep breath. "Uncle Colfax, you're not yourself lately and..."

"Who am I?" he teasingly interrupted.

"This is nothing to joke about. You know what I'm talking about. You tire too easily. You rarely go out in the evenings. You seem preoccupied much of the time and you're often quiet and withdrawn." She swallowed with difficulty. "Are you sick, Uncle Colfax? Are you seriously ill and not telling me?"

"My dear child, you've always had an overactive

imagination," he gently scolded. "No. No, I am not ill," he said, shaking his head. "I've been blessed with excellent health and you know it."

Madeleine tilted her head to one side. "Then what is it?"

"Old age?" he offered, with a cherubic smile.

"You aren't that old," she said. "I think you're not feeling well and you're just not telling me."

Colfax Sumner turned the tables on his worried niece. "What about you, dear? Is everything okay? Lately you look a bit pensive when I come upon you unexpectedly. As if something is troubling you."

Madeleine reached out and affectionately patted his age-spotted hand. "The only thing worrying me is you."

"Then you have no worries," he said, assuring her that there was absolutely nothing wrong with him.

But Madeleine was not fully convinced, so she took matters into her own hands. She contacted Dr. Ledette, told him of her concerns, asked if he would come around to the town house one evening after dinner and examine her uncle. Dr. Ledette graciously agreed. He said she could expect him at eight sharp on the evening of January 5.

After conferring with the physician, Madeleine had decided that she wanted to be at home during the doctor's visit. Furthermore, she wanted to stay until after he had thoroughly examined her uncle. Lord Enfield had understood. He'd smiled then and added, "Surely we can live without seeing each other for one evening."

"Then you don't mind?"

"Not at all, my dear. It's so cold and raw, I'll just stay in Thursday evening. It'll give me a chance to catch up on some long-neglected paperwork."

"Thank you, Desmond."

"You're very welcome, my love."

"I don't like this. I don't like this one bit."

"Kindly stop complaining. Remember you promised."

"God, what was a mistake that was," muttered a highly agitated Lord Enfield.

He frowned and pulled his woolen greatcoat tighter as the pirogue slid silently through the murky, muddy waters of the bayou.

Desmond Chilton was fuming and cursing himself for agreeing to this absurd adventure. It was foolish and dangerous to go into the swamp at night in a flimsy boat that could overturn at any minute. He should have put his foot down. They were placing themselves in serious jeopardy so that the superstitious Dominique could visit an old black woman who claimed to have mystical powers. Desmond snorted at the thought.

Behind him, standing with his feet braced apart and poling the pirogue through the vine-tangled swamp, was the muscular Barton Smallwood. Barton's older brother, Burton, absently rubbing the long scar down his sunken cheek, sat in the bow of the pirogue, on the lookout for tree stumps and alligators.

The Smallwood brothers were Lord Enfield's hired minions. They were, in a sense, on call to the nobleman. Years ago he had bought their way out of Parish Prison with a generous bribe to the night jailor and ever since he had used them for odd jobs. From the beginning he had warned that if either of them ever so much as mentioned his name to anyone, justice would be sure and swift.

The Smallwood brothers had never betrayed this confidence. It was not that they were so loyal. They were simply afraid of Lord Enfield. They had seen a side to him no one else had ever witnessed. They knew better than to cross him. They would do anything he asked without argument.

Dominique, snuggling close to Desmond in the pirogue, was unconcerned with Lord Enfield's black mood. She could hardly wait to reach the remote place where the famed voodoo priestess held secret rituals and performed incredible feats of wizardry. Dominique felt sure that all their troubles would be over once she had enlisted the help of Mama Cecile. She would ask Mama Cecile to use her great powers of sorcery to cast an evil spell on Colfax Sumner.

Dominique wanted Sumner dead. She was tired of waiting for the huge fortune that Desmond promised would be theirs once Sumner was gone. She had attempted, by using her own less potent gifts, to sicken Sumner so severely he would die, but her plan had not worked. She needed a much stronger magic. She needed the omnipotent black magic of the undisputed queen of voodoo, the much-loved, much-feared, Mama Cecile. Dominique had the utmost faith in the awe-inspiring powers of New Orleans' most celebrated voodoo priestess.

The pirogue continued to glide deeper into the gloom and ghostlike atmosphere of the miasmic swamp. A thick, cloaking mist hung in the heavy air, perilously limiting vision. Each jab of the guiding pole into the muddy bayou bottom threatened to slam the little boat into a tree stump, causing the boat to capsize. Spanish moss, dripping down from the cypresses, further impeded vision.

Snakes were also a very real danger. The murky waters were infested with deadly cottonmouths. And not all the snakes stayed in or under the water. Overhead, long, black slithering vipers wound themselves around the low limbs of trees and hung suspended, poised to drop down onto the unsuspecting interloper.

"Damnation!" muttered Barton Smallwood as his pole struck the back of an alligator, angering it.

Dominique screamed in terror when, a few short feet from her, the alligator's great head pierced the water's surface and it snapped its huge jaws menacingly, the sound echoing through the stillness.

"Christ!" Lord Enfield swore. "We're going to be eaten alive!"

"Take it easy, boss," said the scar-faced Burton Smallwood. "We're almost there. Around that next bend we should see the lights."

The younger Smallwood carefully maneuvered the pirogue through a greatly narrowed stretch of the marshy waters. Tangled vines and draping Spanish moss slapped their faces and made them wince with horror. Shuddering, Desmond and Dominique closed their eyes and clung to each other.

The pirogue rounded the last bend.

"We're here," Burton Smallwood announced and the anxious couple cautiously opened their eyes.

They saw, glimmering in the mist, the lights of a weathered old chapel that sat on the banks some fifty or sixty yards away.

When the boat's bow touched the vine-choked banks, Burton Smallwood jumped out and pulled the pirogue up onto the grass. Then he held out his hand to Dominique.

"You know better than that, Burton!" Desmond snapped angrily, and both Burton and Dominique were well aware of his meaning.

Both Smallwoods had been warned never to touch Dominique. Not even her hand. If Desmond learned that either of them had touched her, they would wish they had never been born.

"Sorry, Lord, I forgot," said Smallwood.

He stepped back as Desmond got out of the boat. Desmond turned and lifted Dominique out and set her on her feet. Holding her firmly by the arm, he addressed the brothers.

"You are to stay right here until we return," he instructed. "Do not venture a foot away from this spot. You understand me?"

"We understand," Burton answered for them both.

That wasn't good enough for Desmond. He looked directly at Barton. "You're not to even consider going anywhere near that old chapel. Do you understand me?"

"Yes, Lord," said Burton.

"Very well," Desmond softened a little, glanced again at the chapel and added, "You won't have a long wait."

He meant what he said. He had a low threshold of boredom, and so had no intention of spending an evening sitting in a drafty, ill-lit chapel, listening to an old black woman spouting gibberish. He could think of nothing quite so dull and tedious and he'd be dammed if he would hold still long for such tiresome foolishness.

He had promised Dominique he would come here to visit the voodoo queen. He hadn't promised her how long he would stay. "We won't be gone for more than a half an hour," he said to the Smallwoods.

Twenty-Four

Dominique secretly smiled.

She knew that it would be hours before they returned to the pirogue. She knew as well that Lord Enfield would not be bored.

It was deathly still and quiet as they made their way toward the chapel through the overgrown underbrush and the cloaking fog. No sound came from within the chapel. Only the croaking of the frogs in the marshes broke the eerie silence.

Dominique took the opportunity to give Desmond strict instructions on how he was to behave once they were inside the building.

"Darling, you will be only an observer to the rituals, not a participant," she pointed out.

"I should hope so," he said flippantly.

"You will remain silent and seated throughout no matter what you see or hear."

"My dear, I'll be as quiet as a church mouse," he said, "but I can't promise that I won't fall asleep."

She gave him a sly smile. "I can."

They reached the crumbling chapel and climbed the rickety steps. Dominique drew a deep breath and knocked on the splintery wooden door. Long seconds passed. Dominique grew nervous. But she did not knock again. She waited patiently.

The lord was not so patient. "Let's go back, Dom. I've changed my mind. I don't want to go inside."

"Shh!" she warned, making a face at him.

The warped door slowly opened and a tall, muscular black man holding a smoking flambeau high above his head admitted them into the chapel's shadowy vestibule. He said not one word but pointed, indicating that they were to proceed forward to the closed door on their right.

The black man did not escort them to the chapel proper, but remained where he was, on guard. Anxious to get this pagan exercise in futility behind him, Lord Enfield reached around Dominique and forcefully pushed the door open.

They stepped inside.

The lord blinked and looked around. It was dark inside. The chapel was lit only with burning wicks floating in clay pots of oil. The pots formed a large circle. He saw no one beyond the lights, yet felt their presence and wondered how many people were in the room. A dozen? A hundred?

He squinted, trying to see, and jumped when a thin black woman emerged from the deep shadows and escorted them to their seats.

They followed the woman who stayed on the outside perimeter of the lighted candlewicks. At last she touched Dominique's arm and pointed to the plank floor. The woman left them and Desmond realized, with rising irritation, that there were no chairs. He started to protest, but remembered Dominique's warnings. He was not to say a word inside the chapel.

Lord Enfield stood for a long moment, looking about for a bench or something to sit on. Anything. There was nothing. Exhaling with disgust, the nobleman finally sank down onto the hard wooden floor beside Dominique and once again cursed himself for agreeing to come this god-awful place on this cold winter night.

Seeing that he shivered, Dominique quietly directed his attention to a *govi,* a baked clay pitcher with a small spout that sat at their feet. She whispered that the pitcher was filled with *clairin,* a strong white rum. She did not tell him that the rum contained an infusion of aromatic herbs. She suggested that perhaps if he had a drink of the rum, it would warm him. Desmond was tempted, but refused. There were no glasses or cups from which to drink.

So he shook his head and, as he had done in the pirogue, pulled his greatcoat closer around his ears and sat there, cross-legged, aggravated, waiting for something to happen.

He didn't have to wait long.

The faint clattering of the *asson*—the sacred rattles—began. Then came the slow, steady throbbing of the drums. His eyes adjusting to the darkness, Desmond looked across the room and saw an altar upon which rested a myriad of strange-looking jars and jugs, various shaped rattles, holy emblems, stones swimming in oil, playing cards and bottles of liquor.

And bones.

Human bones. Desmond shuddered at the

thought. He was suddenly very uneasy. He wished that he could leave. He had the eerie feeling that barbaric and inhuman practices took place in this remote sanctuary all in the name of sacrifices offered up to the gods.

Above the altar was a large black cross. And on the floor directly below, resting in the regal pose of the mighty sphinx, was a coal-black cat, its golden eyes gleaming in the shadows. The cat threw its head back and hissed loudly, then yawned and lay its face on its outstretched paws.

It dozed.

At the room's center was a large straw basket with a lid covering its contents. Desmond wondered what was in the basket, but only for a moment, before something more intriguing caught his eye.

To the left of the altar stood a wood carving that looked like a man's engorged sex organ. His mouth agape, Desmond stared at the highly polished wooden object that stood at least a foot tall and was as big around as a man's closed fist.

Fascinated, he leaned closer to Dominique and nodded toward the mysterious object. "What in heaven's name is that?"

"A *boa*," she calmly whispered back.

"*Boa?*"

"A phallus used to symbolize the sex of the great god, Legba."

Desmond was about to ask what it was used for when a ripple of excitement swept through the chapel and his attention was drawn to a tall, stout black woman who was now crossing the room to take up her position before the altar.

Mama Cecile.

Staring, Desmond realized that the celebrated Mama Cecile was nothing like he had expected. He had imagined her to be a skinny old crone, bent and brittle, with dull eyes and a wrinkled face. Mama Cecile was exactly the opposite. Big and strapping though she was, she was quite elegant and agile. She walked with an almost queenly bearing. Her hair was as white as snow, but her broad ebony face was smooth and unlined. She was dressed tastefully in a long gown of dark-colored wool. Her great, dark eyes held a look of quiet serenity.

Draped around her broad shoulders was a wrap and Dominique whispered to Desmond that it was a magic shawl that had been sent to Mama Cecile by the emperor of China.

Mama Cecile, seating herself on a makeshift throne to the right of the altar, began the strange ceremony by calling on Legba, the god who opens the gates that separate the profane world of the living from that other sacred world.

"Atibo Legba, open the gates for me," she intoned. "Papa Legba, open the gates for me. Open the gates that I might enter...."

She spoke in a low, cultured voice that sent chills up Desmond's spine. He stared in awe as several zombielike acolytes emerged from beyond the burning candlewicks into the circle of light. Making their way around the huge wicker basket, they moved toward the altar and fell to their knees before their revered voodoo queen.

"What are they doing?" Desmond whispered.

"Shh!" Dominique warned.

"Shouldn't you join those kneeling before her?"

Desmond asked. "To tell Mama Cecile why you've come here."

Dominique shook her head. "I will speak to Mama Cecile after the ceremonies have ended and the others have gone." She touched his arm. "Have you the gold?"

Desmond patted the small bag containing ten twenty-dollar gold pieces that rested inside his coat pocket. "I do, but I think it's foolish and frivolous of you to be giving money to that old woman."

Dominique's dark eyes blazed. "That old woman is a mistress of the god! She has unlimited powers of sorcery, so you had best hold your blasphemous tongue."

Desmond shrugged, but fell silent as she watched Mama Cecile rise from her throne, her big body beginning to shake from head to toe as if she were having some kind of seizure. Those kneeling before her were totally motionless, petrified in sacred awe. Desmond now also sat motionless with wonder and fear.

Mama Cecile began to sing and pirouette and, quite suddenly, she produced a huge cutlass. The sharp blade caught the candlelight as she brandished it over her head. There was a pronounced silence as everyone, including Desmond, waited with bated breath, eyes fixed on Mama Cecile.

At that moment a squealing black pig was produced. Its loud frantic grunts filled the chapel. But not for long. With one vivid thrust the voodoo priestess plunged her cutlass into the pig's throat. Blood spurted. And was quickly gathered into a waiting clay pitcher.

Horrified and half-nauseated, Desmond watched,

eyes wide and mouth open, as the slaughtered pig was placed on the altar. Its blood was mixed with alcohol and the sickening concoction was then passed amongst the kneeling believers. Each drank of the blood. And each swore to never reveal the sacred secrets imparted under the seal of the blood. All agreed that there would be unfailing punishment of anyone who broke the code. Repulsed, Desmond had an overwhelming desire to get up and leave this place where profane rituals were carried out. He felt apprehensive and anxious. Afraid of what might come next.

Mama Cecile was now moving about, sprinkling magical powders from a hollowed-out gourd. Desmond stared, still gripped with horror, at the voodoo queen. Her eyes were wide-open, but her eyeballs were rolled back in her head until only the whites showed. She was chanting strange incantations, soliciting the spirit world, casting a spell.

Performing her evil magic.

Desmond felt the hair on the back of his neck rise. He was relieved when those asking for help from Mama Cecile began returning to their places beyond the pots of light. Soon all had faded back into the shadows and the chapel fell totally silent. It remained so for several long, tense moments.

The white-haired voodoo queen now sat rigid on her throne. The coal-black cat sat rigid by the altar. And Lord Enfield sat rigid on the floor. Nothing stirred. The silence was deafening.

Finally, from beyond the circle of light, the calabashes began to rattle. A lone drum began to beat a slow, steady rhythm and an intense kind of tension filled the air. Caught up in the mood, Desmond felt a strange tautness in his limbs and his heartbeat quickened dramatically. He anxiously reached out for the clay pitcher of *clairin,* put his lips to the spout and took a long swallow.

A loud shout from out of the darkness startled him and he almost dropped the pitcher. He nervously set it down and reached for Dominique's hand, wondering what terrible thing was going to happen next. The throb of the drums grew more rapid and it was as if the dark denizens beyond the circle of light were suddenly holding their collective breaths.

All at once a bright flash of light lit the room as a charge of gunpowder was detonated and the worked-up spectators gasped loudly. Then from out of the thick acrid smoke stepped an incredibly beautiful black woman.

The woman was totally nude.

Twenty-Five

Her only adornment was a white feather in her ebony hair.

Desmond's eyes instantly fastened on the magnificent specimen of proud femininity. She was young, no older than sixteen or seventeen, but she had the ripe, tempting body of a woman. Her dark, luxuriant hair was unbound and it fell to well below her slim waist. Her legs were long and shapely and her breasts jutted straight out from her chest. The dark nipples were large and soft. All her body hair had been removed, shaved totally clean, leaving her most intimate parts glaringly exposed.

Desmond felt his groin stir as he gazed upon her. He liked the way she looked with no thick thatch of curly hair between her firm thighs. He found it incredibly appealing. She was so slick, so smooth, so tempting. And her body was gleaming, as if she were wet, from head to toe.

His heart pounding, Desmond heard Dominique whisper, "This girl has been given a cleansing balm bath. The bath has removed everything mental, spiritual and physical so that she may be utilized as a pure vessel by Mama Cecile. No soap was used on her body, but a secret potion made from the extract of roots was mixed with rich oils and carefully mas-

saged into the girl's naked flesh." Dominique
paused, glanced at the shimmering black girl, then
added, "The sweet scent from the roots is the very
odor of seduction."

Desmond did not reply. He nodded, bewitched
by the sight of the bare young woman who was
beginning to gently thrust her pelvis forward ever
so subtlety. He itched to touch her. All over. His
belly grew tight as she began to slowly move
around the room inside the circle of light.

She didn't walk, but undulated like a snake. Her
glistening body literally moving in waves, she slithered slowly about, a wild, not-of-this-world expression in her huge black eyes, as if she were in a deep
trance.

When she had finally made her way fully around
the circle, curving her malleable body throughout,
she turned and went directly to the large straw basket at the room's center. She sank to her knees before it and lifted the lid.

At once the head of a huge, hissing snake
emerged and Desmond groaned aloud. But the
beautiful girl showed no fear of the large reptile.
She stared unblinkingly at it and the serpent continued to hiss and dart its long tongue out, its fangs
dripping deadly venom.

A twitter of fresh excitement swept through the
hidden crowd when the girl rose to her feet, reached
out with a lightning fast movement and grabbed the
snake's head. She then nimbly climbed inside the
basket with the reptile.

"Jesus," Desmond swore, "is she trying to commit suicide?"

"No," Dominique calmly assured him. "She is

perfectly safe. The snake is the voodoo. The god. The spirit. He will not make known his will, except through Mama Cecile. Therefore Mama Cecile has ordered the girl to please the god so that we may make full use of his potent powers.''

Speechless, Desmond watched as the writhing snake wound itself around the girl's satiny body. For the next heart-stopping few minutes, serpent and woman writhed together in a bizarre exercise that was akin to orgasmic ecstasy.

It was frightening.

It was obscene.

It was entrancing.

Abruptly the girl, continuing to hold the snake's head so that it couldn't bite her, shook herself free of his great coiled body and got out of the basket. She released the snake's head and it hissed and spit, but she calmly turned her back on it and moved away in unhurried, undulating steps.

Desmond's eyes widened in anticipation when she approached the wooden phallus. He was already so aroused from watching her with the snake that he was uncomfortable. He had shed his greatcoat, loosened his cravat and unbuttoned the top buttons of his shirt. Still he was much too warm and was perspiring freely. He lifted the clay pitcher again and took a long swig of the doctored rum. He swallowed and took another. He could feel the effects of the *clairin* heating his blood, but was unaware that the herbs which had been added to the rum worked as a powerful aphrodisiac.

His intense gaze never left the girl. What, he wondered, would she do with the carved phallus? His throat grew dry as he envisioned her attempting to mount it. He grabbed up the pitcher and took another drink.

The girl danced lithely around the wooden symbol of sex for a time before sinking to her knees before it. She stared at the giant phallus for a long moment, spellbound. Then she took the white feather from her hair and sinking back onto her bare heels, began to flick the feather back and forth over her nipples.

Desmond swallowed convulsively. He thirstily drank again.

Her head thrown back, her eyes closed, the kneeling girl continued to flick the feather rapidly over her breasts until the stimulation caused her large nipples to stiffen and stand out like twin bullets. She then dropped the feather.

She came back up on her knees, leaned forward and rubbed her hardened nipples back and forth against the phallus. Bent on pleasing the god so that he would use his great powers, she teased the wooden object as if it were flesh and blood. The distended nipple of her left breast resting against the polished wood, she lifted her hands and gently wrapped her fingers around its thick carved base.

She might have been wrapping her hands around his own swollen erection from the way Desmond responded to her actions. He could feel her stroking him, arousing him, so excited was he from watching.

His excitement intensified as she continued to toy with the wooden phallus. In a deep stupor, she arched her back and pressed her pelvis to it. She bent her head and kissed the tip. Desmond felt the perspiration beading in his hairline and above his upper lip.

The girl abruptly rose to her feet and stepped directly over the carved object. His breath ragged, his heart pumping fiercely, Desmond stared as the girl stood unmoving for a time, a bare foot planted firmly on each side of the wooden phallus. As it happened, the girl was facing Desmond and Dominique, so Desmond was rewarded with an unobstructed view of the erotic show.

And what a show it was.

The girl masqueraded with the wooden symbol. She danced obscene dances around it, and abandoned herself to prurient play. Her behavior was lustful, lascivious, lewd. The enchanted spectators loved it. Especially Desmond Chilton.

She tossed her head, setting her long black hair to dancing. She spread her hands on her thighs, bent her knees and began to lower her bare bottom down toward the thrusting phallus. Her legs wide open, her undulating body moving ever closer to its target, she stopped just as her shimmering flesh brushed the very tip of the wooden object.

The observers, electrified by what she was doing, urged her on. Shouting and chanting, they begged her to impale herself upon the sexual symbol of their all-powerful god.

"Do it," Desmond was shouting with the rest of them. "Take it inside you! Mount it, mount it!"

Beside him, Dominique smiled and she too egged the girl on.

For what seemed an eternity, the girl stayed crouched just above the wooden phallus, hands on her knees, head thrown back, bare bottom undulating a scant half inch above the thick smooth tip of the carved erection.

She teased her rapt audience, but never fully delivered. All, including Desmond, loudly voiced their disappointment when she suddenly shot to her feet and moved away from the phallus. But she quickly reclaimed their approval when she began to dance to a wild, fast rhythm of the throbbing drums. She darted out her tongue and crawled on the floor in sinuous movements.

She turned onto her back and moved into a position wherein only her shoulders and the soles of her bare feet were touching the floor. She stayed that way for several long moments while her appreciative audience cheered and applauded. Then she moved and began twisting her body into unbelievable shapes. Desmond was panting now, so excited he was beside himself.

Apparently others shared his excitement because all at once the girl was no longer alone in the circle of light. Electrified by her erotic display, the thralls from beyond the circle of light became participants, sharing the black beauty's madness and chanting wildly as they took to the floor.

The drum rhythms grew savage as those who were now as possessed as the naked girl began to dance the infamous *banda,* that well-known dance that was unique for its violent agitation of the hips and lascivious positions.

Desmond fully approved. Clapping his hands and chanting, he watched the pagan dance unblinkingly. He saw things he had never seen before. Things he would never forget.

He continued to drink thirstily of the white rum

and he grew so warm that he shed his shirt. Soon rivers of perspiration made his chest and shoulders gleam.

Caught up in the carnal excitement, he wanted to join the dancers, but was afraid to test Dominique. He glanced at her, saw that she too was mesmerized by the uninhibited dancers. She was focused on the young black girl who moved around the floor dancing first with a man, then a woman, then by herself.

The wild dancing lasted for what seemed an hour, ending abruptly when Mama Cecile rose from her throne and clapped her hands loudly. The dancers stopped dancing immediately and returned to their seats.

Moments later the supplicants began to drift away.

At last Desmond and Dominique were alone in the remote chapel with Mama Cecile and the exotic young girl.

Desmond, now very drunk, stayed where he was while Dominique spoke privately with the voodoo queen. He could see Dominique talking rapidly, making her point, asking for the high priestess's help in casting an evil spell. Desmond knew it was nonsense and a waste of money, but he was glad now that he had humored Dominique.

His attention quickly strayed from the voodoo queen and Dominique to the girl who had so dazzled him with her lewd dancing. She sat now on the throne vacated by Mama Cecile, one long leg casually thrown over the throne's wooden arm, carelessly exposing all her feminine charms. She hadn't bothered to put on any clothes.

In her arms, against her naked breasts, she held

the coal-black cat. She lovingly stroked the purring feline and the contented cat slowly swished his tail back and forth and nudged the girl's chin with his head.

Desmond trembled and, with shaking hands, put on his discarded shirt. Then he looped his clasped hands around his knees and continued to observe the girl, glancing occasionally at Mama Cecile and Dominique. Finally, he saw Dominique smile, shake her head, and give the high priestess the velvet bag of coins.

This was his golden opportunity. Dom was in a receptive mood and he sensed that the black girl had aroused her just as she had him. He grabbed up his greatcoat and hurriedly crossed to Dominique.

"We can go now, Desmond," she said smiling.

He glanced at the girl on the throne, then back at Dominique. "Darling, I was wondering..."

"Yes? What is it?"

"Don't you think it would be enjoyable to take that beautiful girl home with us?" He gave her a hopeful look. "Just for one night. One time only."

Aroused by the erotic rituals, hopeful that she now possessed the powerful magic she needed, Dominique said, "An excellent idea, my lord."

Twenty-Six

Lady Madeleine was disappointed.

She had assumed—and fervently hoped—that with the passing of the Christmas holidays, she would see less of Armand de Chevalier. That had not happened. Much to her annoyance and dismay, it seemed she ran into the impertinent Creole every time she left the town house.

If she went down to the French Market with Montro, de Chevalier mysteriously turned up, to tease and flirt and upset her.

An afternoon with Desmond at the Metairie Racetrack was spoiled because the Creole was there, in a box adjoining theirs. It was evident that he hadn't been there to see the races. He hadn't watched them. He watched her, boldly looking at her through a pair of field glasses while everyone else watched the Thoroughbreds round the oval track.

An evening of frivolous gambling had been spoiled when a lean brown hand casually placed a black chip atop hers at the roulette layout. She'd recognized those long tapered fingers and, frowning, had looked up.

Armand de Chevalier had smiled down at her and

said, "You'd get a better gamble at my place, Maddie."

At a late dinner at Antonies, Madeleine lost her appetite when, no sooner was she seated, than she looked up to see the handsome Creole devouring oysters at a nearby table.

And now, even at the opera—the last place on earth where she'd expected to have seen him—de Chevalier was present. Handsome in impeccable evening clothes, he was surrounded by a pride of New Orleans' most influential doyennes. The regal Baroness de Pontalba, the legendary opera diva, Madame Julia Calve, the formidable Delphine Larie and others encircled him, nodding, laughing, listening to his every word.

Madeleine, taking her seat in the dress circle very near to where Armand was seated, could overhear bits and pieces of his conversation. Armand was regaling the enchanted ladies with tales about last summer's ill-fated ocean voyage on the S. S. *Starlight*.

Madeleine's heart stopped when, in answer to one of the ladies' questions, he said with a wink and a grin, "Why, there was only *one* occurrence of misbehavior."

"Oh, tell, tell," chimed the ladies in unison.

Before he could speak, the lights dimmed. The music rose. And Madeleine released her held breath.

Since the moment Armand had shown up at last autumn's masked ball, Madeleine had lived in constant dread that sooner or later he would expose her.

Ruin everything. Reveal her for the terrible sinner she was.

Added to that nagging worry was the unwanted, steadily growing physical attraction she couldn't help but feel for him. Where the handsome de Chevalier was concerned, common sense did not dictate. There was no denying that each time she saw him, her heart beat too fast and her hands trembled.

She was, she knew, unquestionably foolish.

But she was not a fool.

She was well aware of the danger the Creole presented and made it a point to never offer him the opportunity of catching her alone and vulnerable. She would be safe so long as she exercised constant caution.

But exercising caution in her normal routine had never been one of Madeleine's strengths. In fact, one sunny January morning, when her uncle requested she stay at home for the day since he was taking Montro with him to visit one of his many Delta plantations, she had smiled and said nothing.

Madeleine had made plans weeks ago and she fully intended to keep them. She had promised Madame Simone, New Orleans' most accomplished French modiste, that she would come to the Madam's shop for fittings of her many trousseau gowns. If she broke the engagement it might be days, even weeks before she could get in to see the renowned dressmaker.

Madeleine wisely waited a good half hour after Uncle Colfax and Big Montro had gone. When she felt comfortable that the pair had left the city behind, she went in search of Avalina. She found her idly dusting the dining table, with an expression of worry on her face.

"Avalina, let the dusting go. You know we're due at Madam Simone's in a half hour."

Avalina looked sharply at her. "Are you forgetting that Montro has gone to the country with the master?"

"No, but it's broad daylight and Madam Simone's shop is only four blocks away. Let's go."

Avalina nervously twisted the handle of the feather duster and shook her head. "Please, Lady Madeleine, let's stay home today. I've got a bad feeling. Last night I saw a *baka* in the courtyard outside my window. A *baka* is an evil spirit that takes on the form of an animal and roams at night."

Madeleine stared at the superstitious woman. "I see. And what form did this particular *baka* take last night?"

"The form of a cat. A coal-black cat."

Madeleine smiled and affectionately put her arms around the shorter, stouter woman. "Avalina, dear Avalina," she said soothingly, "it was no evil spirit. It was just a stray cat. You know very well that strays roam the city streets." She released the servant.

Avalina again shook her head and said, "It was no stray cat. It was a *baka*."

"Well, even if it was, it's gone now and the sun is shining and there's nothing to be afraid of."

Unconvinced, Avalina nonetheless agreed to accompany her willful mistress to the dressmaker's shop. When the two women walked through the porte cochere and exited the heavy iron gates, Avalina abruptly stopped and anxiously grabbed Madeleine's arm.

"Look!" said a big-eyed Avalina. "There on the banquette directly in front of the house."

Curious, Madeleine, drawing the reluctant Avalina along with her, went straight toward the strange-looking bundle resting on the cobblestones.

"What is it?" she asked, and started to pick up the bundle.

"No, don't touch it," scolded Avalina, her eyes wide with fear. "It's *gris-gris*," she said, placing a hand on her hammering heart. "Voodoo." She looked nervously around as if expecting some frightening apparition to appear.

"Voodoo?" Madeleine repeated.

Avalina nodded. "And it is not the first time."

"What does it mean?" Madeleine asked.

"That somebody out there—" Avalina indicated the bustling city "—wants somebody in this house...dead."

Madeleine laughed it off. Kicking the bundle away with the toe of her leather slipper, she said, "That's nonsense. Who could possibly want any of us dead? Besides, I don't believe in black magic or casting spells or anything foolish like that."

"Maybe not," Avalina replied, her expression filled with fear, "but we should stay home since Montro is not here to escort us."

Out of patience, Madeleine said, "We are going, Avalina, and that's that!"

By noon the fidgeting Avalina was becoming increasingly bored with sitting in the modiste's Dauphine Street shop while Madeleine was fitted with an expensive trousseau. Madeleine sympathized with Avalina. The black woman was not one to enjoy idleness. At the town house she stayed constantly occupied.

Taking pity, Madeleine suggested, "Why don't you go on home, Avalina. I'll be here the entire afternoon and it's not fair for you to sit here with nothing to do."

"I don't mind, Lady Madeleine," Avalina said, but did not sound convincing.

"Yes, you do, and I don't blame you. Go on now, I insist. Uncle Colfax and Montro should be back in town well before three. You know Uncle Colfax, he'll go straight to his office and Montro will come home. You can send the carriage for me around four."

Eager to get home, Avalina reluctantly agreed. But she warned Madeleine not to venture out of the salon and to promise never to tell Master Colfax that she, Avalina, had left her there alone.

"I won't tell."

"Very well then," Avalina said.

She left as Madeleine continued the task of choosing various fabrics and trying on half-finished dresses.

By early afternoon the sun had disappeared. Dark, ominous clouds rolled in low over the river. By three o'clock it had begun raining, that driving torrential downpour of the semitropics.

At a quarter of four, a tired Madeleine said, "That's enough for today, Madame Simone."

"*Ah, oui, oui,*" Madame Simone was quick to agree. "You must be exhausted." She smiled then and said, "But we have made much progress, no?"

"Yes, we have," Madeleine replied. "Thank you so much."

Taking the umbrella Madam Simone so kindly offered, Madeleine hurried down the stairs, stepped from the door, but saw no sign of the Sumner carriage through the driving rain.

There was, however, a carriage parked at the banquette directly before the salon. Its rear door swung open and a man holding a huge black umbrella alighted. Madeleine's borrowed umbrella slipped from her hand and fell to the banquette.

"My apologies, Maddie, but your uncle and Montro have not yet returned from the plantation," Armand said. "Luckily, Avalina informed me of your dilemma."

Furious with Avalina, Madeleine said, "If you think I'm getting into that carriage with you…"

Ignoring the statement, Armand firmly took her arm and when she balked, he effortlessly lifted her up inside the carriage and climbed in over her.

It was dry and dark and warm inside the roomy conveyance. The side curtains were tightly drawn. Madeleine couldn't see out. No one could see in. Nervously she settled herself back onto the softness of the seat, as far away from Armand as possible.

Her mind racing, she decided that she should get out of this dangerous situation as quickly and as diplomatically as possible.

"Mr. de Chevalier," she said calmly, "I do so appreciate your giving me a ride on this rainy afternoon." She cleared her throat needlessly, and added, "You know where I live, it's just—"

"Yes, I know," he interrupted, his deep, rich voice rising above the fierce pelting of the rain pep-

pering the carriage's roof. He moved closer to her,
let his knee fall against her thigh and asked, "Do
you know where I live?"

Madeleine swallowed with difficulty. "I understand that you have more than one abode," she replied.

"I do, indeed," he stated, "and I want to take
you to every one of them."

Her head snapped around and she stared at him.
"You, sir, will take me nowhere but home! Is that
clear?"

Armand grinned. "Crystal clear, my lady." But
he raised an arm, placed it along the seat back behind her head and added, "You know what that
means though, don't you?"

Flustered, she said, "No, I...what on earth are
you talking about?"

The Creole edged closer still, lifted and spread
his hand across her delicate throat, gently urging
her head back. He looked directly into her eyes and
said, "We'll have to make love right here."

"Make love?" she gasped. "You *are* mad! Totally insane! I have told you repeatedly that I am
an engaged woman and I..."

"You told me," he whispered, then kissed her.

At first she manfully fought it. She turned her
head from side to side in an attempt to free her lips
from his. She pushed forcefully on his solid chest.
She stomped on his foot with her heel. She made
whimpering sounds in the back of her throat.

But, oh, his marvelous, breath-stealing kisses. So
passionate. So penetrating. So hard to resist.

Surely it couldn't do any real or lasting harm to
share just a few stolen kisses.

Twenty-Seven

Armand immediately sensed what was running through Madeleine's mind. He knew that if he continued to kiss and gently coax her, she would surrender to him.

His lips brushing butterfly kisses to the sensitive hollow of her throat, he raised his arm and tapped three times on the carriage roof. He'd instructed his trusted driver to take the longest possible route to the Sumner town house.

The rain, hammering the carriage roof and windows in great cascades, continued and so did Armand's blazing, probing kisses. Heart racing, wits scattered, Madeleine finally tore her puffy lips from his, laid her head back against the velvet seat and closed her eyes.

"Armand, Armand, we—we mustn't," she murmured breathlessly. "*I* mustn't."

"Open your eyes," Armand softly commanded. "Look at me, *chérie*." Reluctantly, Madeleine obeyed. His lips were a scant two inches from her own. His tone low and non-threatening, he said, "Look into my eyes and tell me that you don't want me."

"I—I don't want you," she managed to reply

weakly, wanting him so badly she could hardly speak.

Holding her gaze with his handsome, mysterious eyes, Armand deftly opened the buttons of his white cotton shirt, exposing a broad expanse of his chest. He took her hand and placed it directly over his heart. At once she thrilled to the touch and texture of the warm smooth flesh, the steely muscles, the crisp black hair.

And most of all, to the rapid, heavy cadence of his heart beating against her open palm.

"See what you've done to my heart?" he said. "Does yours beat as mine? With mine?"

Madeleine made no reply. She couldn't speak. She couldn't think clearly. Snared by his humid eyes and mesmerized by the feel of his hot flesh beneath her fingertips, she remained silent. And she remained perfectly still. She didn't even move when his lean tapered fingers began to skim adroitly over the buttons going down the bodice of her blue woolen dress. Before she fully realized what was happening, Armand had bared her left breast and was pressing her flush against his warm, naked torso. The sudden sensation of flesh against flesh made her gasp and tremble.

Into her ear, Armand whispered, "You see, *chérie,* our hearts beat as one."

Madeleine was lost. He was too persuasive. She was too weak. Overcome with longing for this dark seducer, she felt herself giving in to his stirring kisses, his caressing hands, his deep voice murmuring words that both shocked and thrilled her. She was drifting dangerously close to all-out surrender and she had little or no will to fight it.

Still, she weakly tried one last time to stop him, and herself, before it was forever too late.

"Please, Armand, we must stop. We cannot do this. It is not...proper."

"It may not be proper, but it's right," he whispered. "So right."

He bent his head and his heated lips moved enticingly downward over her pale throat and bosom until they were at her bared breast.

He brushed a closed-mouth kiss to her nipple and said, "Did you think I could hold you in my arms once, then never again?"

Flattered by his confession, she whispered breathlessly, "Oh, Armand, we must forget..."

"I can't forget," he stopped her in midsentence. "Can you?"

Her pulse pounding, breath short, she admitted truthfully, "No. No, I can't."

"Let me love you again, sweetheart," he whispered. "Say you will."

His mouth then opened over her stinging nipple and she involuntarily emitted a little gurgle of startled elation.

"I...will, oh, I will," she finally murmured and her trembling fingers went into the thick hair at the sides of his head.

Lips parted, heart racing, she gazed down on the head bent to her and felt her cheeks grow hot with a mixture of embarrassment and excitement. She could have closed her eyes, but she didn't. She wanted to look at him. She bit her lip at the dazzlingly erotic sight of his dark face at her pale breasts. His beautiful eyes were closed, the long black lashes resting on his cheeks. His mouth was open wide on her tingling nipple and his lean jaws were flexing rhythmically as he suckled her.

Madeleine sighed and frantically gripped his head, feeling as if all she had ever wanted—all she had been born for—was to have this irresistible man's heated lips tugging on her nipple, his sleek tongue circling it, his teeth nibbling on it.

This was, she blearily decided, all she wanted. This was enough. She needed nothing more.

But as cold winter rains continued to fall across the cloud-covered city, darkening the skies and sending great torrents of water rushing down the banquettes, Armand easily convinced Madeleine that she needed a great deal more.

While the carriage rolled over the rain-slick cobblestones, the couple inside completely shut out the world—forgetting everything and everyone—and made hot, sweet love in the dark, warm privacy of the closed conveyance.

Madeleine was so aroused she was hardly cognizant that as Armand kissed and caressed her, he was deftly undressing her. The first thing she knew, she was naked in his arms, while he was still clothed. For a time she didn't object to the disparity. It was, truth to tell, quite sensual and stirring to be the only one who was naked, the only one whose bare, sensitive flesh was being caressed and kissed.

Sighing, wiggling, silently urging him on, Madeleine sat on Armand's lap, leaning back in his strong, supporting arm, her legs stretched on the plush seat. She found it wildly exciting to be rolling along in a carriage in the pounding rain while this handsome, fully-dressed man touched and stroked and adored her.

She loved the feel of his fingertips toying with her nipples and skimming over her contracting belly and drifting down her sensitive thighs. Armand knew she was enjoying this bit of sexual play. She wasn't alone. It was heaven to hold her naked in his arms and be allowed to touch and cherish her while she snuggled trustingly to him.

He gazed at his dark hand on her white stomach and exhaled heavily, feeling as if this was all he had ever wanted—all he had been born for—to have this tantalizing woman lie naked in his arms.

This was, he dazedly decided, enough. He needed nothing more.

But as he continued to kiss her honeyed lips and caress her silken skin, the hot-blooded Armand knew that it wasn't enough. He had to have more. He had to have her completely, to be inside her, to make her his own, to love her with all the passion he felt for her, a rash, relentless passion that tortured him night and day.

Armand bent and kissed Madeleine's lips. As his mouth settled warmly on hers, he moved his hand between her legs, urging them apart. Gently he cupped her, caressed her, then parted the flaming russet curls with his middle finger and tenderly touched the wet, pulsating flesh beneath.

Madeleine's body jerked in response to his light touch. But Armand deepened the kiss and began to slowly, gently massage that most feminine part of her. Soon Madeleine's hips were surging up to meet the promise of those stroking fingers. Armand took his lips from hers and Madeleine let her head fall against his chest. His supporting arm tightened around her and together they watched while he pleasured her.

A skilled lover, Armand knew just how to bring her to the threshold of orgasm. He kept her there for several long, breathtaking moments before she finally began to squirm and toss her head and beg him.

"Armand, Armand," she pleaded, "please, please, I…"

"Yes, my love," he said and swiftly, expertly gave her the blinding ecstasy she sought.

He gazed at her lovely face as she climaxed. He saw a flash of fear in her emerald eyes and knew, that just as it had been on the doomed ship that August afternoon, she was half afraid that he might take his hand from her before she was ready for him to stop. Before the spiraling elation was fully attained.

"*Chérie,* I've got you," he murmured soothingly, his tone low, "I'll always take good care of you."

"Oh…oh…oh…Armand," she gasped, then began to cry out his name as her building orgasm exploded through her with a shocking intensity.

Afterward, Armand held her until she was calm, brushing kisses to her forehead and whispering words of love in a mixture of French and English. Then he kissed her one last time, picked her up, and sat her beside him. Madeleine purred and stretched and watched as he anxiously shed his clothes.

Once naked, Armand reached out and caught her hand in his. He laced his long fingers through her slender ones and let their hands fall and rest on the seat between them. For a time they stayed just that way, riding along in the falling rain, holding hands, heads resting against the seat back, smiling at each other.

But it did not escape Madeleine's dreamy notice that Armand was fully aroused, his throbbing erection thrusting horizontally against his flat brown belly. It occurred to her then that he was truly a caring, unselfish lover. He had taken great pains to please and pleasure her while she had done nothing for him. Even now, when he was surely hurting, he didn't roughly pull her beneath him and forcefully take her. He was waiting for her. Waiting until she was ready again.

That knowledge went a long way toward making her ready again. She softly said his name, slipped her entwined fingers free of his, scooted closer to him and laid a warm hand on his hard flesh. Her heart skipped a beat when that blood-filled erection surged up to meet her touch. Feeling powerful and giddy and longing to please him, she let her hand slide down between his legs and gently cupped him, just as he had cupped her.

Armand groaned aloud.

She looked up at him. "Did I hurt you?"

A vein pulsing on his high forehead, he managed a weak, "No. You didn't hurt me, sweetheart."

He ground his teeth as she playfully ran her fore and middle fingers up the bobbing length of him. His throat muscles worked convulsively as he tried to swallow when she skimmed her thumb back and forth over the jerking tip, leaning up to kiss his mouth as she did so.

By the time that penetrating, protracted kiss ended, Madeleine was straddling Armand and his throbbing flesh was buried deep inside her. On fire, Madeleine was so completely lost in her compelling lover, she never for a second considered what might have happened if the carriage had had a mishap on the rain-slick streets.

Nothing and no one intruded on their feverish lovemaking. Just as it had been that stormy afternoon at sea, they were the only two people on earth. Madeleine was so awed and aroused, she never once gave a thought to the blond nobleman to whom she was engaged.

And she would never know that, as fate would have it, the lord's crested carriage passed them on the street while she and Armand were making love.

At the very moment that the two big black broughams were side by side, going in opposite directions, the naked Madeleine was astride the equally naked Armand, literally impaled upon him. Her knees were pressing against the seat back and her arms were wrapped around Armand's dark head. Armand's hands cupped Madeleine's bare bottom and his lips were on her swollen nipples. Their perspiring bodies slipping and sliding sinuously, they moved together rhythmically in an erotic, abandoned dance of pure lust, taking and giving from each other with an almost animalistic wildness.

They climaxed together and Armand had to kiss Madeleine to keep her cries of joy from being heard out on the street. Clinging to him as if she would never let him go, Madeleine could feel the hot, thick liquid spurting up inside her and gloried in the sensual sensation.

"Oh, God," Armand groaned, tearing his burning lips from hers. "Baby, baby," he rasped. His arms tightened around her when she started to move. "No, *chérie,* stay where you are a while longer." He brushed a kiss to the curve of her neck and shoulder. "Stay where you are forever."

Twenty-Eight

When Armand's carriage finally rolled through the pillared entranceway of the Royal Street town house, it was dusk. The rain had completely stopped. The pair inside the carriage were completely dressed.

The mood was completely somber.

Painful lucidity had returned to Madeleine and she had said little or nothing for the past twenty minutes. His dark eyes seeking her approval, Armand had spent those moments urging her not to be so melancholy, not to lament what had happened.

He had gotten no response, but Madeleine was keenly aware of him and what he was saying.

From the lowered veil of her thick lashes she covertly studied the classic features of Armand's handsome face. Her focus settled on his tempting mouth and she felt a sob of despair rising within her. He had, as he made love to her, murmured sweet words of love and made such stirring vows.

But lips that kissed like that could lie with ease.

And did.

This sinfully handsome man who had just made such passionate love to her would hold another woman in his arms that very night. And make love to her with the same heated urgency. That hurtful thought sent a sharp stab of pain through her chest, but Madeleine knew she had to face the distasteful truth.

Making love was nothing but a merry game to Armand de Chevalier, an amusing pastime. A pleasant way to spend a rainy afternoon. And while he gave freely of his magnificent body, his heart, she was certain, always remained untouched.

Madeleine forced herself to look away from him.

On the seat between them rested the faded satin garter that she had tugged from Armand's muscular arm earlier in a frenzy of desire. Blushing at the vivid recollection, she gazed at the garter and impulsively reached for it. Armand's hand shot out and closed over hers.

"No, *chérie*. You may not, for the garter belongs to me," he said.

She nodded and when she turned her sad eyes back on his face, Armand saw the unshed tears shining there. He felt like a terrible heel for making her so miserable.

"Ah, sweetheart," he softly entreated, "Don't be sad. This was my fault, not yours. All the blame belongs to me and I'm genuinely sorry."

"Are you?" she asked, meeting his gaze. "Are you really sorry?"

"I am," he said and meant it. "You may not believe this, Madeleine, but the last thing I want is for you to be unhappy."

A tear slipped down her cheek. She impatiently brushed it away. She said, "If you mean it, then *please* Armand, from this day forward, leave me alone." It was a tortured plea and it touched his already aching heart. She candidly admitted, "I don't know what's wrong with me, I—I—I'm weak and vulnerable and…when you…when we…are together, I—I—" She bowed her head. "I beg you, please don't ruin my life. Don't let me ruin my life. Help me, Armand. Promise you'll stay away from me."

His dark eyes clouding with hurt, he said in a low, firm voice, "If that's what you really want, then I promise, Maddie." He drew a painful breath. "I swear I will *never* bother you again. You have my word." She slowly raised her head, looked at him to judge his sincerity. He added, "And you needn't worry that anyone will ever know about us. I've told no one. No one. I never will."

Relieved, Madeleine gave him a weak smile and said, "Thank you, Armand."

"You're very welcome, Countess."

"Now, goodbye," she said anxiously, and not allowing him to assist her, leapt down out of the carriage the minute it came to a complete stop.

She rushed across the windswept courtyard, up the outside stairs, anxiously yanked the front door open and disappeared inside.

Madeleine couldn't trust herself to hide her emotions. The minute she closed the door, she dashed anxiously toward the stairs, calling out as she went, "Avalina, I've a headache and I'm going straight to bed!"

Avalina immediately appeared in the foyer. Frowning, she looked after her as Madeleine hurried up the stairs and said, "I'll be right up with a cold compress and…"

"No! I need nothing but to lie down and rest,"

Madeleine's tone was sharp. She could hardly keep her tears at bay. "When Montro gets home, please have him convey my regrets to Lord Enfield. I simply cannot go out nor entertain this evening." She went inside her room and slammed the door.

Avalina continued to stand there, arms folded over her chest, looking up the stairs. She felt as if she were responsible for Lady Madeleine's distress. After all, she was the one who sent a messenger to ask Armand de Chevalier if he would kindly drive Lady Madeleine home. Had it been a terrible mistake?

Avalina was thoughtful for a long moment, then she began to smile slyly. She returned to her kitchen certain that she had done the right thing. If the handsome Creole had no effect on Lady Madeleine, then why was she so upset from merely riding home with him?

Avalina's smile broadened. She could hardly wait to tell Montro. To report that she firmly believed a small measure of progress had been made on this rainy afternoon. He would be pleased.

Avalina and Montro shared an unspoken desire to break up Lady Madeleine's engagement to Lord Enfield. Neither wanted her to marry the cold nobleman, although they had never actually said as much to each other. Avalina wasn't sure why Big Montro was opposed to the marriage and she had never asked him to explain. As for herself, she had a sixth sense about people and she had always strongly suspicioned that Lord Enfield was, beneath that veneer of blue-blooded nobility and gentlemanly behavior, an evil man.

Lady Madeleine deserved better.

* * *

At half past ten that evening, Madeleine sat motionless in the gloom of her darkened room. An untouched supper tray rested on a table at her elbow.

The tears of shame and regret had finally stopped falling, but she was still sick with self-loathing. Dry-eyed, she stared unseeing into the orange flames dancing in the fireplace before her. Her head throbbed from prolonged weeping. Her eyes were red and swollen. Her chest felt as if a steel band encircled it.

Madeleine was in pain.

Mentally and physically.

She suffered from the raw, fresh guilt of what she had done that rainy afternoon. But the pain of her unforgivable indiscretion was not her only sorrow. She was confused and torn by conflicting emotions. She was genuinely sorry that she had again broken her allegiance to Desmond. At the same time she was saddened to know that she would not be in Armand's arms tonight.

Or ever again.

Madeleine rubbed her stinging eyes, questioning her sanity. She must surely be insane to have behaved as a common wanton with a man who cared nothing for her. If she were in her right mind, would she once again have risked her secure future with Desmond for a few moments of stolen ecstasy with Armand?

Madeleine wearily laid her head back against the chair and closed her scratchy eyes. A heavy, hurting sadness weighed down on her. For the first time, she admitted to herself that Armand de Chevalier meant too much to her.

He was often in her thoughts. Her heart skipped a beat every time she caught sight of him. The sound of his deep, resonant voice was enough to stir her senses. When he touched her, she had the overwhelming desire to melt into his arms.

Madeleine's eyes opened and she again stared into the fire. It would, she realized, be easy to fall helplessly in love with Armand de Chevalier. And she could well imagine the agony that would come with loving the carefree Creole. She had seen the way women, young and old, beautiful and plain, looked at him with barely disguised longing. She supposed dozens of women had been in love with him. She seriously doubted he had ever loved any of them. One woman would never be enough for Armand. He loved all women.

Unless one enjoyed having a broken heart, falling in love with the Creole would be the worst thing that could possibly happen.

Well, it wouldn't happen to her. She'd had her heart broken once, long ago, when she was a young, impulsive girl. She was far too wise to ever let it happen again. While the Armand de Chevaliers of this world might be charming and exciting and almost impossible to resist, they were, just as she'd known from the first moment she'd set eyes on him, nothing but trouble.

Armand had promised that from that day forward he would leave her completely alone. But she held out little hope he would actually do so. Promises meant nothing to him. She couldn't count on him to obey her wishes. Which simply meant that she would have to be very strong. Much stronger than she'd been in the past. Strong enough to rebuff any future advances.

Madeleine sighed wearily and shook her aching head. She couldn't fully trust herself to be that strong. So she knew that she must never again— under any circumstances—allow herself to be caught alone with Armand de Chevalier. She would take the necessary precautions to prevent such an occurrence and if it meant having to rudely insult him, then she would…

A knock on the door drew Madeleine out of her painful reveries.

"Yes?" she said, not rising from her chair.

"It's your old uncle," he spoke through the door. "Are you all right, child?"

"Yes, Uncle Colfax. I just have a splitting headache and didn't feel like coming down for dinner. I'll be fine by morning."

"Did you eat the meal Avalina brought up?"

"Yes," she lied.

"Is there anything I can do for you?"

"No. No, not a thing. Don't worry about me. I just need a good night's rest."

"Then I'll see you at breakfast," he said and went back downstairs to his own room.

The next afternoon—a cold, damp day with leaden skies and a raw wind off the river—Colfax Sumner, the collars of his coat turned up around his ears, left his Canal Street office early. He had a bad case of the jitters—an impossible-to-shake feeling that something was amiss.

And it was not the first time he had been plagued

with such an unsettling feeling. Even his sleep was often disturbed of late with frightening nightmares.

When he reached the security of his town house, Colfax stepped into the foyer and called out. "Madeleine? Avalina? Anyone home?"

No answer. He shrugged out of his coat, hung it on the coat tree and called out again. Then he remembered. No one was home. At breakfast that morning Madeleine had reminded him that she, Avalina, and Montro would be out that afternoon. She had an engagement with the city's most talented daguerreotypist. The *New Orleans Picayune* had requested a daguerreotype to run with the formal announcement of her engagement.

Well, they should be home soon.

Colfax began to relax. The house was quiet and empty, but a warming fire burned in his study and the lamps were lighted. He went to the fireplace, stretched out his hands to its welcome warmth. The uneasy feelings he'd had earlier were lifting. He exhaled with relief.

Colfax stretched, yawned, turned away from the fire and crossed to the mahogany bar. He took down a cut-crystal decanter of fine Kentucky bourbon and a leaded shot glass and poured himself a stiff drink.

Across town, inside a neat white house on Rampart Street, Lord Enfield's quadroon mistress was also alone on that dark, wintry afternoon.

The curtains were tightly drawn over the windows. The doors were securely locked. Naked, Dominique sat cross-legged on the carpeted floor of her small sitting room.

Around her, in a perfect circle, were tall white

tapers in crystal dishes. Carefully, one by one, Dominique had lighted the wicks and the darkened room had brightened, the candles' tiny flames casting wavering illumination on the shadowy walls.

Dominique had shaken out the sulphur match and dropped it into a dish. She now put her hands on her spread thighs, tilted her head back and called on the spirit god, Legba. She patiently waited until she could feel his power beginning to flow into her tense, naked body. Her nipples stiffened. Her belly tightened. Her entire body tingled. Legba was taking her over, making her his own.

For a long moment Dominique sat rigid, then began to jerk uncontrollably as the great god took total control. She was no longer herself, but a vessel of the mighty voodoo deity.

Dominique waited until her body stopped vibrating.

She then picked up a long, sharp knitting needle. She smiled demonically and lifted a tiny, perfect miniature likeness of Colfax Sumner.

Holding the doll in one hand, the long needle in the other, Dominique chanted a monotonic song, swaying her shoulders to and fro, feeling her long, loose hair brushing her bare back.

All once she stopped smiling, stopped chanting and said loudly, clearly, "You must die, Colfax Sumner. You *will* die!"

And she plunged the needle into the stomach of Colfax Sumner.

At that instant, the leaded shot glass slipped from Colfax Sumner's hand. He clutched his stomach in severe pain and sank to his knees. Cold terror enveloped him. The frightening premonition was stronger than ever. Although Dr. Ledette had declared him in perfect health, Colfax knew that he didn't have long to live.

Clammy perspiration dotted his face and his heart hammered painfully in his chest. He was so weak he could hardly move. With great effort, he dragged himself to the sofa and lay down. Trembling, his teeth chattering, Colfax was more afraid than he had ever been in his life. He could fool himself no longer. Somebody wanted him dead.

But who could it possibly be?

Later that afternoon, when everyone had returned home, Colfax quietly called Madeleine into his study. He offered her a drink of brandy, but she refused. Puzzled, she warily sat down on the sofa, wondering what was on his mind. Had he, somehow, learned of her terrible indiscretion? The prospect filled her with sick dread.

Colfax took a seat beside her. Wasting no time, he shared his concerns with her.

"Dear, you know I would hate to alarm you unnecessarily, but I am almost certain that my life is in danger."

Madeleine was stunned.

"No!" A stricken look came into her eyes and she asked, "Who would want to harm you?"

"That I don't know," he admitted. "But I am not imagining the danger, child. Age brings an awareness of these things. I have felt a terrible sense of doom since that night last autumn when we attended the masquerade ball at the St. Louis Hotel."

"For that long?" she said, eyes widening.

"Yes. That's why I was late to the ball that evening. And several times since then, I've known that same crushing fear. Someone—something—is after me."

"Oh, Uncle Colfax," Madeleine said sympathetically, laying a comforting hand on his arm.

"I have been followed on more than one occasion in the past few weeks," he continued. "Only yesterday I just managed to duck inside an apothecary shop on Exchange Street before the footsteps caught up with me."

"Dear Lord, no," she murmured.

"Worse," he reluctantly informed her, "I have a strong feeling that someone has been here inside the house while we were out."

Eyes growing even wider, she asked, "Is anything missing? Did they take valuables and…"

"They took nothing," he interrupted. "But I'm positive that certain things have been moved—only slightly. Whoever it was just wants me to know that I am safe nowhere. Not even in my own home."

Madeleine was silent for a moment, then said decisively, "We must go straight to the authorities!"

Colfax shook his graying head. "And tell them what? That a foolish old man is seeing hobgoblins behind every door?"

She understood and said, "I shall send for Lord Enfield. He will know what to do."

Twenty-Nine

When Lord Enfield arrived at the Royal Street town house, Madeleine met him in the foyer. Hoping the nagging guilt from her latest indiscretion didn't show in her eyes, she said, "Desmond, I'm sorry about last night."

"No need for apologies, my dear." He was gracious. Brushing a kiss to her cheek, he inquired, "Feeling better? Headache gone, I hope."

"Yes, much better," she replied, nodding, then ushered him directly into her uncle's study where Colfax awaited.

"Colfax." Desmond smiled and acknowledged the older man. "How are you this evening?"

"Not as well as I'd like to be," Colfax answered solemnly. He poured drinks for Lord Enfield and himself.

"Oh?" said Desmond, giving the older man a questioning look. "What seems to be the trouble?" He glanced from Colfax to Madeleine.

She drew a quick breath and began, "Desmond, Uncle Colfax and I need to speak with you about something that is of great concern to us both." Lord Enfield frowned, puzzled. Lady Madeleine sat down on the sofa and said, "Please, sit down."

Taking the drink Colfax offered, Desmond sat

beside her and waited tensely to learn what was going on.

"Someone is threatening Uncle Colfax's life," she stated simply.

"What? But that can't be!" Lord Enfield declared, registering shocked surprise. "Why, I can't believe it. Surely you're mistaken, my dear." He looked from her to Colfax, who stood before the fire, quietly drinking his whiskey.

Colfax nodded his gray head. "She's not mistaken, nor am I."

"We need your help, Desmond." Madeleine drew his attention back to her.

"Why, certainly. You shall have it," he said without hesitation. "Now, tell me exactly what has happened. Tell me everything."

Together Madeleine and Colfax told an attentive Lord Enfield all the strange things that had taken place—that someone had followed Colfax on the streets, that someone had been inside the house—revealing all the events that had given them cause for concern.

When they had concluded, Colfax Sumner said, "I realize it all sounds quite foolish and that we certainly don't have anything concrete to take to the authorities, but I'm telling you, my boy, someone means to take my life."

His brows knitted, Desmond nodded. "Surely no one actually means to harm you, Colfax. But, obviously, someone is attempting to badly frighten you. Why, I cannot imagine."

"I'm telling you, Desmond, someone in this city means to kill me," said Colfax. "And I've a terrible sense of foreboding that whoever it is will be successful.''

"No. No, that isn't going to happen," Desmond stated decisively. "While I agree we can't very well go to the police with nothing more than we have, we can and will take greater precautions than we have in the past." He rose from the sofa, went to the bar and poured himself a fresh drink. Turning, he said, "We will immediately implement a plan of action to ensure your safety. First, Colfax, you must *never* be here in the house alone. Further, you must insist that Big Montro escort you to your office each morning and back home each afternoon."

"Yes," Madeleine wholeheartedly agreed. "You can't be out on the streets alone, Uncle Colfax."

"And," Lord Enfield continued with impressive authority, "Madeleine and I will start spending all our evenings here with…"

"No, no, Desmond," Colfax interrupted, shaking his head. "That's not fair to you two and surely it's unnecessary."

"No arguments," said Desmond, smiling now. "Tell him, my dear." He looked at Madeleine.

"Desmond's absolutely right, Uncle," Madeleine quickly seconded the idea. "We will spend our evenings here at home with you, starting tonight. Should it be necessary for us to attend important social events, you will go with us."

"Exactly," Desmond agreed. "Mardi Gras is coming up and it would look suspicious if we failed to attend various parties and balls. So the three of us will go to those events together. We don't want whoever is threatening you to know we are on to them, now do we?"

"No, we don't," Colfax acquiesced.

"There you have it," said Lord Enfield to Colfax. "Meantime I will check around to see if I can learn anything." He paused, rubbed his chin thoughtfully and continued, "It's so hard to believe that *anyone* would actually want to harm you, but…" He shrugged his shoulders.

Madeleine smiled at Desmond. She was grateful that he was so understanding and sympathetic to her uncle's fears. Once again, he had displayed the kind of admirable character that made her more ashamed than ever that she was not half as honorable as he.

"How is he? Is he dead yet? Is he sick?"

"Scared, but perfectly healthy," Lord Enfield reported, stepping into the Rampart Street cottage. "I left there not fifteen minutes ago and Colfax Sumner was feeling just fine."

"Damnation!" the disappointed Dominique swore, whirling about to stalk off to the bedroom, muttering under her breath as she went. "I don't understand. When I stabbed the pin into the Sumner doll, I could feel the awesome power of the Legba flowing through me! I was so certain that the old man felt the terrible pain of the sharp needle going through his stomach! He should have immediately fallen ill!"

Shrugging out of his heavy coat, Desmond tossed it over a chair back and followed his thwarted mistress into the bedroom. He smiled indulgently as she paced about, arguing that Colfax Sumner should be dead or dying. She had done exactly what Mama Cecile had told her to do.

"Darling," Lord Enfield said, catching her arm

and drawing her to him. "Listen to me. This mumbo jumbo voodoo foolishness of yours is simply not going to do the job."

"Don't say that! The spirit god will hear you! It *will* work. I know it will." She was adamant. "Perhaps I forgot something, did something wrong. Maybe we should go back to Mama Cecile and ask…"

"We're not giving that old charlatan one more cent," he stated emphatically. "Be reasonable, Dom. I gave you your chance. It didn't work and that's the end of it." He released her, stepped back and began unbuttoning his shirt. "*Now* we will do things my way. Sit down and listen to me."

Reluctantly, the frustrated Dominique sank down onto the edge of the mattress. Her dark eyes flashing with anger, she said, "I am tired of waiting for…"

"Be quiet!" Desmond warned with such firmness, she blinked up at him. He stepped close, calmly took his shirt off, and dropped it to the carpet. Then he sank down onto his knees before Dominique, took both her hands in his, and said, "My darling, we've been over all this before, but I will point out one more time exactly how it is going to be. You will listen and you will not interrupt me."

She nodded, afraid to speak.

"As you are well aware, Colfax Sumner is one of the wealthiest men in America and I mean to lay claim to all that is his. In order to do so, I must marry his niece and sole heir, Lady Madeleine." He paused, and a hint of a smile touched his lips when he continued, "The marriage is necessary, unless, that is, the old man's last will and testament should mysteriously disappear."

Dominique withdrew a hand from his, laid it on his cheek. "If that were to happen, you wouldn't marry her, would you?"

"I would not," he assured her. "There would be no need. If the final will—the one in which the entire estate goes to Madeleine—were to disappear, the provisional will would take effect." He began to grin cunningly. "All other executors of the provisional will are...deceased. I alone would have control of Colfax Sumner's vast holdings and the power to dispose of any and all of those holdings as I saw fit."

Dominique skimmed her thumb back and forth over his bottom lip. She said, "We would be very, very rich, wouldn't we, my love?"

"Beyond your wildest dreams," he replied.

"But when?" she asked.

"Soon. Very soon," he promised. "A month from now it should all be settled."

She smiled, pleased. "You intend to steal the will?"

"Indeed," he said, and together they laughed.

When the laughter subsided, Dominique asked, "Then why must you continue to be engaged to Lady Madeleine?"

"Ah, because I leave no stone upturned, my love, you know that. I cover all bets. Should something, God forbid, go wrong, should I be unable to get my hands on that final will, then I'll simply marry Madeleine."

Dominique made a face and pressed forcefully

on his lip. "I don't want you marrying that pale British bitch."

"Silly girl," he scolded. "You needn't be jealous. I have no intention of staying married." He playfully bit Dominique's thumb and said, "Louisiana is one of the few states wherein a woman can inherit and own property in her name. Upon his death, everything Sumner owns will be Madeleine's." He grinned wickedly and added, "Until, that is, her loving husband can convince her to be the devoted and dutiful wife and have everything transferred into my name."

Dominique studied his smiling upturned face and murmured thoughtfully, "First—before any of this can happen—we must get rid of Colfax Sumner."

"Leave it to me," he said and slowly rose to his feet. He reached out, twisted a long, thick portion of her lustrous dark hair around his hand and said, "Are we going to talk all night or make love?"

"Why wait?" asked the bearded, grinning Barton Smallwood before he took a long swig of whiskey from a half-full glass and wiped his mouth on the back of his hand.

"Barton's right," said his scar-faced older brother, Burton. "Hell, we'll just go into town and take care of him tonight."

"You'll do no such thing," Lord Enfield commanded sternly.

The three men were seated at a square wooden table in the Smallwood brothers' clapboard lean-to. It was after two in the morning. Lord Enfield had made his way to the swamp directly from the Rampart Street cottage. As soon as Dominique had satisfied his sexual hunger, he had dressed, slipped out into the dark night and ordered his driver to the Smallwoods'.

The lord now looked from one of his hired henchmen to the other. "I was with Sumner and his niece earlier this evening," he said. "We've got the old man scared to death. He's seeing ghosts everywhere he looks. Which is good. That's what I wanted. Dominique's been casting spells and having *gris-gris* left on his doorstep, which might have helped spook him, I don't know. I do know that the two of you shadowing him have succeeded in terrorizing him and for that I congratulate you."

"Why, thanks, boss." Barton grinned foolishly.

"Quiet, Barton!" Desmond Chilton demanded sharply. "Sumner is extremely nervous, but unfortunately, his health has not been impaired as I had hoped. The old bastard apparently has a very strong heart." He exhaled heavily and added, "Looks like we're not going to be able to scare him to death."

"Too bad," said Burton.

"Yes, it is," Desmond replied. "But I digress. He's presently edgy and badly frightened. He's expecting something to happen to him at any minute, so he'll be on the lookout."

"Then it would be best to wait a while," Burton commented.

"I think so. I told Sumner and his niece that I will start spending my evenings with them at the town house. I could see the relief in the old man's eyes when I suggested it. I'll make him feel safe, put him at his ease."

"So we stay away from him until you give us the word," said Burton.

"Exactly. We want him lulled into a false sense of security. So we'll wait. We'll wait until he's settled down, becomes complacent. I'll see to it he begins to relax and lets down his guard."

"How long?" asked Burton.

"About a month. On the last Saturday in February, I will be escorting my lovely fiancée to the opera. That is the night you two will take care of Sumner."

Barton Smallwood took another big drink of whiskey and asked worriedly, "What about that big bodyguard?"

Lord Enfield smiled. "Montro will not be at home that evening. He will accompany us to the opera. Avalina, the housekeeper, will retire to her private quarters around nine. You will go to the mansion at precisely ten o'clock. Sumner will be there alone."

Burton nodded.

Desmond reached inside his breast pocket and produced a key. He handed it to Burton. "Make sure no one sees you enter the town house. Quietly let yourself in. Slip up on Sumner, surprise him. Then quickly suffocate him. Make it look like his heart failed."

"That all?" asked Burton.

"No, not quite," said Desmond. "There's a small round wall safe behind a picture of Lafayette than hangs in the old man's study directly behind his desk. I won't give it to you now, but hours before you are to kill Sumner, I will tell you the safe's combination. You're to open the safe and take Sumner's last will and testament." His voice took on a harder edge when he added, "Make damned sure you take the correct will from the safe. There are two. Look at both carefully and leave the provisional will. Shut the safe. Put the portrait back in place and get the hell out of there. Understood?''

"Understood," said Burton. Barton nodded as he poured himself another glass of whiskey.

"One more thing," Desmond added as his lips thinned. "Should you get caught, you do *not* know me! If you ever so much as mention my name to anyone, you know I'll have you both killed."

"Why, we wouldn't tell off on you, would we, big brother?" said the tipsy Barton.

"Mum's the word," agreed an unsmiling Burton.

Lord Enfield got to his feet. "All right, lads, that's it. Lie low and I'll be in touch."

"So you ain't gonna marry that pale English countess with the red-gold hair?" asked Barton.

"That is none of your concern," said the lord, annoyed by the impertinent question.

As if he hadn't spoken, Barton whistled through his teeth and said, "Dang, I'd like to get my hands on her just once. She's got a pair of the prettiest breasts I ever..."

The sentence was never finished. With a swiftness that caught Barton off guard, Desmond backhanded him with such force that bright-red blood spurted from the drunken man's nose and split lip. Eyes round with shock and fear, Barton sat there in his chair, nervously lifting a hand to wipe the blood away. He didn't dare say a word. Neither did his brother.

Desmond Chilton reached out and angrily swept the whiskey bottle and half-full glass off the table. They crashed to the rough plank floor and broke, the liquor trickling over the splintered shards of glass.

"Lay off the whiskey, Barton," commanded Lord Enfield, glaring down at the frightened man. "Don't make me have to warn you again."

Thirty

February came to the Crescent City with a welcome warming of the weather and the rowdy, week-long celebration of Mardi Gras.

Colfax Sumner had reluctantly agreed he would accompany his niece and her fiancé to the nightly rounds of spirited celebrations. Big Montro was to escort the trio to each of the galas and stand guard outside until they were ready to return home.

Still, had Madeleine had her way, they would have attended none of the carnival's activities. She was in no mood to celebrate. She was greatly troubled and knew that she would have to force herself to appear gay and happy. Concerned for her uncle's safety, Madeleine felt it would have been wise for them all to have remained in the security of his home.

And there was another reason she would have much preferred not to attend the Mardi Gras parties. She was sure that Armand would be among the merry celebrators and his presence always posed a threat. Thus far he had kept his word and had stayed away from her. But if they were present at the same party, how would he behave? How would she?

She didn't trust Armand or herself.

So Madeleine was overly anxious when they arrived at the very first of the week's many scheduled Mardi Gras soirees. The black-tie affair was at the mansion of Dr. Jean Paul Ledette and his genteel wife. The city's monied elite had turned out in force to savor the elaborate buffet, drink chilled champagne and dance the night away.

Throughout the evening, while the well-heeled guests laughed and danced and enjoyed themselves, Madeleine kept an eye on her uncle as she nervously searched the glittering crowd for the Creole.

"I'm just so mad I could spit," Melissa Ann Ledette, pretty in a fussy ball gown of pale lavender satin, confided to Madeleine midway through the evening.

"Why? What's wrong?" Madeleine asked, glancing at her uncle, before turning her full attention to Melissa.

"Armand de Chevalier sent his regrets. That's why!"

Madeleine hoped her smile was casual. "Perhaps Mr. de Chevalier had a prior engagement."

"How could that be?" Melissa said. "I invited him to this party ages ago, long before the official invitations went out. I think it's very rude of him to renege, don't you?"

The Ledette soiree was not the only party Armand missed. As the week's many festivities continued, Madeleine had yet to see him. She was both relieved and puzzled—she'd expected that the hedonistic Creole would be the first to arrive at every single Mardi Gras celebration.

Fat Tuesday finally came and with it with colorful parades through the city, followed by a massive masked ball on Decatur Street directly in front of Jackson Square. The final affair of the season, Madeleine was more nervous about attending this ball than any of the others.

Her uncle would surely be in peril at an outside gathering with large milling crowds of people, many of whom he did not know. And she would surely be in peril since Armand would undoubtedly make an appearance, masked and handsome and dangerous.

As it turned out both she and her uncle were quite safe at the open-air dance. Big Montro stayed near Uncle Colfax throughout the evening and Armand stayed away from the ball. Madeleine looked for him all evening, tensing every time she saw a tall, dark-haired man in a harlequin mask.

None were Armand.

He was not at the ball, yet she felt as if he were watching her, as if his dark, mysterious eyes were resting on her.

And they were.

Armand stood on the darkened balcony of his Pontalba apartment on St. Peter, silently observing the dancers below. In his hand was a shot glass of whiskey and in his heart was a hollow emptiness. Half-drunk, he broodingly watched the russet-haired woman, who should have been his, turn about in the arms of the vile Lord Enfield.

A muscle spasmed in Armand's lean jaw.

He gritted his teeth and went back inside. He poured himself another glass of bourbon and drained it in one long swallow. He poured another. He was swaying on his feet now. He knew he was getting quite drunk, but he planned to get a lot drunker. He snagged the heavy liquor decanter and took it with him when he went back out onto the balcony.

Stumbling slightly, he lowered himself onto a padded chaise longue. Hugging the decanter to his chest, Armand de Chevalier stayed there on the darkened balcony until everyone had left the dance and Decatur Street was silent.

He was still there the next morning when a strong February sun turned the vast Mississippi the color of rose and shone down on Armand's closed eyelids. Slowly, painfully, he cocked one eye open and moaned. His head ached dully. His stomach was sour. His left arm was asleep. His unshaven face was itching.

He was downright miserable.

He stayed where he was for several long minutes, not sure he could get up. Not sure he wanted to. Hell, he might just stay there forever and let the world pass him by.

But his naturally sunny nature soon surfaced. Recalling his long, tortured night of drinking and feeling sorry for himself, Armand began to smile. And then to laugh at himself. To make fun of himself for behaving like a simple-minded, lovesick schoolboy.

It wouldn't, he vowed, happen again.

The warm balmy days and mild nights of February passed by with no further threats to Colfax Sumner's safety. Gradually he began to feel indomitable once more, confident that no one could harm him. It was as if the dark cloud that had hovered over him had finally blown away, leaving only the bright, warm Louisiana sunshine and a wonderful sense of well-being.

Madeleine was delighted with her uncle's elevated mood, but she did not fully share it. She was, of course, relieved and thankful that he seemed more like his old self, but she was not totally convinced he was out of danger. The possibility that he was letting down his guard too soon concerned her.

She had also begun to question the wisdom of her decision to marry Lord Enfield. She was not in love with him. Never had been. And lately the prospect of spending the rest of her life married to the earl seemed like a long prison sentence stretching endlessly before her.

Unsure, unhappy, she carefully hid her feelings and kept her own council. The problem was hers to solve and she needed to give it a great deal of thought. Plagued with indecision, she nonetheless went about her business as the blushing bride-to-be.

Almost daily she and Big Montro ventured out to take care of the many tasks associated with planning a large church wedding. Each time they left the town house, Madeleine worried that they might run into Armand. And, on several occasions, they had.

But he hadn't behaved like the devilish Armand she had come to know. He had simply nodded politely and went on his way, complying with her wishes to be left alone, as if he were actually a considerate gentleman.

Ironically, his indifference hurt.

Made her heart ache dully.

But she firmly reminded herself—once again—that to care for Armand would be courting disaster. There was, she felt sure, nothing admirable about him. He was, after all, a gambler, a disbarred attorney, a lazy libertine. She had little respect for him. He had no character or conscience. He hadn't hesitated for a second to make love to another man's fiancée. He lived only for the moment, taking his pleasure where he found it, never really giving of himself.

These thoughts were running through Madeleine's mind as she and Montro strolled along the banquette toward the engraver's at Dumaine and Chartres. As they neared the little corner shop, Madeleine paused and asked, "What is all that noise? Where is it coming from?"

Montro smiled and said, "The new children's hospital being constructed over on Ursulines Street."

"Oh, yes, now I recall," she said. "There was an article in last week's *Picayune* about the hospital. A handful of generous donors put up the money with the strict proviso that their identities remain a secret. Most commendable."

"It sure is," Montro agreed. "Want to walk over and have a look before you order the wedding invitations? It's only a couple of blocks away."

"Well, we are early," she said. "Yes, why don't we?"

They quickly walked the two short blocks to the corner of Chartres and Ursulines. A large, half-framed building took up an entire city block. Laborers, sweating in the warm February sunshine, were scrambling over the structure like industrious ants.

Montro, who had been at the site many times, showed Madeleine where the main entrance was to be, directly across the street from where they now stood. He told her the number of patients' rooms the hospital would have and exactly how many sick children could be treated at once.

As Montro continued to talk excitedly and to point out various features of the rising structure, Madeleine shaded her eyes, tilted her head back and looked up to where the rafters joined at the highest point above the building's main entrance.

She blinked and her lips fell open in disbelief.

A shirtless laborer was high up on the steeply slanted rafters, hammering nails into the new, fragrant lumber. He was tall and lean and lithe. His raven hair shone blue-black in the sunlight. The slight expansion of his chest with each indrawn breath brought a rhythmic play of muscles across his smooth olive back, which in turn caused a rising and falling measure of pain in Madeleine's heart.

"What on God's green earth is Armand de Chevalier doing up there on that roof beam?" she said.

"Helping build the hospital," said Montro, his tone matter-of-fact.

Madeleine tore her eyes from Armand, looked at Montro, and said, "De Chevalier engaged in manual labor?" She smirked and added, "I'll bet he doesn't last an hour."

Montro grinned. "Perhaps you've misjudged him. Armand's a talented carpenter and he's not afraid of a little hard work. He works on this project every day."

Skeptical, Madeleine said, "Why? Why is he doing this?"

Big Montro shrugged his massive shoulders. "Maybe because he cares about the city's sick children."

"He cares about no one but himself," Madeleine stated, more to herself than to him.

"You're wrong, Lady Madeleine. Armand is a fine man."

"A fine man?" Madeleine was incredulous. "I think you're the one who has misjudged him. Are you aware that he was once an attorney and that the magistrate disbarred him for some loathsome misdeed?"

For a long moment Montro stared at her. Quietly, he said, "I am aware that he was an attorney and that he was disbarred. And I know the reason it happened." He paused, narrowed his eyes and asked, "Do you?"

"Well, I don't know the ugly details, but Desmond said that Armand did something so contemptible…"

"Contemptible?" Montro interrupted, his eyes flashing now. "I'll tell you exactly what Armand did to get disbarred. He represented—for free—a poor young black man who had been accused of rape by a prominent white woman and was being railroaded to the gallows. Armand firmly believed that the man was innocent and so he defended him in court. Armand proved that the woman was lying, that she had seduced the handsome black man, then quickly cried rape to save her own precious hide. Armand got the poor devil off. But in so doing, he lost his license to practice law in the state of Louisiana.''

"But that can't be," Madeleine said, outraged. "Desmond led me to believe that—that—'' She frowned. "If what you say is true, there were no grounds for disbarment.''

"I know. They had no grounds so they made some up.''

"I don't understand.''

"The rich white lady who lied in the case was from one of the South's most politically powerful families. It was easy for them to get phony charges trumped up against Armand, which allowed them to strip away his law license.''

Thirty-One

On the last Saturday evening in February, Colfax firmly insisted that Montro escort Madeleine and Desmond to the opera, without him.

At Madeleine's worried look, he said, "Now, dear, I will be fine here. Nothing out of the ordinary has happened for weeks, you know that." He smiled and added sheepishly, "Perhaps I was imagining the whole thing."

Reluctantly, Madeleine agreed, but the last thing she said before leaving was, "Lock the doors tight."

"Of course, child. Now, go and enjoy yourselves."

At shortly after nine-thirty, more than an hour after the couple had left the town house, Avalina entered the study and asked, "Can I get you anything, Colfax? Do anything for you?"

"No, not a thing, thanks. I'm just going to read for a while before bedtime."

"Well, I'll just sit here with you until you're ready to got to bed."

He gazed at her and frowned. "You look very tired, Avalina," he said, studying her drawn face. "Is there anything I can get you?"

She smiled at him. "No. I'm not the least bit sleepy, so I'll—"

"You may not be sleepy, Avalina, but you are tired. Why don't you go on out to bed? I'm not going to stay up long myself."

"No!" she said emphatically, shaking her head, setting the points of her white *tignon* to dancing. "I intend to stay right here with you until Madeleine and Montro are back home." She took a seat on the leather sofa.

Colfax smiled indulgently at this loyal black woman of whom he was so fond. She had been with him for more than thirty years and he had no better friend.

He said softly, "You don't fool me any more than I fool you. You're concerned about my safety, isn't that it?"

Her dark eyes flashing, she stated, "Montro shouldn't have gone to the opera, he should have stayed here to look after you."

"I was the one who sent him with the children, Avalina," he pointed out. "And I'm glad I did. While there are always dangers out on the street, I feel confident that here at home we are all quite safe." He smiled and said, "Now go on out to bed."

Avalina pursed her lips, but she rose from the sofa. She crossed the room, turned and softly said his name. "Colfax."

"Yes?"

"Get up out of your chair this minute. Walk with me and as soon as I've gone out the door, lock it behind me."

Rising, he said, "I swear, the women in this

house are getting mighty bossy." But he followed her down the hall.

At the front door, Avalina again paused, looked at him and said, "I could just stay and keep you company until…"

"No," he said resolutely. "And you needn't be scattering any of that magical voodoo powder of yours around the door, either."

"I have no idea what you're talking about," she said haughtily.

Colfax laughed accusingly and she laughed, too. He knew all about her strong belief in black magic and sometimes he teased her about it, but he was never really scornful or derisive. He patted her upper arm affectionately.

"Nothing is going to happen to us," he said, still smiling. "Good night, Avalina."

Throughout the performance of *La Traviata*, Madeleine fidgeted. She was too agitated to appreciate that the diva who was playing Violetta perfectly executed portamentos and roulades. She wished they hadn't come. Wished it was time to leave. She felt overly anxious, worried. And she was feeling increasingly conflicted. She had begun to strongly consider telling Lord Enfield that she could not marry him. That would, she knew, be the decent thing to do.

Unable to sit still a moment longer, Madeleine leaned over to Lord Enfield well before the opera's end and said, "Can we please leave, Desmond?"

Surprised, he fished his gold-cased watch from his evening-vest pocket, opened it and checked the time. Eleven o'clock. "Why, certainly, darling."

By the time they reached the town house, Madeleine was extraordinarily nervous. Her hands were icy cold and there was an insistent pain in her stomach.

When Big Montro unlocked the front door and stepped back, she rushed anxiously into the house shouting, "Uncle Colfax, we're home! Where are you?"

"Dear, he's probably in bed asleep. Perhaps you should stop shouting," cautioned Lord Enfield. He glanced over his shoulder and was annoyed to see that Montro followed them inside.

"Uncle Colfax, answer me!" her voice lifted as she hurried toward his study.

She came to an abrupt stop in the open doorway and screamed. Colfax Sumner lay unmoving on the floor in front of the flickering fireplace. Montro stepped swiftly around her and went directly to the prostrate man. He fell to his knees and laid a hand on Colfax's face. The skin was chilly. Montro moved his fingers down and checked for a pulse in the throat.

There was none.

"Montro, is he…?" Madeleine was now on her knees beside Montro.

"I'm so sorry, Lady Madeleine," said Big Montro. "He's gone."

"Oh, dear God, no, no!" she began to sob uncontrollably, taking one of her uncle's lifeless hands in both of hers and pressing it to her cheek. "My uncle is dead! Desmond, Uncle Colfax is dead!"

"Are you certain?" asked Lord Enfield, joining Montro and Madeleine on the floor, bending to press his ear to Colfax's chest to listen for a heartbeat. After a long moment, Desmond raised his head and said, "He is dead. My God, he's dead."

Rising to his feet, Montro said quietly, "I'll wake Avalina and then go get Dr. Ledette." He turned and left, his eyes filling with tears.

"It's my fault," Madeleine cried, nearly hysterical, "I shouldn't have left him alone."

"Now, dearest," Lord Enfield comforted, as he knelt beside her and drew her into his arms, "there's nothing you could have done. Colfax has apparently had a weak heart and..."

"No!" she protested, pulling away from him, "Uncle Colfax did *not* have a weak heart. His heart was sound. He was perfectly healthy, I know he was, Dr. Ledette told me he was." Tears streaming down her cheeks, she sat down on the floor and gently drew her uncle's head onto her lap. Affectionately smoothing his wispy gray hair, she sobbed, "Dear God, someone killed my uncle."

"Now, Madeleine, you have no reason to think such a thing," Desmond gently scolded. "You're upset, you don't know what you're saying."

"I do, I'm saying that someone has murdered my beloved uncle right here in his own home," she wailed, inconsolable. "Oh, God, we should have left Montro here with him! Why did we leave Uncle Colfax alone?"

A pale, puffy-eyed Lady Madeleine placed a lone red rose atop the new marble vault in the old St. Louis cemetery. She kissed her gloved fingers, laid them on the shiny white marble, bent and whispered a final goodbye to her dear, deceased uncle.

A veil covering her stricken face, a large black

umbrella held over her head by the solicitous Lord
Enfield, Madeleine allowed him to lead her away.
Directly behind them, Big Montro supported the
grieving Avalina as they all made their way to the
waiting carriages.

Despite the heavy rain a large crowd of mourners
had gathered to say their final farewells to the dear
old friend they had loved and admired for so long.
Armand de Chevalier stood alone at the edge of the
gathering, dry-eyed and solemn. He purposely
slipped away before Madeleine could spot him.

Back at the town house after the funeral, friends
began arriving immediately. Montro and Avalina
capably stepped into the roles of host and hostess,
knowing that Madeleine was too upset for the task.
They greeted the many visitors at the door and
guided them into the dining room where a sumptuous spread had been laid out.

After taking a while to compose herself, Madeleine had graciously visited with the guests. Many
stayed all afternoon and some well into the evening.
She was exhausted when finally, at shortly after
nine o'clock, the very last couple departed.

Madeleine sighed with relief, sank down onto the
sofa and secretly hoped that Lord Enfield, too,
would go. He did not. He stayed and after a reasonable amount of time suggested that she should—
if she knew where it was kept—have a look at Colfax's last will and testament.

"Or perhaps you would prefer to wait and have
an attorney present," he said.

"No," she said. "As you know, Uncle Colfax's

lawyer left for Europe last week. Norris Maddox is not expected back for a couple of months.''

''Ah, that's right. No need for a partner to step in,'' he said. ''So…you know where the will is and…''

''Yes, of course,'' she said, wearily rising.

Lord Enfield followed Madeleine into the study. Arms crossed over his chest, he watched silently as she moved the portrait of LaFayette aside, worked the combination of the small round safe and swung the door open.

His heart hammered when Madeleine reached inside and withdrew a legal-looking document. He watched closely as she unfolded it, quickly glanced over it, then tossed it atop the desk. She again reached inside the safe and felt frantically around the chamber.

An expression of shock instantly flooding her features, she withdrew her hand and exclaimed, ''Dear God in heaven!''

''What? What is it, my love?''

She shook her head, stunned and bewildered. She leaned down and peered into the empty safe. She straightened and began to tremble violently.

''Madeleine, what is wrong?''

''The will,'' she said, her face pale, her eyes wide, ''it's gone. My uncle's last will and testament…it…it's missing! My God, the will is not here!''

''Oh, my love,'' soothed Lord Enfield, hurriedly stepping forward to move around the desk and take her in his arms. ''Surely there's a logical explanation. Perhaps Colfax placed the will in his safe deposit box at the Delta State Bank downtown.''

"No, no he did not," she said, quickly freeing herself of his arms. "He showed me the will last summer, shortly after I arrived in New Orleans. He brought me in here and told me the combination of the safe and showed me the will."

"I see," murmured Lord Enfield thoughtfully. Then gesturing to the document she'd carelessly tossed onto the desk, he asked, "And you're sure that's not it? Have you looked at it carefully?"

"I don't need to, I know what that is,' she said, starting to pace restlessly. "That's just an old, out-of-date provisional will he had drawn up years ago. The one naming you and those other gentlemen the executors of the estate when I was still quite young. It has no value."

"No real value whatever," Lord Enfield agreed calmly, hardly able to hide his excitement. Everything had gone just as he had planned. The vast wealth left behind by Colfax Sumner was now—or very soon would be—completely under his control. Demonstrating his deep compassion, Desmond again took the reluctant Madeleine in his arms and said soothingly, "Don't worry about this, darling. The will is bound to turn up. The thing for you to do now is to just forget about it. Go to bed and get some rest."

"Yes," she quickly agreed. "I'm so tired I can't think straight."

"Bless your heart, I fully understand," he sympathized. "Tomorrow we'll look for the will and we'll find it, I promise you."

"You're very kind, Desmond," she said. "You won't mind if I don't see you to the door?"

"Of course not," he replied, brushing a kiss to

her forehead. "Good night, and please don't worry. Everything will work out nicely."

She nodded and left him, hurrying out into the foyer and up the stairs. In the privacy of her room, Madeleine paced worriedly back and forth, sad and confused, trying to figure out what could have happened. How could the will not be there? Why one will and not the other?

Only the provisional will had been in the safe. The other was missing. The will naming her, Madeleine, the sole heir to everything Colfax Sumner had owned. Who on earth could have taken that final will? And why had they taken it?

Upon leaving the Royal Street town house, a self-satisfied Lord Enfield had his driver take him directly toward the swamps below the city. Dominique could wait. He wanted to visit the Smallwood brothers.

This was the first opportunity he'd had to speak with them since before the murder. He wanted to commend them on a job well done. And, he was anxious to get his hands on Colfax Sumner's will, the will that the Smallwood boys were to have taken from the safe on the night they'd killed Sumner.

He wouldn't be completely content until he could watch the will burn and warm his hands over it.

At the pleasant prospect, Desmond laughed out loud and then he felt his groin stir slightly. Seeing the will go up in flames would be gratification akin to sexual pleasure.

Lord Enfield was out of the carriage the moment it came to a stop before the weathered shanty where the Smallwood brothers lived. He didn't bother to knock, but pushed the warped door open and stepped inside.

He frowned when saw that Barton Smallwood was drinking. A whiskey bottle sat on the table before the younger brother and when he looked up at Desmond, Barton's eyes were liquor-clouded.

Desmond, in a gregarious mood, let it pass.

He turned his attention on Burton, who rose from the table to shake hands.

"We been expecting you, boss," said Burton, unsmiling.

"I have your money," Desmond stated, reaching inside his breast pocket. "And I wanted to tell you how very pleased I am with the job you did. Sumner's death was ruled natural causes and no one suspects a thing."

Burton shook his head, smiled weakly, but nervously rubbed the long scar going down his right cheek. "We were in and out in no time," he said.

Desmond smiled, nodded. "Good work, men. I'm proud of you both. I knew I could count on you."

"We done just like you told us," Barton offered hopefully.

"I know you did," said Desmond, looking down at the seated man. "Now, where is it? Give it to me." Barton Smallwood swallowed convulsively and quickly bowed his head. Desmond looked at Burton. Burton shrugged his narrow shoulders and a worried expression came into his eyes, but he said nothing. "Dammit to hell," roared Desmond, "where's that will? I want the will!"

"Boss, you're not going to believe this," Burton spoke at last.

"Not going to believe what?" Desmond's face was growing flushed, "What are you trying to tell me?

"We did just as you said. We quietly smothered the old man then went right to the safe." Burton exhaled and made a face. "There was only one will inside. That provisional will you'd told us about. That was all. Just it, nothing else."

Desmond's flushed face immediately paled. "Just one will— No, that's not…that can't be! You said you'd get that will and bring it to me! Where is it? I have to have it!"

"I'm telling you straight, boss, someone beat us to it," Burton said. "The will was not there."

Desmond felt suddenly sick. His knees buckled. He pulled out a wooden chair and sat down. If the will was not in the safe, that meant somebody had already taken it.

But who?

And why?

Thirty-Two

A long and sleepless night.

Come morning, a haggard, but determined Madeleine had dressed and set off to visit the law offices of her uncle's attorney, Norris Maddox. With Big Montro at her side, she had walked the few short blocks, arriving at the Orleans Street building at 9:00 a.m. sharp.

Inside Blake Forester's plush, paneled office, Madeleine sat quietly as the silver-haired attorney carefully studied the provisional will.

Forester frowned and looked at her in alarm.

The attorney said, "Surely, Lady Madeleine, this is not the last will that your uncle…"

"No. There was another, drawn up much later. It was kept in the safe at home, along with this one. But, mysteriously, the final will is missing." She looked Forester squarely in the eye. "Please, sir, tell me exactly what this unexpected turn of events means to me."

The attorney hesitated. Then he explained that unless the last will and testament was found, the provisional will would stand. He paused, frowned and admitted, "It means, Lady Madeleine, that the Sumner estate—lock, stock, plantations, warehouses, sugar refineries, gins and presses, everything—will be controlled by the only surviving executor, Lord Enfield.''

"No...that can't be," she choked.

Attorney Forester gave her a fatherly smile and soothed, "Now, now, surely there's a copy of the other will in Norris's office which will, of course, make this one null and void. We'll go in right now and have a look."

There was no copy of the final will in Norris Maddox's office. A thorough search turned up nothing.

Seeing the look of growing distress on Lady Madeleine's pale face, Forester said, "We'll send a letter to Norris in Europe. It will take a while, but..." The attorney shrugged.

Madeleine rose to her feet. "Thank you, Mr. Forester."

"We'll get a post off to Norris today. If there's anything else I can do..."

"You've been most helpful," she said, rising unsteadily to her feet.

Dazed, Madeleine exited the law offices. Montro stepped forward, saw that she was upset. "If you're not up to walking home, I can—"

"No, I am. I'd rather walk, try to clear my head," she stated, exhaling heavily.

They started home. Montro waited for her to speak. Soon they were discussing the sad events of the past couple of days. Considering him a loyal friend, Madeleine told Montro of the missing will.

"The only thing that was in the safe was an old provisional will written years ago," she explained. "The other will was there late last summer. Uncle Colfax showed it to me."

Montro listened carefully, nodding, asking a question or two, trying to help her solve the puzzle. "Why didn't the master destroy the provisional will?"

"He meant to, just never got around to it." Thinking out loud, she mused, "Who would have taken the will? Who could have taken it?"

"A good question," Montro responded. "Who, besides you, had the safe's combination?"

"Well, Uncle Colfax's attorney, Norris Maddox."

"Maddox is in Europe. Who else?"

"No one that I know of. Just me and…and… well, Desmond." Montro's eyebrows knitted and his eyes narrowed. Madeleine easily read his thoughts. She immediately stopped walking. Montro paused beside her. "Don't be ridiculous!" she defended Desmond. "Lord Enfield is above reproach! Why, he's the one who insisted on carefully watching over Uncle Colfax. He had been a good and loyal friend to both Uncle Colfax and to me. How dare you suggest that Desmond—"

"Lady Madeleine," Montro softly interrupted, "I didn't."

"You did. You didn't say it, but I know what you're thinking." She started walking again. He followed.

"With the final will missing," he asked, "who stands to gain control of Colfax's entire estate?"

Madeleine made a sour face at him. "Desmond, of course, but he—he—" She paused, swallowed, and added, "Lord Enfield would *never* take advantage of me! Besides, he is a very wealthy man and…"

"Is he? Are you certain of that, Lady Madeleine?"

For a long moment Madeleine stared at the giant who was raising unsettling questions in her mind. "Yes, yes I am. Desmond has made wise investments and—and—"

She fell silent. She had never discussed Desmond's business or net worth with him, had never seen any reason to do so. Uncle Colfax had told her that the earl was comfortably well-off. She had never seen or heard anything to dispute that observation.

"Anyone *else* have the safe's combination?" Big Montro asked as he took her arm and urged her on down the banquette.

"Not to my knowledge. But obviously someone does." She stopped again, turned to him, and said, "I don't care what Dr. Ledette says, I think someone murdered my uncle. And I think that whoever is responsible for his death, took the will."

"If that's true, how did the murderer get into the house? And how did he get into the safe?"

"I don't know," she replied. "I don't know. Someone must have known the safe's combination."

"And has a house key?"

"Yes. Someone we don't know about."

"But why would anyone want Colfax dead? Furthermore, why would they want the will? What good would it do them?"

Again Madeleine said, "I just don't know. It's a mystery that I fully intend to solve."

"When did the earl ask you to marry him?" Montro asked.

"The summer before last when I came for a visit. Why?"

"I see. When did your uncle draw up the last will and testament?"

"Mmm, let's see if I can remember. Yes, I recall now, it was in the spring of '54. He wrote me a letter to tell me he had done it."

"He drew up the will in the spring of '54," Montro repeated thoughtfully. "And Lord Enfield proposed in the summer of '54."

"Yes, that's right." She frowned and said, "But it had nothing to do with—with—"

"We're home, Lady Madeleine."

A week had passed since her uncle's death. A long, miserable week in which Madeleine had had far too much time to grieve and fret and worry. Much as she hated to admit it, Montro's questions had raised nagging doubts in her mind.

There was no denying the fact that Desmond could now dispose of everything her uncle owned without so much as consulting her.

But he would never do such a dishonorable thing. He loved her, and besides, he had no need of her fortune. He was a rich man. He had gained great wealth in shrewd futures dealings in cotton, sugar, tobacco and lumber.

Montro was dead wrong about Desmond.

But *who* had taken the will? And why would anyone have taken it? No one could profit from the theft except—except—

But that made no sense. Desmond wouldn't have done such a thing. After all, he was going to marry her and she would inherit her uncle's vast estate. Or, she would have, if the will still existed.

She was, she repeatedly told herself, absolutely certain Desmond had nothing whatsoever to do with her uncle's death or missing will. Nonetheless, she was greatly troubled and she didn't know where to turn. She badly needed the advice of an independent attorney with only *her* interest at heart.

But she couldn't afford one. She didn't have any money. All of her uncle's assets had been frozen, leaving her with only the small sums he kept at the town house.

The courts, strictly following the Napoleonic Code, had given her approximately three months— until the first day of June—to locate and present a will that superseded the provisional one.

Without it she would lose everything.

Thirty-Three

The messenger arrived at the Royal Street town house with an invitation requesting Madeleine's presence at Lord Enfield's that evening as the earl lay naked in Dominique's comfortable bed. The blond nobleman had a purpose for inviting Madeleine to his home for dinner. He needed privacy for what he intended. It was, he reasoned, time he seduced his aloof fiancée. Starting tonight he was going to give her the kind of hot, urgent sex that would leave her limp and sated in his arms.

And tonight's tryst would be just the beginning. He would continue—day and night—to make passionate love to her until she was so besotted with him she would do anything he wanted, give him anything he asked for. He knew how to break down a woman's resistance, make her his uninhibited love slave.

And he fully intended to do that to the haughty Lady Madeleine.

Of course he knew such an undertaking might prove to be totally unnecessary. With Sumner's final will missing, he held all the cards. But he was a cautious man. He didn't know where the will was and he had no idea who had taken it.

Desmond had to have Madeleine absolutely mad

about him and ready to hand over everything she'd inherited in case the will mysteriously reappeared before the three months had passed. Besides, he mused, the prospect of keeping the beautiful russet-haired woman naked and yielding in his bed for the next several weeks wasn't all that distasteful.

He smiled at the pleasant prospect, then immediately sobered when Dominique came crawling into the bedroom on hands and knees, alternately moaning and purring, pretending to be a sleek feline in heat, eagerly seeking out her mate.

Desmond hurriedly rose from the bed and wrapped a sheet protectively around his body. Shaking his head fervently, he said, "I haven't time for games, love. I'm already late. I must go."

The angry kitty rose up to her knees and hissed loudly at him, but he paid no attention.

Montro left Lady Madeleine at Lord Enfield's Dumaine Street home shortly before eight. She was shown to the upstairs drawing room and left there alone to wait. The servant returned to the lower floor.

Madeleine sat for a time, but when Desmond hadn't arrived in ten minutes she began to look about for something to read. There was nothing. She rose, walked across the hall to Lord Enfield's darkly paneled study. Just as she started toward the wall-to-ceiling bookcases, a slight breeze, coming through an open window, blew a piece of paper off Desmond's desk.

She bent and picked up the paper.

And she looked it.

It was a bill for a large sum of money from a

New Orleans jeweler. And it was marked urgent, with a Please Submit at Once stamp across the top. Madeleine frowned. She walked around behind the desk and placed the bill on its top. She started to turn away, but didn't. Glancing up at the open double doors to be sure she was alone, she picked up some papers, riffled through them and immediately saw, to her shock and horror, that they were all bills. There were stacks and stacks of unpaid bills scattered across the desk top. Notices of intent to foreclose on Desmond's home. Duns from a dozen banks on overdue loans.

Madeleine's hands began to shake as she realized that Lord Enfield was completely insolvent.

But the bills were not the only damning documents she found. Mixed in among the numerous bills and duns were shockingly graphic love notes written on scented lilac paper and signed "Dominique."

Madeleine flushed hotly as she read some of the stunningly shameful sexual secrets shared by a woman who was undoubtedly Lord Enfield's adored mistress.

Madeleine felt sick.

Her hands shaking badly, she hurriedly put everything back in place, but did not move away. Her mind racing, heart hammering, she stood there in that paneled office as a terrible truth began to dawn.

She remembered all those evenings when Desmond had left her early with barely a good-night kiss. Now she knew why. He had been anxious to get away from her and go to the arms of his lover. At once, Montro's damning words came back to her. *When did your uncle draw up the last will? When did Lord Enfield propose?*

In the blink of an eye it was all coming clear. Desmond Chilton was not wealthy! He was deeply in debt and badly in need of money. Pieces of the puzzle falling quickly into place, Madeleine realized that Lord Enfield was after her uncle's fortune, had been all along. He didn't love her. She was merely insurance on the Sumner estate. Which he meant to steal! *He* took the will! He took it and if she looked long enough, she would probably find it right here in his house.

But there wasn't time.

Desperate to get away before Desmond arrived, Madeleine rushed to the stairs and started down, waving away a servant's questioning look. She reached the foot of the stairs just as the front door opened and Lord Enfield stepped into the foyer.

"My dear," he greeted warmly, starting toward her.

"No!" Madeleine threw up her hands in a defensive gesture. "Don't come any closer." She was trembling violently and breathing rapidly.

Desmond frowned, baffled. "Darling, darling, what is it? What has happened? You look as if you've seen a ghost."

"Not a ghost, Desmond," she said, eyes flashing, "a thief. I am looking at a thief!"

Lord Enfield glanced at his servant and said sharply, "Leave us, Rolland!" Then turning his attention back to Madeleine, he softened his voice and said, "You're obviously very upset about something, dear. Come upstairs with me and let's get to the bottom of this." He attempted to take her arm, but she shook his hand off.

"Where is it, Desmond? What did you do with my uncle's will?"

He gave her a blank look. "Why on earth would you ask me a foolish question like that? You know very well that I have no idea what happened to the will. Are you forgetting, I was there with you when you opened the safe and found it missing."

"You took it before that night," she angrily accused. "You took it at just the right time, didn't you? As if you knew when my uncle was going to die. Did you, Desmond? Did you know?"

"I'm not sure what you're accusing me of, Madeleine, but I strongly resent—"

"I'm accusing you stealing my inheritance. I'm accusing you of asking me to be your wife only so you can get your hands on the money! I'm accusing you of persuading my dear, trusting uncle to name you executor so that—"

"Dearest, dearest," he soothed, interrupting, "you should listen to yourself. You're raving like a madwoman. You're making no sense. None whatsoever."

"Why did you ask me to marry you, Desmond? Tell me that."

"Because I love you very much and I want to spend the rest of my life with you. What other reason could there be?"

"Money," she stated firmly. "You knew I would one day be very, very rich."

He snorted and said, "You're forgetting, Madeleine, I, too, am quite wealthy and—"

"No, you're not. You have nothing. You need my—"

"I am rich!" he thundered. "Do you hear me? I don't need your money."

"I'm glad, because you are not going to get it."

Desmond's eyes narrowed and his face flushed. "I don't know what's gotten into you, but I do know what to do about it." He reached out, took her arm and shoved her toward the stairs.

"Let me go!" she shouted, angry and frightened. "It's over between us, Desmond. I am breaking the engagement."

"You're breaking nothing, my spoiled pet," he said through thinned lips, roughly pushing her up the stairs before him. "I'm going to show you how much I love you. I will make love to you until—"

"You will do nothing of the kind!" she screamed at him, kicking at him, furiously attempting to free herself from his steely grasp. "You'll never touch me, you deceitful bastard!"

"Ah, but I will," he promised, struggling to subdue her, angry and worried. "It's time you learned a lesson. I am the master here and you'd best start getting used to the idea."

"My, God, you're evil!" she snarled and, desperate, impulsively leaned over and bit his hand viciously.

He yelped in pain and reflexively released her. She seized the opportunity, spun about and raced down the stairs. He started after her, cursing and threatening what he would do when he caught her. She made it to the front door, burst out onto the street and started running as fast as she could.

Furious, Desmond hurried out onto the banquette

and called out, "You little bitch, you'll pay for this! Do you hear me! Madeleine, get back here this instant!" He jogged a few steps down the street, but soon stopped, winded. Aware that the neighbors were beginning to peer out their windows, he went back inside.

Madeleine never slowed or looked back. She ran as fast her weak legs would carry her, frantic to get away from the monster who had finally revealed himself. Terrified that he was racing after her, she kept running and running.

Even when she realized that he was not behind her, that she was safe, she continued to run. Short of breath, a stabbing stitch in her side, she kept running as tears stung her eyes and her heart pumped furiously.

She hardly realized where she was headed until she reached her destination. She paused beneath the large red canopy in front of The Beaufort Club and struggled to catch her breath.

"Are you all right, miss?" the uniformed doorman stepped forward to politely inquire.

"I—I— Is...do you know...if...if...Mr. de Chevalier is at the club tonight?"

"Why, he most certainly is," the doorman replied. "Shall I take you inside and help you find him?"

Nodding, trying to slow her rapid breathing and calm herself, Madeleine smoothed her flyaway hair and said, "Will you, please?"

"Come with me." The young man gently took her arm and guided her through the club's front doorway.

Inside, he paused and stood for a moment on the

wide marble lip of the club's imposing entrance and searched the crowd below for its dark-haired owner. Not spotting Armand, he said to Madeleine, "Wait right here. I'll find out where the boss is."

She nodded, tried to smile, and gazed out over the large room while the doorman stepped over to speak with the man in the coat-check booth. In seconds the smiling doorman was back at her side.

"Sam said Armand is taking a little break upstairs in his private quarters. I'll take you right up, if you wish."

"Yes, I—I need to speak with him. Tell him it's Lady Madeleine."

Unaware and uncaring that heads were turning and people were staring as the tall, uniformed doorman guided her through the crowded, cavernous gaming palace, Madeleine attempted to stop the chattering of her teeth, to still the pounding of her heart.

Reaching the back of the room at last, the doorman indicated a set of wide, curving stairs along the wall, carpeted in lush blue velvet. Beside him, Madeleine ascended the stairs, wondering anxiously if Armand would even agree to see her.

Filled with doubts now, wondering why she had run to him, she was ushered down a wide corridor until they stood before a heavy carved door.

The doorman lifted a hand and rapped firmly.

From inside came that deep, familiar voice, but with a sharp edge to it that she'd never heard before. "Unless the joint's on fire, leave me the hell alone."

Undeterred, the smiling doorman called back,

"Boss, it's Lady Madeleine. She needs to speak with you."

The carved door opened almost immediately and Armand de Chevalier stood before her, smiling. The doorman quickly backed away, leaving them alone. Armand saw the bright tears shining in Madeleine's green eyes and his smile instantly fled.

"*Chérie,*" he said softly, his dark eyes wide with worry, "what is it?"

"Oh, Armand." She began to sob, unable to hold back the tears one second longer, "I—I—" she choked.

"Come to me, sweetheart," said Armand, gently drawing her into his strong, comforting arms. "Let me hold you, let me help you."

Thirty-Four

Armand gently guided the weeping Madeleine into the spacious apartment, closing the door behind them. Madeleine clung to him and attempted, between racking sobs, to explain what had happened. But she was so upset, so out of breath and crying so violently, she ran her words together in a burst of confusing revelation, hardly making sense.

"...began to suspect...took the will...found all those bills...has no money...accused him...grew angry and violent...said he was going to...to..."

"Shh, shh," Armand soothed. "I've got you now, you're safe, Maddie. Don't cry, sweetheart."

"I'm...n-n-not crying," she sobbed, burying her face on his chest. "I...I...oh, Armand...I came here because...I wasn't sure if you'd...what am I going to do?"

"You're going to have a stiff drink of cognac," he said with calm authority and guided her to a long black-and-white-striped sofa.

But when he attempted to sit her down, to release her, the trembling Madeleine clung desperately to him and pleaded, "Don't let me go, please don't let me go."

"Never, *chérie*," he said softly and, with his

arms wrapped firmly around her, Armand ushered her across the room to the long black-walnut bar.

He didn't go behind the bar. He stepped up in front of it and, keeping her within the safe, protective circle of his arms, reached around her, poured a snifter of brandy and insisted she drink it. Between sobs and coughs she drank the fiery liquid and immediately felt its welcome warmth flow down into her chest and out into her arms. Before she had emptied the snifter, she began to calm somewhat. She stopped crying. She sighed wearily and took the last sip of the brandy before placing the empty snifter on the bar.

"Feeling a little better?" Armand asked, slowly turning her about in the circle of his arms until she was facing him.

Madeleine merely nodded, slipped her weak arms around his trim waist and again laid her aching head on his chest. Armand held her in a close, but unthreatening embrace. She had come to him for solace and that's what he would give her.

For a long, peaceful moment the couple stood there before the bar, gently embracing, saying nothing, sharing a brief interlude of serenity.

Then Madeleine slowly raised her head. She pulled back and gazed up at Armand. In his dark, beautiful eyes she saw genuine compassion. It touched her heart as nothing had in ages. Made her regret that she had come to the club and upset him.

She drew a shallow breath, raised a hand and laid it on his smoothly shaven olive cheek. "Armand," she said, "forgive me. I'm sorry, I shouldn't have come to you with my problems."

His handsome face a study in concern, he said in

a voice rough with emotion, "Sweetheart, I'm honored that it was me you turned to in your time of trouble."

She tried to smile at him, but failed. She moved her hand from his face, slid her fingertips along the satin lapel of his evening jacket and let her hand come to rest on his chest. At once she became acutely aware of Armand's hard, lean body pressed so intimately close to hers. She wondered if he was as aware. She lowered her gaze to his mouth. His sensual lips were slightly parted over perfect white teeth and the tip of his tongue came out and nervously licked his full bottom lip.

She shivered involuntarily.

"Cold, sweetheart?" he inquired, tightening his arms slightly around her.

She shook her head. She swallowed hard. She could feel his heavy heartbeat beneath her spread fingers. Saw the throbbing vein in his tanned throat. They stared at each other as a new, raw kind of tension rose between them and swiftly escalated.

Finally, Madeleine murmured, "Armand, oh, Armand."

That was all it took.

His dark face began to slowly lower toward hers. Purposely, he gave her ample time to stop him if she so desired. She didn't. She sighed when his smooth, warm lips touched hers softly, seekingly. Her response was totally receptive. Still, Armand held back, kissing her so tenderly for a few moments that she relaxed completely and felt as if she were floating in a sweet dream. Incredible warmth spread through her entire body and she sighed once more.

Armand continued to kiss her softly, gently. His mouth moved slowly on hers. He took her bottom lip between his teeth and caressed it with his tongue. She swayed against him. He swiftly deepened the kiss, his tongue going into her mouth to explore and examine and excite. Madeleine's arms slipped around his neck and she eagerly clasped handfuls of the silky raven hair at the back of his head.

With his tall, solid body, Armand pressed her up against the walnut bar, insinuating his knee between hers. A little gurgle of excitement escaped her and Madeleine instantly pressed against his trousered leg, anxiously seeking the partial relief the stony hardness of his muscular thigh provided.

Madeleine finally tore her burning lips from his to take a breath. She shivered when Armand immediately bent his dark head and kissed the bare curve of her neck and shoulder, his lips gently sucking and spreading heat over the sensitive flesh.

Their simmering passions swiftly erupted and they kissed and touched and clung to each other until, very quickly, the barrier of their clothing became too burdensome. Each began to tear at the other's garments in a frenzy of growing desire. They were half dressed, half undressed, when Armand swept Madeleine up into his arms and carried her into the bedroom.

There the only light was the flickering flames in the black marble fireplace directly across from the turned-down bed. In the sensual firelight they finished disrobing and when both were blessedly naked, they again stepped into each other's arms and kissed hotly, hungrily.

Madeleine was overwhelmed by the heat and hardness of Armand's bare beautiful body pressing so insistently against her own. He was so incredibly strong and masculine and she felt very weak and vulnerable against such potent virile power. But she was not afraid of his throbbing strength, she was thrilled by it.

As for Armand, he experienced again that electrifying shock that had swept through him the first time they had come together naked. His already aroused body got a fresh jolt of excitement as he held her sweet softness against him. His body's response was immediate and automatic. Blood rushed to his groin, causing it to expand painfully, and then pounded upward to spread a suffocating heat all through his body.

Madeleine felt herself being lifted from the floor and then gently lowered to the bed. She put up no resistance. Armand placed her in the very center of the big, square bed and she sighed with erotic pleasure as she settled herself comfortably against the black satin sheets and pillows. She sighed again when Armand joined her on the bed, bending to press a long, openmouthed kiss to her responsive lips.

When their lips separated, Armand's mouth slipped down over her chin to her throat. He pressed a kiss to its delicate hollow and then began to leisurely kiss his way down her bare straining body. Madeleine was dazzled by the touch of his lips and tongue on her tingling flesh. When his mouth settled on her left nipple, she raised a hand, started to lay it atop his dark head. She didn't. Instead she drew a deep, ragged breath, raised both arms above her head, folded them, and arched her back, glorying in the tug of his lips, the teasing of his tongue, the sweet sensation of his teeth raking over her stinging nipples.

When his handsome face moved down from her breasts and over her ribs to her waist, Madeleine idly wondered where his mouth's tantalizing exploration would end.

She quivered helplessly when his tongue delved into her navel, and then she held her breath as his hot, open lips moved aggressively on down her flat, contracting belly. She gasped when he nuzzled his nose and mouth into the red-gold curls of her groin. She shuddered as his hot breath stirred the curls.

With his tongue, Armand parted those fiery crisp coils and Madeleine's eyes grew round with a mixture of alarm and arousal. Wanting him to stop, wanting him to never stop, she whimpered when Armand bent his head and kissed her tenderly in that most feminine, secret spot. She felt all the air leave her body in an explosion of shock and excitement. She couldn't believe the incredible pleasure she experienced when his tongue began to slowly circle that pulsing button of flesh where all her raging desire was centered.

Feasting on her, loving her this way, Armand became so aroused he knew he couldn't wait much longer to be inside her. With gentle lips he kissed and sucked, with stroking tongue he licked and lashed, and all the while he was carefully gauging the intensity of her excitement. It was building rapidly. Her legs kept parting wider without his urging. Her pelvis was lifting off the bed, seeking the hot wetness of his loving mouth. Her arms had come down from over her head and her fingers were gripping the black satin sheets beside her raised hips.

Armand gave the pulsing feminine flesh one last kiss, then swiftly rose up over Madeleine. Both were so hot and hungry for each other, he slid into her with no difficulty for him, no pain for her. Immediately they began to move together, as if his lean, brown body and her slender pale one had been fashioned by nature to fit perfectly together.

The hot kisses of burning, questing lips. The deep thrusting of rock-hard flesh into slick yielding softness. The eager hands caressing bare yearning skin. The sleek feel of the black satin bedsheets against sensitized naked flesh.

All conspired to hurl the joined couple to a swift and intense climax. Helpless in the throes of simultaneous orgasm, they clung to each other in their shattering ecstasy, each calling the other's name.

The lovers lay facing each other in the big, soft bed. More than an hour had passed since Madeleine had arrived at The Beaufort. Most of that hour had been spent in bed, making love, the two of them so insatiable they couldn't get enough of each other.

Now the top sheet rested somewhere around their hips and beneath it, their legs were still entwined. Bathed in golden firelight, languid from the loving, they lay unmoving, unspeaking, gazing into each other's eyes, each wondering just how much the other cared.

If at all.

Madeleine sighed and lazily raised up onto an

elbow. She said, "You must be wondering what I'm doing here."

"You're welcome here for any reason, any time, sweetheart," was his gallant reply.

She pushed her tangled red-gold hair behind an ear and said, "I want to tell you all that has happened, Armand."

He nodded, fell over onto his back and folded his arms beneath his head. Madeleine turned onto her stomach beside him and rested her weight on her elbows.

Then she began to talk. "I am not going to marry Lord Enfield," she announced emphatically. Armand immediately felt his heartbeat quicken, but he remained silent.

She continued, "Desmond cares nothing for me, he was after Uncle Colfax's money all along. I was blind to his intentions. I believed that he was an honorable man and that he was quite wealthy, but…"

Talking rapidly now, she told Armand everything she knew, about the missing will and her suspicions that Desmond was the one who had taken it. She told him of her visit to Lord Enfield's home that evening and that she'd found stacks of bills and duns as well as love notes from his mistress.

Madeleine talked and talked and when finally she had told him everything she knew, she sat up in the bed and frowned down at Armand. It did not escape her notice that he had demonstrated no astonishment at any of her shocking revelations.

She asked, "You are not surprised by all this, are you?"

Laying a hand on her silky thigh and patting her

affectionately, Armand reluctantly admitted that he had feared, all along, that the devious Lord Enfield had been up to something.

"You knew?" She was shocked and incensed. "You knew about this and never said anything? Why? Why didn't you tell me?"

Armand drew her down into his embrace, tucking her head beneath his chin, and said, "Would you have believed me? I think not."

"No," she admitted with a deep sigh, "I wouldn't have believed you."

"I tried," said Armand, "on more than one occasion to alert your uncle to Lord Enfield's true nature. I knew Chilton had Colfax fooled and it worried me greatly."

"But if Uncle Colfax didn't know, how did you?"

"I have more contacts than your uncle had. And of a different ilk. When you're in the gambling business, you cross paths with all kinds of characters. While most who come to the club are respected gentlemen and ladies seeking a bit of harmless diversion, others are from the seamy side of society. They usually drink too much, talk too much. I learned, long ago, what few are aware of about Lord Enfield. What your uncle certainly never knew. That Chilton made a killing in black ivory. Illegal slave trade."

"Desmond bought slaves?" Madeleine, horrified, raised her head.

"Bought them cheap and sold them high."

"So he made a great deal of money out of others' misery."

"A fortune," said Armand. "A sizable fortune

which he later lost in reckless market speculation. Chilton has, for years, lived far above his means and has therefore piled up exorbitant debts. The man is probably desperate for cash.''

''That's the only reason he wanted me.''

Armand stroked her lustrous hair, aflame in the firelight. ''I'm sure that's not the only reason, Maddie. But it certainly didn't hurt that you're the heiress to your uncle's vast fortune.''

For a time, Madeleine said nothing more, just lay quietly in Armand's arms, digesting all she had learned since her uncle's shocking death.

When she finally spoke, she asked, ''Armand, do you suppose…could Desmond have had Uncle Colfax…murdered?''

''I wish I could assure you that the answer to that is a firm no,'' he said, his voice soft, low. ''But I can't. Now that I know he's the only living executor named in the provisional will and that the other will is missing…'' He sighed heavily. Then he added, ''If Chilton did have your uncle killed, he'll be found out.''

''You think so?''

''I do. Had he had the guts to do it himself, he might be safe. But when more than one person knows of a crime, somebody, sooner or later, is bound to talk.''

Sickened by the thought Desmond might actually be responsible for her dear uncle's death, Madeleine said, ''My God, I've been such a blind fool. How could I have…?''

''Sweetheart, you're not the only one Lord Enfield has fooled,'' Armand assured her. ''Few in New Orleans are aware of his sins. He's a devious, but very clever man. He has the trust and respect of this entire city.''

"The evil bastard," she said, shuddering at the thought that she had almost married him.

"He's that and more," Armand agreed, "and I want you to swear to me that he didn't touch you, didn't harm you when you encountered him in his home this evening."

"No, he didn't get the chance. I told you, I bit him and was able to get away."

"You might not be as lucky the next time, so…"

"Next time?"

"Maddie, you don't really suppose that this is the end of it, do you? It may well be for you, but not for him, so you must be extremely careful. *Never* go out of the house unless Big Montro is with you. For that matter, never be in the house alone, make sure that Montro is there at all times."

"I will," she said, "I promise and…oh, Armand, what time is it?"

Armand looked across the room to the onyx clock resting on the mantel. "Mmm, about twenty 'til ten."

"Will you take me home? Montro is due at Desmond's town house to collect me at ten sharp. He'll be worried if he doesn't find me there."

Armand rolled up into a sitting position, clasped her upper arms and gave her a quick, sound kiss. "You know I will," he replied and started to get up off the bed.

"One more thing," she said, catching his arm. "I *must* find Uncle Colfax's missing will before the first of June. I need your help."

"You have it, *chérie.*"

Thirty-Five

When Madeleine and Armand arrived at the Royal Street town house, they found the usually calm Avalina wringing her hands and pacing the floor. They quickly learned the reason. An angry Lord Enfield had shown up shortly after nine, demanded to see his fiancée.

Baffled, Big Montro had told the flush-faced nobleman that Lady Madeleine was not home. "It was our understanding that she was dining with you this evening," Montro replied sharply. "I left her at your home shortly before eight and told her I'd return to collect her at ten sharp."

His eyes flashing with anger and frustration, Lord Enfield had shouted at the big, brawny bodyguard, "Am I speaking a foreign language? I said I wish to speak with Lady Madeleine and that is exactly what I intend to do!"

He had irritably brushed past Montro and started for the stairs. Montro had reached out and caught Desmond's arm, stopping him.

"She is not home, sir." Montro's voice had been low, calm. "If you wish to wait here, I will go out and see if I can find her."

Desmond had snatched his arm free of Montro's grip. "If you two know where she is and are concealing her whereabouts from me, I'll see to it that you both..."

"I have no idea where Lady Madeleine might be," said Montro. "Nor does Avalina."

Flustered, Desmond had said, "Very well. I'll return to my home, perhaps she's come to her senses and is looking for me."

"Come to her senses?" questioned Avalina. "Has something happened between...?"

Lord Enfield had given her a scathing look and said hotly, "Servants are *never* to question their betters! You're to mind your own business and keep quiet, do you understand me?"

Desmond had cast one last glance up the stairs, turned and stormed to the front door. "If Madeleine comes here, notify me immediately. I urgently need to speak with her tonight!"

Now, as Madeleine and Armand sat listening to Avalina tell what had happened, Big Montro arrived back at the town house. He came in the front door, heard the voices and stepped into the drawing room.

"They're here and she's safe!" Avalina told him excitedly.

The gentle giant grinned and nodded. He spoke to Madeleine and Armand, then politely excused himself.

"No wait, Montro." Madeleine stopped him. "Please, won't you come in and sit down. There's something I need to tell you and Avalina and I might as well do it now."

The big man took a chair near Avalina. As soon as he was seated, Madeleine began her explanation. "I'll get right to the point," she said, totally composed, her voice firm. "I have broken my engagement to Desmond Chilton and I—"

"You're not going to marry Lord Enfield?" Avalina interrupted, her dark eyes as big as saucers.

"No. No, I am not. Thankfully, I found out in time that Desmond Chilton is not the fine man I thought him to be. I have learned some things this evening that make me suspect Desmond could be responsible for taking Uncle Colfax's will. Unfortunately, the provisional will was never destroyed as it should have been, therefore with the absence of the final will, the provisional will be considered the only one."

"Lord Enfield will control everything!" stated Avalina.

"Exactly. And, since I have broken our engagement, I stand to lose everything Uncle Colfax worked so hard to acquire. Unless, that is, I can find the other will." She glanced at Armand and continued, "Mr. de Chevalier has generously agreed to help me search for the will or any copy of it that might exist." She drew a deep breath and added, "The courts have given me until June 1. If we can't find the will by then..." She stopped speaking, shrugged slender shoulders.

Armand spoke for the first time. "I'm hopeful a copy of the will exists and that we will locate it quickly. However, right now, I believe there is an even more pressing problem for us all."

Madeleine turned her head and gave him a questioning look. He explained, "Lord Enfield will be coming back here no later than tomorrow, perhaps even tonight, to try to change your mind about breaking the engagement."

"Why? He stole the will, he no longer needs to marry me," she reasoned.

"He'll be worried that a copy exists," said Armand. He looked at Big Montro. "You know what to do, Montro."

Nodding, the bodyguard stated, "Avalina and I will both move into the main house." He looked directly at Madeleine. "If you, Lady Madeleine, wish to go out at any time, I will go with you. That is, unless, of course, you are in the company of Armand. You are to *never* be alone, not here at home or anyplace else."

Frowning now, Madeleine said, "You don't actually think Desmond could be dangerous? That he would try to harm me?" She looked from Montro to Armand.

"You've learned what kind of man he is," Armand gently reminded her. "By breaking the engagement, you are interfering with his well-laid plans. Who knows what he might do? I don't trust him."

"Nor do I," said Montro. "But to get to you, Lady Madeleine, Chilton will have to come through me. And that's not going to happen."

"No, it's not," Armand agreed, turning to Madeleine. "Now, since I'm sure you'll be as safe as a babe in her crib, I better be going."

"I'll see you to the door," Madeleine offered.

"Good night Avalina, Montro," Armand said, smiling warmly.

Both beamed at him. He winked at them as if they shared a delicious secret.

At the front door Armand said, "Don't worry, Maddie. Together we'll find the will."

"I hope so." She sighed. "Can we start tomorrow?"

"Tomorrow it is," he replied. Then, lowering his voice, he added, "I wish I could kiss you."

"Well, you can't," she scolded, glancing nervously toward the drawing room.

"Can I kiss you tomorrow?"

She smiled. "Tomorrow it is."

As soon as Armand left, an emotionally drained Madeleine bade good night to Avalina and Montro and went upstairs to bed. When the door closed behind her, Montro and Avalina looked at each other and began to smile broadly. They shook hands, silently congratulating each other. And both offered thanks to the Almighty that their most fervent prayers had been answered.

Lady Madeleine would not be marrying Lord Enfield.

The next morning a huge garland of red roses arrived for Lady Madeleine. The card read, "Dearest, I must see you. Allow me to straighten out this foolish misunderstanding between us."

An hour after the roses arrived, Lord Enfield showed up at the town house. "I must see my fiancée," he announced regally when Big Montro appeared just inside the locked iron gates.

"Lady Madeleine does not wish to see you, Lord Enfield."

Instantly furious, Desmond carefully hid his wrath. "She's upset, I know, but if I can just talk to her for a few minutes, I can explain everything." He laughed as if the whole thing were much ado over nothing. "You know how women are, Montro.

They get upset for no reason and we men have to pet and pamper them out of their sour mood.''

"Lady Madeleine does not wish to see you," Montro repeated.

Desmond exhaled with frustration. He said, ''Did she get the roses?'' Montro nodded. "Good." Desmond gave Montro a weak smile and said, "Please tell her I was here and that I love her more than life itself.''

"Good day, Chilton," Montro said, dismissing him.

For a long moment Lord Enfield continued to stand there in the morning sun outside the locked gates. Finally he turned and walked away, stopping to glance up at Madeleine's window. He was worried as he'd never been worried in his life. He had to get her back. He had to convince her to be his wife in case the final will turned up.

As the warm, rainy month of March rushed too quickly by, Madeleine and Armand were together almost daily, racing the clock in an attempt to save her inheritance. In the beginning Armand was fully optimistic. He reasoned that Madeleine's uncle had written a will giving her his entire fortune. Apparently several people had seen it and heard him acknowledge it; therefore, they could testify to it.

But, no, Madeleine informed him, that would not be possible. All of the gentlemen who knew of the will and its contents were now deceased. There was no one who could come forward and attest to its existence. No one, that is, except Lord Enfield.

Armand and Madeleine went to court and conferred privately with the honorable Judge Baxter, a knowledgeable, levelheaded gentleman Armand had known since finishing law school.

"We need your help, Judge," Armand said to the balding man.

"What do you mean, my boy?" Baxter's bushy eyebrows knitted.

"Colfax Sumner's will has disappeared."

"Oh? I was informed that the will was found."

"But not the latest will," Armand told him. "When Sumner's safe was opened, only an old provisional will was there."

The judge rubbed his forehead. "Contact some of the witnesses to the…"

"All are deceased."

The judge shook his head sorrowfully. "Then we must hope that Colfax left a copy of the will someplace. Without it…what can I say? The law is the law."

The pair returned to court the next day with a petition saying that Madeleine had firm reason to believe that a second will had been made. Armand explained that, frequently, though the law did not require it, family notaries kept duplicates of such documents. Armand, on Madeleine's behalf, demanded that every notary in New Orleans be called in.

It took several weeks before all had finally appeared. Colfax had gone to none of them.

Meanwhile the pair searched a couple of other safes in which Colfax had kept possessions. They spent a full day at the plantation upriver, going through the safe and all the many drawers in the huge mansion.

They found nothing.

* * *

April came to the Crescent City with a profusion of fresh flowers filling courtyards and sweetening the heavy air. The balmy days and warm nights were as near perfection as could be found on earth. New Orleanians, delighted that the penetrating cold and dampness of the winter was behind them and that the heat and mugginess of summer had not yet arrived, eagerly filled the streets and the riverfront. Laughter frequently rang out as good friends gathered outdoors to visit and gossip and bask in the glorious joys of springtime.

While the city's social set were taking full advantage of the warm, beautiful weather, Madeleine and Armand were totally preoccupied.

They visited numerous banks in which Sumner had safe deposit boxes. The boxes were filled with various documents and deeds to land purchased over the years. Both Armand and Madeleine were shocked at the enormity of the estate. Colfax Sumner had been a very good businessman. He had bought up land left and right, in New Orleans and beyond, along the river and bayous.

It appeared that half of the city belonged to Colfax Sumner.

Determined to continue their fight to the bitter end, the pair visited the Spanish structure next to St. Louis Cathedral, the old Cabildo. Once inside the huge room, Armand sought out the clerk of the probate court.

An assistant listened as Armand asked for the succession of Colfax Sumner.

"What is your interest in this information?" he asked.

"May I remind you that these are public records," was Armand's reply.

The clerk pursed his lips, turned and walked away. In minutes he returned with an armload of records.

Armand and Madeleine pored over the old, dusty records. His anger showing in a white circle around his mouth, Armand pointed out that Lord Enfield was already attempting to sell a small downtown parcel of Sumner's land.

"Good God, this is unbelievable," he growled. "Chilton is trying to sell Sumner's property without legal authority of any kind!" Madeleine started to say something, but Armand raged on. "Even if he had the authority to sell the land—which he does not—the law says sales must be held at public auction after full advertisement."

"Does he actually think he can get away with selling the property?"

Armand raised his hands, rubbed his temples. "He must, or he wouldn't be trying. Who knows? Perhaps he has an accomplice inside the law. New Orleans has always been ruled by corrupt and powerful men."

"So I hear," Madeleine said. "That's the reason you were disbarred, isn't it?"

Armand's dark head snapped up and he looked at her in surprise. "How did you know about that?"

"Montro told me. He said you defended a young black man in a rape case and that the woman's family brought false charges against you in an effort to have you tossed out."

Armand shrugged. "The poor devil was innocent."

"I know." Madeleine began to smile. "I know something else about you, Creole." Armand frowned. She said, "You are helping build the new childrens' hospital. I saw you working on the roof."

"I'm a good carpenter." He was nonchalant.

"You're a good man."

Armand colored visibly beneath his olive complexion and murmured, "Let's see, now, where were we?" He picked up one of the big books.

Madeleine's smile fled. She sighed and shook her head wearily. "It looks as though I'm going to lose everything."

"No, sweetheart." Armand closed the huge book and turned to her. "But we've done enough for the day. Let's go to my apartment and have dinner sent over from Antonies."

"They'll do that?"

"For us they will."

Thirty-Six

As dusk blanketed the city, Madeleine and Armand sat on the floor in the spacious drawing room of Armand's Pontalba Building apartment. The tall French doors were thrown open to the coming coolness of the night and a fire crackled brightly in the marble fireplace.

A large white linen cloth was spread on the plush carpet directly in front of the fireplace and upon it was a sumptuous supper catered from Armand's favorite restaurant, Antonies. Rich, highly seasoned *bouillabaisse* was followed with excellent *filet de sole bonne femme*. Madeleine was starting on the rich dessert, blackberries in thick cream, when Armand, rising to his feet, excused himself for a moment.

He was gone for several minutes and Madeleine was growing curious. When he returned she laughed merrily and clapped her hands. He held large silver bowl and ladle in one hand and in the other, a matching silver tray on which several ingredients rested.

Winking at her, Armand again sat down on the floor, placed the empty silver bowl before him, the tray at his side. In the silver dish he put sugar, brandy, cloves, allspice, orange and lemon peel, and cinnamon sticks. He then grinned, rubbed his hands together, lighted a match and set the brandy and ingredients afire in the bowl. Slowly he poured in the coffee and then lifted the blazing silver bowl high into the air while Madeleine applauded.

"Your *café brulot*, my lady," he said, handing her a cup of the hot, delicious brew.

As they sipped the exquisite mixture, the cares of the day faded away and were forgotten. They were alone together and they were content.

When Madeleine took the last sip of her cooling *café brulot*, Armand took the cup from her and set it aside. Without using his hands, he came agilely to his feet and reached for her.

When she stood facing him, he said, "I haven't had a bath since early this morning, what about you?" She smiled shyly and shook her head. "Let's take a bath together."

Not waiting for her reply, Armand laced his fingers through hers. He led her out of the drawing room, directly through his bedroom and into the bath. The giant tub was miraculously filled with hot sudsy water and on a ledge at the tub's foot was a lit candle in a hammered silver holder. A half dozen large white towels rested beside the steaming tub.

"Does a good fairy live with you?" she teased.

"I never give away my secrets," he said, drawing her closer before he began undressing her.

In minutes both were totally naked.

Well, almost naked.

Madeleine laughed and, nodding to the faded blue garter encircling Armand's upper arm, asked, "Do you bathe in that?"

He grinned, quickly slipped the garter down his

arm and off. Tossing it atop a chest, he replied, "No, but sometimes I sleep in it. And I *never* leave the house without it."

"You are crazy, Creole" she teased.

"Crazy about you, countess," he replied.

For a few peaceful, pleasant moments the pair relaxed in the oversize tub, the mellow candlelight washing over them and causing shadows to dance on the walls. Eyes closed, Armand lazed against the tub's high back with Madeleine between his legs, resting comfortably against him. Both had agreed that since they were so exhausted from their long day, they should really rest, not play. Leave each other alone. Just lie and let the warm, soothing water work its magic on their weary bodies.

Very quickly both realized that to lie naked together in a hot tub and not want to make love was utterly ridiculous. Without a word being spoken, Madeleine slid to one side of Armand's wet, solid chest and turned her head to look up at him.

He kissed her and it was a kiss to end all kisses.

Madeleine had never made love while immersed in water, but she found to her surprised delight that it was highly enjoyable. Astride her slippery lover, she ground her hips and clung to Armand's strong neck and looked into his flashing dark eyes. In moments both reached total ecstasy.

Madeleine's burning passion for Armand grew more intense every time they touched, kissed, made love. She felt as if she could never get enough of him, as if the only thing she wanted was to be in his arms forever and ever.

But as they had worked together so tirelessly these past few weeks, the fierce attraction that had been there from the beginning was steadily growing into something much more, much deeper.

Madeleine had learned that this handsome Creole whom she had so foolishly assumed to be a rogue with no conscience, was at heart a good, principled man, deserving of her respect. And she did respect him.

But did that mean she could trust him entirely? Did he really care for her or was their relationship merely a product of their fiery sexual hunger for each other? When the hot, hot passion cooled, would he still want her? And only her?

Lord Enfield, after numerous failed attempts to see Madeleine, had finally given up. He couldn't get past the big burly bodyguard who seemed never to sleep.

Madeleine, Desmond had learned the hard way, was never alone either at home or when she went out. The protective giant was always at her side. And, Desmond had noted with contempt, a regular destination to which Montro escorted his mistress was to the Pontalba apartments of one Armand de Chevalier.

The first time, the shocked earl couldn't believe his eyes. It had happened on an April afternoon when he was crossing Jackson Square after a most disturbing meeting with his broker. He had looked up just in time to see the towering Montro greet a radiant Lady Madeleine outside de Chevalier's apartment. The Creole was at her side, holding her hand as if he owned her, and the three of them were laughing.

His eyes narrowed, unable to abide what he was

seeing, Desmond had witnessed Armand giving Madeleine a kiss on the cheek before she and Montro had turned and walked way. Stunned and livid, he'd had to sit down on a bench in the manicured square to collect himself.

That shameless harlot! That brazen bitch! Openly consorting with the likes of de Chevalier. Callously making him, Lord Enfield, a laughingstock among his friends. Everyone was whispering behind his back; he knew they were. There was no doubt in his mind that Madeleine had told everyone in town about breaking the engagement and they were all speculating about the cause.

Damn her to eternal hell!

Desmond's frustration steadily grew. In the following weeks he saw Armand and Madeleine together several times and while he was half afraid of de Chevalier and wouldn't dare challenge him in person, Desmond decided he wouldn't let the Creole off scot-free. He had no doubt that de Chevalier was putting ideas in Madeleine's head and telling her where to search for the missing will. The meddling bastard needed to be taught a lesson.

After much stewing and cursing and gnashing of teeth, Lord Enfield impulsively paid a late-night visit to his hired henchmens' shanty at edge of the swamps.

"You want us to scare him or kill him?" asked Burton Smallwood.

"Hmm. I hadn't thought of that," Desmond said, cocking his head to one side. "Yes, why not! Kill the sleazy bastard," he decided, slamming a fist down on the table. He quickly added, "But make it look like a robbery. Wait until you can catch him out alone on the street at night. Then grab him, take any money or jewelry he has and beat him unmercifully. You think just you two, you and Barton, can handle it? I don't want anybody else in on this.''

"Barton weighs twice as much as de Chevalier," said Burton. "Sure we can handle it."

Smiling at the prospect, wishing he could be there to see the haughty Creole get what was coming to him, Desmond looked around the cluttered cabin. "Where's your brother now? Where's Barton?"

"Aw, Barton went into town for—"

"Son of a bitch!" thundered Desmond Chilton and shot to his feet. "You let that simpleminded fool go to town knowing damned well he'll drink too much and talk too much!"

"No, no, boss, you got it all wrong," Burton defended his baby brother. "See, Barton needed a woman. Bad. Hasn't had one in weeks and he was about to jump out of his skin. I made him swear to me that he would go straight to a whorehouse and that he'd not take one single drink of whiskey."

"And you believed him?" Desmond snorted.

"I did, because I put the fear of God in him. Made him promise he'd just spend an hour with a woman and then come right back here. I expect him home any minute."

At that very minute, a drunken Barton Smallwood, grinning from ear to ear, haltingly climbed the front steps of a two-story Galletin Street brothel in search of a willing strumpet with whom he could frolic the evening away.

For a ten-dollar bill he got just what he was looking for. A big-bosomed, big-butted woman with pale skin, painted eyes, rouged lips and tinted hair. Gleefully watching the bounce of her ample bottom as she preceded him up the stairs, he asked, "What's your name, sweetening?"

Over her shoulder, "Heaven," she replied. "Miss Heaven Sublime."

"You gonna' take me to heaven, Heaven?" he said, laughing loudly.

"Why sure, big boy."

Inside a small, garish room with walls of scarlet and one low burning lamp, the two of them hurriedly undressed and climbed into bed. Without preamble Barton Smallwood moved between Heaven's plump, parted thighs, pumped a couple of times, heaved, and climaxed instantly.

Out of breath, he rolled off her, fell onto his back, and gasped thirstily, "Pour me a little drink of whiskey, will you, Heaven?"

He gave her bare backside a slap as she got out of bed. Slipping into a not-quite-clean robe, she returned with two glasses and a full bottle of bourbon. She poured for them both, then sipped hers as Barton drained his glass and asked for another.

"Tell me about yourself, Heaven," he slurred and then listened with wide-eyed interest as she made up an interesting background for herself. Her tales of endless adventure and close calls and constant excitement made him surmise that she liked living dangerously and liked dangerous men.

When she concluded, she said, "What about you? You like doing daring things?"

He grinned in his whiskey haze and bragged, "How about murdering a man? Would you consider that daring enough?"

Heaven's eyes widened minutely. "You're teasing me. You never killed anyone. Did you?"

Barton puffed out his hairy chest, downed another glass of whiskey and said, "You ever read the newspapers, Heaven?"

"Why certainly, I pride myself on staying well informed."

"Did you read about an important businessman by the name of Colfax Sumner dying a couple of months back?"

"Yes, yes I did. Mr. Sumner was a very prominent New Orleans citizen. The *Picayune* article announcing his death said that he died of natural causes."

Barton guffawed loudly. "The natural cause he died of was a pillow held over his face until he suffocated. I know because I'm the one who held it there." Laughing heartily, Barton scratched his shaking belly, and said, "God almighty, I thought the old bastard would never stop struggling."

"You murdered Colfax Sumner?" Her eyes grew wider.

"Sure did."

"But why? The paper said nothing was stolen, so why would you want to kill him?"

"Ah, I didn't want to kill him for myself. Me and my brother did it for Lord Enfield."

"Lord Enfield?" She stared at him, aghast. "*The* Lord Enfield? That rich, blond nobleman from England who is engaged to Colfax Sumner's only niece? Is that who you mean? Are you talking about Desmond Chilton, the wealthy aristocrat?''

"That's who.''

Growing drunker and drunker, and talking louder and louder, Barton Smallwood told an entranced Miss Heaven Sublime everything about the murder, leaving out nothing.

Finally concluding, he grinned at her, confident he had greatly impressed her. "Now, darlin','' he said, "you won't go tellin' nobody about this, will you?''

Heaven didn't answer.

Thirty-Seven

The deadline for finding Colfax Sumner's will was drawing steadily closer. And Madeleine and Armand were drawing steadily closer. When they were not searching for the will, they were often in each other's arms, their mutual passion making it difficult to keep their hands off each other.

The Countess and the Creole were falling in love.

And yet Madeleine had never told Armand that she loved him. A part of her was still doubtful, still afraid to give of herself completely, afraid of being hurt.

Armand was just the opposite. He was totally open and honest and loving. He told Madeleine over and over that he was in love with her. That he had never loved anyone else, would never love anyone else. She was the one for whom he had waited all these years. She was the one to whom he would be faithful for the rest of his life. She was the one who held his heart in her hands, now and forever. She never tired of hearing such sweet love talk.

And she found Armand utterly irresistible when he would say to her, "*Chérie,* all I ask is that you love me even *half* as much as I love you."

Madeleine was happy. She did love Armand. She loved him more than he would ever know. And, when she could be absolutely certain that she was not just a passing fling for him, that he honestly, truly did love her and wanted to marry her, then, and only then, would admit she loved him, too. That day, she felt sure, was getting closer.

The only thing marring Madeleine's newfound happiness was the knowledge that she was very likely going to lose her inheritance to an unprincipled man who had callously manipulated her and who had quite possibly killed her beloved uncle.

As for Armand, he cared about the missing will only because he knew it meant so much to her. He, himself, had plenty of property and money, enough to last ten lifetimes. But he couldn't stand seeing her hurt. His greatest wish was that he could protect her from all worldly cares. There was nothing that would have brought him as much joy as finding the will and handing it to her.

But there was little hope of that happening.

Armand was due for a late dinner that evening, the eighth day of May. Last night he had explained to Madeleine that he wouldn't be able to spend the day with her. He had an obligation to work on the new children's hospital—he had been neglecting his duties there and was needed badly. Further, he had said apologetically, once he was finished at the hospital, he had to go by the club. Sign some papers. Check the payroll. Let everyone know the boss was still alive and kicking.

But Armand was running late.

It was well past seven when he finally got home from the construction sight. Sweaty and dirty, he stripped as he walked through the apartment. Allowing himself only a brief time to soak in a hot tub, he was out in a wink and lathering his darkly whiskered face.

Rushing to get dressed, he shoved his long arms into a freshly laundered shirt. He brushed his hair, then took a beige linen suit from the tall armoire. He was dressed and ready in a matter of minutes. Armand took one last glance in the mirror, ran a thumb and forefinger around his shirt collar, straightened his silk cravat and declared himself ready. He turned and hurried from the room.

But Armand forgot something.

Left hanging on a gold-leaf flower framing the bathroom mirror was Madeleine's garter, his good luck charm.

As twilight descended on the Royal Street town house, Madeleine sat at her upstairs dressing table dusting her face with rice powder. Her hair had already been elegantly dressed atop her head by the multitalented Avalina. Madeleine smiled thinking that Avalina's hard work on the elaborate coiffeur had been a waste of time. Armand liked her hair down. Before the night was over he would insist on taking out all the pins and watching it spill down around her bare shoulders.

The prospect made her shiver with anticipation.

Avalina was making Armand's favorite dish for dinner. Spicy shrimp gumbo. She hummed happily as she stirred the thick concoction. In the oven, a huge fresh peach cobbler was bubbling and baking, its pleasant aroma filling the downstairs.

At the kitchen table, Montro sat, keeping Avalina company as he skimmed the evening newspaper.

"Sure smells good," he commented, sniffing the air.

"You're not to even consider taking a taste until Mr. Armand gets here," Avalina warned.

"I won't, but I hope he gets here soon. I'm starving. What time did she say he was coming?"

"Around nine."

Armand stepped out of The Beaufort Club as nine o'clock rang out from the cathedral. He stood for minute beneath the red canopy and exhaled deeply of the humid May air.

"Shall I have your carriage brought around, boss?" the young doorman asked.

"No. Don't bother. It's such a beautiful night, I think I'll walk."

"Very good, sir."

Armand said good night and set out down the banquette as a pale quarter moon began to slowly climb over the rooftops. The heavy scent of jasmine, coming from a nearby courtyard, was powerfully seductive. Somewhere out on the Mississippi, a sidewheeler's whistle sounded faintly and the croaking of frogs came from the marshes along the riverfront. Closer, a pianoforte was being played in an upstairs parlor.

And just ahead on the corner, its fronds gently waving in the night breeze, rose a lone date palm against the night sky.

Armand smiled, recalling the palm's legend. It was said to have sprung from the heart of a maiden who died dreaming of her lover and the happiness

they'd found on a palm-fringed shore of a tropical
isle. The seed from which it grew had been blown
to New Orleans by the wind and it had been planted
by an angel. The tree would not bear fruit until New
Orleans had been cleansed of its wickedness.

Armand's smile broadened.

The lonely palm would never bear fruit because
New Orleans would never be cleansed of its wickedness. But he loved his city just the way it was.
He loved everything about it. He loved New Orleans almost as much as he loved the russet-haired
woman awaiting him on Royal Street. The thought
of Madeleine made his heartbeat quicken and he
picked up his steps.

His heels clicking on the cobblestones, Armand
hurried down the empty street, sweet anticipation
his only companion.

"Hey Creole!" came a gruff voice from out of
the darkness.

Armand stopped in the shadows of the street
lamp. He looked around, saw no one. He looked
up, quickly surveying the tracery of ironworks on
the balconies above. Nobody was there.

Then all at once he groaned in shock and pain
as a heavy blow fell on his back just above the
waist and he felt himself being dragged backward
into a dark alley. With arms pinned painfully behind him, Armand desperately tried to shake off his
attacker. But an accomplice stepped up and forcefully struck him in the mouth. Armand sagged to
his knees, blood pouring from his lips.

He was yanked to his feet with a sudden ferocity
and the bigger of the two assailants pounded both
his fists into Armand's unprotected stomach in a

series of rapid, lethal blows. The moan of pain from Armand brought only laughter from the evil pair pounding him. Another volley of blows followed, to his face, to his chest, to his stomach. Armand sagged, spitting blood and gasping for breath.

Summoning up every ounce of the strength left in him, Armand kicked and struggled and was able to get his arms free for one fleeting second. He managed to land one punishing blow to the big bully mercilessly beating him.

But he paid for it.

His arms were again pinned behind him and he was forced to stand there totally defenseless. More painful blows rained down on him and just as he was about to lose consciousness, the monster battering him lifted a heavy booted foot and shot it straight up into Armand's groin. A shriek of misery passed Armand's bleeding mouth and he clenched his teeth tightly to keep from biting through lips.

While torrents of pain throbbed through him and he fought wave after wave of nausea, Armand's pockets were searched and torn, his money and gold-cased watch taken. Blood streamed down his face onto his chest, saturating his torn white shirt. One eye was already swollen shut and blood from a cut on his forehead blinded him in the other. His weak legs buckled and he could feel darkness closing in.

He heard the stockier of the two say, "I got everything he had, let's finish him off."

And the ruffian raised his big fist and slammed it into Armand's belly just as a laughing couple stepped out of a café and onto the street. Hearing the commotion, the pair came to investigate.

"We got company," said Barton.

"Shut up!" said his brother.

They released the badly beaten Armand. He slumped to the ground as the Smallwood brothers turned and ran down the alley, disappearing into the night.

"I don't know what could be keeping him," Madeleine said irritably, pacing again. "It's after ten. He should have been here by now. You left the iron gates unlocked for him, didn't you, Montro?"

"I did," said Montro. "He'll be able to come right up."

"Where is he?" she mused aloud.

"Why don't I go down to The Beaufort Club and…" Montro began.

"No," she protested. "He knows the way here."

She sighed and sank down onto the sofa. Doubts nagged. Where was he? Why hadn't he come? Had he already tired of her? Had she, once again, been a gullible fool?

It was nearing eleven when the loud knock on the door finally came. Madeleine was up off the sofa and across the room before Avalina could reach the front door.

"Where have you—?" She stopped in midsentence when she opened the door to see a stranger standing before her.

The messenger asked, "Are you Lady Madeleine?"

"Yes, yes I am."

He nodded and handed her an envelope. She stared at him, stared at the envelope.

"Good night," said the young messenger and hurried back down the outside stairs.

Her hands beginning to shake, Madeleine tore the envelope open, took out the note, unfolded it and hurriedly read:

> Lady Madeleine,
> Your friend, Armand de Chevalier, was brought into New Orleans General Hospital a half hour ago after being beaten by street thugs. Armand was unconscious, but he was saying your name.
>
> Dr. Jean Paul Ledette

Madeleine's heart stopped. Then raced out of her chest. She felt as if she might faint. The room started to spin.

"Montro," she managed to whisper.

"Yes, my lady? What is it?" Montro asked, having already come into the foyer.

Both he and Avalina quickly stepped forward to steady the trembling Madeleine. Montro took the message from her hand, read it quickly, and heard Madeleine say, "Will you take me to him?"

"We'll leave at once."

"Yes," she replied, half-dazed, "I must go to Armand."

Thirty-Eight

At the hospital, Madeleine felt icy cold despite the warmth of the mid-May night. She stood stiffly beside Big Montro and watched Dr. Ledette coming toward them. The grim expression on the physician's face was telling. She sagged against the wall, weak and terrified. Dr. Ledette reached them, smiled kindly at her and nodded to Montro.

"Dr. Ledette, is he badly hurt?" she asked, hardly able to breathe. "Will he be okay? Is he awake?"

The middle-aged physician replied, "Armand had been badly beaten, Lady Madeleine. He sustained some vicious blows to the head as well as to his chest and stomach. There's a great deal of swelling and it is, unfortunately, too soon to know how lasting the damage." Seeing the despair that came into her eyes, he laid a comforting hand on her slender shoulder, and added, "I'm so sorry the news is not better, my dear. Perhaps your presence will do what I cannot. When he was brought in, Armand was calling your name."

Madeleine nodded, swallowed hard and, determined she would not cry, asked, "Where is he? I want to see him."

"And you may," said Dr. Ledette, "but I must

warn you about his appearance. Armand's face has been brutally pummeled…he doesn't look like himself. Do you understand?''

"Yes, I do, but I don't care. Please, just take me to him now.''

"Certainly," replied the doctor.

Madeleine glanced up at Big Montro. "Come with me." He nodded.

Her own footsteps and those of Montro and the doctor echoed loudly in her ears as they walked down the silent, shadowy corridor. Madeleine had to carefully concentrate on placing one foot in front of the other. She had to fight down the panic that was threatening to overwhelm her. She had to be strong and responsible for Armand's sake. She couldn't allow him to see her behaving like a hysterical female.

"This is it." Dr. Ledette paused before a closed door at the far end of the corridor. "Are you sure you'll be okay?"

"I'll be fine," she answered, giving him a brave smile. She read the concern on his weathered face and said, "Don't worry, Dr. Ledette. I have no intention of fainting."

"Then I'll give you a few minutes and be back to check on him shortly."

"Thank you, Doctor."

As the physician turned and started back down the hall, Madeleine touched Montro's muscular forearm and said, "You'll stay here? You won't leave?"

"I'll be right here outside the door."

Madeleine drew a long, spine-stiffening breath,

braced herself, opened the door, stepped inside and closed it behind her.

The room was very small and very white. White walls, white bed, white sheets, white curtains. The only light was from a small bedside lamp resting on a metal table.

Her heart in her throat, Madeleine tiptoed toward the bed that was directly across the room. As she neared it and saw Armand, she couldn't hold back the strangled moan of horror that rose to her lips. Her hand flew up to her mouth and she thought she was going to be ill.

For a long moment she couldn't move. She stood several feet from the bed with her hands over her mouth, shaking her head as if to clear it, fighting back the tears that were quickly filling her eyes. When she could function, she moved closer.

She walked around to the right side of the bed, looked down at him and began to sob. The poor battered soul lying so deathly still on the snowy-white bed was not recognizable. He looked nothing like her darkly handsome Armand. He had been literally beaten to a bloody pulp. There was not one square inch of his face that wasn't cut, swollen or bruised.

"My poor, hurt darling," she wept and sank down onto the edge of the mattress, facing him. "I'm here, Armand," she said, knowing he couldn't hear her. "I'm right here, my love. I'll never leave you, never."

No response.

But she hadn't expected any. She leaned closer and gazed at him, blinking to clear her tear-blurred vision. She longed to kiss him, but there was no place on his once beautiful face that wasn't injured.

She wondered if his magnificent body had been battered as badly as his face. The sheet was drawn up around his shoulders. She carefully lowered the sheet to his waist and bit her lip when she saw what they'd done to his chest and ribs and belly. Partially covered with tight bandages, the flesh on his rib cage that was left exposed was black and purple from severe bruising. Raw abrasions decorated his flat abdomen and bare shoulders and long arms.

"Oh, God, oh my God," she cried and gently lifted one of his bandaged hands in both of her own.

She searched for a spot on that long-fingered hand that was not bruised or scratched. There were none. Finally she kissed the inside of his wrist, allowing her lips to linger for a while in an effort to assure herself that he was still very much alive. The faint beat of his pulse against her lips was comforting.

When finally she lowered his hand to the mattress, Madeleine drew the sheet back up over him and said, "Armand, you cannot leave me. I won't let you. I love you, darling. I love you and I'll never let you go."

Long minutes passed with her continuing to gaze down at him, telling him she loved him. Dry-eyed now, she was leaning over Armand's battered face when Dr. Ledette knocked on the door and came inside.

The doctor said, "Why don't you let Montro take you home now, Lady Madeleine. There's nothing you can do here and—"

"I am not leaving," she said softly, but firmly, "until he wakes up."

"But, child, that could be hours or even days."

"I am staying with Armand."

When Madeline had been at Armand's bedside for twenty-four hours straight, Avalina, worried about her, begged her to come home and rest. But Madeleine refused to budge. She asked Avalina to bring fresh clothes to the hospital; she wasn't leaving Armand.

Montro stayed as well.

He patiently stood guard outside Armand's door and it wasn't solely to protect Madeleine. He didn't know who had beaten Armand, but he could tell from the seriousness of Armand's injuries that whoever it was had meant to kill him. It was entirely possible that his attackers might come here and try to finish the job.

Avalina came and went several times each day, worried about all of them.

The warm days and warmer nights dragged slowly by with no change in Armand's condition. Madeleine never gave up hope. She stayed at his bedside talking to him as if he could hear her. Repeatedly, she said she was sorry she had waited to tell him that she loved him. She'd been such a coward and she regretted it. She'd been afraid to admit how much she loved him, afraid she might get hurt and now she realized how selfish she had been.

"I do love you, Armand, more than you'll ever know," she said over and over to the unresponsive man. "I love you, my darling, I'll love you forever."

On the third endlessly long night, Madeleine, wide-awake, was alone at Armand's bedside when the bell in the cathedral tolled the hour of 4:00 a.m. She was, as usual, sitting on his bed, facing him, watching him for any signs of movement or wakefulness. She had been sitting there for hours.

Exhausted, her back breaking, she finally laid her weary head on his chest, taking great care not to hurt him. Her cheek resting on the white bandages encircling his ribs, she whispered, "I will not let you go away, my love. Do you hear me? I love you and I won't let you go."

As she spoke, Armand's dark eyelashes began to flutter as he valiantly tried to rouse himself from the depths of encompassing blackness. Faintly he could hear Madeleine's voice saying the words he had longed to hear. *I love you.* He struggled to open his eyes; when finally he managed to, he saw her flaming hair spread out on his chest. It was the most beautiful sight he'd ever seen and tears quickly sprang to his still-swollen eyes.

He tried to speak, to say her name, but he couldn't make a sound. He attempted to slide his hand across the sheet and reach for her, but even that effort was beyond him. He felt his hand drop back to the mattress, the weight of it too much to lift.

Through the concealing thickness of her tear-wet lashes, Madeleine glimpsed the shadowy movement of his dark hand falling. She reached out and clasped that hand. A low whimpering sound escaped her lips and she drew his limp hand up onto his chest.

She laid her cheek against it and said, "I love

you, Armand. Can you hear me?'' And, as if in response, she felt a slight movement in his hand. Her aching heart began to pound. She quickly raised her head and looked at him. His eyes were open and he was looking at her. "Oh, my precious love," she cried, triumphant, "You're awake. You've come back to me." She saw the muscles in his throat slowly work as he tried to speak, to say her name. Her fresh tears falling on his face, she pressed a tender kiss to his battered lips, and said, "Shh, don't try to speak. Just rest, my love."

As his face became covered with her kisses and her tears, Armand's swollen lips stretched painfully into a semblance of a smile and he croaked, "*Chérie*, have I died and gone to heaven or are you really here?"

"I'm here, Armand," she assured him, laughing and crying at once.

Lord Enfield was finally beginning to relax and stop his constant worrying.

When the Smallwoods had told him that they hadn't been able to finish de Chevalier off because some unexpected bystanders had interrupted, Desmond had been disappointed and furious.

"Damn you both to hell!" he had shouted angrily. "You're telling me you left the interfering bastard alive?"

"He was still breathing," said Burton, "but he won't live through the night."

"He better not!"

The next morning Lord Enfield had read the *New Orleans Bee* with special eagerness and interest. The story he sought was on the first page. Armand

de Chevalier, native son and owner of The Beaufort
Club, the text said, had been badly beaten in an
alley by unknown assailants. De Chevalier had been
found by a passing couple who heard his moans of
agony. The young pair had taken him to New Orleans General where his condition was listed as crit-
ical.

"God in heaven! The son of a bitch is still alive
this morning!" Desmond raged. "Dammit! Can't
the dull-witted Smallwoods do anything right!"

Through his contacts, Desmond kept close check
on Armand. Several times each day he got reports.
They were always the same. No change. Still un-
conscious.

Now, after three full days with no change in de
Chevalier's condition, Desmond felt there was little
need to fret. With any luck, the Creole would never
regain consciousness. And, even if he did, he
couldn't cause much trouble.

Desmond had heard that even with de Chevalier's legal advice and assistance, Madeleine had
been unable to find a copy of Sumner's will. She
wasn't going to find one. It was, admittedly, puzzling that the will was missing. He couldn't imagine
who could have taken it, or why. But apparently
whoever it was had no intention of producing it,
bless them.

The June 1 deadline was drawing close. Only a
couple more weeks. With de Chevalier near death
and Madeleine constantly at his bedside, there
would be no more frantic searching.

Desmond smiled with satisfaction. Life was
sweet indeed. Soon he, the Earl of Enfield, would
have total control over a fortune so vast he could

pay off all his many debts at once. He could buy imposing mansions in New York and Paris and London. He could travel the globe in total luxury aboard his own private rail car and well-manned sea-going yacht. He could buy Dominique diamonds and furs and expensive gowns and move her out of that hovel where he'd kept her all these years.

Best of all, he, who despised labor of any kind, would never have to turn his hand for as long as he lived.

Thirty-Nine

Only six days after being brought into New Orleans General near death, Armand de Chevalier walked out of the hospital. Supported on one side by Big Montro and Madeleine on the other, the weak, pale Armand smiled sunnily as he thanked the frowning Dr. Ledette.

"Son, I really wish you'd stay in the hospital a few more days," said the concerned doctor. "You're far from being well."

"I'll take it easy, Doc," promised Armand.

Dr. Ledette shook his graying head. "See that you do."

Outside the strong May sunlight made Armand wince and blink, but Montro quickly got him into the carriage where the side curtains had been tightly drawn. Madeleine climbed in and wrapped protective arms around him. Montro closed the door, hopped up on the driver's seat, and drove them straight to Armand's Pontalba apartment.

They had discussed their destination before Armand was released from the hospital. Madeleine and Avalina had wanted him to recuperate at the Royal Street town house, but Armand and Montro warned that the entire city would know and tongues would most certainly wag. Madeleine finally agreed he could go to his own apartment, but said there would still be talk because she was going to spend all her time there with him.

As good as her word, she was at Armand's apartment constantly.

Except at night.

At bedtime each evening, for propriety's sake, she reluctantly left him and went home to sleep. But she was up early come the morning and back at his bedside.

Montro, unable to be in two places at once and worried that Armand might still be in danger, enlisted the help of The Beaufort Club's muscular bouncer. The bouncer, glad to be of service to the likeable man he called boss, stood guard throughout each long May night at Armand's apartment.

Dr. Ledette came by to check on his patient every morning without fail. On a couple of occasions, his daughter, Melissa, had joined him. Melissa had hugged Madeleine and whispered, "If I can't have Armand myself, then I'm glad you're the one who has him."

Avalina was there often, as well. She fussed over Armand almost as much as Madeleine. She came each day at noon, carrying a carefully cooked meal for the patient. At sunset she was back again, bringing a nutritious dinner.

Wise enough to know the lovers wanted to be alone, Montro never intruded, never came up to the apartment unless Madeleine summoned him. But he discreetly kept constant watch over the pair from his post across the street in Jackson Square.

The hours Madeleine and Armand spent together while he was recuperating were a golden interlude for them both. The long, warm afternoons belonged solely to them. Between the hours of one and six, they could count on total privacy and it was wonderful.

In cozy seclusion, they relished a relaxed sweet peace together. Madeleine was so happy that Armand had lived through his terrible ordeal, she put aside any lingering despair over her lost inheritance. She had the only thing that really mattered right there in her arms.

During those lazy afternoons the two lovers got to know each other. At his insistence, Madeleine gladly told Armand about her early life in England when she was a happy little girl. She told him that despite being an only child, she had never been lonely because she had the two most loving parents in the world. She had lost them both in the past few years and she still missed them terribly.

Twisting a long strand of russet hair around her finger, she spoke candidly of her marriage to a handsome commoner, an unwise union that had caused her nothing but grief and embarrassment. When she got around to talking about Lord Enfield, she admitted that she had never been in love with him. She had agreed to marry him because she had mistakenly admired him and believed him to be a good, kind man who would never treat her badly, as her first husband had.

"I was horrified," she said thoughtfully, "when his mask of decency fell away and I saw, for the first time, that he was unappealing, unprincipled, unscrupulous. He cared nothing for me, he only wanted Uncle Colfax's money. I will always believe that he is responsible for my uncle's death. It makes my blood run cold to think that I almost married him." She shivered.

Armand reached for her, drew her into his close embrace. "But you didn't and now you're safe here in my arms."

"Yes," she sighed, snuggling closer. "It's ironic, isn't it? The first time I saw you, I thought you were the one who'd be nothing but trouble."

Armand laughed good-naturedly. "I know. You were scared to death of me."

"I was not!" she defended herself. "I'm scared of nothing and no one."

Armand knew better. He kissed her and said softly, "Please don't be afraid to love me, sweetheart."

She looked into beautiful, expressive eyes and answered, "I'm not. I've given you my heart, Armand. I trust you with it."

"You'll never regret it, *chérie.*"

"I know I won't," she said, confident of his love. She sighed with satisfaction, then continued, "I've done all the talking. What about your family? I've never heard you speak of them."

Armand smiled and said, "My father was a brilliant outgoing man who was a respected district judge and my mother was a dark-haired, dark-eyed beauty who loved parties and people. They adored each other, and they adored me, as well. Like you, I was an only child and, as you may have guessed, badly spoiled." A wistful expression came into his dark eyes and he continued, "When I was seventeen, I lost them both in the yellow fever epidemic of '43. They died within hours of each other. I don't know why I didn't contract the fever. I took care of them both, but never fell ill."

"I'm so sorry, Armand," she murmured.

"I wasn't the only one who lost loved ones that summer," he said. Then, quickly changing the subject, he told her, "I grew up fast, Maddie, and I was wild and willful. I have a multitude of faults and a somewhat shady reputation that is probably all too well-earned. I can't deny that there's been too many women in and out my life, but I swear to you that I never loved a one of them." Her perfectly arched eyebrows raised skeptically at the statement. "I mean it. I've never been in love until I met you. I loved you from the first time I held you in my arms. I love you and I don't want anyone else." He paused for a second, and added, "I know I don't deserve you and I'm sure you're disgraced by the fact that I own a gaming palace. I'll sell it, Maddie. I'll get rid of it right away. I have plenty of other properties, including a plantation upriver. If you like, once we're married we can move up there and—"

Madeleine put a finger to his lips to silence him. She said, "No, darling. I want to live right here in the heart of this romantic city with you and I have absolutely no objection to you owning The Beaufort."

"You don't?" he said and she saw the relief flood his features.

Laughing she said, "Of course not. I love you just as you are. You don't have to change a thing for me." She tilted her head to the side, and added, "Well, almost nothing. Let it be understood, here and now and forever more, that *I* will be the only woman in your life.''

"That I guarantee.''

Alone in the spacious apartment, the much-in-love pair spent hours lying in bed together, talking, dreaming, resting, napping. Armand, under Madeleine's unflagging care, was improving remarkably quickly. His face was once again beginning to resemble the man she loved. He was now able to open his blackened, swollen eye a little and his split, swollen lips had healed enough for an occasional kiss if not too much pressure was applied. He was gaining strength daily and he credited Madeleine with his amazing progress.

Madeleine blossomed under his praise and felt very proud of herself. All her life others had waited on her. Now she was waiting on Armand and she was enjoying every minute of it.

So was he.

For Armand it was heaven to have Madeleine's soft, small hands rub his aching back, his arms, his legs. It was pleasurable to have those same soft hands bathe his bruised flesh with gentle loving care and place fresh bandages where they were needed. It was self-indulgent fun to have her feed him as if he were a helpless infant. It was sweet agony to have her—in the sultry May afternoons—climb into bed with him, lower the mosquito *baire* around them, and lie close beside him, so close he could feel every beat of her heart.

It was all he'd ever dreamed of to hear her whisper in the tranquil stillness, "I love you, Armand. I love you and as soon as you're well, I'll show you how much.''

"Show me now," he would coax, knowing it would be unwise for them to make love.

"No." She was always adamant. "The doctor warned that you are not supposed to exert yourself."

"I won't," he teased. "You can do all the exerting."

"Soon, love, soon."

"You're a cruel woman, Countess."

"Yes, but I'm *your* cruel woman, so you wouldn't mind a little torment, would you?"

"What did you have in mind?"

"The tresses torture," she said with a wicked smile, then got up on her hands and knees, flipped her long red-gold hair over her head, lowered her face close to his chest, and slowly, tantalizingly dragged her heavy, ticklish hair down his responsive body.

He loved it and she knew it. The first time she'd done it had been at his request.

But she always stopped when he said hoarsely, "No, baby, I can't stand it. If you want me to get well, you'd better get away from me."

Only twenty-four hours remained until the deadline.

Lord Enfield, ensconced in Dominique's Rampart Street cottage, was rubbing his hands together with glee. Victory was within his reach.

And he deserved it.

For three long, torturous months he had been holding his breath, terrified that the damning will would turn up and shatter all his dreams. But it hadn't. And it wouldn't.

This time tomorrow everything Colfax Sumner owned would be his to manage and dispose of at will—all the vast properties, the many houses, the securities, the gold—and he would be one of the richest men in America.

Happy as he'd never been in his life, he impulsively clapped his hands together in loud applause and gave a great shout of laughter.

Dominique turned from where she was seated at the vanity brushing her long dark hair.

"What is it?" she asked, her brows knitted.

"What is it?" he repeated, tears of laughter spilling down his cheeks as he lay on her bed kicking his feet in the air and pounding the mattress with his open hands. "What is it? I'll tell you what it is, my pet. I, Desmond Chilton, fourth Earl of Enfield, am rich, rich, rich! I have more money than I could possibly spend in ten hedonistic lifetimes." Punctuating the sentence with a sharp howl of laughter, he added, "But I shall certainly try! Ah, yes, for the rest of my life I can have everything I've ever dreamed of. I can go anywhere I please, do anything I please. I can buy anything—or anyone—I desire. I can..." He continued to laugh maniacally and to rant and rave about all the things he could do once he'd claimed his fortune tomorrow.

Staring at him, Dominique began to frown, suddenly displeased. His overly buoyant behavior was beginning to make her more than a trifle nervous. He was acting like a madman, making wild statements.

All this talk about buying anything or anyone he wanted was a bit disturbing. He had always vowed he wanted no one but her. Could she believe him?

What if he decided, once he was wealthy, that he no longer wanted only her?

Or, that he no longer wanted her at all?

Dominique decisively laid the hairbrush aside, rose from the vanity stool and came to the bed. She leisurely untied the sash of her silk dressing gown, but did not take it off. Allowing the lord only glimpses of her satiny brown nakedness, she sat down on the bed and said, "How would you like to experience a new sexual thrill?"

Still laughing uncontrollably, the lord slowly turned his head and looked at her. When he could catch his breath, he said, "Nice try, Dom, but I'm afraid there's nothing we haven't done."

"You're wrong, my love," she said with a sly, catlike smile. "Shall I tell you what it is?"

His laughter had now completely stopped. His full attention was on her. His body was beginning to tense with anticipation. Could it be there was still something erotic that the two of them hadn't tried? Excitement flooded him. Blood surged through his veins. With growing interest, he watched her rise and move seductively across the bedroom to the tall mahogany armoire.

She opened the twin polished doors, pulled out a lower drawer, and took something from it. He couldn't see what it was. She closed the drawer, shut the armoire doors. She turned and came back to the bed with her hand behind her back, concealing what she held in it.

The supine lord's eyes widened when she ordered him to sit up, move to the edge of the mattress, and put his feet on the floor. Obeying, his heartbeat hammered in his chest.

Standing directly above him, her hand still behind her and the silk robe hanging open, Dominique leaned close and put her lips next to his ear. She whispered in the most graphic terms exactly what she was going to do to him. Lord Enfield, so shocked and excited he couldn't speak, could only nod eagerly.

Dominique straightened, smiled, and asked pointedly, "Tell me, is there now, or will there ever be, any other woman for you, my lord?"

"No, God no, Dom, just you, only you."

Forty

The hour had arrived.

Time, for Madeleine, had run out.

The first day of June was steamy, sticky hot in New Orleans. The summer sun beat down with a vengeance and the humid air stirred not at all. No cool breeze blew off the river. No billowy clouds appeared overhead to offer a faint hope of rain.

At straight up noon, a meeting of all concerned parties was getting underway at the Toulouse Street offices of Jay E. Jernigan, a respected New Orleans attorney who had been appointed by the courts.

Lord Enfield, hardly able to contain his excitement, was present with his personal attorney. Smiling, confident, the lord rose from his chair and bowed grandly from the waist when Lady Madeleine arrived. She did not acknowledge him, but he was unbothered by the snub. But when he looked up and saw Armand staring at him with cold loathing, his smile faded somewhat.

He shrugged and sat back down.

At the attorney's instruction, Madeleine and Armand stepped up to the polished conference table and took chairs directly across from Lord Enfield and his attorney. The windows across the front of the office were all open wide, but it did little good. It was uncomfortably warm in the room.

"Is everyone present that is expected here today?" asked Jay Jernigan, looking from Madeleine to Desmond.

"Yes, sir," Madeleine replied, unfurling a fan to stir the still air before her flushed face.

"Everyone's here," said Desmond. "Shall we get on with it?"

Lawyer Jernigan gave Desmond a sharp look over the tops of his wire-rimmed spectacles. The attorney took a seat at the head of the table, opened a folder, and withdrew Colfax Sumner's provisional will. He placed the document on the table before him, folded his hands atop it, looked apologetically at Madeleine and said, "Lady Madeleine, under the terms laid down by the courts of the state of Louisiana, you are aware, are you not, that unless on this the first of June you have in your possession a last will and testament written by your late uncle after the date that this provisional will was made, I have no choice but to…"

As the proceedings continued, Avalina, accompanied by Big Montro, arrived at the law offices. For weeks, Avalina had been eagerly looking forward to this moment.

While Montro waited outside, Avalina went quickly up the steps of the building and, rushing past a startled clerk, forcefully opened the door into the chamber where the meeting was taking place.

The points of her signature white *tignon* dancing, Avalina, with Jernigan's flustered law clerk at her heels, marched directly inside as if she had been invited.

"Sir, I'm sorry," explained the law clerk, "I tried to stop her, but she—"

"It's all right, Benny." Jay Jernigan waved him away. Then turning his full attention on Avalina, he asked, "Madam, what is the meaning of this? We are conducting very important private business here and you are interfering. You must leave at once."

"I'll leave, sir, as soon as you take a look at something I have."

With all eyes resting on her, Avalina smiled, reached into her reticule and withdrew a folded parchment document. She proceeded directly to the seated attorney, shook out the document and declared, "The last will and testament of Colfax W. Sumner!"

A collective gasp issued from all present, including the attorney Jay Jernigan. Armand and Madeleine exchanged surprised glances. Then a moment of stunned silence fell over the gathering.

Commotion immediately ensued.

While the attorney studied the will, Lord Enfield, wringing his hands, began to protest vehemently.

"Have your law clerk alert the authorities at once," said Desmond anxiously. "Somebody needs to get this crazy old woman out of here so we can finish our—"

Ignoring him, an astonished Madeleine asked, "Avalina, where? Where did you find it?"

The black woman smiled sheepishly and admitted, "I have had it all along, Lady Madeleine. I took it from the wall safe shortly before your uncle's death."

"You're lying!" shouted Lord Enfield, his face

bloodred. "You don't have a valid will! The provisional will is the only authentic one! For God's sake, tell them, Lawyer Jernigan, tell them!"

The court-appointed attorney paid no attention to the disturbance going on around him. He was totally absorbed, carefully studying the document that Avalina had produced.

Baffled by Avalina's behavior, Madeleine inquired of the loyal friend and servant, "But why, Avalina? Why did you take the will?"

Avalina said earnestly, "Because I was afraid something terrible was going to happen to Master Colfax. And so it did."

Nodding, comprehending, Madeleine asked, "But why, if you've had it all this time, have you waited until the last moment to produce it. I don't understand."

"There's nothing to understand," Lord Enfield snarled. "The document she's brought here is obviously nothing more than a worthless piece of paper."

But he was growing exceedingly nervous. The will had been missing the night he'd had Colfax murdered. Had this snooping black servant taken it before he could get to it?

As if he hadn't spoken, Avalina said to Madeleine, "I had to do it this way, my lady. If I had not, you might have made the terrible mistake of marrying Lord Enfield." She cast a mean, narrow-eyed glance in his direction and said, "You needed time to see this unprincipled cad for what he really is. And time, as well," she smiled in Armand's direction, "to see Mr. Armand for the kind of man *he* is."

"I see." Madeleine began to nod.

"I suspected that Lord Enfield wouldn't see the need to marry you as long as he thought the provisional will would take precedence," Avalina continued. "It's control of Colfax's money he wanted."

"Bless you, Avalina," the smiling Armand spoke for the first time. "You did the right thing."

Indignantly rising from his chair, the angry, red-faced Lord Enfield, sensing that the vast fortune was slipping through his fingers, began to tongue-lash Avalina. But he got out only a few harsh words before the attorney's office door once again opened and two uniformed officers of the law stepped inside.

"Finally!" bellowed Lord Enfield and pointed an accusing finger at Avalina. "Take her, take this mad black woman out of here at once!"

"It's you we'll be taking, sir," said the taller of the two officers as both crossed directly to Lord Enfield.

"Me?" Desmond's eyes widened and he frantically turned to his attorney. "Don't just sit there, you fool, do something! What's going on?"

"I—I don't know," replied his dazed attorney, rising.

"You can't do this to me! Do you know who I am? Stop it!" shouted Desmond as the officers calmly forced his hands behind his back and clasped irons on him. "God almighty, what is happening? Is everyone insane? Why are you doing this to me?"

One of the officers laconically informed him,

"You, Lord Enfield, are under arrest for the murder of Colfax Sumner."

"Murder?" Desmond choked, truly terrified now. "Why I was nowhere near Sumner's home on the night he was killed." He looked to Madeleine for confirmation. "Ask her! She was with me. We were at the opera and—"

"We know where you were," interrupted the officer, "but your hired assassins were at Sumner's town house carrying out the cold-blooded murder you paid them to commit."

"No, I...that's...you're wrong...that's not true. Sumner died of heart failure, everyone knows that. You're making a terrible mistake. I had nothing to do with his death and—"

"You picked the wrong killers to do your dirty work, Lord Enfield," the officer informed him. "One of them talked, bragged to a lady of the evening about the murder. Told her it was you who hired them to do it. When we went to arrest the brothers, they immediately gave you up. Said it was all your idea, that you wanted Sumner dead so you could get your hands on his fortune."

"No, no, you have it all wrong, I'm telling you," whined a distraught Lord Enfield. "My mistress. Go see my mistress and she'll—"

"We did. We spoke with the quadroon named Dominique earlier today. Under questioning she broke down and admitted that you had masterminded the murder."

"That ungrateful bitch!" groaned Desmond. "She's in on it. Did she tell you that? Have you locked her up?"

"No, we don't think she's responsible, so we

took it easy on her. I believe she's decided to leave New Orleans.''

"She's as guilty as I!" he raged. "She is! She wanted Sumner dead more than I ever did. You should arrest her, not me!"

Cursing and struggling, the handcuffed Desmond Chilton was taken away with his anxious attorney following closely on his heels.

Well," breathed the calm attorney, Jay Jernigan, once things got settled down, "now we can proceed with the business at hand."

He smiled warmly at Madeleine and stated, "This document I hold in my hand is without question the last will and testament of Colfax Sumner and supersedes any prior wills he may have made." The lawyer looked over his spectacles and added, "As you well know, Lady Madeleine, everything he owned now belongs to you."

"Thank you, Attorney Jernigan," Madeleine replied, elated.

"Don't thank me, thank Avalina," he said with a wink and a smile. Then added, "Now, shall we adjourn? It's so miserably hot in here I need something cool to drink."

Forty-One

Sunset on that same hot June day.

A bell tolled in the church tower.

A beautiful woman wearing a lace veil over her gleaming russet hair stood beside a tall, dark man before the lit candles in the old St. Louis cathedral.

Only two guests were present to witness the twilight nuptials. Avalina sat quietly in the front pew, fanning herself and beaming from ear to ear. Big Montro was at her side, his face shiny with perspiration, his mouth stretched into a wide grin.

"I now pronounce you man and wife," said the stooped old priest.

Armand turned, took his bride his arms and kissed her.

Then, with Avalina and Montro tossing rice at them, the happy pair hurried up the aisle, out the heavy front doors, down the stone steps and into a waiting carriage. As Armand pulled the carriage door closed, a flash of lightning briefly illuminated the summer sky, followed by the clatter of thunder.

A light shower began as the embracing couple were whisked directly to the St. Louis Hotel. By the time they entered the luxurious bridal suite, a torrential rainstorm had begun. The sheer curtains in the spacious boudoir fluttered in the wind-driven rain and the heavy air that had been scalding hot all day had cooled dramatically.

"I guess we should close the windows and French doors," said Madeleine.

"No, let's leave them all wide-open," Armand suggested.

"It may rain in, darling."

"Let's take that chance." Then grinning wickedly, he added, "As I recall, you like making love in the rain and the wind."

"Don't you?"

"I do, *chérie.*"

Ignoring the sumptuous wedding supper that had been laid out on the hotel's famed gold place settings, Armand popped the cork on a bottle of chilled champagne, poured two glasses and handed one to Madeleine.

While the rain hissed against the stone balcony outside and the winds rose, the newly married couple toasted each other and vowed their undying love.

Armand asked politely, "*Chérie,* have you an appetite?"

"Not for food," was her smiling reply as she reached up and took the gold clasp from her hair. The lustrous tresses cascaded down about her slender shoulders, the silky ends dancing in the rain-filled wind.

His heart full, his hunger for her potent, Armand took their champagne glasses, set them aside and drew Madeleine into his embrace.

She put her arms around his neck, sighed with bliss, smiled, and said dreamily, "Oh, my love, I am so happy."

Armand swung her up into his powerful arms and started for the bed. Together they laughed when the wind and the rain, blowing into the bedroom, pressed their clothes against their bodies and peppered their faces and cooled the sweet-scented night air.

Beside the bed, Armand lowered Madeleine to her feet, and she said again, "So happy."

Armand kissed her tenderly, and promised, "Sweetheart, I'm about to make you even happier."

From the bestselling author of
THE BABY FARM

MIRA

KAREN HARPER

DOWN TO THE BONE

Deep in the heart of a small Amish community lies a secret someone thought was buried forever. But one woman may have just unknowingly uncovered it....

As Rachel Mast begins to dig up the past for answers, someone is equally determined to keep it buried. Someone who won't stop at murder to keep the truth hidden....

"A compelling story...intricate and
fascinating details of Amish life."
—Tami Hoag on Karen Harper's *DARK ROAD HOME*

On sale mid-July 2000 wherever paperbacks are sold!

NAN RYAN

66521   WANTING YOU   ___ $5.99 U.S. ___ $6.99 CAN.

(limited quantities available)

TOTAL AMOUNT	$_____
POSTAGE & HANDLING	$_____
($1.00 for one book; 50¢ for each additional)	
APPLICABLE TAXES*	$_____
<u>TOTAL PAYABLE</u>	$_____

(check or money order—please do not send cash)

To order, complete this form and send it, along with a check
or money order for the total above, payable to MIRA Books®,
to: **In the U.S.:** 3010 Walden Avenue, P.O. Box 9077, Buffalo,
NY 14269-9077; **In Canada:** P.O. Box 636, Fort Erie, Ontario,
L2A 5X3.

Name:_____
Address:_____ City:_____
State/Prov.:_____ Zip/Postal Code:_____
Account Number (if applicable):_____
075 CSAS

*New York residents remit applicable sales taxes.
Canadian residents remit applicable GST and provincial taxes.

MIRA

      MNR0700BL